OMEGA

ALSO BY PATRICK LYNCH

CARRIERS

OMEGA

PATRICK LYNCH

A DUTTON BOOK

DUTTON
Published by the Penguin Group
Penguin Putnam Inc., 375 Hudson Street,
New York, New York 10014, U.S.A.
Penguin Books Ltd, 27 Wrights Lane, London W8 5TZ, England
Penguin Books Australia Ltd, Ringwood, Victoria, Australia
Penguin Books Canada Ltd, 10 Alcorn Avenue,
Toronto, Ontario, Canada M4V 3B2
Penguin Books (N.Z.) Ltd, 182–190 Wairau Road, Auckland 10, New Zealand

Penguin Books Ltd, Registered Offices:
Harmondsworth, Middlesex, England

First published by Dutton, an imprint of Dutton Signet,
a member of Penguin Putnam Inc.

First Printing, September, 1997
10   9   8   7   6   5   4   3   2   1

 REGISTERED TRADEMARK—MARCA REGISTRADA

LIBRARY OF CONGRESS CATALOGING IN PUBLICATION DATA:
Lynch, Patrick.
Omega / Patrick Lynch.
p.   cm.
ISBN 0-525-94327-7
I. Title.
PR6062.Y596O47   1997
823'.914–dc21   97-12733
CIP
Printed in the United States of America
Set in Transitional 521 BT

F LYNCH

PUBLISHER'S NOTE

This is a work of fiction. Names, characters, places, and incidents either are the product of the author's imagination or are used fictitiously, and any resemblance to actual persons, living or dead, events, or locales is entirely coincidental.

This book is printed on acid-free paper. ∞

This book is dedicated to the staff
of the King/Drew Medical Center
in South Central Los Angeles

ACKNOWLEDGMENTS

We would like to thank the following for their generous help with this book.

At the King/Drew Medical Center in Los Angeles: Dr. Arthur Fleming, Chairman, Department of Surgery and Trauma Director, for opening up a Level One trauma center and guiding us through the detail; Dr. Jessie Sherrod, Chief of Infection Control, for her insights into the war against the microbes; Dr. Pat Fullenweider, Deputy Administrator, for explaining how the system works; Cherie Allmond, Nurse Manager for ER, and her colleagues for walking us through the wards. Thanks are also due to Medical Director Edward Savage, Jr.; Dr. Tessie Cleveland, Director of Public Relations and Social Service, and her assistant, Ronda Durrah, for making it all possible in the first place.

Elsewhere: Lieutenant Raymond Peavy and Deputy Ron Lancaster of the Homicide Bureau, Los Angeles County Sheriff's Department, and Dr. Pedro Ortiz, Deputy Medical Examiner, Los Angeles County Coroner's Office, for their instruction on the conduct of homicide investigations; Kay Atwal, associate editor of *Pharma Business* magazine, for information on the pharmaceuticals industry and its products; the Public Health Laboratory Service in Colindale, London, for access to their medical data; and, last but not least, Dr. Rupert Negus and Dr. Helena Scott for their help on antisense research.

CONTENTS

PROLOGUE   1

PART ONE
THE SHARK'S TONGUE   9

PART TWO
SOMETIMES BAD MEANS BAD   69

PART THREE
POISON   141

PART FOUR
ANTISENSE   187

PART FIVE
THE CZAR   249

PART SIX
OMEGA   301

EPILOGUE   363

If we go on abusing antibiotics as we now do, we are faced with a return to a medical dark age, in which antibiotics no longer work against a vast range of infections, some created by antibiotics, some perhaps epidemic and deadly. . . . Idealists who seek to alert us to the damage done are opposed by an unholy alliance of those who supply and those who demand.

—Professor Graham Dukes
Professor of Drug Policy Studies
University of Groningen

The global pharmaceuticals business is worth at least $270 billion a year.

—Vikram Sahu
Credit Suisse First Boston

PROLOGUE

SOUTH CENTRAL LOS ANGELES

Dzilla was at the corner of La Salle and Florence reading his mail-order catalogue when he saw the Shark coming along the heat-buckled sidewalk, a package under his left arm. The Shark was looking preoccupied, his left hand massaging his throat. Dzilla frowned, not really believing what he was seeing. The whole neighborhood was talking about the Shark, about what he and Tyrone Garret had done over in Walnut Park the night before—talking about the drugstore they knocked over and the girl that was blinded. And here was the Shark, dumb pipehead that he was, walking around like everything was cool.

"Yo," said the Shark. "Wha's happenin', Dzil."

"*Mister* Tibs," said Dzilla, dipping his head, but not moving from his perch on the bench. He pointed at the Shark's throat.

"Look like you swallow' a *ham*bone, brother."

"Man"—the Shark rubbed at his throat—"it's like a . . . like I'm swallowin' glass the whole time, like a *piece* at a time."

Dzilla tapped the tubed catalogue against his thigh, thinking the throat was not the Shark's main problem, thinking maybe he should tell him what was going down.

"So where you been, man?" he said, looking away, making nothing of it. Just talking.

"Oh, you know—aroun'."

"Cos people been aksin for you."

"Yeah? Like who?"

"Just people." Dzilla looked back at the Shark, considered him for a second. "You over in Walnut Park last night?"

The Shark got a shifty look and tightened the hold on his package. For the first time Dzilla wondered what he had in there. Thought maybe it was cash from the stickup.

"Who says so?" said the Shark, focusing on Dzilla's face now, so that his left eye drifted inward slightly.

Dzilla smiled and shook his head. The Shark scored crack from his corner on a regular basis, but the brother's stupidity always came as a surprise because he had what you would pick out as an intelligent face.

"Man, *everybody*," said Dzilla, looking up and down the street, checking on his people. "Whole 'hoods talkin' 'bout what went down last night at that drugstore."

The Shark left off rubbing at his throat.

"Say what?"

"You sayin' you didn't do it?"

"I didn't do *nothing*, man."

Dzilla nodded slowly, pushing out his lips.

"I don't know, man. That's not what they' sayin'. That's not what I'm hearin'."

The Shark tried to swallow. It reminded Dzilla of Wile E. Coyote—it was that kind of noisy, cartoon gulp.

"Who's sayin'? Who's sayin' what?" said the Shark, making a face because of the pain.

"Like I say, man, *everybody*. It's all over the 'hood how you and Tyrone Garret shot up this place—blinded some Chicano bitch."

The Shark started to undo his package, and for a moment Dzilla thought it might be a gun. But then he saw it *was* cash—cash and what looked like tubes of cream and bottles of pills. It came to Dzilla that the Shark had done the drugstore *for* the medicine. Not for the money at all. But that *couldn't* be true. Nobody was *that* stupid.

Making a kind of low moaning sound now, the Shark put all his junk on the ground and started to sort through it. Dzilla got up from his bench and walked away, checking the street. Cars were passing every couple of minutes, and he felt nervous standing near to the Shark when any moment some desperados could drive by and gun him down.

"What's up, man? What you got down there?"

The Shark continued to search.

"I'm . . . I'm lookin' . . ."

Then he was back on his feet, breathing noisily through his nose. He shook out a couple of capsules from a small bottle and crammed them into his mouth. For a moment it looked as if he wasn't going to be able to swallow them—moving his head around, making his Coyote gulps. Then they were gone. Dzilla took the bottle from him and checked out the label.

"Mac-ro-dan-tin. What is this shit, man?"

"Tyrone say it's what I need for my thing. It's a *anti*biotic."

He took the bottle and dropped it back into the bag.

"Some serious shit," said the Shark. "Can't just buy it. You gotta have it *prescribe'*."

He took out a couple more bottles and showed them to Dzilla, Dzilla reading to himself, his lips ghosting the difficult names—*Achromycin, trimethoprim, oxytetracycline.*

"This from the store?" asked Dzilla, looking up.

"Ain't no other way I'm goin' to get it."

Dzilla gave back the last bottle.

"I don't know, man. You got to be careful with that shit. Can't just put any old thing inside you."

But the Shark was rolling up his package now. He didn't want to talk about it anymore.

The show over, he looked down at the ground. It was obvious he didn't know what his next move should be. He didn't know anything about blinding a girl. The whole thing had gotten out of hand. That was all. Eventually, he looked back up.

"Number one," he said, "I didn't shoot nobody."

Dzilla shrugged as though it made no difference to him.

"Number two, it was fucking Tyrone."

"But why Walnut Park, man? Stirring up the goddam Chicanos. Next thing you know it ain't safe on the street no mo'."

The Shark shrugged in his turn. It was all fucked up. That was all he knew. All he wanted to do was get high—at least that way he could forget about his throat. He took a twenty-dollar bill from his pants and pushed it into Dzilla's hand. Dzilla turned to a kid standing twenty feet away.

"Gimme two," he said in a flat businesslike drawl. Without a word the kid jogged off down the street. Dzilla went back to his perch on the bench.

"You say 'blinded'?" said the Shark. Dzilla watched his runner disappear around the corner.

"That's what I hear, Mr. Tibs. Kid lost an eye, anyways."

The Shark shook his head.

"Don't be calling me that, man."

The Shark didn't like *Mr. Tibs*. It was short for *tiburón*, a name the Mexicans had given him in school. *Tiburón* was okay—it actually *meant* "shark" and sounded kind of deadly—but Mr. Tibs was like a cat or cat-*food*, and the Shark didn't like it, whatever people said about Sidney Poitier. Dzilla knew that, but like everybody else in the neighborhood, sometimes he forgot.

The Shark tightened his package again. It seemed he couldn't get it small enough.

"Anyway," he said, waiting for his crack now, stepping from one foot to the other.

"So . . . what?" said Dzilla, bringing his bony shoulders up. "Store-keeper had a gun . . . what?"

The Shark was watching for the runner to reappear.

"Naw," he said. "Wadn't like that."

Then he squared up to Dzilla, planting his factory-fresh Nikes, wanting to get it straight.

"We're leavin', you understan'—walkin' out the fuckin' store—and Tyrone's still waving his .45. Job's *done*, man; storekeeper don't even got a tire tool, but Tyrone he don't wanna put that thing away. He *likes* it. Make him feel *big*. We leavin' and he says to me, '*Look out, look out.*' There's someone coming out of the storeroom or bathroom or whatever it is. And I see it's this kid. This Chicano bitch. Maybe twelve, thirteen years old. She sees Tyrone, and her eyes like pop out of her fuckin' head, man. But she ain't about to *do* nothin' 'cept scream maybe. Tyrone goes and pulls the fuckin' trigger."

"Say what? Tyrone shot the kid?"

"No. He's all gassed up, man—he don't know what the *fuck* he's doing. He pulls the trigger—brings down some ceiling tiles—and then he puts a couple of rounds into this . . . into this baby food. *Baby food*,

man. Like a stack of these little jars up to the fuckin' ceiling. *Bam, bam!*
There's like carrot and shit everywhere, and this kid, this girl, she goes
down screaming. We don't stop to aks wha's wrong, you understan'.
We on our way out."

Dzilla's runner reappeared with his KFC carrier bag, pimp rolling
his way back towards Dzilla's bench. Twenty feet away he dropped the
bag into a trashcan. The deal was done.

"Anyway," said the Shark, setting off to get his bottles.

Dzilla called after him, "Word is she lost a eye, man."

The Shark halted. Turned.

"Yeah, you already say that."

"They took her into the 'Brook," said Dzilla. "And they lookin' for
you, man."

"Who's lookin'?"

"Cos they don't let shit like that slide."

"Who, man?"

"*Locitas.* The kid, the kid got hurt? Her sister's a Locita. You know,
one of them girl gangs in Walnut."

The Shark reached into the trash can and took out his bottles.
Slowly. Trying to look cool.

"Well, let her look, man. I ain't going nowhere. Wasn't me was
carrying the gun. I'll tell her straight."

Dzilla saw the Corvette first. It came gliding along the street—
black windows and a red eagle on the hood. The look on Dzilla's face
brought the Shark round with a jerk, reaching for his .38. But it was
only Tyrone. The door was punched open and he stepped out into flat
morning light, smoothing himself down like the pimp he was. He
nodded in the direction of Dzilla and then looked back at the Shark.

"Get in the car, man."

The Shark's hand came out from under his shirt. Tyrone's hair was
in new dreadlocks, so the Shark knew he'd stopped by to bang Shannel,
his whore.

"Where d'you get the wheels, Tyrone?" he asked.

Tyrone slapped the roof, the proud owner.

"Check it out, nigger. Eighty-three Corvette."

"You hear about the kid?" said the Shark, wanting, as always, to get
Tyrone back down to earth.

Again Tyrone looked at Dzilla before fixing on the Shark.

"Why d'you think I come lookin' for you, man? Word is *out*. You looking to get shot in the head standin' around out here."

He watched the information sink in. Then opened his door.

"Now, you goin' or stayin'?" he said.

They drove back down La Salle to 79th Street, where they took a right, Tyrone explaining about this motel he knew by the airport, the Shark thinking about all the girl gangs that had sprung up in the city, how it didn't used to be that way—thinking also about Tyrone and how he wasn't going to run with him anymore because he was a stickup-artist, sneaker-dealing, crackhead motherfucker.

The problem was the Shark was in the car now and they were making their getaway. He was too scared of Tyrone to just tell him, *"Stop the car, let me out."* He had to find some kind of excuse. Then it came to him.

He slapped his hand against the dash.

"Pull over, man."

Tyrone's head jerked round.

"I said, *stop* the car."

Tyrone pulled over to the side of the road at the next light. Twisting round, he lay his left arm along the back of the seat. He was breathing heavily and the Shark could see that he was real pissed.

"So . . ."—Tyrone shrugged—"what's the problem? You got to take a pee? What?"

"Gotta find me a drugstore," said the Shark.

Tyrone pushed back against the door.

"You shittin' me, brother? Tha's how we got into this mess in the first place."

"No, man. I gotta aks me some questions."

"You gotta what?"

The Shark gave his bag of medicines a shake.

" 'Bout the drugs, man. I been takin' all kinds of shit, and Dzilla says maybe I should think twice."

He tried to get the concern into his face.

"For my throat, man."

Tyrone opened and closed his mouth. He looked as if he was going to blow his top.

"*Fuck* Dzilla, man—*fuck* your throat."

He wrenched the car into drive. But the Shark grabbed the wheel.

"I'm *serious*, Tyrone. I got this throat, man. You don't believe me, take a look."

He opened his mouth as wide as he could. Tyrone turned, looking away.

"Get out of here, man. I don't wanna be lookin' into *that* motherfucker."

The Shark pulled out the Macrodantin.

"I been takin' these, man—like you said—but maybe they' no good for me."

Tyrone reached across and snatched at the bag. He rummaged around inside.

"Ain't you got no *in*structions, man . . . something . . . ? I don't know, on the bottle or on the . . . on the package."

"Tyrone, I just *grabbed* this stuff in the drugstore. This shit's all loose. There ain't no instructions. There ain't no package."

Tyrone looked the Shark in the eye, and for a moment the Shark thought Tyrone was going to see that he was just looking for a way out. But then he checked the rearview mirror and pushed out a big sigh.

"Shark, everybody in the 'hood knows we did that drugstore. Just a question of time before the po-lice come looking for our ass." He looked across at the sidewalk. "That's if the motherfuckin' Locita bitches don't nail us first."

"I just wanna aks a few questions, man. Tha's all."

Tyrone took his hands off the wheel.

"You step out of that door, I'm gonna leave you here."

The Shark met Tyrone's stare. Then he pulled on the door handle.

He walked north on Western, the package under his arm, waiting to hear the shriek of Tyrone's wheels. About fifty yards up he found an old-fashioned pharmacy and paused in the doorway to look back down the avenue. The Corvette was still there. Waiting. Tyrone having second thoughts about letting a key witness to the shooting just walk away. The Shark considered making a run for the next cross street. Then he thought that maybe there was a back way through the store.

Inside the shop he was confronted by a nervous-looking Indian guy standing behind a counter.

The Shark touched his throat.

"Yeah, I jus' wanted to aks you a question," he said, his eyes roving around for a way out. He looked down at the bottle in his left hand and then showed it to the Indian.

"My doctor prescribe' these here capsules for my throat, and I'm worried that maybe they ain't the right thing. You understan' what I'm saying?"

The Indian considered the bottle for a moment, and then handed it back. He looked a little confused.

"For your throat, sir?"

"Tha's right," said the Shark, noticing a door, but thinking it might be a storeroom.

"This is Macrodantin," said the Indian. "It's for urinary tract infections."

The Shark's eyes cut back to the man's face.

"Say what?"

"Urinary tract infections, sir."

"Urinated track? You sayin' this for my pecker, man?"

The Indian shrugged.

The Shark stepped back from the counter, clutching at his throat. Then froze, watching the Indian raise his hands.

He turned.

She was standing in the middle of the store—standing there like she had just beamed down from her starship—smiling, biting her teeth together in a kind of angry smile, and staring at him out of green-glitter eye paint. In her small brown hand the Glock 19 looked like a bazooka. Before the Shark could reach for his .38, she stepped forward and pushed the Glock hard against his throat, forcing his head back.

"Hola, Tiburón," she said. "Got a problem with your throat, motherfucker?"

And she shot him.

PART ONE

THE SHARK'S
TONGUE

1

WEST LOS ANGELES

Dr. Marcus Ford, director of the Trauma Unit at the Willowbrook Medical Center, put down his mug of coffee and looked around the room, trying to locate the source of the noise. It sounded like a hornet maybe, or a big, fat fly. It was flies he hated. Their opportunism, their fixation on decay disgusted him. But this noise wasn't right for a fly. Then he realized it was coming from the clock radio in his daughter's bedroom. He'd bought it himself for her thirteenth birthday, but he was normally dressed and gone long before she woke up, long before the thing switched itself on. He stood there for a moment, listening, trying to catch up with a little part of her life that he'd missed.

Then he reminded himself that he wasn't too pleased with Sunny right now, that he was going to have to say something to her because of the way she'd behaved. If he didn't draw the line, things would only get worse. But he was dreading the confrontation. What would he do if she just ignored him or told him to mind his own business? Or worse? She wasn't above that kind of thing nowadays. She would turn on him at the most unexpected times and places and hit him with a statement of defiance or criticism that was clearly designed to hurt. It caught him out every time, because to Ford it didn't sound like his daughter talking. It didn't sound like his little girl. It was as if a different person had gotten inside her somehow and was struggling to take control. He tried to imagine what Carolyn would have said about it, whether she would have understood it better, handled it better. But then again, if Carolyn were still alive, he reminded himself, there probably wouldn't have been a problem in the first place.

He went into the kitchen and poured a glass of orange juice. Yellow sunlight squeezed through the shutters, and from outside came the faint flutter and hiss of lawn sprinklers. He peered out across the back gardens: a man in a suit, carrying a briefcase, climbed into a Lincoln Continental and reversed out of his driveway. Dan or Don, was it? He'd moved to Kirkside Road about a year before, worked for an investment fund of some kind. Ford recalled standing on the sidewalk in his running gear, hearing the man talk about how thrilled he and his wife were to have found a house in such a safe neighborhood, while burly characters in overalls carried huge boxes into the house. The two men had talked about inviting each other over for drinks or a barbecue. So far it hadn't happened.

Ford took the juice through to Sunny's room, where the clock was flashing 7:30. On the radio a girl was in raptures over the price of the Mista Taco spicy cheese taco with regular diet coke (at participating restaurants), but Sunny looked fast asleep. With her blonde hair mussed—yellow strands clung to her mouth, stirred by her gentle breathing—she looked very grown-up, a little too grown-up for the flowery pink wallpaper. He stood there for a moment, breathing the musty smell of potpourri and shampoo, looking at her latest gangsta rap poster taped up over the dresser: four black kids with diamond-studded teeth snarling at the camera from an urban wasteland of rubble and burned-out buildings. Directly beneath the poster a one-eyed teddy bear looked like an archeological relic—a reminder of a long-lost, more clement world.

"Sunny?"

She squinted up at him through sleepy eyes, then moaned, rolled over, and slapped the clock radio off.

Ford frowned.

"Orange juice. You want it?"

She was silent a moment. Then she slowly pushed herself up on her elbows.

"Yes."

He handed her the glass and went over to the window to open the drapes.

"No, Dad, don't," she whined. "It's too bright."

He opened them halfway. Sunny moaned and rolled over, covering her head with the sheet.

"It's time to get up, young lady."

Sunny pulled her feet up under the bedding, searching for warmth.

"Sunny? What time did you come home last night?"

Now she was very still.

"What?"

"What time did you get in, damn it?"

"I don't know. I don't remember."

Ford folded his arms. He'd come back the night before loaded with groceries, including a good supply of fresh vegetables, all ready to cook a decent supper for them both. Sunny had seemed unhappy about something, but wouldn't say what. Then she'd announced that she was going over to the Wilsons' house for the evening and would eat at the mall. Ford had made her promise to be back by nine-thirty. She hadn't kept her word. It was after midnight when Ford had woken from his armchair slumber to find her asleep in bed.

"It had to be ten-thirty or later, Sunny, and you promised me nine-thirty. I *told* you nine-thirty."

"It wasn't my fault. The others wanted to stay."

"If there was a problem, you should have called me. I was worried."

Sunny flipped the sheet back and looked at him with her pale blue eyes—Carolyn's eyes.

"What about?"

"Anything could have happened to you out there. How did I know you hadn't been mugged or run over or something?"

"In Beverlywood? Oh, come on, Dad. Get real."

Get real. That was the phrase she used all the time now, whenever he said something she didn't like. It was as if she lived in the real world, and he was just visiting from Planet Parent.

"What's real, young lady, is that you come home when I tell you to or you don't go out at all. Is that clear?"

"You're always late for everything," she said, coolly. "And if you don't get a move on, you're gonna be late for work too."

"That's not the point," Ford said. "And for your information I've taken the day off today. The point is—"

"Really?" She sat up, suddenly wide awake. "Does that mean you can come watch the volleyball game this afternoon?"

"Don't try and change the—"

"It's my first time on the team."

Ford blinked. She'd made the junior volleyball team. That mattered to her, he knew that. Yet she hadn't told him until now.

"It is, huh? Why didn't you say so before?"

"Because I'm saying so now," she said, slipping into a kind of petulance she didn't usually show anymore. It was part of what she was going through at the moment—this slipping in and out of girlishness. It was very confusing. "The game starts at five-thirty."

Ford pushed at a coffee stain on the carpet with his toe.

"Well, honey, the trouble is—"

"Oh, *please*. It'll be great. All the parents'll be there."

"Honey, I can't. I'm giving this talk today, at a conference. I told you about it. That's why I've taken the day off: to prepare."

Ford looked at his watch. The truth was he had most of his speech still to write, and he was supposed to get it cleared with the medical director first, not to mention Lucy Patou, the chief of Infection Control.

"Dad," she drawled, stretching the syllable, letting him know he was the worst father in the neighborhood. "So when *will* you be back?"

"About six-thirty, I think. If nothing comes up."

Sunny looked down at the bedspread for a moment.

"Yeah, right," she said—no longer the child, no longer his little girl—and she climbed out of bed. Ford knew he ought to get back to the subject of last night, but his heart just wasn't in it anymore.

"I'm sorry, honey."

She turned and looked at him for a moment, pushing the fine hair out of her eyes.

"How old is that suit?" she said.

Ford looked down.

"I don't know, six, seven, maybe ten years."

"It's too small for you," she said, and she went into the bathroom.

Ford put his hands on his hips and frowned. Then he turned to look at himself in her wardrobe mirror. She was right: the pants pinched around the middle, and there was a little pillow of flesh at the front. In the past he'd always prided himself on staying in shape, but recently he hadn't kept up so well with the jogging and tennis. Now he was paying the price. It had been easier when his wife Carolyn had been alive. They had often jogged together, and Carolyn had been a high school tennis champ. Sunny hit a mean forehand herself, but now she had all the other school activities to keep her busy.

He sighed and walked up close to the mirror. In exactly two months' time he would turn forty. He tried a smile—according to Carolyn his best feature—and then noticed the coffee stains on his lower teeth. He wondered how long it would be before his sandy-colored hair would turn gray—it had already receded a good deal at the temples— how long before the circles beneath his brown eyes would take on the haggard permanence that marked the onset of middle age.

If Carolyn had been alive, she would have told him it was time to get out of Trauma. Seventy-hour weeks and all-night emergencies made it a young man's game. Hardly anyone stuck it out after forty. He tried to imagine her words, how she would have said he should leave the Willowbrook and take up a more comfortable post at double the pay—a post at Cedars-Sinai, for example, or the Columbia Health Care Corporation. Would she have brought Sunny into the equation or not? He tried to imagine what she would have said, and whether in the end he would have done what she wanted.

The Santa Ana winds had come early that year, and in the hills to the north brushfires had been smoldering since the weekend. A brown haze hung over the city, smudging the horizon, tainting the air with a chemical smell like diesel oil and burnt plastic. At noon the temperatures reached a hundred degrees and kept on climbing.

Driving down Robertson towards the Santa Monica Freeway, Ford wrestled with the air-conditioning system in his white Buick Century. After nearly five years he still hadn't gotten the hang of it. Whichever setting he chose, whichever outlets he selected, whichever direction he pointed the vents, he was either sweltering or numb with cold. But that didn't stop him from trying. Every morning, right through the summer, he would spend several frustrating minutes changing the settings, adjusting the outlets, and redirecting the vents, before finally giving up and rolling down the window. It wasn't the only feature of the car that annoyed him: there was the huge turning circle and the bouncy suspension. Not to mention a tacky interior that recalled the worse excesses of seventies sedan luxury. Carolyn used to laugh each time Ford cursed the immovable gearshift. Whenever Sunny had climbed in with muddy shoes or a runny ice cream, Carolyn would say with mock officiousness, "Watch the burgundy velveteen." One way and another they'd laughed a lot in that car.

The Willowbrook Medical Center was half an hour's drive away on the freeway. It had been built as a direct response to the Watts riots of 1965 and the social problems that lay behind them. Although planners and administrators had seen to it that the name Watts had all but disappeared from the city maps, the vicinity of the hospital remained one into which LA's white population rarely, if ever, ventured. Today, thanks to a program of closures, the hospital's service area was stretched over more than one hundred square miles of the city, but still only three percent of its patients were Caucasian. The majority of those remaining were now Hispanic, reflecting the high level of immigration into the area from across the border. Among the Willowbrook staff African-Americans were in the majority, although within the Trauma Unit there was usually a mix, thanks in part to the presence of army surgeons. With two thousand intentional-injury admissions per year— gunshot and stabbings mostly—the Willowbrook offered experience in handling battlefield casualties that was otherwise available only in wartime. In fact, the rotation scheme that brought army doctors in had been Ford's initiative. Formerly a resident at the Walter Reed Hospital in Washington, DC, he had served in the medical corps for eight years, rising to the rank of major.

Despite the violence, Ford no longer worried about driving into South Central, not now that they had Freeway 105. The Willowbrook was just two blocks away from the eastbound exit, six from the westbound. When Ford had joined the hospital seven years earlier, it had been different. Back then, whichever route you took, you were still left with two and a half miles of Imperial Highway to cover or three miles on El Segundo Boulevard. Both roads ran right by the projects and were notorious for muggings, carjackings, and shootings. Of course people were still careful once they were off the freeway. They kept their doors locked and drove in the left-hand lane, away from the sidewalk, but Ford hadn't heard of any drivers being shot at since the '92 riots, and he barely even thought about it anymore.

Finding traffic to be light that Tuesday morning, he flipped on the cruise control and began working on his speech, noting his ideas on a microcassette recorder.

The conference he was speaking at was being held at the Convention Center downtown. *Towards 2000: Priorities for Medical Research and Development* was being organized by the National Institutes of Health, the afternoon session being dedicated to the field of anti-infective agents. It promised to be an interesting forum.

Past experience had forced Ford to face the fact that he was not a natural public speaker. With a small group of medical students he had no problem. It was like a conversation. You could look into their faces, gauge their interest, make contact. But in front of a crowd of strangers it was different: you talked, they listened—provided what you were saying really interested them, provided they could follow your argument, provided your delivery was clear, confident, and free of hesitation. Otherwise they sat there in silence, row upon row of expressionless faces, waiting for you to finish. The thought that he was a surgeon in the company of pharmacology specialists, talking about their field of expertise rather than his, made him even more apprehensive.

Ford was still thinking about his speech as he approached the Wilmington Avenue exit. He was on the ramp, still doing forty, when the pickup in front of him suddenly slammed on its brakes, its tail end drifting sideways, tires screaming. Ford stamped on the brake pedal, but he was too close, going too fast, the mass of the car still surging forward. He felt the wheels lock. He yanked the wheel right and tried to steer into the gap by the rail.

The rail was what he hit. There was a noise like a gunshot, and he was thrown forward against the seat belt. He sat for a moment behind the wheel, his heart pounding, just waiting for his body to tell him if he was actually hurt. But he wasn't. He'd made it. Still feeling a little shaky, he climbed out onto the road.

There were cars all over the junction. In the middle an ambulance was slewed across Wilmington Avenue. A police helicopter swept overhead, tilting as it circled the scene. Ford took in the devastation. People were getting out of their cars to get a better look, fascinated but scared too. The ambulance itself was wrecked. It looked as if someone had pounded the front with rocks and then torched it. Yellow crime-scene tape fluttered in the smoke-tainted air, and Ford noticed a couple of squad cars parked a little way from the junction with a group of policemen standing around a black woman. There was glass every-where and in back of the ambulance dark patches of what looked like blood.

2

Nurse Gloria Tyrell came out of the Emergency Department isolation room holding a pair of blood-spattered Pump Reeboks as Ford entered the corridor.

"Good morn—"

A shout from the isolation room cut off her greeting.

"*Oh! Muh-motherfuckah!*"

The voice crackled with superhuman rage. Gloria shrugged her huge momma-bear shoulders and held up the bloody shoes.

"Boy comes in dusted. I don't think he even knows he's been stabbed. Twice."

Ford looked back down the corridor at the crowds in triage, where wounded people were being prioritized.

"What's going on, Gloria?"

"Didn't you catch the news?"

"On the radio just now I heard something about a young girl. Hammel, was it? Is that what all this . . . ?"

Ford saw Mary Draper, a fourth-year resident, come out of the critical room, radiologist Marvin Leonard's baritone booming out behind her—"*Ra-di-ation, ra-di-ation, ra-di-ation*"—clearing the room while he took his pictures. Seeing him, she smiled.

"I'm glad you could find time to be with us, Doctor."

"I got stuck coming off the 105," explained Ford. "Somebody torched an ambulance at the bottom of the ramp."

"I know. We stabilized one of the paramedics. He's in OR-two now with pretty severe head injuries. Somebody hit him with a baseball bat."

"Ouch."

"Plus we have two auto-versus-peds and a couple of gunshot wounds. A patrolman got a stray bullet in the thigh, and there's a homeboy's been shot through the neck with a nine millimeter—a Glock, I think the paramedic said. Weren't you bleeped?"

"I'm not even supposed to be on today. But I need to talk to Haynes."

Slipping on his white coat, Ford followed Draper back into the critical room.

Four of the six gurneys in the thirty-by-thirty room were occupied, and mixed teams of residents, interns, rotators, all talking at once, were establishing airways, getting in lines, seeking to stabilize the trauma victims. Normally the trauma team of ER physicians, surgical residents, radiologists, and anesthetists responded to the gunshots, stabbings, and car accidents—the so-called Code Yellows—but when logjams developed, support came in from the adjacent departments. The Willowbrook was a teaching hospital, so there were always enough hands in an emergency despite the lack of funds, but things could get pretty noisy at times.

Ford took in a red-faced patrolman who was standing in one corner, a paper cup in his hands, his tired eyes fixed on the gurney where his wounded colleague lay in a pair of inflated medical antishock trousers—or MAST pants.

"Where's the homeboy?" asked Ford.

Mary Draper led him across to one of the noisiest groups, people parting as they saw Ford come through. There was a flurry of good mornings but no let up in activity. The patient had been anesthetized, and a fourth-year surgical resident was cutting through the cricothyroid membrane, seeking to establish an airway without going through the nose or mouth. At the same time this was happening, another resident was cutting off the young man's pants, running the shears up one leg, then the other, cutting through underwear, belt, everything. The pants unpeeled like a banana skin, revealing pieces of lint in the man's pubic hair. Ford noticed the relative absence of blood—a few splashes on what looked like brand-new Nikes, that was all. What was it with these kids and footwear?

"He took a nine-millimeter shell in the throat?"

Draper nodded, pointing to the entrance wound on the right side of the neck.

"Looks like the missile came out through the left jaw."

The anesthetized patient began to gag as a tracheostomy tube was inserted into the incision and the cuff inflated. It sounded as if he were trying to clear his throat, but it went on for several seconds. Then it stopped. Ford's eyes flicked up at the ECG monitor. He was doing okay. Two of the team stepped back, shoulders relaxing, coming down off the buzz of action.

"Nice intubation," somebody said.

"Looks like the bullet missed the major vessels," Ford observed.

There was a sharp ripping sound of stripped adhesive tape. They were taping the young man's head to the backboard.

"Blood pressure was okay, so I guess he's not bleeding too bad. Just the one missile?"

"So far as we can see."

Mary Draper was punching in numbers for the operating room. There were three ORs at Willowbrook, located directly above the Emergency Department on the second floor, right next to the Intensive Care Unit.

Melvyn Hershy, the doctor who had performed the cricothyroid-otomy, came around the gurney as Mary Draper slipped into her ultra-cool, I-cannot-be-fazed telephone manner—*"Hello, Janet. I have a customer for you. Black male in his mid twenties . . ."*

"Glock," said Hershy. "According to a bystander it was a young lady pulled the trigger. Track goes in through the sternocleidomastoid, through the base of the tongue and out through the left mandible. Must have missed the carotid and the jugular by a whisker."

Ford looked at the young man, who was now breathing through the tube.

"And he's got a hell of a throat infection," said Hershy, almost to himself.

"A what?"

"A throat infection. Saw it when I was taking a look inside. Strep throat."

"Well, I guess that's the least of his problems now," said Ford.

Hershy smiled.

"You get held up?" he asked mildly.

"There was some trouble on the freeway."

The other man was shaking his head now, looking back at the patient.

"I'm not surprised."

"Oh?"

Hershy looked back at Ford, confused for a moment.

"Didn't you catch the news this morning?"

"No."

Hershy shook his head again.

"It was a hell of a night. Big shootout in Crenshaw. Fertilizer truck flipped over on the Pomona Freeway. About one o'clock the Mother started sending cases over to us. There was a kid—little girl with appendicitis—got referred to us in the early hours. Appendix ruptured in the ambulance. Kid went into shock, died."

"Jesus."

"Yeah, well, anyway there was media all over the place. Somehow they found out about the girl. Story was all over the networks by dawn. 'Hospital turns away dying black kid' kind of thing."

Ford shook his head.

"So they start burning ambulances."

Mary Draper put down the phone.

"They're ready in OR-three, Dr. Ford."

Ford refocused on the job at hand.

"Do we know this kid's name?"

"The 'Shark' is what he said to the paramedics. Or 'Sharky.' "

Ford looked at Hershy and smiled.

"My first fish of the day."

From the other side of the room there was a sudden spike in the noise. It was always bad in the critical room when more than one gurney was occupied, but when things started to go wrong the shouting took on an edge, a jagged sharpness. Ford turned away from Hershy and entered a new group.

"Pulse going over one-twenty. Tachycardia!"

"Get these fucking pants off him."

"Systolic blood pressure dropping. We're down to ninety."

The patrolman was jerked hard as the deflated MAST pants were pulled away, revealing dark blue polyester pants soaked in blood. The patrolman started fumbling at his oxygen mask and was immediately restrained.

"For Christ's sake, hold him!"

Ford stepped forward, gently pushing a nurse to one side.

"Cut off the uniform. Tourniquet the left thigh. Dr. Ozal, get a line into the distal saphenous vein. I want three liters of volume resuscitation."

The shouting moderated to status-updating level as Peter Ozal, a third-year surgical resident, performed the ankle cutdown required to access the saphenous vein. Ford watched Ozal's nimble hands as he incised the exposed vessel.

"Okay," said Ford, taking a deep breath, making an effort to keep the anger out of his voice. "Here we have a perfect example of why MAST pants create as many problems as they solve. Dr. Ozal, your opinion?"

Ozal frowned with concentration, inserting sterile intravenous tubing four inches into the big leg vein.

"Well, I guess you could say their strength is also their weakness," he said out of the side of his mouth.

Ford smiled. He liked Ozal, but he tended to be a little taciturn.

"You could," he said. "But what would that mean?"

"Well, the MAST pants work by increasing peripheral resistance in the lower half of the body, allowing more blood to get to the upper trunk and head. But the problem is that when you deflate the trousers too rapidly"—Ozal shot a glance across to a diminutive Asian nurse who was trying to avoid his eye by staring at the monitors—"you can get profound hypotension. Patient's blood pressure drops through the floor."

"Exactly. Another problem is you can't see exactly what's going on. Without the MAST pants, we can see clearly"—he pointed to the wound on the patrolman's left thigh—"where the missile entered the leg." Ford looked around at the circle of young faces. "Remember, patients will die of hypoxia before they bleed to death, but in fact, after central nervous system injury, the commonest cause of death is exsanguination."

Ford checked the monitors and stood back from the gurney.

"Is he going to be okay?"

There was a momentary pause in the babble of talk as Ford turned to see the other patrolman, still holding his paper cup. He gestured with it towards the man on the gurney.

"He's goin' to be awright, right?"

Ford took in the weary face of a stocky man in his late forties. Broken veins high on each cheekbone gave the man the appearance of good health, but underneath the threadlike capillaries the skin was sallow and open-pored. There was a smear of dirt across his forehead. He looked as though he'd had a rough night.

"Yes, I believe he is. We'll get him up to the operating room, take that bullet out of his leg."

Ford started to move away, but the patrolman followed.

"Hey, Doctor . . ." They had left the critical room and were out in the corridor now, the patrolman keeping close. Ford noticed the bloody Reeboks still on the floor where Gloria must have left them. He bent to pick them up. "Doctor, there's something I wanted to ask you."

The man sounded hostile, and Ford prepared himself for whatever was coming. He turned, the bloody shoes in his right hand.

"Go ahead."

"I wanted to ask you . . ."—he had to draw a breath, he was so angry—"why it is you'll care for a . . . for a *scumbag* gangster before an officer gunned down in the line of duty."

Ford raised a warning finger.

"Well, first of all, I don't know that the young man with the neck wound is a gangster," he said. "I don't know that he wasn't an innocent bystander."

The patrolman pressed a hand against his mouth, bottling up the hot feeling that threatened to overwhelm him. Ford noticed bitten nails—abrasions and grime on the knuckles.

"And as for the circumstances in which these people are shot, I can't say that that enters into the equation. The neck wound might have been life threatening. You would be surprised how quickly you can lose a patient wounded in that area, so close to the spine, and major blood vessels. I made a decision based on my experience."

This was too much for the policeman.

"But I just watched my partner nearly . . . nearly *bleed* to death, goddammit!"

Ford waved away a concerned-looking Melvyn Hershy. He could handle this on his own.

"It may have looked like that to you. In fact he was momentarily hypovolemic due to a procedural . . . due to a moment's clumsiness. But they got a line into his leg and he'll be fine now."

The patrolman took a step closer, so that Ford could smell his rank breath.

"Do you know what I think, Doctor?"

Ford stared into the man's bloodshot eyes. You didn't need to be telepathic.

"I think that in a . . . in a *war* you have to make up your mind whose side you're on."

Ten minutes later Ford was scrubbing up, preparing to go into the OR. He watched the hot water run over his hands and arms, then pushed the faucet lever with his elbow. He kept seeing the scared faces of the people in their cars, looking out at the burning ambulance. He knew exactly what they had been thinking: a couple of hours earlier, and it could have been me. Night after night the TV pumped out stories of rape, murder, drive-by shootings, recreational killings, riots, but it wasn't until you smelled the smoke, saw the blood on the sidewalk that it came to you what a violent city LA really was.

"What's up, Doc?"

Ford turned and saw Conrad Allen, a senior surgeon specializing in cardio-thoracic injuries. Allen was gloved up and ready to go, an unconscious Mexican with a bullet lodged in his colon waiting for him in OR1. Ford shrugged, taking in his old friend's face. Allen had a rich caramel complexion flecked with dark freckles that went right up into his short frizzy hair. His playful, relaxed demeanor belied the dedicated professional and superb surgeon that he was: decisive, cautious, quick when necessary, qualities he kept steel-hard and blade-sharp right through to the end of a twelve-hour shift. He was one of the few people in Trauma Ford felt he could rely on one hundred percent.

"A police officer just told me I had to decide whose side I was on."

Allen's smile crimped the skin around his intelligent brown eyes.

"The good guys or the bad guys, right?"

"I think he had in mind the good guys or the black guys."

"Riiight." Allen dragged out the monosyllable, still smiling. "I thought maybe it was Loulou Patoulou put a dent in your morning."

"You've seen her?"

"She was going in to see Haynes."

Dr. Lucy Patou (Loulou Patoulou, the Culture Vulture or simply the Vulture) had been the control of infection officer for the Willowbrook since 1990. She had been brought in to tackle what the county considered to be elevated mortality levels due to nosocomial infection—infections caught by patients *inside* the hospital and to a degree encouraged by hospital conditions.

The year Dr. Patou joined the Willowbrook, there had been an outbreak of *Staphylococcus aureus* on the neonatal ward in which four infants had been infected, one fatally. The staph bacteria in question proved resistant to treatment with penicillins, but had responded to high doses of cephalosporin. Despite this, Dr. Patou had instituted a draconian regime that included stripping out all organic material—curtains, sheets, rubber fittings on equipment such as ventilators and trolleys—and scrubbing down of the whole ward with disinfectant. The staff didn't know what had hit them.

Patou's background was in pediatrics, where infection was one of the principal enemies of the clinician. In Ford's view she tended to apply the pediatrician's perspective to every other aspect of hospital care, and it was this that so often put her in conflict with the Trauma Unit, where sterility was frequently sacrificed to speed of intervention.

Five years at the Willowbrook had taught Patou to stay away from Trauma and the unedifying spectacle of *dirty* people coming into the hospital with *dirty* wounds. Unfortunately that just meant that the frequent clinician versus infection officer spats were staged in the Intensive Care Unit, where Dr. Patou was forever asking for items to be cultured (hence the nickname) in order to see what bugs might be getting established. IV lines were removed and replaced, mattresses taken away and, on some occasions, without explanation, incinerated. Even respirators were taken out of commission in order to be stripped down, cultured, and then put back together again. In the opinion of some of the Trauma staff, Dr. Patou would have preferred it if the Willowbrook could be run without the patients. It would have been so much *cleaner*.

"You saw her?" asked Ford. "You didn't speak to her?"

"No sir."

Ford let out a sigh. He had been anticipating some acerbic message or other. Then he noticed Allen's expression.

"What?"

"I didn't speak to her. Lady spoke to me, though. Gave me that beady eye just as she was going in to Russell and said, *'Tell Dr. Ford I'm onto him.'* "

"Oh, Lord."

Allen looked at Ford's upraised hands inquisitively, as though searching for dirt.

"You better be sure you're clean because she's gonna be *culturing* your ass."

Ford watched Allen's receding back and reflected on the potential calamity of having Lucy Patou *onto* him. Their relationship, fragile from the very start, had taken a turn for the worse at the beginning of the year when he had published an article in *The California Medical Review*. The article had focused on some unusual infections afflicting abdominal-wound patients at the Willowbrook where the principal pathogen had been *Enterococcus faecalis*, part of a community of anaerobic bacteria found in the lower digestive tract. Despite treatment with a broad range of antibiotics, including vancomycin, the infections had proved impossible to check. Over a ten-week period, four intensive-care patients had succumbed to blood poisoning and died.

That abdominal wounds should become infected was not in itself unusual. Whenever the bowel was punctured, whether by blade or bullet, the risk of contamination was great. Below the stomach, the digestive tract was heavily populated with bacteria. In fact more bacteria lived on a single square inch of the human intestine than there were humans on the planet. Indeed, there were more bacteria in the human body than there were *human cells*. As long as the bacteria stayed in the intestine, they could, for their own purposes, assist in the breaking down of fats, sugars, proteins, and unwanted chemical waste. That was the deal that had been struck between bacteria and primates over millions of years of evolution. In a sense, the intestinal bacteria did the jobs that nobody else in the body wanted to do, and for that service they were tolerated. But when they got outside the circumscribed confines of the bowel, they became dangerous. That was why abdominal-wound patients were immediately given broad-spectrum antibiotics as a prophylactic.

What had worried Ford about these particular cases—what had pushed him to write the article—was firstly the inexorable progress of the infections, the inability of the ICU team to stop them, and secondly the compressed incidence of cases, there having been four of them in a matter of weeks.

A few days after the article was published, Ford had been summoned to the medical director's office. Though Russell Haynes himself had not seemed unduly bothered by what he called Ford's "disregard for the niceties," it had become clear that Lucy Patou had lodged a complaint. Ford, as a representative of the hospital, had publicly spoken of a matter and of a domain that, properly speaking, was hers to monitor and, if she felt like it, to comment upon.

There had followed an awkward meeting in which Patou had sought to put Ford in his place. She had drawn his attention to a string of resistant *Enterococcus* cases at St. Thomas Hospital in New Jersey in 1994. The cases Ford had encountered, she said, were nothing new. More to the point, the fact that the cases were multiple was not necessarily indicative of a general spread of resistant bacteria among the community at large, as Ford seemed to be suggesting in his article. In fact, the resistant bacteria in New Jersey were proven to have been passed from patient to patient within the Intensive Care Unit via contaminated equipment. In other words, true to form, Lucy Patou was pointing the finger at ward procedure and hygiene. And this despite the fact that thorough investigation at the Willowbrook had revealed no evidence of *Enterococcus* contamination in the Intensive Care Unit.

Thinking it over now, pushing his hands into the latex gloves, Ford began to understand what Patou had meant when she said she was *onto* him. She knew all about his invitation to speak at the conference organized by the National Institutes of Health. Indeed, Ford had more or less agreed, under duress, to go through his speech with her prior to the conference. She wanted to be sure that he at least qualified his remarks with some of the doubts she had expressed. Now she suspected him of going back on their agreement and of deliberately avoiding her. Of course she assumed that the speech must be written by now.

The problem was that the whole subject had become more complicated in the past few weeks as a result of a rash of new resistance cases. This time the microorganism concerned was not an *Enterococcus* but a strain of *Streptococcus pneumoniae*.

The first victim had been a twenty-three-year-old black male named Andre Nelson. A known user of cocaine and PCP—the police claimed that he was also a dealer—he had arrived at the Emergency Department after suffering an acute asthmatic attack at his home in Lynwood. Although the medical emergency team was able to stabilize him, it later emerged that he was suffering from a lung infection. That infection proved as impossible to halt as the others, and after a week on a ventilating machine Nelson had suffered complete respiratory failure. Since then, two more resistant pneumonia cases had appeared at the Willowbrook, one of them admitted via the Emergency Department, the other through General Surgery. Although it was too early to draw conclusions, Ford was convinced that the high incidence of resistant infection encountered at the Willowbrook was a cause for concern. At the very least it suggested that the selective advantage enjoyed by resistant bacteria was somehow being accentuated in the South Central community as a whole.

It was because he had felt it vital to incorporate these new cases into his speech that Ford had run out of time. If it had simply been a matter of going over the ground covered in the original article, it would have been fine—he would have been happy to discuss it with Lucy Patou. But as it was, there was no time left, and the disturbance that morning—the extra cases it had generated—had snatched away any chance of a last-minute briefing. He was going to have to deal with the Shark's neck injury and run if he was going to make his three o'clock slot.

Ford entered OR3 and said his good-mornings. The Shark had been positioned to allow rapid, wide access to the upper thorax in the event it became necessary. He was on his back, a bolster between his shoulders, his head tilted away from Ford. Apart from the entry wound and the tube in his throat, the Shark looked as if he might be sleeping. Ford made the first long cut along the sternocleidomastoid, starting just below the Shark's right ear. As the young man's blood welled, he gave a little shake to get his mind off Lucy Patou, but it was impossible. He prayed that she would not find herself a front-row seat at the conference.

3

The traffic was sparse on the Harbor Freeway. Ford drove fast, listening to the news bulletins on the radio. Things had been quiet since noon, they said, but the police remained on full alert right across the city. As Central Los Angeles slid past him, street after street of squat brown houses on plots of parched brown grass, Ford could not help feeling vulnerable. He felt as if he were crossing a no-man's land. When he saw a pair of patrol cars up ahead, he got on their tails and stayed there until the downtown tower blocks loomed tall through the gray-brown haze.

The Convention Center parking lot was the size of Dodger Stadium, but there weren't many cars in it. Maybe the news of the disturbances in South Central had put some people off coming.

For Ford the failure of antibiotics was a more profound and disturbing threat than that of civil unrest, even if it never got a mention on the radio. For surgeons of all kinds it was a dark cloud that loomed over the future of their profession. The spread of drug resistance among more and more bacteria threatened to turn the clock back more than half a century, to the days when the most trivial infections could turn lethal and when surgery of any kind was more hazardous than Russian roulette.

Ford had been just ten years old when the U.S. Surgeon General of the day had declared that medical technology would soon be able "to close the book on infectious diseases." At the time, this optimism had appeared well founded. As Ford later learned in high school, since the discovery of penicillin in 1928, one disease after another had succumbed to the power of antibiotics, among them scarlet fever, pneumonia, syphilis, typhoid, meningitis, and the industrialized world's biggest killer, tuberculosis. At the same time, the ability to keep open wounds free of infection by common but potentially lethal bacteria such as *Staphylococcus aureus* had turned surgery from a last-ditch option to a central pillar of medicine. Unmentioned in the curriculum was the fact that, with the days of infectious disease numbered, drug companies were already devoting their resources to other health problems, in particular those afflicting the longer-lived populations of the developed world: heart failure, arthritis, and cancer.

Yet the victory had proved surprisingly short-lived. In the early 1960s penicillin-resistant strains of *Shigella dysenteriae*, a bacteria that causes dysentery, began to appear in Japan, killing fifteen percent of those infected. While Ford was applying for college, lethal strains of *Streptococcus pneumoniae* were surfacing in neonatal wards all over the world, proving fatal to three quarters of infected babies under two months of age. In South Africa a strain was found to be resistant not only to penicillin, but to most of its successors, including ampicillin, streptomycin, methicillin, chloramphenicol, and tetracycline. By the time Ford transferred to the Willowbrook in 1989, multidrug-resistant bacteria were responsible for the return of such lethal or crippling diseases as cholera, septicemia, rheumatic fever, gonorrhea, leprosy, and tuberculosis—which was claiming around three million lives a year, most of them in the Third World. Although a succession of new antibiotics had been brought onto the market, many pathogens were proving able to cope, among them *Staphylococcus aureus*. In many hospitals strains of superstaph, as it became known, were proving resistant to every antibiotic yet developed—except one, vancomycin. As far as Ford was concerned, when staph overcame that final hurdle, the post-antibiotic era would have arrived.

That species of bacteria would over time acquire resistance to the antibiotics used against them was not surprising in itself. According to evolutionary theory, random changes in bacterial genes would, sooner or later, produce strains capable of surviving any given form of attack. These new strains would enjoy an enormous competitive advantage over the rest, gradually displacing them until they became dominant. What the medical profession had not anticipated was the rate at which

these genetic mutations would take place: not over centuries and mil-
lennia, but over years, months, and even weeks. Even more alarming,
bacteria proved capable of transmitting resistance genes *between
species*, something unheard of in the animal kingdom. This was a particular concern in hospitals, where people suffering from different types
of infection came into contact with each other via shared facilities or
via the medical staff themselves. Drug addicts, diabetics, and people
with AIDS—the so-called immunocompromised, who made up such a
large proportion of Marcus Ford's patients—posed the same problem
in microcosm, often suffering a number of different infections at the
same time because their immune systems were not strong enough to
resist.

What Ford found most disturbing was the way that the misuse of
antiobiotics accelerated the spread of bacterial resistance. Instead of
being employed sparingly, when a patient's natural defenses looked
likely to be overwhelmed, they were still distributed en masse as cure-
alls, used to tackle sore throats, toothaches, acne, and the common
cold. They were fed by the kilogram to chickens and pigs and sprayed
on the walls of hospital wards. In the developed world, public demand
and determined marketing campaigns by manufacturers put doctors
under intense pressure to prescribe the latest drugs, rather than let
nature take its course. Studies in Europe and the United States suggested that between a third and a half of all antibiotic prescriptions
were either inappropriate or unnecessary. In the developing world, the
situation was even more serious. Driven by hunger for market share,
manufacturers pushed their products as hard as possible, even though
the medical profession in these countries was ill equipped to supervise
their use.

Self-medication on a vast scale was the result. Ignorant of the consequences, many people would continue a course of antibiotics only for
as long as their symptoms persisted and not the for the full period
needed to kill all the bacteria causing them. The small colonies left
behind would, of course, be the ones that had proved best able to cope
with antibiotic attack. The cost of antibiotics, especially for the poor in
developing countries, often made this false economy inevitable. But
whether through poverty or ignorance, human beings had been selec-
tively breeding for resistance bacteria just as surely as if laboratories had

been set up for the purpose. In spite of this, the use of antibiotics around the world continued to grow. The National Institutes of Health had estimated that by the year 2000, a total of fifty thousand tons of antibiotics would be used on humans, animals, and plants, a mass genetic manipulation without parallel in the history of life on Earth— unplanned, unregulated, and beyond control.

The afternoon session was already well under way by the time Ford arrived. In the foyer a team of young women in scarlet jackets presented him with a name badge and a chunky document folder. On either side of the foyer stood tall displays of flowers, brilliant beneath the discreetly recessed lighting.

"We were afraid you weren't going to show, Dr. Ford," said a tall fifty-year-old woman with taut, face-lifted skin. Her green eyes fixed on his tie. It was on crooked; it had to be. "I'm Julia Lacey, conference manager."

Her hand felt smooth and remarkably cold, but then the air-conditioning in the center was almost enough to make you shiver. Ford realized how clammy his own hand must feel.

"I hope you didn't have any problem getting here," she said. "Were the directions clear?"

"No problem," he said. "I'd have arrived sooner, but things were a little busy at the hospital. I'm sure you can imagine."

"Yes, of course," she said, returning him a professional hospitality smile. "Please follow me and I'll show you to your seat."

She led him along a passage that ran parallel with the side of the hall. Ford could hear a speech in progress, a man's amplified voice bouncing off the walls. He felt a flutter of nerves in the pit of his stomach. The hall seemed big. Just how many people were in there? When Julia Lacey wasn't looking, he reached up and adjusted his tie. The knot had tightened into an awkward little ball. He really needed to undo it and start again, but there wasn't time.

Lacey opened a door giving onto a brightly lit stage. He saw a long cloth-covered table, at which sat five men in dark suits, each one with a plaque in front of him bearing his name. At the front of the stage another man was speaking at a lectern. Ford couldn't see the audience.

One of the men behind the table saw the two of them and came over. It was Marshall West, an old med-school friend of Ford's who had recently been appointed to a top job at the county health department. It had been at West's prompting that Ford had been invited to address the conference. Most of the speakers at conferences such as this were microbiologists and pharmacologists, experts in the research and manufacture of drugs. Surgeons, mere users of drugs, were not usually asked to participate. West had thought it a good idea to get the perspective from "the front line," as he put it. Ford didn't want to let him down.

Although the two men were the same age, Ford couldn't help feeling that the years had been kinder to West. His full head of dark hair had only just started to turn gray, and there was a brightness in his eyes, a glow to his skin that suggested a healthy diet and regular sleep. Always a keen track-and-field man—he had been a champion hurdler at Michigan—he had kept himself in remarkably good shape. His tailor-made suit and crisp white shirt accentuated his athletic build. The sight of him left Ford feeling more disheveled than ever.

"Marcus, so glad you could make it," West whispered, shaking Ford's hand with a double-handed politician's squeeze. "I was afraid with all the trouble you'd be snowed under. What's happening down there? Are you coping?"

"Yes, yes," said Ford. "We're on top of it. Last night got pretty hectic, though. You heard about the girl?"

"I don't think we'll ever be allowed to forget it. The switchboard's been jammed all day. I came down here to escape."

"I thought the media was concentrating on the hospitals. We've had them camped on the parking lot."

"Yeah, but now they're making a big resources issue out of it, and that's my territory." West inched closer. "Actually, I'm wondering if it might not be helpful in the long run. I mean, this Hammel story is national news, especially with the disturbances. And national issues determine congressional votes, if you get what I mean."

Ford nodded. Politics was West's strong point, federal politics in particular. That was why the County Board of Supervisors had set him up above the entire administrative structure of the Health Services Department and granted him complete operational autonomy. His title was simply Health Czar. They'd hoped that with his experience and contacts he might be able to squeeze more funds out of the federal and state governments, helping to prevent the virtual dismantling of the public health-care system in a county more heavily populated than the entire state of Georgia.

Ford and West had not seen much of each other after med school, although their careers had taken both of them from Ann Arbor to Washington, DC. Drawn to the pace and the variety of work in trauma, Ford had joined the army medical corps. West had taken up a research job for a Democratic senator named Hal Burroughs, an early exponent of health-care reform and a friend of the West family. For a few months Ford and West tried to keep in contact, but as time went on, it had become harder and harder for both of them (as an intern, Ford's leisure time was all but nonexistent). By the time Ford left for California, their relationship was down to Christmas cards only.

It was at his next job in Washington, at the Department of Health and Human Services, that West had acquired his reputation. In particular he was credited with a key role in an emergency response program set up to tackle an epidemic of multidrug-resistant tuberculosis (MDR-TB, as it was known). The epidemic had originally centered on prison inmates in Miami and New York City, but had spread rapidly to the general population, especially in poorer neighborhoods where drug addiction and HIV infection were rife. After extensive tests one antibiotic was found to be effective against the bacteria: streptomycin, the first antibiotic to be discovered after penicillin. But there was a problem: nobody made it anymore. Pressuring the industry into restarting mass production was a difficult proposition. Existing, profitable product lines had to be suspended to create the necessary capacity, and given the absence of patent protection, the outlook for profitability was poor. The fact that most of the demand would be in the Third World only made matters worse. It was a tribute to West's powers of persuasion that these objections had been overcome.

The invitation from the board of supervisors came in response to another crisis, this time a financial one. The previous year, like neighboring Orange County before it, Los Angeles had been facing the prospect of bankruptcy. After four years of overspending, thanks in part to the 1992 riots and a string of natural disasters, the county found its creditors unwilling to lend it any more money. A downgrading of its long-term debt by the credit-rating agencies made the search for alternatives hopeless. The board of supervisors had no choice but to order an immediate twenty percent cut in spending so as to bring the county's $11 billion budget into balance. In order to meet its allotted share of the cuts, the county health department was faced with the outright closure of its biggest hospital, LA County/USC Medical Center, all mental health facilities, and virtually the entire network of health centers and clinics. This network provided the bulk of immunization, pediatric, and preventative health care for the community, as well as a range of emergency services. Outpatient care was also to be radically cut. As one journalist had put it, without a restructuring plan and money from Washington the Los Angeles public health-care system would be able to do little more than gather the dead and wounded off the streets.

By the time the invitation went out from LA, rumors had already begun that West might soon stand for elected office, although he still seemed a little young to run for Congress. Nevertheless his decision to accept had come as a surprise. The newly created post of Health Czar was a political hot potato. Although job cuts and closures were inevitable, it was the czar who would play the key role in deciding where and when these should happen. It was not a job for a man who was anxious to be popular.

But West had surprised everyone. Following discussions with the President's staff and his old colleagues at the Department of Health, he had been able to come up with extra federal funds of $350 million. The money was contingent upon the implementation of a restructuring plan that placed an emphasis on outpatient and preventive care, rather than care within hospitals, which was far more expensive. Many people still opposed what became known as the West Plan—at the Willowbrook they had received bomb threats—but most people recognized that the alternative was far worse.

Ford had finally met West again on a fact-finding visit to the Willowbrook six months earlier. Ford was struck by how little West had changed.

"What's the turnout like?" he asked. "Has everybody stayed at home?"

"Some have," said West, "but most of the industry people are here, and some journalists. Are you going to be okay to go ahead? Otherwise, I'll have to say something. I'm supposed to be chairing this session."

"I'll be fine. I just wish I'd had more time to prepare. I'd planned—"

"Don't worry. After Dr. van Brock and his Australian ants you'll be a breath of fresh air. We could use a little reality check, I can tell you."

"I'll do my best."

West clapped him on the shoulder.

"Knew I could count on you. We'd better go."

He led Ford to an empty place behind the long table and resumed his own seat in the middle. At the lectern Dr. van Brock, a tall man with a neatly trimmed beard and a Teutonic accent, was delivering the conclusion to his speech. According to the program, it was entitled "Anti-infectives in Nature—Alternative Strategies for Research." In front of him sat an audience of maybe one hundred and fifty people, although the auditorium was designed to hold three times that number.

"Over the years we have come to think of antibiotics as an invention of modern science," he was saying, "the sole purpose of which is to protect human beings and livestock from bacterial infection. We forget that antibacterial defenses were developed by bacteria themselves long before the evolution of plant or animal life on Earth. The weapons developed by certain species of fungus were the basis for the earliest antibiotics, including, of course, penicillin." He spoke directly to the audience, not even glancing at his notes. "What I hope our work on the Formicidae of Australasia will demonstrate is that the antibacterial struggle has also been waged by more complex species, including that most diverse class of species in the animal kingdom, the *Insecta*. Research into their antibacterial strategies may provide us with some exciting new insights in the years ahead."

He gathered his papers and acknowledged the audience's applause with a smile. In spite of what West had said, Ford got the impression that the audience liked Dr. van Brock and his work. He had a reassuring, avuncular manner, like one of those Middle European professors that always turned up in old sci-fi movies. And maybe he was really onto something. Maybe there were useful lessons to be learned from the insect world about how to deal with microbes. It had to be worth a try, if only because, during the past few years, conventional pharmaco-logical research had come up with very little that was new.

West was on his feet, thanking Dr. van Brock, when Ford saw her sitting in the second row—Lucy Patou. She was looking straight at him, her upturned head accentuating her smooth jawline and high cheek-bones. He felt the color rise to his cheeks. She thought he'd been delib-erately avoiding her, and now she was down here at the conference, watching him like a member of the health department Thought Police. A man sitting next to her leaned over and whispered something, and she smiled. Ford thought about giving her a wave, trying to ease the tension a little, but he had a feeling she wouldn't wave back. Loulou Patoulou was *onto him*.

He got through the first part of his speech pretty well, summarizing the work of the Willowbrook's Trauma Unit and the type of commu-nity it served. A grim silence descended upon the audience as he described the high proportion of patients who were on welfare, and the growing number of so-called undocumented people—mostly illegal immigrants from Mexico. He hammered home the point that many of these people had virtually no other contact with professional health care, either because they lacked any form of insurance coverage, or because they simply did not know how or where to get it. Many of them showed clear signs of malnutrition, a proportion comparable, in fact, to that in many developing countries. This was as true for the children as for the adults—and children now made up around a third of the Willow-brook's trauma admissions.

He made sure there was no trace of emotion in his voice. He didn't want his speech to sound like a charity appeal or, worse still, a political call-to-arms. He was setting out the parameters of his experience, not appealing to anybody's conscience. Even so, as he went on, he sensed a growing restlessness, an embarrassment. Maybe it was just his imagination, but it was something he'd become sensitive to over the years. When he talked about his work to neighbors and old friends—prosperous middle-class people, with careers and families—he had often felt the same thing. For them, hearing about South Central and its problems was like being told about another famine in Africa as you sat down to your evening meal. You felt guilty, not because you were responsible, but because you knew damn well you weren't going to do anything about it.

He avoided Lucy Patou's eye as he moved on to the incidents of drug-resistant infection he had witnessed during the last year: first the *Enterococcus* and then *Streptococcus pneumoniae*. This was her field, and the certainty that she was keeping track of his every word made it harder for him, but he described each case in detail: the progress of symptoms, the tests carried out, the treatments attempted. He also described how, in each case, a thorough search of the Intensive Care Unit and its equipment had been carried out to see whether the source of the infections was nosocomial—originating inside the hospital itself.

"Since these searches came up negative," he said, "I think it fair to assume that an uncommonly high incidence of resistant bacteria now exists among the South Central population, and perhaps beyond. There are a number of possible explanations for this, but high among them has to be the lack of supervision in the distribution and use of antibiotics. That is why I believe resistance is, at least in part, a resources issue."

Several people shifted in their seats. Lucy Patou's arms were now folded, and she was perched on the edge of her seat, as if struggling with an urge to interrupt. Ford ploughed on: "But lack of resources here in the U.S. may only be part of the problem. More than twenty years ago a strain of *Salmonella typhi*, the microbiological cause of typhoid, killed hundreds of people in Mexico and threatened to spread into this country. A U.S. Senate committee investigation concluded that the bacteria had mutated into a superbug because the drug industry had aggressively promoted chloramphenicol for a wide variety of infections in Mexico and other developing countries. That early warning does not seem to have been heeded. Latin America today plays host to an alarming number of resistant pathogens, including the El Tor strain of *Vibrio cholerae*, which is now carried by at least a million people in the Western Hemisphere and has killed at least nine thousand to date."

Ford looked up from his notes. In the audience people were exchanging glances. Ford wondered what it meant. It couldn't be that they were surprised at the information—the outbreaks he'd referred to were well known and well documented—but for some reason they seemed surprised to be hearing it now, as if it somehow had nothing to do with them. Ford felt his pulse accelerate. He had to stick to the argument, get to the point. Maybe he was simply going on too long. He turned over a page of his notes, but found himself looking at an abbreviated version of his opening remarks.

"What I want to say . . ."

Someone in the audience cleared their throat. Ford turned over another page. It was upside down.

"What I want to say is simply . . ."

It was another part of the speech he'd already done. He'd dropped some pages somewhere or left them at the office—or . . . Then he remembered: *they were still on the microcassette recorder.*

He looked up at the audience, at the rows of upturned faces. One hundred and fifty people. Industry executives, health-care experts, biotechnology entrepreneurs. Professional people, successful, *civilized.* They sat there in silence, waiting politely for him to have his say, to get his lungful of the clean, cool, civilized air before returning to the inner city, to a world of violence and barbarism that they had despaired of long ago. They were probably wondering where he'd gone wrong.

"The point is this: we can go on looking for new drugs, magic bullets to tackle each new crisis, but that's what we've been doing for the last twenty years, and it isn't working."

He saw several heads pop up around the auditorium. Suddenly people wanted to get a look at him.

"We're not winning the war. Sure, we need new antibiotics urgently, but the way things are going at the moment, the bugs are developing defenses faster than we can develop weapons. What's the use of coming up with new products, new approaches, if two years down the line they don't work anymore?"

There was an audible murmur from one side of the auditorium. Maybe in front of a conference of pharmaceutical producers this line of argument seemed a little hostile. Suddenly Ford felt hot.

"I realize that the drug companies are businesses. They have to sell their products. But there's a conflict here: the more widely their products get used—I mean in the antibiotic field—the less effective they become. Mass distribution might be profitable in the short term, but the resistance that results may pose a threat to all of us. Microbes don't care about borders any more than they do about race or . . . income."

Ford glanced round at Marshall West: his face wore an expression of muted surprise mixed with amusement.

"This conference is about priorities for medical R and D, and you've asked me to give you the view from the intensive care unit. Well, for the R and D, priority is to change the way these drugs are handled. Yes, I want to see more resources put into health care—what surgeon doesn't? I want to see more independent information made available about drug-resistant infections, so that at least we know what to expect. But most of all I want to see much closer control of how and where antibiotics are used. It may not be a fashionable word, but what I'm talking about is government regulation, of sales, of exports, whatever it takes. Given what we now know, I think that's the logical next step. If hospitals like the Willowbrook are to go on saving lives as they do now, I don't see any alternative."

Ford gathered up his notes. He'd planned on sounding more professional, less strident. He'd planned on presenting a step-by-step argument, instead of galloping to the end the way he had. But it was too late now. From the audience came a hesitant spatter of applause.

"Thank you very much," he mumbled and turned to go, but immediately Marshall West was on his feet.

'I'm sure Dr. Ford will take questions. Would anyone . . . ? Yes, sir."

A smartly dressed man with ash gray hair and heavy-framed glasses stood up. He was handed a microphone by one of the young women in the scarlet jackets.

"Ed Sampson, Biofactor Research," he said. His voice was gruff, with a faint southern drawl. "Dr. Ford, surely you don't expect pharmaceutical companies to be responsible for controlling the way drugs are prescribed in the Third World. How do you expect us to do that?"

It was an obvious objection, and one that Ford had anticipated.

"Well, I think the reality is that pharmaceutical companies, and their local representatives, will sell their products as aggressively—and, if I may so, irresponsibly—as the local conditions allow. Chloramphenicol in Mexico was one clear illustration of that, and I don't believe very much has changed. What's more, when developing countries have tried to set up centralized and rationalized distribution systems, these have been opposed by the major drugs companies as an infringement of their free-market rights. In fact, our government has on occasion threatened to withdraw aid from Third World countries whose drug policies it considers overly restrictive. I'm not an expert on the drug industry, or any kind of industry come to that, but as a doctor it seems to me that if companies cannot or will not ensure that their products are used appropriately in a given country—and will not let anyone else do it for them—then they must refrain from distribution in that country altogether."

There was a murmur of dismay from the audience. Several more hands went up, but Ed Sampson was not finished: "Dr. Ford, pharmaceuticals is a competitive industry. It has investors, shareholders, *employees.* Doesn't it worry you that even more government regulation would simply kill off any incentive for companies to spend money on research? What with the time it takes to get drugs approved by the FDA, it's getting harder and harder to justify R and D spending as it is. I mean, this is *shareholders' money.* And they need to see a return sometime, don't you think?"

The rest of the audience seemed to like this question, if it was a question.

"The profit motive is important, I'm sure," Ford replied. "But a profitable drugs industry doesn't necessarily mean a . . . a healthier world. Over the past thirty years there's been a massive increase in the consumption of medical drugs, yet I see no real improvement in public health. In fact, here in the U.S.A. our infant mortality rate is now the highest in the developed world and the incidence of chronic infection is rising all the time. If we look at the global picture, the industry's record is even worse. By the time drug-resistant tuberculosis hit the U.S.A., three million people a year were already dying of the disease in the Third World, yet the one drug that was still effective against the bacteria had gone out of production."

Marshall West was nodding slowly, no longer smiling, but watching Ford with an unfamiliar intensity.

"Like you say, sir, pharmaceuticals is a business. It devotes its attention to the most lucrative markets: people with money to spend, people who are willing to pay top dollar for the latest products. But it ignores the interests of everyone else—the majority. Because it is they, the poor, who are least able to deal with the new generation of resistant pathogens. I worry that this—how can I put it?—this *narrowness* of focus may come back to haunt us."

Sampson did not look happy, but West was moving things along: "Another question? Yes, sir. In the second row."

It was the man who had been talking to Lucy Patou. He had short blond hair, glasses, and a bow tie. The way he smiled gave Ford a bad feeling.

"John Downey, Jr., Mirada Technologies, Dr. Ford,"—he held the microphone in one hand and kept the other deep in his trouser pocket—"as I understand it, your view is based upon the experience of the cases you've handled at the Willowbrook, the cases you've described today."

"That's correct," said Ford.

"You believe that more resources, more medical supervision, and tighter government regulation of the pharmaceuticals industry would prevent such cases from arising. Is that right?"

"I think it would help, yes."

"Yes"—Downey rocked forward onto the balls of his feet, seeming to ponder the issue for a moment—"I see. But as I understand it, Dr. Ford, most of the cases you describe concerned addicts, narcotics dealers in fact, people who wantonly abused and weakened their systems with heroin, PCP, and the like. Of course, the fact that you and your colleagues devote yourselves to the care of such people is commendable, but is it right, do you think, to overturn the whole industry, at huge cost, to protect the well-being of people who seem to have little or no regard for it themselves?"

John Downey, Jr., was suddenly the most popular man in the room. All over the audience people were nodding and muttering their agreement. Several people in the audience actually clapped.

"A patient is a patient," Ford stammered. "It is not my job to discriminate between . . . Besides, the fact that some of these particular individuals may have been immunocompromised does not alter the fact that the bacteria infecting them proved resistant to a wide spectrum of antibiotics, possibly all antibiotics. It is only to be expected that the immunocompromised among a community would succumb to infection ahead of the rest."

People had started talking. At the back a couple of people walked out, buttoning their jackets. More arms were going up. Ford felt as if he were drowning. Suddenly West was on his feet again.

"On the question of cost, I would just like to add one point," he said calmly, waiting a moment for the silence to return. "Studies have shown, both here in the United States and elsewhere, that close super-vision of patient medication can be done cheaply and is actually cost effective. First, it generally results in fewer and cheaper drugs being prescribed. Secondly, it may prevent the creation and spread of the kind of resistant strains Dr. Ford has described. To give you an example of the economics involved: in the mid 1980s both federal and state administrations slashed their budgets for tuberculosis control and sur-veillance, saving I believe two hundred million dollars in all. A few years later we were hit with an MDR-TB epidemic, which cost at least one billion dollars to rein in via an emergency response program, not to mention the cost in lost productivity and human lives."

John Downey, Jr., was already sitting down.

"That is why," West went on, "here in Los Angeles County, we have set up what we call a Directly Observed Therapy, or DOT, pro-gram in spite of our very tight financial position. Yes, it is relatively labor intensive, but we believe it makes good sense in the long run. So, while I take the gentleman's point, I think the cost issue is, at the very least, open to debate."

He looked around the auditorium. Suddenly no one wanted to ask any more questions. Debating with a South Central surgeon was one thing, with Marshall West quite another. Ford had the feeling he had just been rescued from the schoolyard bullies by the deputy principal.

"Now, if there are no more questions, I think we're due for a break," West said. "I suggest we continue this session at four."

They were serving tea, coffee, cold drinks, and pastries. The net-working was back in full swing, taking up where it had left off at lunch. Ford eased his way through the crowd, catching one solitary nod of acknowledgment. He helped himself to coffee and scanned the room for a friendly face. West had disappeared and he recognized no one, except Lucy Patou. She was over by the door, talking to John Downey, Jr., laughing in a lazy, distracted way. Ford didn't want to talk to her, but it was only going to make things more awkward if he ignored her. He took a mouthful of coffee and started making his way over.

"Excuse me. Dr. Ford?"

Ford turned and found himself facing a tall man, maybe sixty years old, with deep-set brown eyes. There was no name badge on his lapel.

"I just wanted to tell you . . . what you said, it interests me very much. I read your paper on the *Enterococcus*. It's . . . It's rare to find a surgeon who's so . . . who's alert to these issues."

He spoke quietly, almost nervously, as if he didn't want to be overheard.

"My name's Novak. Charles Novak."

"Yes, of course. Professor Novak. I read your paper in *Science* last year. It really got me thinking about this issue."

They shook hands. Now that he knew who the man was, Ford was struck by his rumpled appearance. He wore an old-fashioned green suit that was shiny on the lapels, and his loud striped tie had a grease stain just under the knot. It looked as if he had slept in his clothes. He certainly didn't look like one of the drug industry executives.

"So, what brings you to the conference?"

Novak shrugged.

"I like to keep abreast of developments. But that wasn't . . . Actually, I wanted to ask you something. This *pneumoniae* you've had at the Willowbrook—has it shown up at any of the other hospitals in the area?"

"Not as far as I'm aware, but that doesn't necessarily mean very much. We report resistant infections to the CDC in Atlanta, and they're supposed to keep us posted if anything dangerous is going around. But, frankly, the local lines of communication could be better."

Novak nodded. "Yes, I see. And I suppose a lot of the people that come in—I mean in that area—they're often at an advanced stage of infection. Is that right?"

"Absolutely."

"So that they could die before the full properties of a particular pathogen have been discovered."

"It can take two weeks to culture out a sample and find out for sure what you're dealing with. A lot of our patients never last that long. As I tried to explain earlier, a high proportion have no regular access to health care. They come to us as emergencies."

"Still, I'd welcome a chance to go over the data with you," Novak added. "If you could spare the time."

"Yes, of course. If you'd like to give me a call at the hospital. I'm usually . . ."

A woman had approached them. She was standing a few feet away, holding a cup and saucer in both hands, waiting for him to finish. Ford was surprised he hadn't noticed her before. She had abundant dark hair and dark, almost Arabic eyes. Ford guessed that she was probably in her mid-thirties. She was power-dressed in a gray outfit that accentuated her Mediterranean complexion.

"You did say you take sugar, Professor Novak?" she said, smiling at Ford.

Novak looked distinctly uncomfortable.

"Yes, I did, thank you. Dr. Ford, this is . . ."

He hesitated, unable, it seemed, to remember her name.

"Helen Wray," the woman said, holding out her free hand. "Stern Corporation. A pleasure to meet you, Dr. Ford."

They shook hands.

"Congratulations on your speech," she said. "I think you made quite an impression."

"I'm not sure I made myself very popular," he said.

She smiled.

"It certainly woke us all up. What did you think, Professor Novak?"

"It was interesting," said Novak. He looked down at his coffee.

But Helen Wray persisted: "Would you favor greater regulation of the industry? Dr. Ford seemed to want export controls."

Novak frowned. He was suddenly very reluctant to talk.

"Resistance is a serious problem. How to deal with it . . . That may be a matter for politicians, but certainly not for biochemists like me. Dr. Ford, do you have a card, by any chance?"

"Yes, I do." Ford took one from his top pocket.

"Thank you. I hope you'll excuse me. I have to . . ."

"Of course," said Wray.

Novak turned and wandered out of the room. Helen Wray watched him disappear and frowned.

"Hell, I hope it wasn't something I said."

Ford smiled.

"I don't think so. Do you know him?"

"Not really. Know *of* him. He's actually an incredibly difficult person to get to meet. Almost a recluse these days."

"He's retired, then?"

"Very. You should be flattered that he wants to talk."

Ford shrugged.

"Well, then, I guess I am."

She looked at him hard.

"He used to work at a biotech company we took over a few years back. High-powered back then—as in gigawatts."

"But still keeping his hand in, it seems."

"Yes," she said, again fixing Ford with her dark eyes, "so it seems."

Ford smiled and wished he weren't looking such a mess. Sunny was always telling him to "get out and meet some girls," but one way and another it never happened. Now it finally was happening and he was in a hundred-year-old suit that made him look fat.

"So how long have you been working in South Central?"

"Seven years."

"Jesus. And how long are you going to stick with it?"

Ford hesitated. It was clear from the tone of her voice that in her view no one would stick with it for a moment longer than necessary, no one who had a choice.

"I enjoy my work," he heard himself saying. "It's what I chose. Trauma, I mean."

She studied him for a moment, as if doubtful of his sincerity. He felt a faint buzz of tension travel up his spine. It was her eyes. They had a hard mineral quality that reminded him of . . . volcanic glass. Obsidian. Yes, that was it. Hard, but hot rather than cold. She was really something.

"Sure, why not?" she said. "That's great."

"It's really not as—"

He was interrupted by his beeper. It meant he was needed. A Code Yellow cardio-thoracic, probably. And he hadn't even had a chance to find out what she did for a living.

"I'm sorry," he said. "I've got to go. Do you know where there's a phone?"

"No problem," she said, reaching into her jacket pocket. "Use mine."

4

Turning into his street, Ford forgot to slow down to the obligatory crawl, dropped into the speed dip at the intersection and clunked the front fender of the Buick. It was still seesawing from the impact when he rolled up in front of his house. With a disdainful wrench he pulled the gearshift across to PARK and snapped off the ignition. Four hours working on the Shark, then the conference, then another two hours in the critical room had taken its toll. It had been a very long day.

He sat for a moment, staring at the fine layer of dust on the burgundy vinyl dashboard. Sweet, grassy, suburban air drifted in through his open window, still warm two hours after sundown. And over the smell of the newly mown grass he caught the leafy tang of the Spanish oaks that grew thickly along the sidewalks. In the distance he could hear the stuttering hiss of a sprinkler. He looked up at the house, half expecting to see Sunny's face appear through the living room drapes. But the window was empty, and out of nowhere he was hit by a feeling of loss strong enough to make him grab the wheel, as if the car, though stationary, was swerving out of control. He snapped the ignition back on and turned to KKGO, hoping for something soothing. Gary Hollis was introducing the next piece in his sleepy drawl. Mozart. A piano concerto.

Ford listened to the opening bars, waiting for the bad feeling to go. It was a sensation he knew well, a sudden cold squeeze that crept up on him at odd moments like this. Returning home, seeing the lights on in the house, was always difficult, but normally he was ready, prepared to get over it the way he negotiated the dip at the end of the street. But if he was really tired, if he wasn't really paying attention, he could hit this little pocket of despair, a depression he had to get out of straightaway or it could deepen into a gloomy evening in front of the television or, worse, feelings of guilt about not being around more for Sunny.

It had been three years since Carolyn's death—three years and two months, in fact, since the call from the LAPD notifying him of the smash on 405—and he had more or less gotten over it, indeed had been *obliged* to get over it, if only for Sunny's sake. But there were still moments like this, when he felt complete and utter incomprehension—so that the idea that Carolyn was not behind the living room drapes, and never again would be, seemed absurd. For him, in the moment of confusion, gripping the wheel, she *was* there, sitting with Sunny, waiting for him to come in through the door.

He switched off the Mozart and climbed out of the car. Still there was no face at the window. Sunny was either out with friends or sulking—angry with him for being so late. When she was younger, she always used to wait for him at Mrs. Ellerey's, two doors down, but nowadays she didn't bother unless he called to say he'd be late. She insisted she was old enough not to need a baby-sitter. He stepped onto his own patch of carefully manicured grass and checked out what looked like a little moss, pushing at it with his foot.

The front door opened.

"I thought Conrad was coming back."

Ford looked up and saw his daughter framed in the doorway. She was wearing faded jeans and a T-shirt through which you could clearly see her developing breasts.

"He got held up. He'll be along in a minute. How did the game go?"

"Oh, okay, I guess. I made dinner."

"Thanks, honey." He closed the car door. "Did you use the vegetables I bought yesterday?"

"Nope."

She gave him what he knew she *felt* was a winning smile.

"Why not?"

Saying nothing, she took his hand and led him into the house, where there was a warm smell of tomato and melted cheese. He followed her into the kitchen, where she had prepared the breakfast nook for supper. She had thrown a blue cloth across the little pine table and had set out knives and forks for three people.

"*Mmmmm* delicious," he said. "Monosodium glutamate, anti-caking agent, preservative, mood stabilizers, plutonium. Let me guess."

Sunny opened the oven door on a huge pizza she had taken from the freezer.

"Come on, Dad. You know Conrad likes it."

And he did. He turned up five minutes later, and they sat right down to eat. Allen's wife, Ellen, was going through a Creole cuisine phase, and he said it was great for him to eat something that didn't involve rice. That Sunny should have remembered this—apparently Allen had mentioned it the last time they had eaten together—was not surprising. She was particularly fond of Allen, and he seemed to return the affection. Seeing them together, Ford often got the feeling they were somehow on the same wavelength, while he was tuned into something else altogether.

But although supper went well, with Ford telling them all about the conference, Sunny was more reserved than usual. She was also clearly having trouble swallowing her food. When she refused a second slice of the pizza, Allen asked her what was wrong.

"What's up, sugar? You in love again?"

"No, I am hungry, but I've got this . . ."—she rubbed at her throat—"this killer pain in the throat." She made a face, pressing her lips into a hard line and gulping. "I can hardly swallow."

Ford reached across the table and gently tilted back her head.

"Let's have a look."

Sunny opened her mouth, rolling her eyes at the same time for Allen's benefit.

"You should have made soup," said Ford, letting go of her chin. "We could have had soup."

"So, what about my throat?"

"It's a little inflamed. That's all. You should have made something a little easier to swallow."

"I *wanted* pizza."

"We could always put yours in the blender," said Allen, smiling, his mouth full of food.

"Very funny," said Sunny, delivering a playful slap.

She swallowed another piece, frowning with the effort.

"Just chew for a while, sweetheart," said Ford.

She made a show of elaborately chewing, watching him out of the corner of her eyes.

"So, how was your speech?" asked Allen. "Do you think they understood it?"

"Oh, I think they managed to follow most of it," said Ford. "You know what a paragon of clarity and concision I am. Marshall West was there. He seemed to share a lot of my views, actually."

Allen nodded noncommittally. Like most of the staff at the Willowbrook, he viewed West with a mixture of suspicion and gratitude. As health czar West was so powerful it was good to have him defending your interests, but *because* he was so powerful, and because he moved in political circles, any interests he might be defending came down to being his own. Who knew when health-care provision in South Central might drop off his personal agenda? When West visited the Willowbrook, people smiled a lot and were careful about what they said.

"Did you meet any nice women?" said Sunny out of the blue.

Ford pushed back from the table, faking surprise.

"Honey, conferences are for professional people to exchange ideas."

"I heard they were where businessmen went to have parties and pick up girls."

Ford looked across at Allen for his reaction to this and was surprised to see him looking very serious.

"I think that's more conventions," said Ford, frowning. Allen caught his expression, tried to smile, and then looked down at his plate.

They finished the pizza in silence, Ford preoccupied with what had been said at the conference, thinking also of the woman he had spoken to. He wondered if she was the type Sunny would consider nice. She was certainly good looking.

"What was your speech about, anyway?" asked Sunny, putting a tub of ice cream on the table.

"I told you. It was about medicine—the way we take it."

Sunny raised her eyebrows.

"Right. But you never really went into details."

She scooped expert round balls of mint chocolate chip into three bowls. She had begun to take an interest in biology at school, but Ford was always wary of talking too much about his ideas and his work. He worried that one day she would reject it all precisely because it was an interest of his. He preferred to let her find her way into it herself.

"Didn't I?" he said, adopting his usual fake indifference. "Well, it was about antibiotics, specifically."

Sunny pointed at Allen with the scooper, dripping melted ice cream onto the tablecloth.

"That's what *I* need," she said.

"What for?" said Allen.

"For my throat, silly. There's a kid at school says his mother gave him some and his sore throat just went, poof!" She clicked her fingers with a surprising snap.

"Oh, really," said Ford. "What did he take exactly?"

"I don't know *exactly*. All I know is he doesn't have a sore throat anymore. Everybody's got it, though. The throat, I mean. Mr. Buckley said it was strep throat. Is that right, Conrad?"

"Probably it is."

"What is it, strep?"

"It's a bug. Its real name is *Streptococcus*. But it isn't very powerful. Your immune system knows how to deal with it."

Sunny looked at Allen for a moment, considering this information. She had her mother's eyes. Gray-blue with flecks of gold radiating out from the pupil.

"Dad, can't I have an antibiotic like Carl Merriman?"

"Do you know what they say about strep throat, Sunny?" said Allen.

Sunny made a little adjustment on her seat, squaring her shoulders to face Allen, getting ready for the information. Even though she was becoming more of a teenager everyday, she still occasionally reverted to the mannerisms Ford had grown to love in her as a child. He sometimes wondered if she didn't do it just to please him, to reassure him that she was still his little girl. He smiled and ruffled her hair, something that, officially, she didn't allow anymore.

"They say that properly treated strep throat can be cleared up in seven days, but left to itself it can hang around for a week."

Sunny frowned for a moment. Then she smiled.

Ford and Allen sat for a long time after Sunny had gone to bed, talking about the Hammel case and about the situation in South Central generally. Since catching that odd, sober look at the table, Ford had been watching Allen and sensed that there really was something wrong. He asked himself if there had been anything recently that Allen might have said—about his home life, for example, his marriage with Ellen. But whatever it was that was bothering him, Allen didn't seem to want to get into it, and so the talk stayed fairly general. They were planning a fishing trip in October, just the two of them alone, and for a while they discussed different options, with Allen, as always, preferring the most expensive.

At ten-thirty he stood up to go.

"Oh, man," he said, stretching his arms. "She's growing up so fast."

It was a moment before Ford realized he meant Sunny.

"She sure is," he said. "Too fast, maybe. You know I go into her bedroom sometimes and it's like somebody else's kid has moved in their stuff."

"She's just growing up," said Allen, reaching for his jacket and car keys. "Just moving on."

He looked at Ford, and for a moment Ford thought he might be about to say what was on his mind. But he didn't.

5

Despite the wired jaw and the pressure dressings, the Shark was looking alert when Ford went in to see him the next day. There was even a flicker of disbelief—or maybe it was anger—in his eyes when Ford stood at the end of bed three and told him how lucky he had been.

"Guess he doesn't feel so lucky," said Conrad Allen, coming up behind Ford, a clipboard in his hands. Allen was in the ICU to check on the previous day's casualties. He and Ford reviewed some of the cases together. Ford was especially relieved to see that the patrolman who had been shot in the thigh was making good progress.

They reached the end of the ward and stood talking for a moment. Allen wanted to know if Lucy Patou had caught up with him at the conference.

"I was going to ask you last night, but it went out of my head," he said.

"No, I didn't talk to her. She was there, though. She was also in ER yesterday, or so I hear. Sent home three of our best people."

"Oh?"

"Gloria and two of the other nurses have this strep throat infection that's going round."

"Oh, right. Like Sunny."

Allen looked down at the floor for a moment. Ford could see he had something on his mind.

"Yeah, I spoke to Gloria yesterday afternoon," Allen mumbled. "She mentioned something about that. Some discomfort . . ." He looked back up, shrugging, raising his eyebrows. "Oh, well. I guess it's in the patients' best interests. Don't want your nurses breathing bacteria all over them."

"It's a pain in the ass is what it is," said Ford, watching Allen now, waiting to see if he was going to get to whatever it was on his own. "The roster gets screwed up, for one thing. And anyway, I can't see—"

"Marcus."

Allen paused for a moment, frowned at his scribbled notes.

"I've been meaning to talk to you. I wanted to say it last night, but I . . . I just couldn't get into it somehow."

"What . . . what is it?"

Allen moved towards the door. He waited until they were outside in the corridor before speaking again.

"Look, I've been meaning to . . ."

"To speak to me, yes. I think we've established that."

Allen laughed an uncharacteristic, nervous laugh. Then his face fell. Ford had never seen him look so serious.

"So," said Ford. "What is it?"

Allen watched a nurse coming along the corridor.

"Is it Ellen?" asked Ford. "Is there something wrong at home?"

Allen looked back at him, a puzzled expression on his face.

"Has she spoken to you?"

"No. No . . . I just. I don't know, you've been acting kind of strange lately, and I just thought . . ."

Again Allen looked away. He nodded a greeting as the nurse went past.

"Well, she isn't too happy about our situation," he said. "That's for sure. It can be real hard. Sometimes . . . sometimes I get home and I'm too tired even to talk, even to eat. I sit down in front of the TV and watch the news about all the shooting I've been dealing with all day. You know how it is."

Ford looked at the floor. He knew how demanding Ellen could be. She was very proud of Conrad, of what he had accomplished, and loved to hear Ford sing his praises, but she could be critical too and wasn't above suggesting that Ford exploited her husband sometimes, using their friendship to exert pressure.

"Sure, I know," said Ford, hoping that if he made sympathetic noises, Allen might get into a little more detail. "It's hard. Carolyn used to hate it too. The hours, I mean."

He looked up at Allen's face, and waited for him to speak. But Allen seemed to have run out of steam now.

"Maybe we should call off the fishing trip," said Ford. "Maybe you should take Ellen somewhere instead. Get away from it all. You know, just the two of you book into somewhere nice. The Kempinski in San Francisco is supposed to be romantic."

Allen shook his head. Then he lifted his foot and put it down firmly, as though making a decision. But at that moment Ford's pager sounded. He checked the number.

"We'd better get down to Trauma," he said.

Three days after surgery, the Shark's condition began to deteriorate. His temperature was spiking at 104 degrees and his white-blood-cell count shot up in response to bacteria in his system. Although he was still pretty much immobilized in bed, his discomfort was obvious. When Ford came to see him in the ICU, the dark, angry eyes never left his face.

There was distinct redness around the entry wound, which was warm to the touch and tender enough to close the Shark's eyes and make the air whistle in his throat tube. There was also pus at the site of the entry wound and in the vacuum bottle of the surgical drain Ford had established as a precautionary measure. Fearing the formation of an abscess somewhere inside the missile track, Ford took a sample of the exudate drained from the entry wound and was able to identify a gram-positive coccus, which the lab later narrowed down to *Staphylococcus aureus* through fluorescent antibody staining and a blood plasma coagulation test.

The Shark wasn't so lucky after all.

Not that staph infection was unheard of. The infection rate for so-called *dirty wounds* at the Willowbrook—all trauma wounds were classified *dirty*—was running at around fifteen percent, and staph was the most common pathogen in wounds of that type. It was a nasty bug that despite being present in the nostrils of around thirty percent of healthy adults was little understood in terms of its ability to wreak havoc in the human body. Through the production of a variety of toxins and enzymes, staph caused boils, abscesses, conjunctivitis, and a condition known as scalded skin syndrome in which the skin came away in sheets.

Ford's immediate worry was that the infection appeared to have developed despite the high dose of a so-called scattergun antibiotic given to the Shark prior to surgical intervention. It wasn't a reason to panic. Drug-resistant staph was unfortunately fairly common. It was one of the most successful bugs in the microbial war against antibiotics, a dark champion that had gone from being totally helpless against penicillin back in the early fifties to winning nine out of ten battles against the same drug by 1982.

But the bug teeming inside the Shark's wound was not necessarily of that sort. The fact that it had failed to respond to cephalosporin, the antibiotic initially used, did not mean it was invulnerable to other forms of attack. But because of the position of the wound and the potential for complications should a deep abscess form somewhere inside the Shark's neck or mouth, Ford decided that he was not going to have the luxury of running through a series of drugs to find out which one worked best. There was a possibility that the cephalosporin resistance indicated broad resistance to other penicillin substitutes. This, Ford felt, ruled out the use of methicillin, a drug that, nine times out of ten, continued to be effective against staph.

In the end he decided on a radical change of tack. In his view, the Shark's best chance of beating the pathogen was vancomycin. Administered intravenously, it was an unpleasant drug to take, and there was a risk of serious side effects. Because of this, it was rarely prescribed, and therein lay its power: the microbes didn't see it often enough to develop defenses. Like penicillin, vancomycin inhibited cell-wall synthesis, but it did so using a different mechanism, one for which—Ford felt sure—the staphylococcus in the Shark would find no answer.

Ford instructed the attending nurse to set up bed number three for the administering of vancomycin and then paged Dr. Lucy Patou. The Willowbrook's internal guidelines obliged him to notify the chief of infection control of any resistance problems, whatever the pathogen involved. The case would eventually come to Patou's notice anyway through the hospital records, but by notifying Patou immediately, Ford was giving her an opportunity to institute any measures she might feel were necessary.

She came back to him immediately on one of the ICU phones, sounding professional and chilly. Ten minutes later they were in her office.

Not surprisingly, given the events of the past week, Patou was not in a very friendly mood, although, Ford was relieved to see, she did not raise the issue of his professional discourtesy. For most of the interview she looked down at her notes, meeting Ford's gaze only when he had trouble recalling what exactly had gone on in the critical room, and then in OR. From time to time she leaned forward in her swivel chair to check her microcassette. It was there to remind him that this was all *on* the record.

She wanted to know everything about the Shark and procedure prior to the infection declaring itself. She did nothing to disguise the fact that she suspected a nosocomial source. After half an hour she came to her concluding questions.

"Regarding the closing stages of the operation, Dr. Ford, did you encounter any problems?"

Ford smiled.

"You mean did I leave any swabs in there, any IV tubing?"

Ignoring the gibe, Patou consulted her notes.

"You say you closed the soft-tissue injuries of the lining mucosa and worked outwards, finishing with the damaged jaw."

She looked up.

"That's right," said Ford, "inside out, bottom up—the way I always do, Dr. Patou."

"Using debridement, cutting away damaged tissue?"

"A little. But the missile track was actually very clean. I instituted a surgical drain to draw off any residual fluids or pus."

"There were no fragments left inside?"

"Not that I noticed."

Again she looked up.

"Not that you noticed, Dr. Ford?"

"Dr. Patou, rummaging around for fragments in this area is not recommended. A broad rule of thumb we surgeons use is that, all things being equal, a bullet ceases to cause damage when it ceases to move. Nothing showed up on the x ray. As these things go, it was a pretty clean wound. Getting shot in the neck is bad news because there are so many blood vessels. But provided the bullet misses the major ones, you're in fair shape from an infection point of view precisely because the tissue is so well supplied with blood and thus oxygen."

Patou gave a little sniff. She didn't need an anatomy lesson.

"As for the exit wound," Ford went on, "it was a little more complicated."

Patou waited.

"The missile punched a hole through the left mandible. There was a degree of avulsion."

"Avulsion?"

"Tissue, teeth, and bone fragments punched outwards."

"And?"

"Well, it actually looked worse than it was. And I was able to . . . I basically molded the fragments with my fingers into the best anatomical position and wired his jaws together."

Patou looked momentarily alarmed. Ford realized he should have expected her not to like this. If she had ever studied surgical procedure, it was a long time ago. She had obviously forgotten how messy it could sound.

"That's right," said Ford. "I don't know how much of med school you remember, Dr. Patou, but that's how you do it. You don't go in there with a knife and start stripping soft tissue away from the bone, putting in clamps and plates and so forth. You repair the gum and mucoperiosteal tissue as accurately as you can to minimize bone loss. If you debride too much, you just end up losing bone. Bone is tissue too, remember. It has to have blood."

Patou seemed to be accepting his account, so Ford moved on.

"Once we got to the outside, I was able to verify the viability of injury flaps with pressure blanching."

"Pressure blanching? What does that involve?"

Ford smiled. She wasn't going to like this either.

"You pinch the tissue with your fingers, press the blood out. If the capillaries refill afterwards, you probably have healthy tissue there. I mean viable tissue. There was actually very little outright tissue loss. Then I closed him up."

"You closed him up?"

"Not too tightly. Sew them up too tight and you can get distortion later on. That's when they come back looking for you."

He tried a smile, but Lucy Patou was not about to relax.

"And postoperatively?"

"He went into ICU with firm pressure dressings to stabilize soft tissues. Tube fed to maintain oral cleanliness. I took him off cephalosporin and put him onto vancomycin."

Patou raised an eyebrow.

"That's a pretty direct route," she said.

Ford shrugged.

"I didn't feel I could waste time finding out if something else worked."

"Well, let's hope he pulls through."

"Amen to that."

Patou pushed her notes aside and in doing so knocked over a framed photograph she kept on her desk. Ford caught a glimpse of a young boy's smiling face, and it suddenly dawned on him that Patou was probably a single parent, just like him. He had no concrete reason for believing it, but seeing her alone with the child, it was like the last piece of a jigsaw. Suddenly a lot of things, a lot of impressions made sense. He had never really thought about Patou's private life. Apart from the NIH conference, the only time he had ever seen her outside the walls of the Willowbrook she was coming out of a store at Farmer's Market one Saturday morning. She had been carrying too many shopping bags, struggling with the weight, but keeping her usual tight-lipped dignity. Recalling the incident now, he felt his intuition was being confirmed. Of *course* she had been shopping on her own, she was living on her own, or living with this child, the kid in the photograph—her son probably. He experienced a little squeeze of fellow feeling, of compassion for her.

Patou looked up from her papers and caught something in his expression that made her narrow her eyes.

"So what went wrong, Dr. Ford?"

Ford sat back in his chair.

"You know the statistics, Doctor. It's a dirty wound. There's a one in six chance of infection."

"So you think he brought it in with him?"

"Maybe."

Patou made a wry mouth.

"Well, I'll tell you the problem I have with that, Dr. Ford. The chances of a cephalosporin-resistant staphylococcus coming in off the street is rather less than one in six. In fact in the whole of Los Angeles County there are only around one hundred cases of multiresistant infections, and a large percentage of those are TB."

"We don't know that this is multiresistant. We've only tried one drug. It may be that methicillin would—"

"You're right. We don't know. But we have to err on the side of caution. As chief of infection control, I am obliged to do so."

She fixed him with her cold green stare.

"No. I think it is more likely that he picked this thing up in OR. I know you don't want to hear this, but there are, it seems to me, two pertinent considerations. Staphylococcus is unlikely to develop multiple resistance outside. That's just the way it is, *despite* theories to the contrary."

She waited a moment to let this sink in, to see if he had the nerve to get into any of his conference bullshit with her one-on-one. He said nothing.

"But inside the hospital," she went on, "there is sufficient contact between the bugs and the drugs for resistance to develop. Now, as I'm sure you are aware, the most common vector of infection is dirty hands."

Ford moved around in his chair, offended, despite himself, at being accused of poor hygiene. Patou went on, apparently oblivious.

"Fortunately in this hospital surgeons scrub for ten minutes before going into OR."

She said this as though she didn't believe it for a second.

"And wear sterile gloves and gowns, and face masks," added Ford.

Patou acknowledged this with a nod. She waited a beat and then asked, "Do you suffer from eczema, Dr. Ford?"

The question caught Ford off guard. For a moment he was at a loss for words. Patou went on. Clipped, cool, looking him straight in the eye.

"Or any other lesions? Boils, fungal infections of the groin?"

Ford felt the blood rise in his face.

"No . . . No, I don't believe I do."

Patou brought her notes together and shuffled them into a neat stack.

"I'm obliged to consider the possibility that somebody in OR passed the staphylococcus to Mr . . . to the patient. Eczema can be a factor in a carrier haboring high concentrations of bacteria."

"You're saying I'm a carrier?"

"A *broadcaster*, more to the point. Someone who sheds large numbers of staphylococci into the air. And, no, I'm not saying that you are. I'm saying that you, or someone else on the team that attended the patient, may be."

She smiled.

"Staphylococcus can be isolated in the anterior nares of around thirty percent of healthy individuals," she said, "and occasionally the perineum."

"The perineum?" Ford could hardly believe his ears.

"That's right, Doctor. You know, that little strip of skin between the anus and the genitals?"

Ford could see that Patou was beginning to enjoy herself. Allen had been right. She *was* planning to culture his ass. Involuntarily he clenched his buttocks.

"Other areas get contaminated from a carrier site. The face and neck, sometimes the hair and hands of a nasal carrier. Or the buttocks, abdomen, and um . . . the *fingers* in the case of a heavy perineal carrier."

Ford was beginning to feel very dirty.

"But with lesions of one sort or another, contamination can be more—"

"Yeah, I'm beginning to get the picture, Dr. Patou. Well, I don't have any lesions or fungal infections of the perineum. Not the last time I looked, anyway."

Patou smiled brightly.

"Fine! That's great. In that case testing you will probably be a very straightforward matter."

Ford sat up straight.

"Testing me?"

"That's right. You and the other members of the team. Well, it's the only way to be sure about this."

"What kind of test are we talking about?"

"It's very simple. Broadcasting is measured by air sampling in a small room or plastic chamber while the person in question carries out some standard exercises—without their clothes, naturally."

Ford swallowed.

"You want me to take my clothes off in a plastic cubicle while you suck the air out."

Patou nodded encouragingly.

"But we're all wearing gowns, masks, gloves, for Christ's sake. Even if one of us did have some organism, it wouldn't be able to get onto the patient."

Patou was shaking her head, disappointed at this lack of cooperation.

"Unfortunately, standard protective clothing doesn't stop infection from happening. But, now that you mention it, there *is* a form of plastic diaper on the market that surgeons with this problem wear when operating."

Ford briefly considered the prospect of standing under the OR lights for six hours wearing plastic diapers.

"Let's do the test," he said.

In the early hours of Sunday morning the Shark woke with the feeling that his whole body was on fire. He blinked up through stinging eyes at the white ceiling, squeezing his fists, focusing on a strip of shadow thrown across from the curved curtain track. It was getting harder to hang on to the here and now, to be present, to be where he *knew* his body was. In bed. At the Willowbrook. He kept seeing the Chicano bitch who had shot him, seeing her vividly in the moment she bit her teeth together in a sort of angry smile, pushing the gun at his face. Sometimes she was more real to him than the bed. He kept seeing the white doctor, Ford, kept hearing his voice telling him how lucky he had been. Colored lights jerked behind his eyes. He dreamed that he was shouting and then woke up with his jaws wired solid, all sensation in his face gone, so that his whole head felt like a stone and the only thing that was still human were his eyes. He drifted in and out of consciousness, coming to in the mesh of tubes with the feeling that they were there to stop him floating away forever. And all the kaleidoscope craziness wasn't just the drugs they had given him to kill the pain. Somehow he knew that.

The cocci were perfect spheres, like eggs or dark spawn. Simple even for bacteria. There were no hairs or rotors or whips, which more sophisticated bacteria use to move around in the wash of chemical signals. The cocci did not need them because they did not move. They did not form complicated chains or strings or tetrads. They clumped. And they doubled. Tricks they had been repeating since the beginning of Life. Doubling every twenty minutes and clumping together in grape-like clusters. At the base of the Shark's stalled tongue, in the smashed bone of his jaw, along the track left by the bullet. Clumped in clusters that numbered eight million and then sixteen million and an hour later one hundred and twenty eight million perfect peptidoglycan-plated spheres. All doing the thing they had always done. Perpetuating themselves. Twenty times smaller than the cells that surrounded them, they were nevertheless redoubtable enemies. Pushing out their poisons and their powerful enzymes, struggling against the onslaught of the Shark's immune system and the vancomycin, breaking up the surrounding cells and tissue, until soon they were doubling and doubling in abscesses the size of walnuts—pockets of serum, dead cells, and obliterated tissue.

The curtain had been pulled around the Shark's bed, and he was looking up at the ceiling, his eyes partially closed. He had gone into a coma at around four-thirty that morning. The duty nurse had discovered his condition when she had come to check his temperature. Ford pulled back the sheets and looked down at the young black boy. The contrast between the lean youthfulness of the torso and the ugly swelling of the neck and head was striking. It was like a Halloween mask, a monster's head. It was the work of less than a week.

"I thought you might like to take a look before they took him away," said Allen, keeping his voice to a whisper. "This is unusual, I think. I've never seen anything quite this fulminating."

He leaned forward and pulled back the dead man's dehydrated upper lip. Ford covered his nose and mouth and leaned forward himself, hardly able to believe the quantity of thick, yellow pus pushing through the wired teeth.

The two doctors were silent for a moment. Then Allen said, "I hope you agree we have to open him up. See exactly what happened inside."

Ford nodded.

"The autopsy and lab reports are going to make for interesting reading," said Allen. "I'd bet my bottom dollar this thing ate his tongue."

PART TWO

SOMETIMES BAD MEANS BAD

1

THE WILLOWBROOK MEDICAL CENTER

Medical Director Russel Haynes took the emergency meeting in his office. He was a small man in his mid-fifties, with a puckered, sour-looking face and tightly curled gray hair he kept militarily short. To disguise his lack of stature, he tended to stay seated behind his teak veneer desk, which was always piled high with papers and reports. On the front edge of the desk, threatening to topple off, was a small marble plaque on which was written:

> *God grant me the serenity*
> *to accept the things*
> *I cannot change, courage*
> *to change the things I can*
> *and wisdom to know the difference.*

The Code Yellow team and staff from the ICU were crammed into the space on the other side of Haynes's paper barricade. Mary Draper was there along with Melvyn Hershy and Marvin Leonard, the radiologist. Marcus Ford sat close to the door next to Conrad Allen and three other interns who had been on duty when the Shark had entered the ICU. Dr. Lionel Redmond, the Willowbrook's affable PR person, was also present. It was stiflingly hot in the office, and there was a strong smell of vanilla from a plastic air freshener Haynes kept on one of the bookshelves.

Although Haynes had called the meeting, it was Lucy Patou who was running the show. She was sitting in the corner on the couch Haynes slept on whenever the paperwork kept him from home. She had cleared herself a little space on a low coffee table and filled it with her own documentation. She looked keyed up.

The Shark's death was not the only cause for alarm. Four other patients in the ICU were now showing signs of resistant infection, including the patrolman, Raymond Denny. Denny's leg wound had failed to heal and was now inflamed and purulent, as was the cut into his saphenous vein. He, like the other problem cases, had been put onto vancomycin two days before. In every case the principal pathogen isolated from wound exudate was *Staphylococcus aureus*. What the staff was looking at was an outbreak.

After a few prefatory remarks from Haynes, in which he made it perfectly clear he expected everyone to cooperate with Dr. Patou one hundred and ten percent, she addressed them herself: "I don't have to tell you why this meeting has been called, so we'll get straight on to what we are going to do about what I think you'll agree is a very grave situation."

She checked them all over with her pale eyes, except for Ford, who was magically invisible to her.

"I'm treating this as an outbreak of methicillin-resistant *Staphylococcus aureus*, or MRSA. I know that Dr. Ford's patient was given vancomycin prior to his death, but it seems to me far more likely that the vancomycin was prescribed too late, than that it was ineffective per se."

"How can you be sure, Dr. Patou?" asked Ford, glancing across at Haynes's face to make sure he wasn't out of line.

"I can't be sure. We can't be sure. We are going to wait for the lab to tell us exactly what we are looking at in terms of resistance. The patrolman, Raymond Denny, is also receiving vancomycin, as are the other two infected patients. Their injuries are less serious, and I am counting on them responding to the vancomycin in the next few days."

"What if they don't?"

It was Draper who had spoken.

"If they don't, the Willowbrook will be making medical history and

I will be contacting the CDC. At that point our response will be coordinated with them."

The Centers for Disease Control, based in Atlanta, was the institution of last resort in cases of outbreaks of infectious disease. The CDC compiled statistics, carried out laboratory work on lethal pathogens, and even entered the field if circumstances called for it. Their experts were also available as consultants and, where necessary, as expert backup in situations requiring containment.

"In the meantime," Patou continued, "we will approach this problem with the utmost caution. This will entail a number of measures which, though inconvenient, must be put into effect to safeguard our staff and the general public."

There was a general movement in the room of people preparing themselves for bad news.

"Whatever the definitive characteristics of this thing turn out to be, what we appear to be looking at for now is a multiresistant strain of *Staphylococcus aureus*. Given the clustering of cases in ICU, we have to assume either a propensity for the pathogen to spread fairly easily or a common source of infection *inside* the hospital. This may turn out to be a member of staff or it may be a machine, a curtain, a mattress. Over the next few days I will be carrying out a survey of relevant staff and equipment. Now . . ."

She paused for a moment to consult her sheaf of notes.

"With a view to finding a broadcaster, I will be taking nose swabs from all staff in Trauma, in the ORs, and in ICU today. I will also be sampling air during operations performed by the suspect teams, and I will be sampling the OR floor with contact plates at the end of operations."

"At the end of each operation?" asked Hershy.

"No, that won't be necessary. I will also be culturing equipment, bedding, and other fomites in the ICU. Just in case I don't get a result from the swabs or from the OR air samples, I will also be testing each one of you individually today. I know this is going to hamper you in your work, but it has to be done. We have set up an isolation room for this purpose. All it involves is undressing and going through some movements while we sample the air. As I have already explained to Dr.

Ford"—she gave Ford a look—"this thing can be carried on the perineum, and we won't necessarily pick it up unless we get tough."

Allen and Ford exchanged a look.

"Men are more likely to carry this than women, so I am going to start with them. Dr. Ford has already agreed to go first."

Several heads turned to look at Ford.

"I want the rest of you to agree on who comes at what time."

"What about the infected patients?" asked Dr. Draper. "What do we do about them? They are a source too now, right?"

"I'll come to that in a moment," said Patou.

She exchanged one set of notes for another. She was going to get through this in her own time.

"Now, we can reduce the immediate danger by assuming that everybody is a carrier." She looked around to see what effect this news might have. The room was completely silent. "This is not as serious as it sounds. All it means is that, starting tonight and for the next week, I want you *all* to take *daily* baths with an antibacterial agent."

She reached down and produced a four-liter plastic bottle of what looked like industrial detergent, thumping it down on the coffee table. Nobody had noticed it until now. Mary Draper's mouth dropped open.

"This is a hexachlorophene detergent. It probably doesn't smell like your usual brand, but, as I keep saying, we have to get tough if we are going to beat this thing. I also have cetrimide shampoo, which I want you to use twice weekly. Finally, I will be supplying you with a nasal cream which contains one percent chlorhexidine and point five percent neomycin. You put the cream into the anterior nares—there's no need to shove the stuff right up your nose. And you use it four times a day for one week."

She looked around at them, a faint smile on her lips.

"Of course, it may turn out that we isolate our carrier immediately from today's tests, the results of which should be ready by tomorrow lunchtime. At that point you can bring all the stuff back to me and proceed as normal."

She put the detergent back on the floor.

"Now, regarding the infected patients. We will be cohorting them in the two isolation rooms adjacent to the ICU. It'll be a squeeze, but as long as we don't get any more cases in the immediate future, it should be manageable. We will continue whatever systemic support is necessary with sterilized equipment. The equipment used so far will, as I have already said, be cultured for evidence of contamination."

There was a moment's silence, and then Patou said, "Are there any questions?"

It was Conrad Allen who spoke: "Dr. Patou, your base assumption seems to be that this outbreak has been generated in-house."

"That's right. As I have already discussed with some of you, it is extremely unlikely that MRSA will have come in off the streets. In my experience, it just doesn't happen like that."

"You don't feel there may be a connection between this outbreak and the problems we had a few weeks ago with the *Streptococcus pneumoniae*?" said Ford. "Remember one of those cases came in through General Surgery. It had nothing to do with the Trauma Unit."

Patou smiled.

"We are all aware of your theories on this question, Dr. Ford. Unfortunately, we have to deal with the reality of what is happening in the ICU, and as Dr. Haynes's plaque says"—she reached across and took the marble plaque from Haynes's desk, something nobody else in the room would have dared do—"give me the 'courage to change the things I can.' If your theory is correct, if South Central is shaping up as some kind of microbiological flashpoint, then we are obviously in a lot of trouble. I think it would be irresponsible to air your theory overmuch—in public, I mean—without having some pretty solid proof."

Russel Haynes stood up.

"Thank you, Dr. Patou. On the issue of public information, this is probably as good a time as any to get our game plan in place. Now, an outbreak of multiple-resistant infection stands a fair chance of attracting the attention of the press, especially since a law enforcement officer is involved. If Officer . . ."

"Denny," said Patou.

"If Officer Denny succumbs to this thing, and I pray to God he doesn't, we may attract a degree of scrutiny. Now, I am nominating Dr. Patou to provide information to the media. She will work with Lionel on any press releases, while Lionel will, as always, field any telephone or fax inquiries."

Haynes came round to the front of his desk and leaned on it.

"If we work as a team, we'll get through this thing with the minimum of disruption," he said.

2

Ford had just squeezed a fat loop of nasal cream into his right nostril when Nurse Gloria Tyrell came through on the interior phone announcing a visitor. The cream smelled of chlorine and produced a burning sensation that made his eyes water.

"Who is it?"

Gloria put on a truculent voice.

"What am I, your social secretary? Just straighten your tie, Mister, 'cos she looks like she means business. And she's on her way right now."

"Gloria, what did . . . ?"

There was a soft knock at the door and then Ford found himself looking at the woman from the NIH conference. If anything she was more impressive than before. She looked completely out-of-place in the bare, functional world of the Willowbrook. For a moment Ford could do nothing but stare.

"Dr. Ford? I hope I'm not disturbing you. I just thought I'd come and say hi on my way out."

He stood up.

"Yes, yes please, come in. Sorry, for a moment there I couldn't . . ."

"Place me? Helen Wray. We met at the . . ."

"Yes, no I know, I just didn't expect to . . . I mean . . ."—he pointed to his nose and bloodshot eyes—"Sorry about the . . . It's an antibacterial thing we've having to use, only I think I've overdone it. Here, have a seat."

"You're not sick, I hope."

"No, no. It's just a precaution. Our Control of Infection Officer thinks we're breathing bugs over our patients—not that we are, don't worry. It's just . . ."

"Routine."

"Exactly. Excuse me."

He fumbled in his pocket for a handkerchief. He had definitely used too much cream. It had to look awful stuck up there.

Helen Wray sat down opposite the desk. She was dressed in a smart red jacket, a knee-length black skirt, and a white silk blouse through which the outline of her brassiere was faintly visible.

"I've just been meeting with your in-house pharmacy people," she said.

"Oh, great."

"Yes. We're introducing some new formulations for Lodanol, our top analgesic, and I wanted to tell them about it."

"Lodanol?" said Ford, keen to show interest. "Yes, I know it well. We use it to deal with postoperative pain. We like it. Less side effects than the steroidal anti-inflammatories."

"I'm glad you've found that. Well, now we're about to launch two new formulations: a topical gel and a transdermal patch."

Ford nodded positively, although he wasn't sure about the benefits of either new product to him. The kind of operations patients underwent in the Trauma Unit required heavy doses of painkillers, doses that could only be administered intramuscularly or intravenously. A gel would be better suited to general conditions like arthritis and injuries like sprains.

"Well, I'm sure they'll look with great interest at those," he said. "I'm sorry, I'm forgetting my manners. Can I get you coffee or something?"

"If you're sure it's no trouble."

"Of course not." Ford stood up again. "There's a machine right outside. We have freeze-dried instant coffee, freeze-dried instant tea, or freeze-dried instant hot chocolate-style beverage."

"Oh . . . well . . ."

"It doesn't matter which. They all taste the same pretty much."

"I see. Well, how about some freeze-dried instant water?"

"I'll see what I can do."

He went out into the corridor and hastily fed a dollar into the big vending machine. Why had she come to see him? Was it something in his speech that interested her? That seemed unlikely, because she was clearly in sales, and people in sales didn't care about anything except selling. On the other hand, if that was the case, why had she been at the conference at all? The machine sucked up his crumpled dollar bill, thought about it for a moment, and then pushed it back at him. Ford cursed under his breath and reached into his pocket for another. Maybe she just wanted information. Maybe she was going to ask him to participate in some dreary marketing survey. As the machine dispensed two fizzing cupfuls of club soda, he realized that this was probably exactly what she was going to do. Hadn't she launched straight into a marketing spiel about Lodanol? Or maybe she was looking for an endorsement for something, using her charms to get him on her side. Certainly a purely social visit was a little too much to hope for. Of course it was. He sighed and sipped at one of the club sodas. It tasted as flat as he felt.

"So you're in marketing, then, I take it?" he said, sitting back down.

"I'm sorry," she said, reaching into a slim briefcase. "I should give you my card. Here."

Sure enough, under her name the card read: *Assistant Director, Marketing (West Coast)*.

"So you probably visit a lot of hospitals, I imagine."

"Well, some," she said. "Actually, I don't get out on the road as much as I'd like. It's important to hear from the front line now and again. Clinical trials don't tell you everything about how a drug really performs or how useful it's likely to be."

"I believe it. So you like to get as much information as you can from . . . well, people like me."

She hesitated, the paper cup just touching her lips, then drank. Ford watched the gentle undulation of her throat as she swallowed, reminded for an instant of the Shark and the wound that had taken his life, a wound he should have survived.

"Well, we always welcome our customers' opinions, that's for sure."

"But people aren't always as cooperative as you'd like, I suppose. I mean, there's not much in it for them."

"Well, if people have an opinion, they usually don't mind telling you about it."

"Okay, okay," Ford said. "You've probably got a questionnaire, right? You can leave it with me. I'll pass it around. I just hope it's multiple choice, because my team doesn't have a lot of time to write essays."

She smiled.

"There's no questionnaire, like I said—"

"Well, I don't do endorsements. I'm against all that on principle. Doctors shouldn't have a financial interest in preferring one product over another. The patient's interests should be the only consideration. You'd have more luck at Cedars-Sinai, I'm sure."

Wray carefully put down the cup on Ford's desk.

"I know how busy you must be. I've obviously come at a bad time."

"Not at all," said Ford. "It's just I think you should know where I stand, that's all. I don't think patient care and big business make comfortable bedfellows."

She stood up.

"I didn't come on business," she said, still smiling.

"I see. Then, why . . . ?"

She looked at him for a moment, and then headed for the door.

"It was nice seeing you again, Dr. Ford."

Ford stood up, red-faced. She'd come to see him because she *wanted* to, because in those few minutes they'd been together at the conference she'd sensed something of the same attraction that he had. But, unlike him, she had actually gone out and done something about it. Maybe the visit to the Willowbrook had already been scheduled and maybe it hadn't, but either way she had made the first move. She had been the one to take a chance on humiliation or rejection, and all he'd done was throw it back in her face.

"Wait, please, there's"—she stopped, her hand already closed around the door handle—"there's no need to go. I'm sorry, I didn't mean to be . . . Look, if you knew what kind of a day I've had, really." Wray turned, fixing him with her dark eyes. "My team is in danger of falling apart; they're being paid half what they could get at other hospitals, and there's nothing I can do about it; now there's a suggestion that they're actually *dirty*, and this afternoon each one of them had to strip naked and do squat jumps while . . . I can't even tell you. So you see, morale is not as high as it could be."

She smiled.

"I understand," she said, "but that's okay. I've got to be going, anyhow. I'll just call for a cab and be out of your hair."

Ford checked his watch. It was a quarter after six.

"Which way are you going? I'm all through here. If you like, I could give you a ride."

"Honest to God, that woman hates me," said Ford as they rode the freeway into Santa Monica. "I don't know why. I can't believe it's just because I didn't consult her about my paper."

The sun was low over the ocean, bathing the city in pure Californian gold. A convertible went past with the top down; inside were four kids wearing sunglasses. Ford could feel himself beginning to unwind.

"Maybe she thinks you don't belong there," said Helen. "Maybe she feels threatened."

"Threatened?"

"You could do a lot better anywhere else—you said so yourself—but you choose to stay. That gives you a kind of moral superiority, quite apart from your status as a professional. And maybe, in a way, she feels patronized."

"Patronized?"

"Could be."

Ford didn't want to argue about it. He wanted to try and enjoy the ride with this lovely woman, this beautiful woman—he still couldn't quite believe it—who had sought him out. The only problem was what to talk about. Flirting had never been his strong suit, and by now he had lost the knack completely.

"So . . . what can I do about it?" he said. "How do I make her feel *un*patronized?"

"You can't. That's just the way it is with some people. You just have to leave them alone."

"I wish I could, but with this infection problem in ICU she's breathing down my neck all day."

"She say anything about your speech? To your face, I mean."

"No, just the odd sideswipe in meetings. She thinks these resistance cases all come down to sloppy procedure and that I just don't want to admit it."

"Well, Dr. Patou may think you're out of line, but Professor Novak seemed to take you pretty seriously. And he's a much bigger gun altogether, at least he was. Next exit, Marcus. Lincoln Boulevard."

It looked like a nice neighborhood. The streets were lined with shady trees, and there were plenty of open spaces where people played ball or just sat around in groups. The houses ranged from prewar clapboard bungalows to miniature hacienda-style condos, their patios and windowsills crammed with pots of colorful bougainvillea. As they went north, crossing Santa Monica Boulevard, the properties became larger and more expensive-looking, with lush lawns and hedges lining the sidewalks. Just a half a mile from the beach, the neighborhood was a couple of steps up the real estate ladder from Beverlywood, where Ford had his home. You could tell that from all the European cars parked by the side of the road.

"Has he been in touch with you, by the way?" Helen asked.

"Who, Novak? No."

"Didn't he say he'd call?"

Ford shrugged.

"Yes, but he's retired, right? Probably decided to go fishing."

"Probably. What was he interested in, particularly? Did he say?"

"He said he wanted to go over the data, on the *pneumoniae* cases I talked about especially. Why, what's your interest?"

Helen flipped down the visor on her side.

"Oh, nothing in particular," she said. "He's just such a character. He intrigues me."

They drove past Lincoln Park. A small outdoor stage was being set up for a concert, and people were already gathering. A turquoise Frisbee cut through the air.

"So Novak must have worked in anti-infectives, is that right?" Ford asked.

"That's what they say. He was one of a group of biochemists and genetics people who founded Helical Systems."

"I remember the name, I think."

"Stern bought them out maybe five or six years ago. It was before my time, but it was supposed to have been a really high-powered outfit, scientifically at least."

"So our Professor Novak retired a rich man."

"I don't think so. Helical was big in the brains department, but businesswise I think it was a nonstarter. I'm not sure they ever came up with a marketable product. Stern wouldn't have paid a whole lot, I'm sure of that."

"Which explains why Novak was at the conference," said Ford with a grin. "He's probably doing a little moonlighting to pay the rent."

"Or to get a new wardrobe," said Helen. She pointed a manicured finger. "Just another fifty yards on the right."

Number 940 Lincoln Boulevard was a Mexican-style whitewashed villa divided into four spacious apartments. A woman tending the roses by the front steps turned and waved as they pulled up outside.

"Well, thanks for the ride," said Helen, slowly unbuckling her seat belt.

"Any time," said Ford, feeling that he had to say something now if he wanted to see her again, but not sure what it should be. "It was nice of you to drop by. A nice surprise."

"Well, it's not every day I make a trip into South Central, that's for sure. I have to admit it: normally I'm strictly West LA."

Ford looked up at the house.

"It sure is nice here. I'd forgotten how nice. We used to talk about moving to Santa Monica, I mean my wife and I did, when she was alive. We never planned to stay where we are for long. It's just that, well, we're kind of used to it now. And Sunny has friends in the neighborhood."

He didn't say any more. He hadn't meant to talk about Carolyn, but somehow it had slipped out. And now he felt awkward.

"How long ago did she die?" Helen asked.

Ford kept on looking at the house, at the woman pruning the roses. She wore white gardening gloves and a pristine sky-blue apron.

"Three years. Road accident. Kind of ironic in a way, I suppose."

"I'm sorry," she said. "It must be tough, especially with the job you do."

"I prefer to stay busy," he said. "Keeps me from moping around. To tell the truth, I don't really like free time, except with my daughter of course."

"Everyone needs free time. You can't function without it. You lose your sense of perspective."

Ford looked at her. She seemed genuinely concerned.

"Well, I plan to take a week off at Thanksgiving. Take Sunny off to see her grandparents in Michigan. That should be fun."

"That should be cold," said Helen. "Can she skate yet, your daughter?"

"No, but I plan on teaching her, sometime."

"She'll love it. I used to do it in New York. Went round and round the Rockefeller Center rink every Christmas, just like in the movies. You bump into some very interesting people, literally."

And with that she opened the car door. Ford smiled at her as she climbed out, knowing that his chance was gone. He was supposed to have been flirting, and he had ended up talking about Carolyn. What did he expect?

Helen was out of the car, her briefcase in her hand, when she leaned down and said, "Say, can you make some free time tomorrow night? Because if you can, we could go out to dinner. If you'd like to."

3

"Turn around," said Sunny. She tilted her head left and then right, clearly unsure what to think.

"Isn't it a little formal, Dad?"

Ford looked down at the sports coat. To him it looked, if anything, a little *casual*.

"Honey, we're going out to this tony Italian place on Melrose, not to McDonald's."

He raised his left arm and stared hard at the cloth as if that were going to help. It was a jacket Carolyn had always liked. But now he asked himself if that was a good reason for putting it on.

"Maybe if you took off the tie. Just wore a sweater underneath." She snapped her fingers. "I know what you need."

She bounced up off the couch and ran through to his bedroom. Ford stayed where he was, wishing now that he hadn't accepted Helen Wray's invitation. What had he been thinking of? He hadn't dated anyone since Carolyn, and that was—he could hardly bear to think—*fifteen years* before. Fifteen years. Where had the time gone? Sunny walked back into the living room holding up a black turtleneck sweater he had never seen before.

"Now," she said with all the authority of a couturier, "in this you can look cool or dressy, whichever way you want to go."

Ford took it from her. It smelled powerfully of mothballs.

"I don't remember this."

"Mom bought it for you for your birthday. It's been in the bottom drawer for years."

He stared, still unable to recall.

"Oh, of course," he said, doing an it's-all-coming-back-to-me slow nod. "I don't know. Don't you think it's a little pretentious? Like I was trying to look like a jazz musician or something."

Sunny put her hands on her hips and let out a theatrical sigh.

"Dad, pretension is okay. Just think of it as *ironic*. And it really is versatile. Look, if you take your jacket off . . ."

She started to tug the jacket off his shoulder. It was halfway off when she stopped. She took a step back, wrinkling her nose.

"What is that?" she said.

"What?"

"That smell."

"Like a soap smell?"

"A *detergent* smell."

He sniffed hard at his shirt and underarms.

"You're right. It's this stuff I'm showering with."

"The insecticide stuff?"

"*Germ*icide. It's bactericidal."

Ford read despair in his daughter's eyes.

"Look, there's nothing I can do about it," he said, beginning to feel annoyed. "If it comes up during the evening, I'll just have to explain. It's not as if we're going to be necking."

He shot Sunny a glance, hoping this—the *prospect* of necking—was okay with her, at the same time hoping it would make her back off.

"How do you know?" she said boldly. "What if she decides to take the initiative?"

Ford felt his stomach flutter. He gave Sunny a look, something between irony and reproof, not really knowing what he wanted to communicate. She stood her ground.

"And she *won't* mention it. You can *count* on that. She'll just notice and keep quiet, and the next time you call her, she'll be out."

"Look, I'll try the sweater," said Ford. "Maybe the smell of mothballs will kill the detergent."

He had the sweater over his head when the phone rang.

'That'll be her," said Sunny. "She's calling it off."

It was Charles Novak.

"I hope you don't mind me calling you at home," he said. Ford looked at himself in the living room mirror. The surgeon pretending to be a jazz musician. Sunny was giving him the thumbs-up and nodding encouragingly.

"No, that's fine, Professor. I'm glad you did."

"We didn't really have a chance to talk the other day."

"No, that's right."

There was a pause in which Ford thought he heard the rustle of papers.

"Well, anyway, as I think I said at the time, I read your piece on the *Enterococcus*. It was interesting to get the physician's perspective."

"Well, I'm very flattered to hear . . . that a man of your standing—"

"And I have to say, my curiosity was piqued by the speech you gave. That was what I really wanted to talk about, the *pneumoniae* outbreak. I haven't seen any reference to it in *M and M Weekly*."

Morbidity and Mortality Weekly was a CDC publication that served to disseminate information on the incidence and spread of disease, part of the published information being collected nationwide from the fifty reporting states.

"I think we were slow in getting the stuff through to Atlanta," said Ford. "Reporting tends to get neglected when we're really busy on the wards."

"So can we go through the details now?"

Ford sat down on the couch.

"What did you want to know exactly?"

Novak sighed into the receiver.

"Well, everything, I guess. Perhaps you could start with the cases. There were three, as I understand it."

Sunny pointed at her watch. Fortunately, Ford was ahead of time. Wanting to return the favor of his lift from the hospital, Helen had said she was going to "swing by" in her car at seven-thirty. It was now just after seven.

He went through the whole outbreak, from Andre Nelson's admission and subsequent death to the deaths of the other two patients. Novak listened quietly, occasionally interrupting to get more detail. He wanted to know the exact when and where of each case regarding clinical expression of the disease and suspected original infection. He seemed particularly interested to find that all three cases lived fairly close to one another: Nelson in Lynwood, and the other two in the neighborhoods of Vernon and Huntingdon Park. Again Ford heard the rustle of paper. Was he consulting a map?

"And did you come to any conclusion regarding the vehicle of infection or a possible etiologic agent?"

"Do you mean a possible source?"

"Yes, I'm sorry," Ford heard Novak move around in his chair, "I'm looking at a descriptive epidemiology sheet. It's a little heavy on the jargon."

"Right," said Ford, beginning to wonder exactly what Novak was after. Ford had hoped they were going to talk about his ideas regarding the spread of resistant pathogens in the South Central community. But it looked as though Novak just wanted raw data. "No, not really. There was some speculation. The problem with Nelson was that his immune system was in such a state he could have picked the thing up anywhere."

"I guess that's typical where drug users are concerned."

"Yes. Professor Novak?" Ford checked his watch. "Forgive my asking, but your interest in all this, is it academic? I mean, are you preparing another paper? If so, you might want to consult our chief of infection control. She likes to have an input into these things."

There was a moment's silence.

"I've thought about it. But . . ." Novak pushed out a sigh, swallowed. It sounded as if he was drinking. "I don't think it would do any good."

"Do any good? I'm sorry, I don't—"

"No, I'm not going to write a paper."

There was a trace of bitterness in Novak's voice. Ford was puzzled.

"Then what did you have in mind?"

"I can't say right now. . . . But to answer your question, my interest is *not* purely academic. I wanted to talk to you about this outbreak because I was interested in your . . . in how you read the situation. It struck me at the conference, that you . . . that we are on the same wavelength. . . . I mean regarding the situation in Los Angeles—from a microbiological standpoint."

Ford looked at his watch. Helen would be arriving any minute, but his curiosity was aroused now. Novak's sudden change of tone was more than intriguing.

"You can't say, Professor? Is that because we're talking complex epidemiological projections or . . . ?"

"No. No . . . it's not that."

Ford listened hard.

"No, it's . . . the thing is I have to talk with some people before we get into this any further."

"What people?"

Novak's tone hardened.

"Look, I'm coming across as mysterious, and that's not . . . It's a question of professional etiquette, protocols. You understand."

Yes, Ford understood. His experience with Lucy Patou had taught him. But then, he was a part of a professional team, an employee. According to Helen Wray, Novak was retired. So which people could he be talking about? Ford wondered if he could draw Novak out by telling him about the Shark and the possibility of vancomycin-resistant staphylococcus at the Willowbrook. It would be very unprofessional, of course, but Novak wasn't going to go to the press with a scare story. Thinking this through, Ford suddenly realized that Novak was saying good-bye.

"I'll be in touch in the next couple of days," he said.

"Professor Novak?"

But it was too late. He had hung up.

When Helen finally arrived, just before eight, it was Sunny who got to the front door first.

"Hi!"

They were shaking hands, smiling broadly when Ford reached them.

"This is Sonia, my daughter," he said over the top of Sunny's head.

"And you're Helen, right?"

"That's me," said Helen with a big grin.

They went through to the living room. Helen took a seat on the couch next to Sunny. She had pushed her hair up into a soft knot, revealing a slenderness, a fragility that was surprising. Dressed in her corporate shoulder pads, she came across as so strong, so dynamic, she looked as if she might be an aerobics nut—all freckles and sinew—but the sleeveless black cocktail dress she was wearing revealed a paleness, a pearly sheen, that struck Ford as exotic, distinctly old-world. She was like some beautiful French courtesan. For a moment he could only stare. Helen smiled.

"We'll have to go pretty soon. They won't hold the table for long."

"I'm ready when you are," said Ford.

"You might want to put on some shoes," said Helen, pointing at his feet.

"And maybe some socks," said Sunny.

Ford stared down at his naked feet, and suddenly Helen and Sunny were laughing.

He shrugged.

"What? What's so funny?"

"Oh, Dad." Sunny tried to catch her breath. "It's you. You're so . . ." She looked at Helen, hoping for some help.

But Helen was staring at Ford, smiling warmly.

"Perfect," she said.

He left them on the couch, still laughing. When he returned five minutes later, they were getting to know each other, Sunny obviously struck by Helen's sophistication. As he entered the room, they both turned to look at his feet.

"I hope those socks are matching," said Sunny.

4

"You know, this was the first proper restaurant I came to in LA," said Helen, once they were installed in the intimate back room of the restaurant. "And I saw Andie MacDowell sitting at that table right behind you."

"No kidding."

Ford looked round. The back room seemed to be the preferred area for couples. Not counting the odd bottle of I-love-you champagne, Ford guessed that Chianti did its real business out front in the *cucina* section, where it was brighter and noisier and where there were big groups.

"That was actually a year and a half ago," said Helen. "I've been wanting to come back here. I *love* pasta, and this place has the best."

"But you only live a few miles away," said Ford.

"I know, I know."

"Do they keep you that busy at Stern?"

"Most of the time, yes. But that isn't the only thing." She shrugged. "I mean, it's the kind of place you go to on a date, isn't it? Not just when you're hungry. It's a place you dress up for."

This was a signal even he could pick up: she hadn't been out on a date for eighteen months. He had been thinking that she was maybe on the rebound, looking to replace in a hurry someone she'd lost, and that was why she had asked him out. But after eighteen months? And the way she was looking at him . . . Every time he spoke, her dark eyes drifted down to his mouth.

"So you don't like dressing up?" he said innocently, trying to make it seem as if he drew no inference from her words.

"Yes, I like to dress up," she said, smiling. "I just haven't had any one to dress up *for*. Not since I got here. You needn't look surprised, though I appreciate the gallantry. To tell the truth, it hasn't been a priority."

"Did you . . . ?" Ford hesitated, unsure whether he should be candid just because she had been. "I mean, were you involved with anyone before you came here?"

"In New York? Sure. The last four years. His name was Ted. Worked for the *Wall Street Journal*."

"Four years," said Ford. "That's a long time."

"Long enough."

"What went . . . Sorry, I shouldn't—"

"What went wrong? Nothing really. Nothing dramatic. I wanted to take the job out here. It was a big step for me. I'd worked hard for it. He didn't want to come with me. I mean, things were starting to work out for him on the *Journal*, so . . . well, we decided to call it quits."

Ford didn't know what to say. She was so open about everything that it was disconcerting. And yet there was a soft-spoken weariness in the way she talked about her life that touched him. It was as if she were tired of pretense, of trying to make a good impression, as if she just wanted to be honest about everything from the word go, so that no one could say they'd been deceived later on. Maybe his being a doctor helped.

"Does that seem terrible?" she said. "To split up because of a job?"

"No," said Ford. "It just . . . It does seem a little sad, after four years."

"I don't know. I probably could have been persuaded to stay. But as soon as I talked to Ted about it, I mean that was it. He wouldn't even *think* about moving out West with me. There was no way he was going to take a chance with his career just because it suited the little woman. You know. He even had the gall to say I'd probably give up work once I was married, so what was the point? Not that he was offering, of course."

"He sounds a little . . . unreconstructed."

"That's one way of describing him. I can think of some others. The way I look at it, my going for this job kind of smoked him out. I found out what our relationship really meant to him."

"I see. Do you still keep in touch?"

"He sends birthday greetings on E-mail. Now I heard he's going with some girl from the *Christian Science Monitor*, can you imagine?"

"Not really."

"Blonde. Twenty-four. Loves to cook. It's a perfect match."

"Oh," said Ford. "That's too bad."

"No, it isn't. I made the right decision. I put my work first, and it's paying off. My boss may be moving out to Europe in a few months. It's not in the bag, but with a little luck I think I could be taking his place. At this rate, three more years and I could make the executive board. It beats baking bread and changing diapers."

The waiter brought them their starters and the bottle of chardonnay Ford had selected from the more expensive end of the list.

"Well," he said, raising his glass, "here's to—what shall we say?— the executive fast track."

Helen watched him as she drank. Ford felt suddenly self-conscious, as if it were now his turn to open up, to explain his circumstances. Instinctively he reached up and tugged at the neck of his sweater. Helen's look softened.

"I know what you think," she said. "You think I've got my priorities wrong."

"Not at all. I—"

"It's okay. I mean if money was the important thing for you, you wouldn't be at the Willowbrook. You'd be raking it in at Columbia Health Care or somewhere."

"You're assuming they'd have me."

"Yes, I am, because they would."

Ford reached for his knife and cut into the succulent *crostini* on his plate.

"All right, maybe so. But that's a decision I made. A career decision. You moved out to LA because there was a job you wanted to do here. So did I. Maybe the Willowbrook doesn't pay as well as other organizations, but it pays better than the army did, and in its own way—I mean in trauma—it's a leader in its field. Almost everywhere else is a step down."

"Sure," said Helen. "I can see that."

"I don't mean it's the number one in terms of technology or even necessarily expertise—though I think we have the best of both—but in terms of *experience*. We deal with just about the biggest range of injuries and emergencies you could think of. And every one is different, every *day* is different. So we're constantly developing new techniques and responses. That to me, as a trauma surgeon, is worth one hell of a lot. I guess in the end it's just a question of what gets you out of bed in the morning."

Helen looked at him, a smile forming on her lips.

"Nice try," she said. "But that's not the whole story, and you know it. I heard your speech at the conference, remember? I got the impression that it was, I don't know, a cause for you—I mean, in a good way. You felt you were fighting for something."

Ford frowned. "I was trying damned hard *not* to make it sound that way. I was trying to stay factual."

Helen shook her head. "Sorry, Doctor. It got pretty obvious, I'm afraid, the way you felt, especially once you stopped reading from your notes. You became pretty polemical, as a matter of fact. People started to sit up."

"People started to leave."

She laughed, tilting her head back.

"I think that was just too much to drink at lunchtime."

"Are you sure?"

"Well, maybe some people thought you were a little too . . . political."

"Political? What did I say that was political?"

Helen reached for her wineglass, rotating it gently by the stem.

"With a small *p*, everything."

"Is that what you think?"

"It's nothing to be ashamed of. You're entitled to your opinions. Anyway, I like that, I really do."

She fixed her eyes on him, and he felt it like a physical pressure, as if she were sending a thought wave across the table.

"But I've never taken the slightest interest in politics. I just think . . ."

Ford sighed. She was forcing him to explain feelings, instincts that until that moment had never been put into words. "Maybe it's all those years in the army, I don't know, but . . ."

"But what?"

"But I still believe in this country. I can't put it any other way. I still believe in a United States. You know, one nation and all that." He gave a shrug. "Listen to me. It probably sounds a little old-fashioned."

"No, it doesn't."

He leaned forward, putting his elbows on the table.

"The way I see it, we're all of us immigrants here. Our ancestors came from every corner of the earth. Out of all that diversity they built one country. They didn't roll out the barbed wire and divide the place up. Yet today, I see exactly that happening, bit by bit, don't you? The gay community, the African-American community, the dog-owning community. I mean, with all those communities what happens to society? You stay on your side of the fence, and I'll stay on mine. I wonder what kind of future we're making."

Helen frowned.

"I don't know. I guess I've never really thought about it."

"No one seems to think about it. Or if they think about it, they don't say very much. All you hear about is rights—my rights, my freedoms—but you never hear anything about responsibilities, about duty. Those are always for the other guy."

Helen watched him closely. Ford looked down at his food, beginning to feel self-conscious again.

"You really believe all that stuff, don't you?" she said. "Ask not what your country can do for you . . ."

"Yes. More or less. I think a lot of people do. It just isn't very fashionable to admit it." He laughed, trying to lighten things up a little. "I guess I'm not a very fashionable guy. Sorry."

"Don't apologize," said Helen. "I'm not sure I like fashionable guys." Suddenly she was serious. "It's rare to find someone who actually believes in something. I think it's great."

Ford looked at her. The pinpoint reflections of her eyes seemed to add to their darkness. It was a darkness, he sensed, that came from depth. Her openness revealed only a surface; it did not open a way to the interior. Yet that was what pulled him towards her. Beauty aside, it was the sense of her hidden self that made her so fascinating.

Suddenly there was a loud crash from the front of the restaurant. A waiter had knocked over a whole dish of pasta. Another waiter said something as he passed, and a ripple of laughter went round the tables. Suddenly the atmosphere felt lighter, partylike. Helen and Ford exchanged a smile.

"By the way, I got a call from our friend Professor Novak this evening," he said, deliberately changing the subject. "Just before you arrived."

Helen took the wineglass from her lips without drinking.

"Really?"

"Yes. He said he and I were on the same wavelength."

"Oh? What did he mean by that?"

"He didn't say exactly. He wanted to know all the details of those resistant *pneumoniae* cases I talked about at the conference."

"Why?"

"I don't really know. I asked him, but he just gave me a lot of hot air about protocols and professional etiquette. He was pretty secretive, actually."

Helen sipped her wine, thinking. She was intrigued, Ford could tell.

"Do you think he is doing some kind of study?"

"I don't know. He did say his interest was not just academic. So maybe he isn't quite as retired as we thought he was."

"Perhaps not."

"You said Novak was a biochemist, right?" Ford asked. "Did research on medicines?"

"Yes, that's right."

"So epidemiology was never his field in the past?"

"Not really, at least not directly."

"Not directly?"

Helen put down her glass. Her Parma ham was almost untouched. Ford was about to say something, but stopped himself just in time. He wasn't out to dinner with Sunny, and Helen Wray wasn't out to dinner with her father. This was a date. And he was having more fun than he'd had in a long time.

"Well, at Helical Systems the main focus of research became anti-infectives," she explained.

"I remember now, you told me."

"That's right. Actually I did some asking around a few days ago, because all this was before my time. Apparently they started out hoping to make headway against cancer, but switched their focus to antibiotics later."

"That's quite a switch."

Helen smiled, shaking her head.

"Medically yes, biochemically no. You see, the Helical team, the whole venture, was based on research into genetic medicines, medicines that are supposed to work on the genes of diseased cells—like cancer cells—or bacteria. The theory, the biochemical technology was basically the same. The difference was between the type of target."

"And bacteria turned out to be easier targets than cancer cells."

"They must have thought so, I guess. Or maybe the cancer field was just getting a little too crowded."

"Crowded? How do you mean?"

"I'm just speculating. You see, the theory behind their work had actually been around for a few years. By the late eighties a number of people had started trying to develop these synthetic DNA drugs— antisense and triplex agents they're called—but they were all concentrating on human cells. Their main targets were viral infections like HIV and various forms of cancer, especially leukemia. That work's still going on. Nobody ever thought about focusing on bacteria, probably because developing new antibiotics didn't seem like much of a priority at the time. I think maybe the Helical team saw a gap in the market."

"A gap they never managed to fill."

Helen put her knife and fork together neatly at the side of her plate.

"So the story goes," she said. "I mean, no."

"But you're not sure?"

She shrugged.

"Well there've been rumors, rumors that Helical had been ready for clinical trials on a new antibiotic. I mean, before the Stern takeover. Expectations were certainly running high for a time. They had a great team there: Scott Griffen, Lewis Spierenberg, not to mention Novak himself, some real hotshots. They were supposed to have overcome some big obstacles."

Ford hastily swallowed a mouthful of bread and pâté. He wanted to get this straight.

"Do you know how the drug was supposed to work?" he asked.

"In theory, sure. These agents all do the same thing, in essence: they interfere with the synthesis of proteins that contribute to disease."

"Sounds good. How?"

"Well, just think back to how proteins are made inside a cell. Every protein is coded for by a particular gene in the cell's nucleus. For a protein to be made the gene must be copied from the double-strand DNA into individual molecules of single-strand messenger RNA, right?"

"Right. That's transcription."

"And then comes translation: outside the nucleus the messenger RNA gets converted into the required protein. Essentially a two-step process. Well, triplex and antisense agents are strands of specially designed DNA. They call them oligonucleotides. Triplex oligonucleotides insert themselves inside particular genes, turning the double helix of DNA into a triple helix, hence the name. That messes up the first step, the transcription. Prevents the transcription of the messenger RNA."

The waiter reappeared to take their plates. He looked almost hurt at the sight of Helen's barely disturbed salad, but said nothing.

"And antisense agents?"

"They mess up the second step. They're designed to bind to specific types of messenger RNA. Once bound, the RNA becomes impossible to translate."

"To translate . . . to make sense of, I suppose."

"Right. Antisense. So you get no translation. If I remember right, antisense agents were thought likely to be more promising, because they don't have to penetrate the nucleus, which is quite tricky biochemically. But whether you follow the triplex strategy or the antisense strategy, the result should be the same: the protein that's causing the problem—spreading the cancer or the virus or whatever—doesn't get made. The same principle applies to bacteria, except that there you'd be looking to stop the synthesis of proteins that the bugs actually *need*, to survive or to replicate. That's it."

"I must admit it, it sounds beautiful, in theory."

"A real magic bullet. You go right to the heart of your disease. You reach right in and switch it off at the source. It would be like hitting the enemy's command center with a laser-guided missile. You paralyze their whole army without losing a man. There'd be little or no toxicity either, so no collateral damage. Revolutionary, if you could actually manage it in practice."

"I can see why Stern would be interested," said Ford.

"Well, I'm not so sure that was what prompted the deal. I mean it was clear Helical was having major problems well before the takeover was finalized. I mean, there were no trials or anything. In fact, there were even suggestions that Helical had been deliberately talking up their progress so that they could get more money for the company. It wouldn't be the first time. Anyway, you can bet that if they'd had any kind of usable product, they'd have come out with it. There'd be no sense keeping it to themselves."

Ford felt disappointed. It was fun to speculate about secrets and things that were not what they appeared to be. It was less fun to be confronted with the obvious, prosaic explanations.

"So where were these problems, as a matter of interest? I mean, scientifically."

Helen hesitated.

"It's not confidential or anything, is it?" asked Ford.

"No, not really," she said. "Novak and his friends published quite a few articles on their work, as a matter of fact, especially in the early days of the venture. They talked about the problems then. Degradation was a big one, I think. These oligomers are very complex compounds, and they tend to be unstable, apparently. They're also very expensive to produce. The researchers probably found a whole lot more problems as they went on. We don't really know."

"You don't?" said Ford. "How come?"

The waiter was back. Helen smiled at him as he placed the seafood linguini in front of her.

"I mean you—Stern—you *own* Helical, don't you?" Ford persisted.

"Yes, what's left of it. But you see, well, the original Helical team, not just Novak, they moved on very quickly after the company was sold. I mean, all the senior guys, anyway. By the time the rumors started going around about Omega, it was too late to ask them about it. And the information they left behind on the computers was inconclusive, to say the least. Or incomplete."

"Omega? You said Omega? What's—?"

"I'm sorry, didn't I say? That was supposed to be the name of the new antibiotic, or rather the name of the project—Omega. I guess it was kind of prophetic in a way."

"How do you mean?" said Ford.

Helen laughed. "Well, it was the last thing Helical ever worked on. You could say it finished them off."

5

Nobody was carrying the staph. Patou tested the twelve people likely to have infected the Shark and came up with nothing. It turned out that Marvin Leonard did carry elevated levels of the bug in his nose, but he was not a broadcaster and anyway the bug was not the resistant strain responsible for the Shark's death. He was sent home for a week with instructions to carry on washing with the antibacterial agents. Culturing of fomites and equipment from the Critical Room and the ICU was continuing but without significant results.

But in the isolation rooms on the second floor the staph seemed to be thriving. Ford monitored Officer Denny closely, paying him regular visits in the isolation room where, as the most serious of the three cases, he was being kept on his own.

Raymond Denny was a powerfully built man in his mid-twenties. About thirty pounds overweight, he had a neck like a bull and tight biceps that suggested regular gym workouts. At first he was chirpy, bantering with the doctors and nurses, behaving as if everything was going to be okay. But when they put him onto the vancomycin, explained the dangers of the drug itself, the gravity of his predicament began to sink in.

Ford told him that because of his youth and health, his immune system and the vancomycin would soon knock the staph on the head, and it was clear that Denny believed it. The bantering was replaced by a desire to cooperate and a modified, keeping-my-spirits-up cheerfulness. All he wanted to do was get better and get out of there.

He never asked why he was in a room on his own. He seemed to think it was for security reasons, many of the other patients being either black or Hispanic gangsters.

When Ford called on him Wednesday morning he was struck by the clear signs of deterioration. Denny's boyish features were puckered in a frown, and his chunky fingers were restless on the blanket, working away at his severely bitten nails as if he wanted to remove what was left of his cuticles. The two men exchanged their, by now, habitual good-ol'-boy greeting. But as Ford checked his status chart—at no point since his operation had his temperature come off 103 degrees—Denny fell silent.

"So how're you doing, Raymond? Sleep okay?"

Denny didn't reply for a moment. He was staring at the bump made by his feet. Then he looked at Ford, giving his head a shake.

"What I don't understand is how such a little slug can be giving me so much trouble," he said.

Denny's optimism regarding his prospects for recovery had always been based on the fact that the bullet they had removed from his thigh was from a .22. Somewhere in his personal lore was a rule that said a .22 slug in the thigh could not kill you.

"I know guys had much worse and they were okay in a couple of weeks," he said. "Incredible stories, stories you would not believe. Guy I know from Operation Safe Streets—you know, the gang people—busts into this apartment and there's this character holding an M52. You know that handgun?"

Ford shook his head and replaced the charts. He sat down to examine the two wounds in Denny's leg.

"It's an automatic. Anyway this character starts blazing away. Puts the guy down—the Safe Streets guy—and then walks across the room to finish him off. Fires a round into the guy's *chest* before the guy's support come in through the door and take out the gangster. Now, the bullet—the bullet the scumbag fired?—it goes through the body, through the floor, through the ceiling downstairs, through a *table*—can you believe this?—it lodges itself so deep in the floorboards, the forensic people have to take up the floor and saw off a piece of wood to retrieve it."

"Sounds like a powerful weapon," said Ford, pulling back the dressing on Denny's ankle. Even though he was prepared, he could still hardly believe his eyes. The wound that had been cut by Peter Ozal in order to access the saphenous vein was now swollen and full of pus. The cut had not been made in optimal conditions, but Ozal had been careful to clean the skin with alcohol before proceeding and the blade was perfectly sterile. After three days on vancomycin, this surgical wound looked as though it had been made with a dirty can opener and then left to fester.

"Czech," said Denny. "Seven-point-six-two-millimeter bottleneck cartridge. Muzzle velocity of sixteen hundred feet per second."

He was silent for a moment, watching Ford's face. Ford struggled to adopt a neutral expression.

"And the guy who got shot, the guy on the floor?" Denny continued, "He goes into Harbor. He's in surgery for eight hours, where they take four slugs out of him, two of them in the *bowel*, one in the left lung. Three months later he's back on the job."

"Those are the breaks," said Ford, turning to the gunshot wound on the thigh. "Bullet can hit one thing or it can hit ten things on its way through. Makes all the . . ." He peeled back the dressing and had to catch purulent fluid with his sleeve rather than soil the sheets. The smell was surprisingly bad. "Makes all the difference."

"Stinks don't it?" said Denny, trying to sound cheerful.

"Yes, it does," said Ford, again as neutral as possible. He looked up at Denny's face and saw how frightened he really was.

Ten minutes later Ford was back in his own tiny office, with its dying houseplants and stacks of reports, papers, and medical records up to the ceiling.

"I realize that, Dr. Haynes," he said into the phone, looking across his desk at Mary Draper, who had come in for a chat. "All I'm saying is that if we don't operate, we are going to lose Denny. We may lose him anyway."

After seeing the state of Denny's leg, Ford had immediately gone to call Haynes. It wasn't something he would normally do—consult the medical director on a clinical issue—but he was aware of the wider importance of Denny's case. It was Haynes's secretary who had given him the mobile phone number. Haynes's Lexus was stuck in traffic somewhere. Every now and then the signal broke up, but there was no mistaking the tension in Haynes's voice.

"Well, I hope you're right, Dr. Ford. Because this is going to be all over the networks this evening. I hope you've thought it through."

Ford nodded.

"Sir, very little thought is required here. The drug is not working. *Vancomycin* is not working on Denny or on the others. That is *also* going to be all over the networks, if not today, then tomorrow. Denny's infection has not been checked. At this stage I believe the leg is no longer viable. If we don't amputate and transfuse, the patient will be dead in a couple of days. He'll go the same way Shark did."

"And how do you know the amputation will not also be complicated by infection?"

"I don't. All I can say is that as the doctor responsible, I firmly believe that amputation is his best chance."

There was a long silence in which Ford heard the honking of horns and what sounded like a quiet curse.

"Okay," snapped Haynes, and the line went dead.

Ford hung up and leaned back in his chair. There was a knock on the door.

"Go away."

The handle turned and Conrad Allen stuck his head into the room. Seeing Mary Draper in the chair, he started to back away.

"I'm sorry; am I—"

Ford waved him on.

"No. Come in, come in. I wanted to talk to you, in any case."

Because of the boxes of records—Ford had been holding out for a decent set of filing cabinets for two years with no luck—there was very little room and Allen had to perch on the edge of the desk. He handed Ford a sheaf of notes from the Shark's autopsy.

"This just came back. It's sobering stuff."

"Oh?"

"When they opened him up, they found necrotizing fasciitis along the missile track."

Necrotizing fasciitis was an infection caused by either streptococci or staphylococci focused on the opposed planes of wounds. The Shark's infection had spread with remarkable speed, replacing healthy tissue with a gangrenous mush.

"I spoke to Ben Prosser. He did the autopsy. He told me the tongue was actually discovered to be detached when they unwired the Shark's teeth."

"Jesus," said Draper. She stood up to leave.

The phone rang.

"Hello, Ford speaking."

There was some rustling and then a voice Ford didn't recognize. Mary Draper slipped out through the open door.

"You don't know me," the voice said. "My name is Dr. Wingate, Nathaniel Wingate. I'm the chief consultant at the Trinity Clinic."

The voice was assured, professional, yet there was an edge to it, a breathlessness that suggested to Ford some kind of heart condition, or maybe just an attack of nerves.

"I'm sorry to bother you during working hours. I wouldn't have dreamed of calling if I didn't think it was a very serious matter."

"The Trinity Clinic?" said Ford. "I'm sorry. I'm not sure where that is."

"*Um*, Beverly Hills," said Wingate. "We're in general practice up here. Mostly just local patients, actually."

The way Wingate said it, you'd think Beverly Hills was some hick town on the wrong side of the Appalachians, where all the inhabitants wore dungarees and plaid shirts. It was as if he was afraid of a hostile reaction.

"So what can I do for you, Dr. Wingate?"

"Recently one of my patients—Edward Turnbull—came to me with a small wound. You've probably heard of the Turnbulls. They're, well, you know, old Oscar Turnbull's family. At one time they practically *owned* the Valley."

Ford looked up at Conrad Allen and pressed the hands-free button so that Allen could hear.

"Hello?"

"Yes, I'm still here, Dr. Wingate. What exactly is your patient's problem?"

"He sprained his wrist falling from a horse on the weekend. At a polo match, actually. Do you know the Will Rogers Country Club?"

Allen folded his arms, suppressing a grin.

"I've heard the name," Ford said.

"Well, that's how it is with the Turnbulls. They don't trip on the sidewalk or strain themselves lifting patio furniture. They fall from horses. Anyway, besides the sprain, he got a small puncture in the palm of his hand. He may have fallen onto a nail or something."

"I take it the wound became infected, then?"

"Yes. I treated it with penicillin, but it didn't respond. The hand started to look bad, very bad. I isolated *Clostridium perfringens* from the wound exudate. I believe there's a . . . I believe there's a danger of myonecrosis."

Ford and Allen exchanged a look. Suddenly Allen wasn't smiling.

"Dr. Wingate, I'm very sorry to hear about your patient, but—excuse me for asking—but what made you decide to come to me? How did you get my number?"

"I was talking to a colleague at the clinic about the case, and he told me about the speech you gave at the NIH conference. He said there'd been cases of resistant infection at the Willowbrook. The thing is, I've never seen anything like this before. I was hoping to get some advice."

"Well, without seeing the—"

"I have already recommended amputation. I told the mother this morning."

Again Ford and Allen looked at each other.

"That sounds pretty drastic," said Ford.

"I know. But I couldn't see any safe alternative, and I was concerned to cover myself. You know how it is. You have to understand this thing started from nothing. And in two days it developed into a full blown clostridial infection that was apparently completely resistant to the penicillin I prescribed."

"Did you try any other drug?"

"I felt that time was a factor. I didn't want the gangrene to take ahold of the boy's arm. What do you think I should have done?"

Ford pondered for a moment, thinking about the Shark's tongue.

"Have you seen resistant clostridia at the Willowbrook?" asked Wingate.

"No," said Ford. "No, we haven't. We have been having problems with staphylococcus—both *pneumoniae* and *aureus*." Ford stared at his cluttered desk, thinking hard. "What did the mother say? When you recommended amputation?"

"She was very upset. Understandably. Said she was taking him elsewhere."

Ford shrugged.

"Look, Dr. Wingate, I'm afraid I don't see that I can be of much help to you right now. It may be that there is some general problem in LA, but it's a little early to say exactly how general . . . how serious the problem really is. It may be that your patient's clostridium will respond to another antibiotic and is not actually multiresistant at all. All I can say is that I am reporting my cases to the health authorities and suggest you do the same. The people at the CDC stand more chance of putting together some kind of epidemiological picture. If you learn anything, though, please let me know."

Wingate said good-bye and hung up. For a moment Ford and Allen sat in silence, listening to the hum of the disconnected line.

"*Clostridium perfringens?*" said Allen at last. "This is beginning to get a little scary. What the hell's going on?"

Ford shook his head. Allen was right. It was like something out of a horror film where nature suddenly turns nasty, like the birds in the Hitchcock film.

"Look, whatever the . . . thing Edward Turnbull has, it may not even be multiresistant. Anyway . . . ." Ford gave himself a shake, tried to concentrate on business at hand. "Conrad, what I wanted to speak to you about was Raymond Denny. I took a look at him this—"

The phone rang again.

Ford snatched it up irritably. It was Patou. She had been reviewing the staph cases in the isolation rooms and wanted to go over the facts, she said.

"I was in with Denny this morning," said Ford. "He doesn't seem to be responding to the drug."

"I agree," said Patou. "It may be that the initial infection was far greater than we thought."

Ford was puzzled for a moment. Was she going to drag him through an account of the operation again? Try to accuse him or his team of sloppy technique?

"I'm sorry, I don't—"

"Well, I understand from a reliable source that there was a problem with Denny when he was admitted."

"Dr. Patou, I—"

"Oh, come on, Dr. Ford, somebody inflated the patient's MAST pants too quickly and he became hypovolemic. As you know, the chances of infection are greatly increased after this kind of event."

Ford could not believe it. They were staring a powerful new pathogen in the face, one against which they had no effective weapon, and Patou was still going on about procedure. And what did she mean, *a reliable source*? Why not just name names?

"That's right," he heard himself say, trying to keep the anger out of his voice. "I was there at the time, along with six other people, all of whom you might consider reliable sources."

"Well, we won't go into that now. All I wanted to do was arrange a time to meet, perhaps later in the day. I can fit you in at around six o'clock."

Ford closed his eyes, unable to believe the woman's arrogance.

"What for?"

"Well, I wanted you to take me through the operation you performed on Raymond Denny."

Ford felt his face grow abruptly hot. Suddenly he was standing.

"Dr. Patou, something is killing the patients in the isolation rooms, something that cannot be treated with vancomycin, which, in case you have forgotten, was the last reliable weapon we had. I have just received authorization from the medical director to go ahead and amputate the leg of Raymond Denny, an otherwise healthy twenty-five-year-old. Before doing that, I would like to notify his family. This being the case, I may not have time to sit and talk with you about what we did to Officer Denny the first time round. But in order to save time in future, I suggest you come to the OR and *watch* the amputation, suck air samples, culture the floor, culture any frigging fomite you feel inclined to, but *don't* bother me with any more of your ridiculous requests!"

He slammed the phone down and stood there trembling. Allen smiled.

"Attaboy," he said quietly. "Tact and charm. Wins 'em over every time."

6

Raymond Denny's wife and five-year-old daughter came down to the hospital at four o'clock to see him before he went into the OR. They were accompanied by Michael Rickman, the police officer who had confronted Ford in the critical room when Denny was first admitted. The family went quietly into the isolation room in a state of shock, but Rickman stayed outside with Ford. He wanted a word.

Once again Ford found himself standing closer than was comfortable to the policeman's tired face with its network of broken veins.

"I thought you told me he was going to be okay?" said Rickman.

"In normal circumstances I would have been right," said Ford. He looked up and down the ICU ward. "What we are dealing with here is completely new."

Rickman pushed his head over to one side.

"Oh, it's not your fault. Is that what you're trying to say?"

"That's right. This pathogen has not responded to any of the drugs used. It is something which is beyond—"

"And what about those antishock pants?"

Ford stared.

"What about them?"

"He nearly died when you were getting those things off him. I was there, remember?"

"Mr. Rickman."

"*Officer* Rickman."

"Officer Rickman, the deflation of the MAST pants has no bearing on the development of the staphylococcus infection in Raymond Denny's leg."

"That's not what I hear," said Rickman. He stood back, tapping the side of his nose and smirking. For a moment Ford had a paranoid flash of Rickman and Patou talking together on the phone. "I know a doctor who says that hypervolema—"

"Hypovolemia."

Ford bit his tongue. The last thing he wanted to do was provoke this man.

"Whatever. That hyper-whatever-it-is significantly increases the chances of infection. In other words, what happened in ER does have a bearing on what followed. In other words, *your* negligence is going to cost my partner *his* leg."

Ford's silence drew a satisfied smile from Rickman. But he couldn't hold it. His lip was trembling, and he looked as though he might actually cry. He pointed towards the door of the isolation room.

"And I owe it to that woman . . . and to that . . . little girl to make sure this hospital pays for what it has done to them."

Ford looked away as Rickman brushed the tears from his eyes with the back of his fist.

"Officer Rickman," said Ford, suddenly tired, suddenly struggling under the weight of events. "You'll do what you feel you have to. In the meantime I must ask you to excuse me. I have to go scrub up."

The day following the operation, Raymond Denny died of septicemia, his blood seething with staphylococcus and its destructive toxins. Several Los Angeles television stations covered the story, showing pictures of the distraught wife standing outside the Willowbrook's main entrance. At eleven o'clock that evening KNBC Channel 4 News carried an item on the Willowbrook's recent record in postoperative infection and talked about a killer bug that was claiming lives in the intensive care unit. Curtis Lipperman, a spokesman for a South Central urban regeneration group known as the Brotherhood, appeared on KTLA news, raising the question of the treatment of blacks in South Central and at the Willowbrook in particular. Invited into the studio to air his views, he pointed out that a number of African-American patients had recently succumbed to resistant pathogens at the Willowbrook, and wondered why it was that a white policeman's death had attracted media attention when the others had gone unnoticed.

"As the recent tragic death of Jessie Hammel proved, African-Americans are being sacrificed in South Central to government budget cuts," he shouted. "The health-care dollar is stained with African-American blood."

The morning after the KTLA program, Ford was unable to park in the area reserved for staff cars. The whole parking lot was jammed with local and national media teams. Vans bristling with satellite dishes and antennae blocked access to the main entrance, while camera crews roved back and forth getting local reaction to the news about budget cuts, Jessie Hammel's death, the danger of incurable disease in the Willowbrook, and anything else that might excite an angry response.

Ford spent ten minutes trying to park somewhere that would not be in the way of other cars, but it was hopeless. He rolled down his window.

"Excuse me!" he tapped a cameraman on the back. "EXCUSE ME!" The guy turned and Ford found himself staring directly into a lens. "Excuse me. Do you think you could get out of the way? I'm trying to park my car."

Out of nowhere a microphone was shoved into his face. It had a dirty protective cover that looked like yeti fur. Ford tried to push it away. At the same time somebody slapped the roof of the Buick hard.

"I said, I'm trying to get through to park!" Ford shouted.

A young woman's face was suddenly crammed into the window along with the mike and the lens. Somebody started rocking the car, pressing down on the trunk and letting go, so that Ford was bouncing, still trying to push the mike back out the window. His heart started to pound.

"Karyn Schaeffer, CNN," said the young woman.

Ford pulled away from the mike and was astonished to see that other lenses were now staring at him through the windshield. A flash went off. Then another.

"Sir?" said the woman, struggling to keep some composure in the mob that was developing. "Are you with the hospital staff?"

Ford nodded.

"Yes, and I'm here to go to work."

From behind the woman somebody shouted, "It's Ford! He's the one that took that cop's leg off!"

A camera bumped the windshield with a sharp crack, and then suddenly questions were being shouted through the growing babble of angry voices.

"Is it true that the Willowbrook is a hotbed of disease?"

"What have you got to say to the wife of Officer Denny?"

"Why were sick patients crammed together in a single room?"

"Is there a danger to the local community?"

"Is there racial discrimination in the—"

"Look," shouted Ford, holding up his hand against another barrage of flashes. The dirty mike was pushed against his mouth, so that he had to lean back. Magically the questions had stopped. He was being given a chance to speak. Trying to sound as professional as possible he formulated his reply: "There is no danger to the South Central community, or to people inside the hospital."

There was a pause, and then an explosion of new questions. Ford held up his hand.

"We have recently . . . We have recently been encountering instances of infection with a . . . with a very common pathogen, a bacteria which many of us carry all the time without any harm to ourselves or others. This bacteria was, I believe, responsible for the death of Officer Denny and—"

"What is it called?" shouted a man's voice.

"*Staphylococcus aureus.*"

"Superstaph!" somebody screamed. This was a devil they knew.

"Is it a mutant strain?" shouted Karyn Schaeffer.

"Our lab people are working to culture and identify the precise biochemical characteristics of this bacteria, and as soon as they have results, I'm sure they will make them available to the press."

"You mean, you don't know what it can do?"

Ford shook his head. All they wanted to do was sensationalize.

"We know it is seriously pathogenic. It produces infection rapidly in open wounds and appears not to respond to any of the available drugs."

"You mean there's no cure?"

Cameras started to flash again, and somebody fell against the front of the car, making it rock.

"It's a little early to say, but nothing we have tried so far seems to have an effect."

"Professor Ford, you recently gave a speech at a conference saying that LA is in danger of being overrun by drug-resistant pathogens. Is this the beginning?"

Ford was a little taken aback at this. He felt as though somebody must have singled him out. They had already been digging around.

"My title is Doctor," shouted Ford, "not Professor, and I didn't . . ."

He was momentarily blinded by flashing cameras. It was time to get out.

"I didn't say that. I said that the way antibiotics are distributed can encourage resistance, especially where there's inadequate medical supervision."

He snapped off the ignition and opened the door, having to push hard to get out. For a moment he was staring into the tiny red eyes of a dozen microcassettes.

Karyn Schaeffer was still right in his face. "Is this the beginning of an outbreak, Dr. Ford?"

"I, well . . . it depends how you define an outbreak," said Ford, pushing forward towards the main entrance now.

"What do you mean?" shouted Schaeffer, following him—walking backwards, completely oblivious to any obstacles that might be behind her.

"Well, a small group of patients in a ward that all suddenly come down with the same thing—if the disease in question was fairly unusual—that would be considered an outbreak."

Ford ploughed forward, blinking against the flashes. He reached the glass doors of the main entrance and was glad to see two of the hospital safety police on guard.

"So this is an outbreak?" Schaeffer persisted.

Ford turned in the doorway. He looked over to where he had left the Buick. He hoped it was going to be okay.

"Is it an outbreak?" repeated Schaeffer.

Ford looked at the young woman's face.

"In the technical sense I defined, yes, it is," he said.

For the LA media the Willowbrook story was like a temporary license to print money. News that there was an outbreak of an incurable disease, a mutant strain of a bacteria that around one third of the population carried all the time, gave television ratings and newspaper circulation a much needed boost. Many journalists focused on the serious issues raised by the incident, but many more reveled in the lurid details of what superstaph could do to its unfortunate victims.

Mary Denny, the dead policeman's widow, was paid $40,000 by UPN News 13 for a live interview, while several of the Willowbrook staff received offers from journalists wanting to know what was really going on inside the wards and operating rooms.

The media feeding frenzy was matched by the panic in South Central among people who had friends or relatives inside the Willowbrook. Hospital security was strained to the limit controlling the crowds that turned up seeking clarification and reassurance. Many demanded that their loved ones be transferred elsewhere. Amateur video of a young woman wheeling a bed across the Willowbrook parking lot at three o'clock in the morning, complete with saline drip and wounded boyfriend, was broadcast all over the country by CBS, while a still from the same video appeared in newspapers and magazines across the country.

Three days after Officer Denny's death, another nine gunshot and stabbing victims were discovered to be infected with the strain of staph that had killed the Shark.

7

Ford was summoned to see the medical director at ten o'clock in the morning, but when he got there, he was told he would have to wait. Russell Haynes was on the phone, his door firmly shut. In the open-plan office outside, the normally chatty corps of administrative staff went about their work in silence, speaking only when their work demanded it, and then in whispers. Ford got the unmistakable impression that they were avoiding his gaze.

There came a low-tech electronic buzz, and then Ford heard Haynes's voice coming simultaneously through an intercom and his office door: "Ask Dr. Ford to come in, please."

Ford thought he knew why Haynes wanted to talk to him. The staphylococcus emergency threatened to have a profound impact upon the running of the hospital, not least because such a high percentage of its patients were admitted via the Emergency Department. The presence of a bacterial pathogen in the hospital also posed a particular threat to obstetrics—which accounted for a quarter of all admissions—because babies and mothers in labor were especially vulnerable to infection. Whatever the source of the problem, hard choices were going to have to be made about which facilities stayed open and which were shut down.

"Russell?"

"Take a seat, Marcus," he said, looking not at Ford, but rather at waist-level space a couple of feet in front of him. Haynes's gaunt, pock-marked face wore an expression of impatience, as if the matter before them was not one he was going to spend a lot of time discussing, whether Ford liked it or not.

Ford sat down without saying anything. Haynes was upset about something, and it wasn't just the fate of the patients.

"Marcus, I'm . . ." He sighed and pushed himself back from the edge of his desk, as if trying to distance himself from the seat of his responsibilities. "I'm afraid this situation is getting out of control."

For a moment there was silence.

"I mean, way out of control. I just got off the phone with the chief deputy director at the health department. They're mad as hell down there. Mad as hell about how this whole situation's been handled."

Ford blinked. What did Haynes mean, *handled*?

"Russell, we've done everything we can. We've never had to deal with anything like this before. Don't they understand—?"

"I'm not talking about the outbreak." Haynes was almost shouting. "I'm talking about the press. The publicity, goddammit. In less than two weeks time the board of supervisors is going to decide whether or nor to accept the health department's restructuring plans, plans which stave off the worst of the cuts in return for a leaner system long-term. This crisis could derail the whole deal, not to mention a year's negotiations with Washington."

Ford stared at Haynes, unable at first to take in what he was saying. Here they were, dealing with a medical emergency, and all the health department was bothered about was the press. He could only assume that the death of Raymond Denny had taken on some new political significance.

"With respect, I don't see that we can be held responsible for how the public reacts to what's happened. Our job is to—"

Haynes slapped a copy of the *Los Angeles Tribune* onto the desk. On the front page, just below the latest on a celebrity rape trial, a headline read: EPIDEMIC THREATENS SOUTH CENTRAL. It looked like the most alarmist report so far, but worse than that, it carried a photograph of Ford alongside it, talking into a battery of microcassettes.

"The article cites you as saying that cuts in the health-care budget are contributing to the crisis. It's right there in quotation marks."

Ford stared at the article in horror.

"But . . . but . . ." he stammered, "I never said that. They just asked me what was happening."

"And you told them that the epidemic was at large among the South Central population—in effect, out of control—and that the county was responsible."

"I didn't say a damn thing about the county. I don't know how . . . They must have spoken to one of the people at that conference. I was talking about the need for supervision of antibiotic therapy. About access to health care."

Haynes closed his eyes, shaking his head in disbelief.

"Russell, it was a professional forum." Ford searched for the right words. "Nothing I said was in any way political."

And as he spoke he remembered what Helen Wray had said, that his whole speech had been political, with a small *p*. Suddenly it felt as if his work as a surgeon was no longer just about the patients and their needs. It had levels of significance, touched upon priorities and considerations, that he knew little or nothing about. It was a bad feeling.

Haynes did not look impressed. "Well, I can understand just why Dr. Patou was so anxious to hear what you proposed to say before you gave that speech," he said. "I wish I had taken her objections more seriously at the time."

Ford bit his lip. It was a deliberate dig; it had to be.

"Of course, in making a statement on our infection problem without her say-so, you've strayed onto her territory yet again. I deliberately put her in charge of dealing with the media on this thing."

"Look, they jumped me in the parking lot. I wasn't ready for them. I've refused all calls from the press since then."

"Well, I should damned well hope so."

"I suppose Dr. Patou has complained again?"

"Not to me, not yet. But I'm sure she'll eventually get around to it."

Haynes took a handkerchief from his pocket and dabbed at the perspiration on his brow. The edge had come off his temper. Now he just looked tired.

"Look," said Ford, "if you want me to talk to her, I'll talk to her. But she's got to understand—"

"I'm afraid it may be a little late for that. She's gone over my head this time." Haynes sighed and tucked the handkerchief back into his pocket. "She has connections in the health department, you know. And with this Raymond Denny thing, well, she's got them pretty stirred up—not that they weren't stirred up already. She's also taken her concerns to our chief executive. Of course, I'd have preferred it if she'd have come to me, but . . . well, it's too late now."

Ford didn't know what to say. He felt as if he were staring into the headlights of an oncoming truck but couldn't step out of the way.

"Her . . . her *concerns?*" he managed to say.

"There's to be an investigation. Apparently your handling of the Denny case will be the main issue. The fact that we may face a high-profile legal action makes that essential. The county has to be seen to be taking the matter seriously, especially at such a delicate time with respect to our funding, as I've explained. They'll also look at how the whole Code Yellow team has been operating and its response to the infection threat. The CEO here's being as supportive as he can, but this is a clinical matter and not his direct concern."

Ford couldn't believe his ears. He tried, but he could not understand how all this could have come about. Somehow everything had been blown up out of proportion. It was insane.

"Russell. As I explained to Dr. Patou, what killed Raymond Denny was not the way his MAST pants were deflated, for God's sake, but an entirely new strain of—"

Haynes held up his hands. "I know, I know. It doesn't make sense. But this whole thing is beyond my control now. It's an issue, a public issue, and part of that is your responsibility, whether you like it or not."

Ford found himself staring at the marble plaque on the edge of Haynes's desk: *God grant me the serenity to accept the things I cannot change.*

"In the meantime, I have to tell you it's likely—I believe they're going to reach a decision tomorrow morning—it's likely that they'll want you suspended from your duties, at least for the time being. Until this whole thing is sorted out. It's tough, I know, and I don't like it. But I have no choice."

Ford could not speak, caught between different emotions—fear, anger, disbelief.

"I'm just letting you know this in advance so that, well, so that you needn't be here when the news comes through tomorrow. If it does.

We can let you know by phone. That way your colleagues won't have to
see—"

"I'm coming in," said Ford. "I still have students to teach."

"I just wanted to save you any embarrassment. I—"

"I'm coming in, Russell. This is my job. If they want to suspend me,
that's up to them. I'm staying at my post until I'm told to leave."

He stood up.

"Is there anything else?" he asked.

"Look, the chances are we'll have to shut down most of the Emergency Department anyhow, at least for a couple of weeks. The CDC
will see to that. Their advisers are already on their way."

"So Dr. Patou finally gets what she's always wanted: a hospital
without any sick people."

"Marcus, I think it would be best if you avoid Dr. Patou for the
time being. Any further confrontation can only make things worse."

"Worse for whom?"

"For all of us."

"I'll talk to you tomorrow, Russell. You'll find me on my rounds."

He opened the door.

"Marcus, listen, I know how you must feel. I . . ." Ford turned
around. "I'll talk to you tomorrow."

Returning to his office, Ford found a memorandum from Lucy
Patou in his wire in box. Copies had been sent to all members of the
department, including support staff. It outlined special measures being
taken in response to the superstaph outbreak. Starting at eleven o'clock
that morning—it was already half past—all Code Yellows would be
diverted to other hospitals. The Intensive Care Unit was to be shut
down as soon as practicably possible, pending investigation of the outbreak by the CDC. Two special wards were to be set aside for the isolation of the patients already infected with the staph. These patients
would be barrier-nursed and supervised by a special unit whose members would be strictly prohibited from entering other wards in the hospital or any other medical facility in the county. The memorandum
ended by listing the individuals who would make up this unit. Half of
them were drawn from Ford's own team, including Mary Draper and

third-year resident Peter Ozal. Dr. Patou, it seemed, no longer thought
it necessary to consult the director of Trauma on the disposition of his
own people. Probably because, if she had her way, they were not going
to be his people much longer.

Ford slumped down behind his desk. He felt breathless, stunned.
How could this be happening? After all he'd done, after all the years of
giving—to his patients, to the Willowbrook, to the whole damned
city—suddenly he was on the stand. Suddenly he was a scapegoat for
bureaucrats and politicians he'd never even met. And instead of sup-
porting him, his colleagues were just standing by and letting it happen,
as if it had been *bound* to happen and there was nothing they could do
about it. *Grant me the serenity to accept the things I cannot change . . .*
Maybe he should have seen it coming. Maybe for seven years he had
just been fooling himself: he just didn't belong there. As Conrad Allen
had said, South Central was a war zone—by implication one where
middle-class white people simply did not belong, however good their
intentions. Where they were not welcome.

He needed to talk to Peter Ozal. He'd been present when they
deflated the MAST pants. If there was an inquiry, what he said would
be important. He reached for the phone, but before he could pick it up,
it began to ring.

He hesitated before picking up the receiver. What was he going to
say if it turned out to be Lucy Patou? Or one of his colleagues in
Trauma. What would he say if it was Conrad Allen?

"Marcus? It's Helen."

Her voice sounded as if it came from another world: fresh, clean,
sweet, a world on the other side of the universe.

"Oh, hello. How . . . How are you?"

"I'm fine. Are we still on for a drink tonight?"

They'd arranged to go down to Venice. He was picking her up at
around seven o'clock. Sunny was doing rehearsals for a school play until
half past eight. It had seemed like a convenient window. But what sort
of company was he going to be now? He couldn't expect Helen to share
his burdens so early on. It was asking too much.

"Yes, sure. If you want, only . . ."

"What's the matter? You sound terrible."

"Well, I've had some . . . Things have taken a turn for the worse down here."

"Not your friend Loulou, I hope."

"How did you guess?"

"She's gunning for you again, huh?"

"And how."

And then his side of the story came out: Raymond Denny's death, the newspaper article, the inquiry, the shutdown of the Trauma Unit, and his likely suspension. He needed to tell someone, and she seemed anxious to hear all about it.

"So Haynes just wants you to crawl away and keep your mouth shut," she said at last.

"That's it. As he sees it, my big mouth is what's landed me in this spot. I'm just supposed to cure people. I'm not supposed to have opinions about why they get sick in the first place."

"And if the inquiry goes against you?"

"It can't. I mean, I haven't done anything wrong, at least not medically. It's just a lot of political posturing, Haynes says."

"Posturing that could still damage your career. Even if you're exonerated."

"Well, it isn't exactly a vote of confidence from the health department, that's for sure."

"Exactly. That's why you need to start calling in favors, just in case. They have to know that you're not going to take this lying down."

Ford was surprised to find Helen so interested, so anxious to help. She wasn't just sympathizing, either; she was coming up with ideas, strategies. Already he felt that he was not facing the crisis alone.

"I'm going to talk to the people on my team this afternoon, the ones that treated Raymond Denny. They know what happened."

"That's a good start. But you should go beyond that. The health department is pissed off about the things you're supposed to have said, right? Well, it can't do any harm if you establish that those things were actually true."

"But how do I do that?"

"You can start with Professor Novak. He said he was on the same wavelength as you, didn't he? If he came and supported what you've said, it could only strengthen your position."

"You think so?"

"Of course. They can't crucify you if all you've done is alert the public to a genuine danger. At the very least he'd upstage you. He's still someone they'd have to take seriously."

"Okay. I'll give it a shot. I'll call him. The trouble is, I don't think I've even got his number."

Helen hesitated.

"Somebody here must have it. Just hang on. I'll get it for you."

The tape hiss told him he was talking to an answering machine. The outgoing message gave no name, but the voice sounded as if it could be Novak's. As he waited for his cue, Ford tried to think up the right kind of message.

"Hello, Professor Novak, this is Marcus Ford. I wonder if you wouldn't mind calling me back as soon as possible. There have been some developments which I'd like to—"

There was a loud clunk on the line.

"Dr. Ford? This is Charles Novak."

"Oh, good morning. I hope I'm not disturbing you. I thought—"

"I do screen my calls sometimes. Just a habit I've gotten into. I've just been reading about your problems at the Willowbrook."

"My problems?" Ford couldn't believe that Novak could already have heard about the inquiry. "You mean—?"

"The staph outbreak. Are the reports true?"

Of course, the staph outbreak. In the wake of his meeting with Haynes, Ford had only been concerned about himself. He had almost forgotten about the infected patients. Except, of course, that his services were no longer required as far as they were concerned.

"Essentially, yes."

"The bacteria are showing resistance to vancomycin?"

"Yes, to everything we've tried so far. The CDC'll be turning up any day now."

"To do what exactly, do you know?"

Ford frowned. The truth was Lucy Patou had been solely responsible for reporting to and liaising with the Centers for Disease Control.

He hadn't been asked to comment upon their exact brief, nor was he likely to be.

"I assume they'll look for the source of the problem and advise on appropriate medication for the infected."

"If there is any."

There was something unfamiliar in Novak's voice, a terseness, a touch of defiance, which Ford did not know how to interpret.

"If there is any," he repeated. "Look, Professor Novak. The reason I'm calling is, well, you may be aware that some of my comments at the conference have been reported—or misreported—in the press. I'm afraid that's caused me some problems, I mean with my employers."

"I'm not surprised. Are you?"

"Frankly, yes. I am."

Novak laughed.

"You've been rocking the boat, Dr. Ford. Several boats, in fact. You surely didn't expect it to make you popular."

"I didn't . . . All I know is, it would be helpful if some of those things, the things I've said, received some support. I mean about the source of the resistance problem, about antibiotic misuse in South Central and its consequences. Because at the moment all attention is being focused on the Willowbrook. As if that's where the problem was created."

"As if it was all your fault? Is that what you mean?"

Ford sighed.

"Yes. That's exactly what I mean. I know there's no reason why you should take any interest. You're certainly under no obligation. But if you read the situation the same way I do, now would be a good time to say so, publicly."

There was silence on the line. Ford could hear the faint sound of music. He thought he recognized Beethoven, a late sonata.

"Professor Novak?"

"Yes," he said, seeming distracted now. "I'm here. I'm sorry, but if you're asking me to talk to the press, I'm afraid . . . I'm afraid that's impossible. Besides, I don't think anyone would be interested in hearing what I have to say."

"You're a leading figure in your field. I'm sure you still—"

"According to whom?"

Ford thought about mentioning Helen Wray. After all, Novak had met her at the conference. But then he remembered how unsettled he had been around her. Maybe it was something to do with the Stern connection. Helen had said that all the Helical Systems people had left very quickly after the company was sold. Maybe there had been bad feelings.

"Just people here, at the hospital." Ford seized on a credible lie. "Our in-house pharmacy people, in particular."

Novak seemed to accept it, but he was not persuaded. "The fact remains, I'm retired. I intend to stay that way. But there may be . . ."

"May be what?"

"Something else I can do to help. Provided my name is kept strictly out of it. Can you guarantee that?"

"Yes, of course, if that's your wish."

"Good. We'll need to meet. Give me . . . let's say, a week from now. Next Friday. Can you make it, let's say, nine o'clock Friday night?"

"Yes. You want me to come to your home?"

"No. I'm a long way out of town, hard to find. Besides there's some material I want to show you at the apartment. Information, research. If you use it in the right way, it could be very helpful. It could be helpful for both of us."

"Research?"

"I'm going to give you an address and a number. It's a new apartment block, just finished. I work there sometimes. The entry phone system isn't connected up yet, but this number will get you into the lobby. There's a keypad by the door. Do you have a pen?"

8

Lincoln Boulevard looked different after sundown, swept clean of people by the dark. Ford switched off the engine and sat quietly looking across to number 940, where lights were burning on every floor. He sat like that for a minute, watching, trying to guess which drapes hid Helen Wray, trying to imagine her moving around inside, getting ready for their date. Or maybe she was already dressed, sitting in a chair with a drink, checking her watch with the beginnings of irritation. It was now just after seven-thirty, and he was running late.

The front door of the building opened, and the woman Ford had seen before tending her roses came out, dragging a dachshund by its leash. Afraid of being recognized, he lowered himself in the seat, and for a second considered turning on the ignition and getting the hell out of there. Why? Didn't he want to go in? He forced himself to focus on Helen, to recall the moment—only four nights before—in which they had said good-bye. Electric light had lit strands of reddish brown in her dark hair as she leaned forward to kiss him on the corner of the mouth. He remembered that moment as having seemed perfectly right. But now, sitting in the Buick, still in the clothes he had worn to work— he hadn't had time to go home and change—it all felt alien to him. He was overwhelmingly conscious of how little he knew about the woman he was getting involved with. He was so depressed and tired he didn't know what he wanted.

The dog lady started towards the car. He would have to move now. Either go or stay. He shoved open the door and climbed out.

The dachshund gave a little querulous bark as Ford made his way across the lawn.

"Good evening," he said, waving, trying to sound as hearty and unthreatening as possible.

The woman gave him a steady look.

"I thought that was you," she said. "In the car."

She went back to her companion, coaxing him to do his business.

"Come on, Webster. We're not moving until you do it."

Watched by Webster, Ford scanned the list of names on the keypad and pressed *Wray*.

"She's in," said the woman, still staring down at her dog. "Came back about an hour ago."

The first impression Ford had of Helen's apartment was of intense luminosity and a lack of furniture bordering on the impractical. She was holding the door open when he reached her floor and greeted him with a winy kiss—on the corner of the mouth again, but more than just friendly. Ford was guided through to the stylishly bare living room, where blond light bounced off the stripped pine floor, hurting his eyes.

"I'm sorry I'm late," he mumbled. "What with all this trouble, it's been . . ."

But she was gone again.

"Don't worry about it," she called from the kitchen, returning immediately with a bottle of chilled white wine. She poured two glasses, holding her free hand flat against her stomach.

"I got the picture on the phone. It sounds like the whole hospital is coming apart at the seams."

She was wearing a red cocktail dress and looked, as usual, terrific, stripped to the essentials like her apartment: no earrings, no necklace, not even a wristwatch. Involuntarily Ford looked down at the baggy knees of his pants.

"It's Vouvray," she said, handing him a glass. "I hope that's okay. People are so used to chardonnay out here they find the chenin blanc a little peculiar."

"As long as there's wine in it," said Ford.

He sipped, found the chenin blanc a little peculiar, and smiled, taking in Helen's chic decor. The only provision for seating seemed to be a black leather couch.

"It's nice," Ford ventured. "Kind of minimalist. Or have you recently been burgled?"

Helen smiled, but Ford could see he was making her uncomfortable. He had probably carried his hangdog, doomed look from the hospital. He'd have to shape up or the evening was going to be a disaster.

"I hate clutter," said Helen. She sipped her wine. "I go through a long period of careful accumulation and then wake up hardly able to breathe. I end up giving everything away."

"Oh, really? Does that mean I can have the couch?" asked Ford, making an effort now.

The beginnings of a frown plucked at Helen's forehead. She looked at him for a moment as if she were considering her answer. Then she reached out and touched his face.

"Are they really going to suspend you, Marcus?"

Ford's shoulders sagged.

"Do you think we could . . . ?"

He squinted up at the powerful lights. It was like standing in a photon storm.

Helen set off across the room for the switch.

"I'm sorry," she said. "It's a habit with me. I always have the lights up full in every room. I don't know why. Maybe it was because I was abused as a child."

She shot him a look over her shoulder.

"Just kidding."

She dialed the dimmer switch to a romantic twilight. Then went over to the stereo and brought up a little soft jazz.

"Sit down," she said. She didn't have to ask twice.

This was much better. The half-light and smoochy saxophone made him want to push his shoes off, maybe wiggle his toes a little. He leaned back in the couch, took a good long pull on his wine, and closed his eyes.

When he opened them again, Helen was wearing a white T-shirt and a pair of faded chinos. Chopin had replaced Stan Getz, and there was a good smell of cooking in the air.

"Jesus!"

Ford jerked forward on the sofa, staring at his watch. It was a quarter to ten.

"Jesus, Helen, I must have—"

"It's okay," said Helen, looking up from the book she was reading. "You looked so exhausted I couldn't bring myself to wake you."

Ford struggled to get up, but Helen pushed him gently back into the couch.

"But what about that drink?" he pleaded. "I was going to take you out. Jesus. I just can't . . ."

Helen laughed, openmouthed, throwing her head back. Ford could see she had been at the Vouvray while he was asleep.

"For goodness' sake," she said. "Relax, can't you? There's really no need to get upset. And you weren't *taking* me out," she added, raising a finger. "We were going out together."

"Right."

"And to be honest, I'm just as happy to stay in."

She leaned across and kissed him—flush on the mouth this time. The peculiar grape smell was on her breath, and her T-shirt smelled of something between beeswax and vanilla. Ford kissed her back, liking her mouth and this lovely rich smell she had. Then she was looking at him again, definitely a little tipsy.

"Christ, Helen," he said. "I'm so embarrassed. I make you wait for me, and then I crash on your couch like some old fart. You must think I—"

Helen kissed him again and then leaned away, pushing the hair back from his forehead.

"Marcus, no more talk. Talk is finished. You're working too hard. With all that's going on at the hospital, it's not surprising. God, if I were you, I'd have burned out a long time ago."

Ford looked at his left hand, pale against the black leather.

"You're right," he said. "It's all getting a little crazy down there. This afternoon when Haynes called me into his office—it was surreal."

Helen shook her head.

"I can't believe they're thinking of suspending you," she said softly.

"I think they're serious," said Ford.

He stood up now and started pacing back and forth on the bare floor.

"Haynes thinks I was out of line talking to the press. And he's virtually handed control of the hospital over to Lucy Patou."

Helen nodded sympathetically.

"Look, if they do suspend you, it's only going to be a temporary thing. I know how much they value you down there. That nurse, what's her name, Gloria?"

"Oh, Gloria wouldn't suspend me even if she caught me suffocating a patient with a pillow."

"And she'd be right," said Helen.

Ford stopped in his tracks.

"What?"

"Well, she would know that if you were murdering someone, you probably had a good reason and would be doing it according to sound ethical principles."

"You're probably right. Maybe I should strangle Patou. Sneak up behind her. Get an arm round her throat." Ford narrowed his eyes. "She's not a big woman. It wouldn't be too hard."

"That's the spirit," said Helen, laughing. "But we can plan all that later. First, I think we should eat. While you were sleeping, I made a little salad and tempura. I hope you like fish."

Ford considered her for a moment. With her long legs doubled up, there was something of the foal about her. That's what she was, a thoroughbred, with her glossy black hair and dark eyes. Impulsively he squatted down to kiss her on the mouth, but his knees made such a loud crack, he couldn't go through with it. Helen stared at him, struggling to stifle a laugh, her wine-moistened lips trembling.

"Look at me," said Ford, still squatting. "The old fart on a hot date."

Helen's expression became quizzical. She put her head over to one side.

"Marcus?"

He loved the way she looked at him—there was something so intelligent about her face, a cleverness that was almost unsettling.

"Yes?"

"Did you know you drool when you sleep?"

And before he could cry out or catch hold of her, she was up and gone, laughing at him from the kitchen.

It was then that he remembered Sunny.

He called home, listening to four rings before she picked up.

"Hello?"

"Sweetheart, it's me. Are you okay?"

"Oh. Sure. Why wouldn't I be?"

She sounded pissed.

"It was just . . . I'd hoped to be home when you got back. . . . How did the play go?"

"Rehearsal. It wasn't the whole play."

"Right—so how did it go?"

"It went."

"Did you find the meat loaf in the refrigerator?"

"The small gray thing with sort of perspiration on it?"

"*Honey.*"

"I went out."

"You went out?"

"Yeah, you know. You go out the door into the street. Lots of people do it."

"Don't be funny. You mean you went out to eat? Where did you go?"

"Just a place in the neighborhood."

"Who with?"

"Some kids from school. After the rehearsal we just went across Robinson to this taco place. So you see, it didn't matter that you weren't here. There's no need to feel guilty."

There was a long pause during which Ford gripped the phone with both hands. He did feel guilty. Very. And he didn't know what else to say.

"Dad?"

"Yeah?"

"Where are you? Are you at the hospital?"

"No, I'm at a friend's house."

"Oh."

Another pause.

"I read about the Willowbrook. What's going on?"

"I'll tell you about it tomorrow morning."

"Aren't you coming home?"

The plaintive note in Sunny's voice squeezed Ford's heart.

"Of course I am, honey. But I don't want you waiting up, okay. I'll come in and kiss you good night."

"Not if I'm asleep. I've got to get some sleep, Dad."

"Okay, honey. Love you, sweetheart."

"Sure you do. Good-bye, Mr. Bear."

And she hung up.

Ford stood with the phone in his hand, deep in thought. *"I've got to get some sleep"*—she could sound so adult and then call him Mr. Bear, something she had stopped doing years ago. This flickering between being a child and the beginnings of a woman threw him completely. He didn't know whether he was supposed to be her friend or her dad.

When Helen came back into the room, he was standing at the window looking out.

"What's up?"

"I was going to get back to see Sunny after school."

"Is she okay?" asked Helen.

"Sure. She's fine."

Helen came up to him and held him from behind.

"After all, she is thirteen, isn't she? And she's not the only woman who has a claim on your time."

Ford turned and looked Helen in the face. He didn't like what she had said. It was callous. Then, looking at her, he saw that this hardness was part of her appeal. She looked at you, and you could see she was engaged, genuinely turned on, but there was something else too, something calculating, almost predatory. Out of the blue an image of Carolyn, just before her death, flashed into his mind. He remembered the way she had looked at him in moments like this. The look in her eyes had always been so trusting, so loving. It was always he who had initiated their lovemaking. He sensed that with Helen it wouldn't be like that. When she looked at you, you could see her thinking what she would like to do to you, what she would like to take. With a rush of hot feeling in his loins, he felt as if he wanted her to take him.

"Why don't you go and take a shower?" she asked softly.

She pressed herself against the bulge in his groin and kissed his mouth. Ford smiled. She was so clever. Instinctively. She seemed always to know what he was thinking and knew exactly how to be herself at all times, through a bewildering number of registers. He had an agreeable feeling of being in her power.

They ate in the living room, balancing plates on their knees. The tempura was good, and the chilled Vouvray started to take the edge off his feelings of guilt about Sunny. Pretty soon all he could think about was the great time he was having. They talked softly, laughing from time to time, as if it hadn't been such a bad day, as if South Central were on another planet, as if they were in a bubble that protected them both from the city and their daily lives.

"Raw masculine power aside," said Helen, putting her head on one side and smiling at him. "Do you know what it is that really turns me on about you? I mean *really* turns me on?"

Ford shook his head.

"I always assumed it was the raw power. That's what usually drives women—"

"It's your goodness." She grinned, looking a little drunk and daffy. "You're a good man"—she leaned forward and kissed his mouth—"and you're a real man."

Then she sat back and took a sip of wine.

"I think, working at the Willowbrook, you don't realize how rare those qualities are in this city."

Ford looked down at his hands.

"It's funny," he said. "Just now I was thinking that what I liked about you was something predatory. Something sharp, almost bad."

Helen sat up straight.

"Bad. Gee, thanks."

"Not *bad* bad. I mean . . . bad like the claws in a friendly cat's paws. They're there, but they won't hurt you. Unless . . ." He smiled and showed her his hands curved like a pair of claws.

Helen stared, a serious look on her face, until Ford had to look at his own hands, wondering what was wrong.

"That's another thing I like about you," she said.

"What?"

"This is going to sound too weird."

"No, go on."

Helen looked away, laughing.

"I can't."

"*Go on!*"

She looked at him now with a dark emphasis that he felt like a soft push.

"Your hands," she said. "The idea of what you do with them. The idea of you cutting and reaching in and saving people. I think that is . . . in-cred-ib-le."

They both laughed, Helen laughing until there were tears in her eyes, but shaking her head, wanting to make her point.

"No, I'm serious. There's a line in T. S. Eliot about that. How does it go?" She looked away, recalling. " '*The wounded surgeon plies the steel that questions the distempered part. Beneath the bleeding hands we feel the sharp compassion of the healer's art.*' I mean is that sublime or what? 'The sharp compassion of the healer's art.' "

Ford was speechless, watching her lovely face, completely in her power.

"You know that was the first thing I thought about you," she went on, "when I saw you at the conference. When you looked at me."

"What?"

She smiled, her mouth slightly open, so that he could see the tip of her tongue against her crooked lower teeth.

"That when you looked at me . . . You were talking to Novak and then you saw me and you gave me a real close look. And I had this thrill thinking that you weren't just seeing me, I mean the skin, the surface, but that you also knew exactly how I looked inside, I mean my heart and lungs and everything."

Ford was taken aback. He didn't know what to say for a moment.

"Is that the way it is?" asked Helen. "I mean, looking at me now, looking at my breasts, say. Do you think about what's inside?"

Ford looked at Helen's breasts.

"Not really," he said. "I mean, I *can*."

He watched his hand reaching out, hardly able to believe he was doing what he was doing. He watched his hand gently cup her breast. The nipple was hard under the starchy cotton of her T-shirt. He looked directly into her dark eyes, feeling the contour of the nipple and the round fullness of flesh.

"I can," he repeated, "but only if I want to. But I can see what you're saying. And I guess that, yes, behind what I see is knowledge of how the body is inside. I guess it makes my appreciation of the whole . . ."

Helen leaned across the plates again and kissed him, holding his hand against her breast. After a moment she leaned back and sat quietly. Then, with one simple movement, she pulled the T-shirt up over her head, making her hair crackle with electricity, revealing her sleek courtesan's torso and perfect, pale breasts. She smiled.

"Sometimes bad means bad," she said.

Just after two in the morning Ford got out of bed and went across to the window. The Buick sat in a pool of light next to two trash cans that had been wheeled out next to it. The car looked different somehow, and it wasn't just the big dent in the front. Then he realized that it wasn't the car but he himself that had changed. He was no longer the man that had climbed out of the driver's seat only a few hours before. And what had happened was that for the first time since Carolyn's death he had given himself to someone else. Despite himself, he couldn't help feeling that he had been unfaithful. But he knew too that what had happened was good. It seemed to him that the only way to see it, to evaluate events, was to say that he was now fully alive again, his wounds healed. The car looked like the heap of junk it was. He would sell it and buy another.

"What are you doing?"

Helen's sleepy voice drew him from the window. He turned and looked at her.

"I'd better get back," he said.

"Oh. Okay."

He went and sat on the bed beside her. He pushed his hand into her dark hair. It felt wonderful to be able to do this natural thing without any restraint. It frightened him—how nice it felt. It scared him how much he would miss it when he was home in his own bed.

"That was really nice, Helen. I mean that was really a lovely thing."

Helen smiled. Then her face was serious.

"Marcus?"

"Yes."

"Why did you sit in the car so long?"

"When?"

"When you arrived. I heard you pull up and looked out the window. But you just stayed where you were."

Ford frowned, trying to think how he could answer.

"I don't know," he said. "I guess I had used the last of my energy driving across town. When I turned off the engine, I sort of turned myself off."

Helen watched him, unblinking.

"I thought maybe you were having second thoughts."

"About what?"

"About me."

It was uncanny, the way she could guess what he was thinking all the time. He wondered if, in this poor light, she could see how uncomfortable she was making him.

"No," was all he could say.

"Good," she said.

"It's been hell the last few days, Helen. This is me at my worst in a long while."

She smiled.

"Well, if this is the worst . . ."

"It's not just all those people dying, all those people I haven't been able to help; it's the way the whole thing has become . . . I don't know what the word is. The way it's all become *politicized*. It reminded me of what you said about my speech being political. I realize now what you meant. Everything is a position. I'm not sure I like that. When I was talking to Haynes and he was going on about the budget and the health department and the media, I felt completely . . . completely powerless. Like a fish out of water, you know?"

"Sure."

"And then with the press . . . Suddenly the whole thing's blown up, twisted, distorted."

"The media always sensationalizes. I think most people understand that. They know this isn't the end of the world."

Ford withdrew his hand from Helen's hair and stood up. He walked slowly over to the window and looked out at the street again, resting his head against the cool glass.

"Do they? How can they know?"

Helen lay silent for a moment, then pushed herself up on her elbows.

"What do you mean?"

"Well, people are focusing on the staph outbreak. And that is terrible. I mean if you had seen that guy, the patrolman, Denny. He was . . . You would never have expected that outcome. The guy was young, healthy. A little overweight maybe, and that can sometimes affect the immune response, but the wound he had in his leg . . . you'd never have expected that outcome. But what people are forgetting is that we've had enterococci that have behaved the same way, and more recently *Staphylococcus pneumoniae*."

He turned and faced the room.

"And yesterday I had a call from a doctor in Beverly Hills who thought he had a case of resistant *Clostridium perfringens*."

"The botulism bug? Wow."

"Now, I don't know what the chances are of all this happening at once, but I bet they're pretty small. So, what I'm saying is, there may be something happening here. Maybe, somehow, multidrug-resistance is spreading between species even faster than normal. I mean, it does happen: through conjugation of one kind or another."

"Plasmid transfer . . ."

"Or transposons, jumping genes. Exactly. How staph transfers resistance to something like a clostridium, I don't know, but maybe that's what we're looking at."

"So what are you saying, Marcus? That this *is* the end of the world?"

Ford shrugged.

"No, of course not, but the implications for medicine . . . I don't know how we'd begin to face up to them. They're enormous. It's like planning for the aftermath of nuclear war. Where do you begin?"

"But even if the industry, I mean the pharmaceutical industry, can't find a way to kill this staph—which I doubt—all it would mean is we'd have to go back to the way things were sixty years ago, to the 1930s. Before antibiotics. Sure, surgery would be a lot more dangerous, but on its own that wouldn't put mortality rates up all that much. After all, it was improved sanitation, water treatment, that kind of thing that brought them down, wasn't it? Proper housing."

Ford came back to the bed and lay down on top of the sheets.

"That's the problem," he said. "There is no going back to the 1930s. What you say about housing and sanitation is true, but only in the industrialized West."

"I don't follow."

"Well, the Third World as we know it didn't really exist back then. I'm talking about these vast cities and their spiraling populations— Bombay, Rio, Cairo, Jakarta. Did you know there are now twenty million people in Mexico City?"

"So?"

"Twenty million people, most of them *without* proper housing, *without* proper sanitation. But people who still use modern medicine to stave off illness."

"If they can afford it."

"Twenty million people using the antibiotics pushed at them by the big pharmaceutical companies." He rolled over and looked at Helen's face. "Do you know what the biggest killer of children under three years old is, I mean globally?"

Helen went on staring at the ceiling.

"I don't know. Diarrhea maybe?"

"That's right. About five million deaths every year. And the main cause of illness is squalor, filth. Whether the pathogen involved is viral or bacterial, the best treatment for diarrhea is oral rehydration therapy. But the drug companies have pushed antibiotics as a magic cure for the disease because they see it as a huge marketing opportunity."

"Oh, come on. Now you *are* being political."

"Listen, it's a market worth over five hundred million dollars a year."

"Says who?"

"There was a company—I can't remember the name, this was back in the early eighties—it started marketing an antidiarrhea drug containing chloramphenicol and tetracycline in the form of a chocolate flavored pill. It was a big success in the Third World. And how do you think it was being used? I'll tell you how. Child got sick, Mom got out the candy pills. Symptoms went away, Mom stopped the candy. Millions of people mixing antibiotics and potential pathogens in their guts, year in, year out. It's like having a gigantic project for the development of resistant bacteria."

"But what's that got to do with your problems in South Central?"

"A lot. Because microbiologically the planet is now a world away from what it was in the 1930s too. And because of the way the world has opened up—with international trade and tourism, the ability to fly from one country to another—the whole system is permeable. Add to that the political instability and flows of refugees across national borders, and you have an unprecedented confusion of bacterial ecosystems. The whole thing about being able to rely on proper sanitation and urban planning goes out the window."

He turned and looked at Helen. She frowned for a moment, but said nothing.

"You see my point? I mean what percentage of Los Angeles higher-income establishments have immigrant domestics? You may live in a great neighborhood and have access to the best medicine in the world, but what about the woman in your kitchen cutting vegetables? What are the sanitation arrangements where she lives, and what's her medical history? How about the Sri Lankan guy working as a chef in the Indian restaurant you like to go to? Do we give a damn if they have healthcare even when they're here perfectly legally? I'm telling you, Helen, the planet is a microbiological disaster waiting to happen."

"Jesus. And you say the press sensationalizes."

"They do. And they distort. They emotionalize; they focus on people like the Dennys and then start looking for the nearest scapegoat. They don't understand the detail of what's going on, and they don't have the courage to consider the bigger picture."

Helen turned her head, looking straight at him.

"Is that it?"

Ford smiled, embarrassed. She didn't want to hear it, not now. It was two o'clock in the morning. He kissed her lightly on the cheek, then flopped back on the mattress.

"I'm sorry. I get worked up and then I suddenly hear myself talking, like I was on the other side of the room. Since I wrote that paper, I've been reading all kinds of stuff on resistance. I'm turning into a fanatic."

"I'd say more of a proselyte."

Ford smiled. "That's because you have an education. I'm going to have to try to keep a lid on it, though, if I'm going to talk to experts. I mean like Novak."

Helen sat up. "Did you get to talk to him?"

"I called him this afternoon."

"And?"

"He invited me to meet him next Friday."

"That's great. You're going over to his place?"

"No. I offered, but he said it was too far out. He wants to meet someplace near here, actually."

"No kidding, where?"

"Pacific Palisades. Haverford Avenue. It's some kind of condo, I think."

Helen looked surprised.

"Hey, that's pretty ritzy. Did he say why he wanted to meet there in particular?"

"He said he had something to show me, some research or something. He gave me the entry code to get in. Apparently the entry phone system isn't linked up yet."

He held up a finger. "That reminds me."

He climbed out of bed and went across to the chair where he had hung his jacket. He rummaged in the pockets and came up with a scrap of paper on which he had written Novak's instructions.

"Don't want to lose this," he said.

Ford got home just after three and went straight through to his bedroom. Sunny listened to him close his door. Then, as quietly as possible she went down the hall to the bathroom. She felt terrible. Something was churning in her guts, making the perspiration flood out of her. She kneeled down and leaned over the toilet bowl, pushing the door closed with her foot. Ford slept heavily until the alarm went off at five-fifteen, undisturbed by the sound of his daughter being sick.

PART THREE

POISON

1

The Willowbrook Medical Center

Ford was sitting alone in the cafeteria when Conrad Allen came in, holding his gray cardboard tray in both hands. It was only eleven-thirty and the place was empty, except for a trio of nurses in the far corner.

"Kind of quiet in here," he said. "All it needs is tumbleweed and a gunslinger in a poncho."

Ford looked up from the remains of his salad and gave Allen a weary smile.

"I got tired of sitting in my office waiting for . . . for something to happen."

Allen put down his hamburger and coffee.

"I never thought I'd find myself short of things to do, not in this place. I guess that's what happens when they stop sending you any patients."

"Or medical students," said Ford.

"No students? How come?"

"All student visits to the Emergency Department and ICU are out. Dr. Patou's orders."

Allen shook his head in disbelief.

"She afraid they'll catch something?"

"Yeah," said Ford. "Bad habits, I expect. From me."

Allen laughed. If he knew about the investigation and the threat of suspension, he wasn't letting on. But there was something, a gentleness about his manner, that suggested sympathy.

"So what have you heard?" said Ford. "I mean about me?"

Allen lifted the bun off his hamburger, looked at what lay beneath, and replaced it.

"I heard the county's trying to pin that patrolman's death on you. I heard they're mad about you talking to the press."

Ford nodded.

"Who told you?"

"Everyone knows. Haynes's office leaks like a sieve. I'm surprised you couldn't hear all their ears flapping when you were in there."

"Come to think of it, there *was* a draft," said Ford, trying to keep his composure. He'd suspected that word would get out pretty quickly. That was another reason he'd stayed in his office most of the morning. He could bear the idea of carrying on as if nothing had happened so long as he was the only one who knew. But if everybody knew, it would seem futile, ridiculous to go through all that pretense. Silence, the very fact that he was capable of suppressing his indignation, might even look like an admission of guilt.

Sitting there, he wondered how Conrad Allen would have handled it. In the operating theater he was always a model of cool efficiency. No matter how stressful things got, he was always the same. It took genuine carelessness on somebody's part to get him to even raise his voice.

"Marcus, everyone knows it's bullshit too. I mean everybody who understands anything. There's no way they can blame you."

"But they can suspend me, apparently, pending investigation. I've been waiting for the bad news all morning."

"Well, the team's right behind you. You don't have to worry about that."

"Really? My phone hasn't exactly been humming with messages of support."

Allen waved away the objection. "The Vulture's got everybody running around. But I've talked to them. They'll back you up all the way."

"Thanks, Conrad. I appreciate it."

Allen shrugged and tore open a package of ketchup with his teeth. "No sweat."

"The only problem is . . ."

"What?"

"Well, if the CDC finds anything they don't like about our procedures—and you can bet Loulou'll do her best to see they do— then the whole team will be discredited. And since I'm in charge of the team . . . That's what worries me."

Allen leaned closer, lowering his voice.

"Marcus, there's nothing wrong with our procedures. Loulou hasn't found a thing, and she won't. Have a little faith, will you? This is the Code Yellow team we're talking about. They don't come any better than us."

They exchanged a look. That was how Ford saw it, for sure. He had trained most of the team himself, and their experience, their *belief* made them something special in his eyes. But did Conrad Allen still see it that way? Lately he had seemed so distracted, so preoccupied . . . Ford was sure it had something to do with trouble at home, but they still hadn't gotten around to having the talk Allen had started outside the ICU. Watching Allen season his sad-looking burger, Ford decided the time had come to get things straight.

"Conrad, I . . . You remember the other day? You said you wanted to talk to me. Did we talk? I mean, maybe I missed it, but it seems to me—"

Allen picked up his hamburger in both hands and gave it a long look as though he were counting the sesame seeds. It was easier to do that, Ford knew, than to look at him.

"No, we never got round to that particular conversation," Allen said. "With everything that's happening here, there never seems to be a good time."

He heaved a sigh and put the burger back on the plate.

"Well, this is a good time . . ." said Ford, smiling. "Hey, if Loulou gets her way, you may never see me again, anyway."

Allen tried to smile, but Ford could see that he had become very uncomfortable. He stared at his burger for a moment and then put his elbows on the table, leaning forward a little. Ford decided to take the plunge.

"Look, Conrad, if ever . . . I mean if you ever want to stay at the house, you're more than welcome. Me and Sunny, we'd love to have you."

Allen looked confused.

"I don't . . ."

"No big deal," said Ford, shrugging, pushing back from the table. Then he was confused too. It came to him that maybe he had misread the signs. "I just thought . . . You said Ellen was . . . I got the impression maybe you two were having problems."

"Oh, Christ," said Allen blankly. He looked Ford straight in the eye. "Marcus, I've been offered a position at Cedars-Sinai as director of trauma."

Ford blinked. Tried to smile. Couldn't.

"They're willing to hold the position open for me for a while, but I said I could be free by the end of October."

"The end of . . ."

Ford's voice trailed off. Suddenly he had a headache. Again he tried to smile, tried to understand what Allen was saying. But he just couldn't take it in. The words *this is disastrous* came into his mind with a vocalized clarity. It wasn't just that Allen was the most valued member of the Code Yellow team, his right-hand man. He was also his *friend.* He looked at the other man's face, registering the confusion there. He had an abrupt sense of the way he himself must be looking.

"Conrad, I'm sorry . . . I . . . That's great news."

Allen stared, his face close to Ford's in the harsh light of the cafeteria. It was as if they were speaking in a foreign language.

"You really—?"

"That's great," said Ford again, realizing as he said it that that was exactly the opposite of what he felt. "When are you going, did you say?"

"The end of October. Next month. I thought after our trip. I decided to take your advice about going away with Ellen. We're going walking in the Grand Canyon. This place owes me a little vacation."

"That's fucking great," said Ford, suddenly, irrationally jealous of Ellen. The obscenity seemed to release something, and his voice flooded with anger: "Fucking brilliant. And . . . I can't . . . What about the Willowbrook, Conrad? What about this place?"

Allen appeared to move his tongue around inside his mouth. When he finally spoke, his voice came out squeezed.

"What about it?"

"Well . . ." Ford made a vague gesture, turning his hand to show the empty palm and curled fingers. "Now, of all times. When we're really up against something big."

"Come on, Marcus, I've been planning this for months. It's got nothing to do with what's going on here."

"But I thought this . . . I thought *this* was a commitment. I thought coming in here every day was a commitment. And now you say . . ." Ford realized he wasn't making any sense. He stared at his hand. "I mean, how are we supposed to feel about this?"

"Marcus, the Emergency Department is not going to close down because I leave."

"Don't . . . Don't flatter yourself, Conrad. We'll get along fine. I'm just realizing . . . I'm just seeing how wrong I was about your—"

"Whoa, whoa. Hold on there. Hang on just a second. We're talking about a career here. That's all. I'm a doctor. I'm being given an opportunity to carry on my work somewhere else. So what? It's not like I'm becoming a stockbroker or an arms dealer or something."

"No, but this is where you're *needed*. Here, not in Beverly Hills. A doctor goes where he's needed."

"If they didn't need me, they wouldn't—"

"What about your commitment, Conrad, your *responsibility* to this community?"

Allen smiled, but it was a tight, angry smile.

"You mean my responsibility as a *black* man to the *black* community?"

For a moment neither of them spoke. Ford felt his blood pulsing in his temples.

"That sounds just a bit racist, Marcus. Just a bit. I may be black, but I'm also American. It's *okay* for me to care for Americans."

"You know I didn't mean that."

"I'm not sure I know what you mean."

Allen paused. Seeing Ford's discomfort, he softened a little.

"And what about my responsibility to my family?"

"To Ellen?" said Ford. "She believes in what we do here as much as I do."

"So do I. And I'm not talking about Ellen, or the kids—though God knows they'd be delighted for me to take the job, for me to get out of this war zone—I'm talking about *my* parents. I'm talking about the sacrifices they made to put me through med school. I'm talking about the dreams they had for me."

"Right," said Ford. "Of course the money's got nothing to do with it."

Allen got to his feet.

"*Earning* the money is part of my responsibility. And, since we're on the subject, what about your responsibilities?"

"What about—?"

"Sunny must be the only kid in your neighborhood who doesn't go to a private school. What about your responsibility to her?"

This hurt. Ford felt the injustice of it like a slap in the face. He sent Sunny to Alexander Hamilton not because he couldn't afford a private school—he earned over $100,000 a year, for Christ's sake—but because he believed in the state education system and because Sunny would have exposure to kids from other ethnic backgrounds there. The wrongness of what Allen had said stalled him for a moment. He felt his heart jolting in his chest and didn't know what to say.

"*Fine*," was the word that came out in the end, said with all the bitterness of a curse. "Fine. You want to turn your back on these people, Conrad, that's your business."

Allen drew trembling fingers across his mouth.

"You know what your problem is, Marcus? Your problem is guilt. You feel guilty about what's happening in this city. Well, you want to work out your white man's guilt in this place, that's your problem, man. Not mine."

There was the sound of a tray clattering to the floor and a shouted curse. Then a high, squeaking punt-punt-punt sound. Allen turned. Gloria Tyrell appeared around the corner, wide-eyed, hurrying towards them, her face shiny with perspiration. In all this time at the Willowbrook, Ford had never seen her so much as break into a trot. He got to his feet.

"Jesus, Gloria, what—"

"Dr. Ford, I think you should come with me. I'm sorry, but I didn't want to have you beeped."

It was Haynes. The suspension. It had to be.

"It's Sunny," said Gloria. "She's in ER right now."

The way she said it, the way she looked—Ford felt the blood rush from his face.

"Sunny?" he said. His mouth was suddenly dry. "Here?"

"Taxi dropped her off about a half an hour ago. Looks like some kind of food poisoning. Code Blue team took care of her."

"Food . . . food poisoning? Jesus Christ."

He was already hurrying from the cafeteria, leaving Allen at the table. Gloria followed hard on his heels.

"Dr. Lee said she's okay," she said. "He's gonna transfer her to pediatrics pretty soon."

Dr. Simon Lee was one of the senior residents in the Code Blue team, a group that handled medical emergencies such as heart failure, strokes, and ruptured appendixes. Although he had been at the Willowbrook for nearly five years, Ford did not know him well. One of only two Asian doctors in the Emergency Department, he seemed to keep most of the other staff at a distance.

"What did she eat?" asked Ford. "I mean, *when* did she get sick? I only left the house a few hours ago."

"I don't know. I only just . . ." Gloria was struggling for breath. "I only just found out. I don't think she was fully conscious when they brought her in."

Lee was checking Sunny's blood pressure when they arrived. They found her stretched out on the gurney, her face turned away from the light. It gave Ford a jolt, seeing her plugged into a drip, electrodes stuck to her chest, machines monitoring her vital signs. She looked no different from the critical cases he handled every day, one of the kids laid out by a blade or a bullet or a joyride gone wrong—she looked just like one of the kids who never made it, who flat-lined in the middle of the night and were gone from their beds by morning.

"Sunny?"

He touched her forehead. It felt cool. She turned and looked at him. A faint smile flickered on her lips.

"Mr. Bear."

Her voice was barely audible.

"How do you feel, honey?"

She blinked. The bright fluorescent lights seemed to bother her.

"Not . . . not so bad now," she said.

"She was dehydrated," said Lee. "But we took care of that. Pulse was one hundred five, but now we're down to eighty-five. I don't think it's anything to worry about, Dr. Ford."

"Hear that, honey? You're gonna be fine."

"I took a cab. I didn't want to call an ambulance, in case . . ."

In case they drove her someplace else. Ford carefully reached for her hand, taking care not to disturb the line.

"I wanted to find you."

"You have found me. You did the right thing. Don't worry."

She blinked slowly and smiled again. She looked so small and fragile he felt a sudden surge of remorse that he had not been there to take care of her, that no one had been.

"When did you get sick, honey? Was it when you got up?"

She shook her head.

"In the night. I felt real bad, and then I was sick."

"You were sick in the night? Honey, why didn't you call me?"

She screwed up her face and hunched her shoulders for a moment, as if she were trying to squeeze herself through a gap between the truth and a lie. It was one of her little-girl gestures.

"I didn't want to wake you."

Ford squeezed her hand. It was worse than he'd thought. Instead of looking after his daughter, he'd been out getting laid, had crawled home at three in the morning and crashed—too far gone even to hear that she was getting sick.

"I'm sorry, honey. It's all my fault."

"Dr. Ford?"

Ford could sense a degree of impatience, of disapproval in Dr. Lee's voice. Visitors were not usually permitted in the Emergency Department, and a visitor was what he was, surgeon or not. But, in her own way, Sunny had made sacrifices for the Willowbrook, just like most of its staff. She was entitled to something in return.

"You're gonna be all right now, honey. We'll have you home in no time, I promise."

Dr. Lee drew him aside.

"I did a stain. We've got a gram-negative bacterium," he said. "Probably salmonella of some kind. The lab results'll be with us in about three days."

"You plan to prescribe a prophylactic?"

"Yes, I do. Chloromycetin seems to have the best gram-negative coverage from my experience. And I want to add tobramycin as well. It's got a good record against bowel infections, and I don't think we should take any chances. Her symptoms were pretty severe. It seems she almost blacked out in the back of that cab. I've already given her something to check the diarrhea."

Ford turned to look at Sunny again. Why *hadn't* she woken him? Could it be she thought he might not be alone? As if he would let anyone take her mother's place so quickly. Yet, in a way, he realized with another stab of guilt, he already had.

Dr. Lee was still talking. "In the meantime we need to know exactly what she ate, where she ate it, and when. It should help us work out what we're dealing with. Can you get all that for me?"

Half an hour later Sunny was installed in one of the main pediatric wards, next to a young Hispanic girl with a shattered pelvis from an auto-versus-ped and a fourteen-year-old homegirl with a gunshot wound to the shoulder. The high-pitched crash and twang of the home-girl's stereo headphones was loud in Ford's ear. It felt odd being a visitor in his own hospital.

"I got home about eight-thirty," Sunny was saying, her voice hushed. "I ate some crackers, and then I went out to the MistaTaco on Robertson. About nine o'clock. I didn't touch the meat loaf."

"Wait a second, honey. You told me you went straight from the school to the taco place with your friends."

"Oh," said Sunny, looking down at the end of her bed. "No."

Ford locked his hands together and squeezed them into his lap. She'd lied to make him feel better.

"So you went alone?"

She nodded.

"And what did you eat? Can you remember?"

"A MistaTaco spicy cheese taco," she said. "Plus a regular diet Coke."

"Okay. And what was in this taco?"

Sunny sniffed.

"Just minced meat—like in spaghetti bolognese—chili, and lots of gooey cheese. I didn't like it much."

"And that's all you had?"

"No. I had a regular salad too. You're always telling me not to eat junk. So I had the salad for the vitamins."

"And what was in this salad? Try and think, now."

"You serve yourself. I had lettuce, tomatoes, red peppers, kind of toasty cube things—"

"Croutons?"

"I guess. And an olive oil dressing."

"And that's it?"

"And I had a lot of corn. Dad, how long will I have to stay here?"

Ford looked up and down the ward. It was brightly lit, spartan, like everything else at the Willowbrook. The only concessions to the age of its occupants were a cardboard Fred Flintstone propped up in one corner and some dinosaur stickers along the bottom of the window.

"It's just for one night, probably. As soon as Dr. Lee's satisfied his treatment is doing its job, I'll be able to take you home. And I'll be there to look after you myself. I'm . . . taking a few days off anyway."

"You are?"

Her face brightened up.

"Sure. You'll have your own private doctor."

Sunny closed her eyes. He could see that she was still very weak. He was about to stand up when she said, "What kind of treatment?"

Ford sat down again.

"Well, antibiotics. Two kinds."

Sunny opened one eye.

"Properly treated a bug can be cleared up in seven days. Left to itself it can hang around for a week. Isn't that what Conrad said?"

Ford smiled, though the mention of Allen's name brought a wave of difficult, negative feeling. *You know what your problem is?*

"A strep throat, is what he said. A strep throat can hang around for a week."

"A strep throat, which I still have, by the way."

"Still? Does it hurt?"

"No. I can kind of feel it sometimes. But it's more than a week I've had it, for sure."

"Well, that is a little different. A sore throat is just an irritation. The bug can't do you any serious harm. But a salmonella can. If you were a baby, then it could be serious. That's when you should use antibiotics. When people are actually sick, like you were last night."

Sunny took a deep breath and closed her eyes again.

"That's okay, Dr. Ford," she said. "I trust your prognosis. Just so long as I don't become drug dependent or anything."

Ford leaned over and kissed her on the forehead.

"You get some sleep. I'll come and check on you again in a little while. I have to go tell Dr. Lee about what you ate."

Lee had gone into OR by the time Ford got back to the Emergency Department, so he decided to type up his findings in the meantime. It was important to get Environmental Health on the case before any more people were struck down with food poisoning—if they hadn't been already. It would be something useful for him to do. He was just going into his office when the phone rang. It was Russell Haynes.

"I'm sorry, Marcus," he said. "But things have gone pretty much as I expected at the health department. I'm instructed to advise you that as of midnight tonight you are suspended from your duties at the Willowbrook Medical Center."

2

Charles Novak opened his eyes and squinted across the small sitting room. He had fallen asleep on the sofa, the whisky glass still balanced on his chest, the Mahler still playing full volume on the stereo. But now the Mahler was finished and all he could hear was the ugly, insistent trilling of the phone.

Slowly he sat up, blinking at the weak, yellow lights. How much had he drunk? For sure more than he was used to. He felt all dried up inside, poisoned. He hauled himself to his feet and stumbled towards the source of the noise, kicking over the whisky bottle as he went. He cursed, picked the bottle up, slammed it down on the side table. What time was it? He glanced at the carriage clock over the fireplace: just coming up to midnight.

"Hope I didn't get you out of bed."

Novak recognized the voice at once. It was Scott Griffen, one of the few Helical people he was still in touch with. But it didn't sound as if this was a social call.

"No, I was just . . . I was—"

"So guess who just called me, Charles."

Novak tried to clear his throat. He could hear the anger in Griffen's voice.

"I don't know. How should—?"

"The same person you called a few hours ago. The same person you called up and threatened to put in a very *difficult position*, if I understand it right."

"No, Scott, it wasn't like that. I didn't threaten anything. I—"

"Did you mention my name?"

Novak hesitated. Of course he had mentioned Griffen's name; he'd been trying to make a case, trying to suggest he wasn't alone in feeling the way he did. He'd been well into the booze by the time he'd made the call. Now he questioned the wisdom of what he had done.

"No, Scott. Of course not."

"Charles, did you mention my name?"

"No. No, I didn't. I just voiced my own concern at—"

"To *him*?" Suddenly Griffen was shouting. "Jesus, Charles, are you out of your fucking mind? I thought we agreed to keep all this between us. We agreed that if we were going to do anything, then we'd have to keep it to ourselves."

"But I didn't . . ."

Novak sat down. It had been a mistake, going behind Griffen's back. It had aroused suspicions, that was clear, fears that their silence could no longer be guaranteed. But how important was that when so much more was at stake?

"Look, Scott, maybe I was a little hasty, but . . ."

"Jesus Christ, *hasty*?"

"But I thought he'd support us. I thought he'd see things our way. I've heard his views on drug resistance. I thought he'd be an ally. He could get something done, directly. That has to be better than leaks and—"

"Christ, Charles, how can you be so fucking naive? I guarantee you he was on the phone to Washington within five minutes of your call. Now anything that happens, anything that shows up in the press, any rumors even, they're going to pin them on us. They're going to think we started them. And they're watching now, Charles, thanks to you. You'd better believe it. You see what you've done?"

"I'm sorry, Scott, I . . . I just . . ."

Novak closed his eyes. Somehow it had all gone wrong, gone bad. Yet nobody seemed willing to do anything. Everybody was too worried about guarding their position.

"Scott, listen to me. None of this would matter if they'd take the steps we agreed upon. That's all we're asking, isn't it? That they do what was envisioned all along."

Novak heard Griffen's breath push against the mouthpiece.

"Now *you* listen, Charles. These are powerful people. We made the decision five years ago to bring them in. When we did that, we gave them control. We knew that's what would happen, and it happened. It's too late to try and change the rules now. It's in their hands. They've got control, and they aren't going to let it slip."

"Then why don't they *do* something? People are dying, for God's sake. And they just sit there. It wasn't supposed to be like this. What we did, it was supposed to be for . . . it was supposed to be for everyone."

For a moment there was silence on the line.

"Scott?"

"Too late, Charles. It's too late."

3

At five-thirty the following morning, Sunny called the duty nurse to her bed complaining of a dry mouth. The nurse refilled the carafe Sunny had emptied during the night, then checked her blood pressure and pulse. They were normal, the pulse, if anything, a little sluggish. The diarrhea had stopped, but her stomach was distended and sensitive to even gentle palpitation.

"S'probably jus' my throat," said Sunny. "Strep throat. Thas . . . that's what my da' says I have."

The nurse was struck by the way Sunny slurred her words, but put it down to the early hour and her probable fatigue. She helped Sunny drink, noting that despite her obvious thirst, she seemed to have difficulty in swallowing. Before leaving, the nurse explained that Dr. Lee would be on the ward at around ten o'clock and that she would review Sunny's condition with him at that time.

"Try to rest a little," she said.

Sunny closed her eyes and pushed back into her pillows. It was better with her eyes closed—the faint dizziness she was beginning to feel receded then.

Ford had the key in the ignition, was about to start the car, when he saw it. Chained to one of the two Spanish oaks at the bottom of the drive: an aluminum stepladder, the kind you used for odd jobs around the house. It wasn't exactly in the way, but it was nevertheless *there*. Right where he reversed into the road. He stared for a moment, puzzled. A small aluminum stepladder attached to a tree with a heavy-duty steel chain and shiny new padlock. He got out of the car and walked to the end of the drive.

It was seven-thirty and people were leaving for work. Cars drifted by, slowing down for the dip at the corner. Julian Merrow, the father of one of Sunny's friends, gave a friendly honk as he went past, and Ford offered a distracted wave. He looked up and down the street. Then back at the stepladder. There was a red sticker on one of the steps with the letters *BZZ* written on it.

He was on the Santa Monica Freeway before he started to make sense of the thing. Racking his brains, trying to think of where he had seen something like it before, suddenly he remembered. Three years previously, a short time after his wife's death, he had gone up to Malibu with Conrad Allen on a fishing trip. They had chartered a boat, gotten sunburned and more than a little drunk. Driving back in the twilight, sobered, hungry, they had stopped off at a restaurant Conrad knew. Part of the restaurant, an attractive terrace, shaded by vines, had been given over to a private party, and by the look of the cars parked outside, the clients were a pretty select bunch. Going into the main building, Conrad had pointed out a number of photographers who were standing on stepladders to get a view of the party. "Trying to catch a shot of Julia Roberts's derriere," was what Conrad had said. Ford pushed irritably at the vents controlling the flow of cold air and wondered if that fishing trip had been the last they would ever take together.

Then, like the pop of a flashbulb, Ford understood. Some agency photographer must have heard about his suspension and decided there was a story in it. Assuming that the news would soon be out, and that Ford's modest home would be overrun the way the Willowbrook parking lot had been, he had established a ringside seat in the shade of a conveniently placed tree. He must have come real early, then, seeing that nothing was going on, driven up to Pico for coffee and donuts.

Ford couldn't help laughing. It was so ludicrous. The guy was going to be real disappointed when he saw the car was gone. Ford laughed, but at the same time the realization came to him: his departure from the Willowbrook wasn't going to get him out of the media spotlight after all. And that had been his one consolation in getting suspended.

That and the idea that Lucy Patou would have to face the many-headed monster of LA's press and TV on her own.

Now he realized it wasn't going to be like that. If he was right about the stepladder, the media scrutiny of his professional and personal life was only just beginning. But how had they found out about the suspension so quickly? He couldn't see Haynes picking up the phone to call the LA *Times*. Haynes hated the press, had ever since the riots in '92, when not one of them had come down to the Willowbrook to see what was happening. They'd been too scared. Lionel Redmond might have called them. Or Lucy Patou, of course. But why? Unless the hospital was setting him up for a fall, looking for a scapegoat. Ford had an unpleasant folding sensation in his gut, followed by a cold trickle of anxiety.

"Don't be paranoid," he said to the empty car.

He flipped on the radio, but the music did nothing to soothe him. He was approaching the Wilmington Avenue exit. With a jolt he remembered why he was there. It was Sunny he should be thinking about. What would the press say when they found out about her?

The thought of photographers trying to get pictures of Sunny in her sickbed sent him speeding down the ramp. There was a squeal of brakes and a blast of angry horns on Wilmington Avenue as he raced to beat a red light and lost.

At eight o'clock Sunny was woken by an orderly pushing a cart with the breakfasts. She watched him come to the end of her bed, blinking, trying to get the man's face into focus. But she couldn't do it.

"Good morning!" said the man. He sounded cheerful, friendly, but his voice was strangely muffled as if he were talking to her from behind a cushion.

Sunny struggled to raise herself against her pillow in order to eat, but she was too weak.

"What's up, honey?"

The man put an arm underneath her and helped her sit upright. His breath smelled of orange juice.

"I ca . . . I can't . . ."

She could not form the words. It was as if something were holding her tongue.

"I caaan'—"

Then she started to cry, the tears running down her hot cheeks. She watched as the man's blurry face receded, unable to understand what he was saying. Then there were booming rubbery footfalls echoing in her head and the man was gone. She tried to see where he had disappeared to. His cart was still there. She could see the different colors of the dishes and fruit. But the whole thing seemed to ripple as though she were looking through water. She tried to call out, but the noise she made didn't sound like her at all. Suddenly she was terrified.

Then she was surrounded by people. Hands were everywhere. Warped voices came through to her—insistent, urgent. A thumb was pushed against her eyelid and a bright light came on, a light that seemed to flood her head, making thought impossible.

Dr. Lee had been eating his breakfast in the hospital cafeteria when the Code Blue alert came over the intercom. When he reached Sunny's bedside, when he saw her eyes, he was immediately aware that his initial presumptive diagnosis of the previous day had been wrong. This was no salmonellosis. The girl's eyelids—drooping over fixed dilated pupils in a condition known as ptosis—her attempts to speak hampered by a marked inability to articulate: these two signs alone were enough to set Lee's personal alarm bells ringing. This was not salmonellosis. It was botulism.

He had very little time.

With botulism the danger to the patient came not from the bug itself but from a toxin it released when the cell was broken. If the organism was allowed to mature in food—badly canned vegetables were the classic culprits—it released a protoxin that, in contact with stomach enzymes, became a full-fledged poison easily absorbed by the small intestine.

Clostridium botulinum was in fact a sinister family comprising eight siblings, the subspecies differentiated according to the poison they carried. West of the Rocky Mountains the sibling that held dominion was of the serological type A, the worst of a very bad bunch, a minutely small organism carrying the most powerful poison known to man.

The toxin worked by moving through the blood and lymphatic systems to the peripheral nervous system. Binding into the body's electrical circuitry at the neuromuscular junctions, it started to effect the chemical equivalent of cutting the wires. The initial focus of the attack was in the cranial nerves, resulting in problems with eyesight, hearing, and speech. Overall weakness ensued with creeping paralysis and eventually the collapse of the respiratory system. Given Sonia Ford's symptoms, Dr. Lee knew that there was a grave danger of her asphyxiating before his very eyes.

He stood back from the bed, taking in the serious faces of the nurses and clinicians in attendance. Apart from Carl Doxopoulos and Janet Harbin, both third-year residents, they were all pretty new to Code Blue work. Newer than Lee would have liked.

"Okay, I want this patient moved to ICU, and I want her pulmonary function monitored with particular attention to any decline in respiratory status. I want to *clearly* establish values for baseline vital capacity and forced inspiratory volume, and I want them every two hours. If there is any sign of decline, we will have to intubate and get her onto a respirator."

Lee went straight to his office and called the CDC consultant on the twenty-four-hour hotline. There was a brief conversation in which the consultant set out the sample requirements for the CDC— specifying that stool samples should be taken without the use of enema, and should be kept refrigerated but not frozen—and informed Lee as to where he could obtain the CDC trivalent botulin antitoxin, stocks of which were kept at or near regional airports and Public Health Service Quarantine Stations all over the U.S. Having arranged for the delivery of the antitoxin to the Willowbrook, Lee hurried back to the pediatric ICU, where Sunny was being hooked up to a battery of monitors.

"Okay," he said, taking up a position at the head of the bed. "Unabsorbed toxin-containing food may still be present in the patient's stomach or lower GI tract. So I want upper and lower gastric decontamination and high enemas. Dr. Harbin?"

He faced the young red-haired woman. There was a faint sheen of sweat in the middle of Harbin's smooth forehead.

"Yes, Doctor?"

"Your view, please, on the value of gastric lavage in cases of botulin poisoning?"

* * *

When Ford entered the ICU just after eight-thirty, Sunny was intubated and breathing with the help of a respirator. Seeing everything in the minutest detail, Ford was nevertheless unable to take it in, unable to believe what he was seeing. He had a distinct sensation of falling into the sea of blue linoleum.

"I can't . . . This can't be . . ."

It was Lee who took him aside, leading him away from the bed where his daughter, once merely ill, was now battling for her life.

Lee didn't speak until he had Ford sitting in his office. He pushed a paper cup into his hand, saying something that Ford couldn't understand. He said it again. Ford lifted the cup. Drank. Tasted bourbon.

"Fifty grams of activated charcoal," said Lee, dipping his head, and placing his hands in front of him as though there were something between them. He smiled encouragingly, obviously impressed by whatever it was he was showing with his empty hands.

"I like Super-Char. It really soaks up the toxins. I don't think there's any reason to worry," he said.

This got through to Ford and he felt himself smile. It hurt his face, felt more like a rictus. He was out of control. He could tell. He felt as if he was about to burst into tears.

"No reason to . . ."

He couldn't finish the phrase. Lee made complicated puckering movements with his mouth. Then spoke.

"Relatively speaking. It was unfortunate that it got to this stage. But as you know, botulism is pretty rare and actually very difficult to diagnose. If she had come in with the blurred vision, slurring of speech, and so forth, I would have made the right diagnosis. But as it was . . ."

He looked down at his empty hands. Ford was suddenly aware that Lee was embarrassed, even upset. He drained his cup and poured himself another shot of bourbon.

"I understand," he managed to say.

Lee was absolved. He leaned back in his chair.

"I am taking her off the antibiotics. Aminoglycosides should not be used to treat secondary infections because they can sometimes have the effect of enhancing the toxin-induced neuromuscular blockade.

Also you have to be careful about destroying the bug once it's inside the body."

"Right," said Ford, suddenly anxious to get back to Sunny's bedside. He felt he had reacted badly to her predicament, acted in a way he would not have expected of himself. It was the long hours, the outbreak, the Shark's death, Denny's death, the row with Allen, the press, Patou. . . . Everything was going against him, undermining him. He felt unsteady in a way he had never experienced before. He would have to be careful with his head. He would have to be strong. If only for Sunny's sake.

"The most likely scenario is that Sonia—"

"Sunny."

"Is that Sunny ingested some preformed toxin. Maybe at that restaurant she mentioned."

"Doesn't she need the antibiotic for the bug?"

Lee pushed a hand into his black hair, which grew so thick it was like fur.

"Pardon me?"

"You were saying you wanted to take her off the antibiotics. I don't . . ."

"Ah, yes. No. You have to understand botulinum needs a number of environmental conditions to be able to come to maturity. It's not actually a very robust organism except in spore form."

"Spores, right." Ford was remembering his bacteriology. Botulinum was a spore-forming bacteria, a clostridium, like the bug that had gotten into Wingate's patient.

"The spores are actually tough little mothers," said Lee. "They can survive boiling, freezing, ionizing radiation, chemical attack."

"You sound like you admire them."

Lee paused for a moment. Then went on.

"But once they germinate, they don't do so well."

"You're saying they're going to die anyway. In Sunny, I mean."

"Yes. Even if she had ingested spores, even if they had germinated, become bacteria, they would not be able to survive in her gastrointestinal tract. It's too acidic for them. What we have to focus on is the effects of the toxin."

"Okay."

"As I said, we have cleaned her system out, and as soon as the anti-toxin arrives, we'll be giving her that."

"What's that?"

"Pardon me?"

"I mean what's in the antitoxin?"

"It's developed by the CDC. It comes in twenty-milliliter vials and is derived from horse serum. You can get hypersensitivity reactions from some patients—maybe one in ten—but you don't have to worry too much about that."

Ford stood up to leave. He had to get back to Sunny now.

"You keep telling me not to worry, Dr. Lee. That worries me."

He tried to smile, but he could see from the look on Lee's face that it was not a very convincing effort.

"And how long before she gets better?" he asked.

Lee shrugged.

"Well, there's good and bad news there. I'm afraid recovery from botulism is a fairly protracted process. It could take months. Patients can complain of weakness up to a year after the end of the acute phase."

"And the good news?"

"Well, eventually, with time, with proper care, she should make a complete recovery."

4

When Ford got home in the afternoon, he found two television vans parked in the road and maybe a dozen journalists and photographers waiting for him. It was not quite the crowd the guy with the stepladder had expected, but it was disagreeable nevertheless. Lenses were pressed against the windshield, flashbulbs went off. Ford had to wait, grim-faced, gripping the wheel of the Buick. As soon as he got out, they were at him like a pack of coyotes.

"Dr. Ford, what's the latest body count?"

"Dr. Ford, do you feel you are being victimized by the county health department?"

"What was the reason for your dismissal?"

Reaching his front door, Ford rounded on the clamoring pack.

"I was not dismissed. I have been suspended on full pay pending an inquiry."

"Did you cause Officer Denny's death?"

Ford felt the color rising into his face. He fumbled for his keys, telling himself that he must not get drawn into another to and fro with these sociopathic sons of bitches.

"Dr. Ford, what are your daughter's chances?"

Everyone turned, trying to see who it was who had asked the question. Obviously, they were only just learning about this themselves. A small, bald-headed man with pale eyelashes pressed forward with his microcassette.

"I said what are your daughter's chances of recovering from the disease?"

Ford felt his blood chill. He wanted to grab the man's cassette player and ram it down his throat.

"My . . . My daughter is ill with botulism. It has nothing to do with the outbreak of staphylococcus."

"Will you be treating her?"

This was shouted down by the rest of the group. Obviously he wouldn't be treating her; he had been suspended. Ford took advantage of the momentary diversion to slip inside the house.

Amazingly, the crowd outside continued to shout questions. Ford walked through to the kitchen at the back of the house and poured himself a cold beer.

Closing the refrigerator, he stood with his back against it, the chilled bottle held to his forehead. What were the neighbors going to say about all this? Should he call the police, at least get the bastards off his lawn?

A flash went off. For a second Ford thought he must have imagined it. Then he saw the man standing at the kitchen window. He was focusing to get another shot of the doctor at bay. He would have had to climb over a number of fences to get access to the back of the house. This was the last straw.

"Get the hell off my property!"

Ford ran through to the back door, threw back the bolts, and charged out into the garden. To his surprise, he found the man waiting for him. About six feet tall, he was wearing army-surplus clothing. He was smiling, his camera raised for another picture. Ford blundered forward, hardly knowing what he was doing. He grabbed at the guy's camera, grabbed a fistful of clothing, pulled, twisted—the man not resisting in any way, obviously used to this, just wanting to get away with his pictures. He held on tight to his camera, but otherwise allowed himself to be led through the house, banging against walls, furniture, Ford screaming at the top of his voice, completely beside himself. As he opened the front door, there was a barrage of flashing cameras and shouted questions. It was like the shock wave of a small explosion. Ford pushed the intruder into the crowd. Then stood there shaking, trying to catch his breath.

"You are standing on . . . You are standing on private property," he shouted. "Now, *back* off, or I'll call the police."

"Dr. Ford, is there any danger of the disease spreading?"

It was as if they hadn't heard him.

"Are you going to be leaving your daughter down there?"

Ford staggered backwards into the house and slammed the door—closed his eyes, breathed, struggled to compose himself.

"Will you be resigning?"

"Is the Denny family going to litigate?"

"Dr. Ford—?"

The questions came to him muffled by the door. Walking stiff-legged, sick now, unsteady after the surge of adrenaline, he went through all the rooms, closing the curtains, switching on the lights even though it was broad daylight.

When Conrad Allen called, Ford was in the living room, peeping out through the drapes at the few remaining journalists. Allen sounded tired.

"Marcus, hi . . . I just wanted to see how you were doing."

They had not spoken since their argument. Ford sat down.

"I'm coping, thanks."

There was an awkward pause, and then Allen went on.

"I . . . I'm real sorry about Sunny. I can't believe it. I talked to Lee this afternoon. He seems to think there's—"

"Nothing to worry about, I know. How are things in ER?"

"Patou has cohorted all the resistance cases."

"Uh huh."

"I guess you can imagine the atmosphere on the ward."

He could. Perfectly. Gang members, junkies, a few innocent bystanders, but mostly people who were used to living by their wits and taking direct action to get what they wanted, all being asked to lie in bed and take whatever was coming for the good of the wider community. And they would be watching the news coverage like everybody else, hearing the lurid details of what had happened to Denny and to the Shark's tongue (the autopsy report had been leaked, no doubt for a handsome fee). Ford's guess was Patou would be encouraging the liberal use of tranquilizers.

"Has the CDC been in?" he asked.

"Yeah, we've seen a few bug hunters down here. They walk around looking very serious, shaking their heads. I don't think they know what to make of it."

There was a pause.

"Marcus?"

"Yes?"

"I've been thinking. I know how you feel about me going up to—"

"Conrad, I was way out of line yesterday. It's just that it came as a bit of a shock on top of everything else."

"Sure . . . sure I understand. Anyway, what I wanted to say was that it would be real easy for me to arrange Sunny's transfer up to Cedars if you wanted me to. I'm just saying it because it would make sense for you guys."

Ford gave a sharp nod.

"How's that?"

"Well, what's the point of you coming all the way down here just to visit? That's all I'm saying. If she was up near where you are, it'd be easier for you to call in."

"I've been driving down to South Central for seven years. It's no trouble, Conrad."

"Come on, man. You know what I'm saying."

"I'm not sure I do."

"I think you do, though. But if you want me to spell it out, I'm saying that we don't know what is happening here, microbiologically I mean. And that being the case, I think you would be more than justi-fied in taking Sunny out."

Ford closed his eyes. He should have seen this coming.

"Marcus?"

"Yeah, I'm still here. I was just thinking how that would look."

Allen fell silent. Ford could hear the sound of footsteps coming along a corridor. They were barely audible but perfectly distinct, per-fectly reproduced. Then a door closed. When Allen spoke again, it sounded as if he had gotten closer to the phone. His voice came through in a whispered growl.

"Man, who *cares* how it looks? This is no time to start worrying about principles. Especially after the way you've been treated."

"Conrad, to hell with the principle. I believe in the Willowbrook. I believe in the people who work there, and I'm standing with them through this thing. I'm not gonna jump ship because of a few damned reporters and a bunch of accountants at city hall."

Allen sighed into the phone.

"Okay," he said. "If that's the way you want it. It's your daughter. Your call."

And he hung up. Ford sat staring at the folds of the drapes. He pressed his lips together and closed his eyes for a moment. Allen was right, but at another level he was wrong. You had to care about principles, and that didn't change just because of circumstances or just because you had been given a raw deal. He looked around at the room. It was the first time he had been alone in the house in a while. He had an eerie feeling that he was being watched by Carolyn. What would she have said about his leaving Sunny down in South Central? He picked up the phone again and punched in Helen Wray's number.

"And you know what I felt?" asked Ford, once the dishes were in the sink and he and Helen were installed on the couch with the remains of the burgundy she had insisted on bringing.

"Frustration, I guess. I know that's what I'd feel, all those cameras pointing at me, nobody really listening."

"Sure. That's true too. But it came to me when I was looking at all those people that . . . that they were somehow angry with me. That they wished me ill. They were hoping things were going to turn out badly."

"They couldn't care less. They just want to sell newspapers."

Ford sat forward on the couch, nursing the wine between his hands.

"I guess. But apart from that there was something . . ." He frowned, trying to understand what it was that had disturbed him so much. "Do you know what it was like?" He turned to face her, noticing how tired she looked. She had probably been looking forward to an early night— had come over to be with him in spite of that. "It was like I was something alien that was triggering . . . like, an *immune response*. You know? Like something that the histocompatibility complex had determined was nonself, different."

"An antigen."

"Exactly. And all these furiously active microorganisms, with their cameras and microphones and antennae, were attaching themselves to my surface, worrying away at the membrane."

"Stop. You make it sound like a horror film."

Ford leaned back, pushing his fingers against his tired eyes.

"I swear to God, that's exactly what this is. A horror film."

Helen moved closer until her dark fragrant hair was touching his face. She gently removed his hand and kissed his closed eyes.

"Mmmmnn," growled Ford, but he was just being polite. He could not get excited the way he had been in her apartment. He was too conscious of this being the couch that he and Carolyn had bought. But he was glad she had come, nevertheless. She had put on her battered chinos again and a T-shirt that said YOSEMITE in faded red letters. The clothes had the effect of toning down her almost strident sexuality. It was the way he liked her best.

"You have to keep some kind of perspective," she said. "And you have to be positive."

Ford looked at her. This close her steady, all-seeing predator's eyes were almost hypnotic.

"Like the guy in the joke, you mean?"

"Which guy?"

"Guy falls from the top of an apartment building. He's got ten seconds before he hits the sidewalk, and as he flashes past each floor, he keeps saying—'So far so good, so far so good, so far so good'. . ."

Helen smiled.

"You're not going to fall," she said. "Sunny's going to get better; Novak's going to come up with an answer to the superstaph; you're going to be reinstated."

"Marshall West will find the money for a new trauma center. The hoodlums will hand in their guns. The Democrats will control Congress."

"There you go," said Helen, giving him a friendly squeeze. "Two months from now you'll be up to your elbows in some crack junkie's intestines . . ."

"Everything back to normal," said Ford, nodding, hoping she was right.

5

The taco restaurant at which Sunny had eaten tested positive for *Clostridium botulinum*. The CDC team isolated the bug in canned corn that the restaurant owner had purchased from damaged stock at a warehouse based near Hermosillo in Mexico. Three other cases of food poisoning had been reported in LA that the CDC were able to link to the same source. The establishment was closed.

Despite Helen Wray's reassurance, Ford did fall, was falling. That was what it felt like, anyway. Freefall. With nothing between him and the worst kind of dead-stop definitive ending. Sunny did not react badly to the CDC serum, but it didn't seem to help her, either. He spent hours by her bedside, holding her limp hand, watching the machine feed her air. He talked to her ceaselessly, hoping that his voice would give her something to hang on to.

Three days after initial admission, Dr. Lee once again took him into his office.

He looked tired and overwrought. Everybody was acutely aware of the developing crisis in the Emergency Department. Patou's attempts to contain the outbreak appeared to be working for the time being, but there had been three more deaths among the cohorted patients, and the media had virtually set up camp in the parking lot. Russell Haynes had been obliged to call the county sheriff's department for additional safety police to ensure access for ambulances and staff.

Lee's desk was piled high with medical journals and textbooks, some of which Ford remembered from med school. Seeing Ford's curiosity, Lee picked up one of the fattest tomes.

"Remember this? Haddad and Winchester. As you can see, I've been doing a little reading."

"To good effect, I hope," said Ford, soberly. He wasn't in the mood for professional banter.

Lee shrugged, returning the book to its teetering stack. He leaned back in his chair and brought his smooth, effeminate hands together over his stomach.

"To be honest with you, Dr. Ford, Sunny's case is . . . well, it's causing me some confusion."

So far so bad, thought Ford.

"How so?"

"Well—and you have to understand I've been looking at the detail in close consultation with Rita Benowitz at the CDC; she's their expert on this organism—I . . . Look, I'll start with the facts. Last night, after you left the hospital, the lab people informed me that they had found high levels of botulinum in Sunny's stool. In spore form, but also as mature organisms."

"She's infected. We already knew that."

"No, I'm not talking about the samples we took when she was admitted. This sample was taken *yesterday*. If anything, the bug seems to be present in slightly higher concentrations now than it was when she was first admitted."

"It's multiplying?"

"Apparently. Unless, of course, it has just come down with the last of the food she ingested. But I doubt that. In fact I would say that was extremely unlikely."

"But you said that couldn't happen. You said that her GI tract would be too acidic."

"That's right. Normally speaking, that would be the case. In infants up to six months botulinum can replicate because of the relative sterility of the intestinal lumen and the low acidity. In adults the bug cannot normally survive. However—and this is direct from Dr. Benowitz; this is the current position—for a while now the CDC has been employing a fourth category for the disease, which they term Botulism Classification Undetermined or BCU."

Ford gave a wry smile.

"A classification meaning there's no classification?"

"That's right. They've had cases that were outside the norm, including infected adults. They wanted to describe the indescribable, and that's what they decided to call it. The people in this group—people said to be infected by BCU—have to be over one year old and cannot have any foodstuff or wound as the source of their disease."

"I don't understand. Sunny got it from food."

"Just bear with me a second. The important issue here is not really where Sunny got it but whether or not the thing can replicate in the GI tract. We know where and how she picked this up, but we don't know why it's surviving—apparently even breeding inside her. Now, this is all fairly virgin territory, you have to realize. There are few certainties. Benowitz believes that most cases of BCU represent an adult variant of infant botulism. Usually the patients have some abnormality in the GI tract that could facilitate spore germination. Low acidity or relatively sterile intestinal lumen as a result of pretreatment with broad-spectrum antibiotics are often factors."

"Sunny is a perfectly normal child," said Ford blankly.

Lee watched him for a moment.

"No history of antibiotic use?"

"Nothing out of the ordinary. In fact, I've always discouraged them except where there's no alternative."

Lee looked down at his linked hands. With a slow, meditative gesture he opposed his delicate thumbs.

"So what do we do?" asked Ford.

Lee didn't have to reflect for long. He had obviously already made up his mind about the options.

"It's a difficult call to make. As long as she has the right systemic support, she is in no immediate danger. However, there is a point at which prolonged use of the antitoxin could become . . . problematic. We can go on administering the current levels for a while, but the longer we do, the greater the risks of an adverse reaction. I certainly wouldn't want to step up the doses."

"How long do we have?"

Lee tried to smile.

"Let's see what happens." He was rounding up now, concluding the meeting, looking for the positive payoff. "At some point the number of organisms is going to fall."

"And if it doesn't?" asked Ford.

"Then we will have to consider some way of attacking the bug."

"Attacking? With antibiotic therapy, you mean?"

"Right. Penicillin is theoretically contraindicated because if you rupture the cell wall of this thing, you release more toxin, and her system does not need more toxin. But there are alternatives. Chloramphenicol, metronidazole . . . vancomycin."

Ford was starting to get a feeling of déjà vu. The names came up like road signs leading to disaster. Getting a grip, he told himself that Sunny's infection had *nothing* to do with what was going on in the Emergency Department. Lee was still talking.

". . . giving us a degree of leverage. Chloramphenicol, as you know, inhibits peptide bond formation; it stops the bug in its tracks without tearing it to pieces. I think that that's what I'd go with initially."

Ford stared hard and long at Lee's face. He wanted to find something there that would give him hope.

Lee looked away.

They tried chloramphenicol. But material and fluid from Sunny's GI tract continued to culture positively for botulinum. Four days into her illness she suffered a brief and alarming episode of cardiac fibrillation. At two o'clock in the morning her heart's normal sinus rhythm was lost, as the heart's muscle fibers flickered in spasm. A Code Blue was called, and the doctors administered digoxin. Within two minutes normal contraction resumed.

Ford was by Sunny's bedside that morning when he was told what had happened. It sent him into a flat spin. Raising his voice, drawing looks from other patients on the ward, he insisted that he was not going to leave Sunny's bedside again.

"I should have been there," he said. "I'm a doctor, for Christ's sake. I could have helped. What if the Blue team had been dealing with something else? What if—?"

"They were here within a minute of the call," said Lee firmly. "There's nothing you could have done that they didn't do."

Ford could not understand. He stared at Lee's impassive face. The smaller man's lips were moving, sounds were coming out, but Ford could make nothing of it. Then he found himself being eased into a chair next to Sunny's bed. A nurse appeared with a cup and what looked like a tranquilizer. It was crazy. They were treating him like a patient. With a flush of embarrassment, Ford realized that this was because he was behaving like one. He was behaving like someone who had no understanding of what was going on, someone for whom the only reference points were emotional. He took the tranquilizer and washed it down with the tepid water.

"Okay," he said, wiping his mouth. "Okay. It's all right now. I understand."

Lee backed off a step. Ford turned and looked at his daughter. He stroked her fine blonde hair. Her irises were just visible under the prolapsed eyelids. She looked impossibly fragile.

"You're only going to make yourself ill," said Lee.

"The doctor's right," said a deep, maternal voice.

Ford turned and saw Gloria Tyrell. She was standing at the end of the bed, a legal pad clutched to her matronly bosom.

"You've got to be strong for her," she said. "She's goin' to be needin' you when she gets out of here."

Ford got to his feet.

"Jesus, Gloria," he said. "It's good to see you."

Gloria shrugged her heavy shoulders. She too was looking tired.

"Just thought I'd say hello," she said.

"How're things in ER?"

She rolled her eyes expressively.

"Aren't you breaking quarantine?" asked Ford.

Again there was the expressive roll of the eyes.

"Dr. Allen told me you'd be here. So I thought you ought to have this."

She handed him the legal pad. On the top of the first sheet of paper, a telephone number had been scribbled and next to it the name *Wingate*.

"Man keeps calling. I explained about what's going on here. He wanted your home number, but I thought it would be better if you called him."

"Okay. Yes. Thank you."

Ford looked blankly at the sheet. It was a moment before he made the connection between the name and the doctor who had called from Beverly Hills. He tore off the page and folded it into his pocket.

"I'd like to look after Sunny," said Gloria, addressing herself to Lee.

Ford looked at her big friendly face. He found himself smiling again, partly at the warmth, but also at the confidence she inspired. Looking at her, this mountain of a woman, with her large, practical hands, you could believe that there was no illness she couldn't nurse you out of.

"I'm afraid that would not be allowed," said Lee. "Not my decision, of course. The chief of infection control would have to be consulted."

Once it was clear that Sunny's botulinum was multiresistant—neither chloramphenicol nor metronidazole appeared to have any impact—Patou was brought into the case, as a matter of course.

There was a terse interview in Lee's cramped office, Patou for some reason sitting in Lee's place, while the two men perched on the other side on plastic chairs. Patou was clearly uncomfortable talking to Ford as the parent of a patient rather than the professional rival—enemy even—that she had come to see him as. Ford, numbed by the news of the botulinum's resistance and the prospect of Sunny's going onto vancomycin, listened quietly to Patou's evaluation of the situation in the Emergency Department. There had been another death during the night. This time of a young woman thought to be part of a local gang. She had been admitted with two stab wounds to the lower abdomen four days ago and had succumbed to a staphylococcus infection in the early hours of the morning. The superstaph had now taken eight lives in two weeks.

Finally Patou came to the subject of Sunny. As she spoke, she kept her eyes on the page of her notepad.

"It now appears that Dr. Ford's daughter is suffering from a multiresistant pathogen. Of course, we don't yet know how it may respond to vancomycin, and I'm sure we all hope for a . . . *positive* outcome. If, however, it does not respond, it will clearly represent an alarming new departure. Resistant wound infections are one thing. Staph, as we know, comes into constant contact with antibiotics, especially within the hospital environment, but botulinum does not. According to the

CDC, there has been an increased incidence of wound botulism particularly among the intravenous drug users where a degree of pathogen/antibiotic interfacing may have taken place. That, I think you'll agree, is a matter for reflection."

Ford sat up at this. It seemed to be an acknowledgment of his own views on the development of resistant bacteria.

"But whatever the mechanisms involved, I suggest Sonia Ford be isolated. Not with the cohorted staph cases, obviously, but on her own."

Ford nodded his appreciation of this.

At the end of the interview, rounding up, Patou mentioned the fact that three other hospitals in the metropolitan area had reported cases of resistant staphylococcus.

For a moment Ford thought he must have misunderstood. To him it seemed like headline news, but Patou had slipped it in like an aside, a footnote. She was shuffling papers, making ready to leave.

"You mean resistant to vancomycin, to everything?"

Patou stopped what she was doing.

"I believe so."

"I don't understand."

"What don't you understand, Doctor?"

"You're saying this is happening all over the city? Where?"

Patou calmly addressed her notebook.

"Saint Francis, Daniel Freeman, Centinela."

Ford sat back in his chair, making it crack.

"But this changes everything."

"Oh?"

"Well . . ." Ford gestured with his hands, his mind racing. "Well, it means that your theory that this thing was nosocomial, that we somehow, through sloppy procedure, cooked it up in-house . . . that all goes out the window."

Patou watched him with her green eyes. Completely inscrutable.

"I'm not sure I follow."

Then there was a flicker of something. Ford could see it in the tilt of her head, the way she was holding herself. She was afraid, backed into a corner. Not that she was at fault. She had taken action to contain the outbreak. She had done the right thing. But now she was faced with the possibility that *he* had been right all along. Something big was happening in Los Angeles, something that had nothing to do with the Willowbrook or its staff. Ford felt a steadying contraction of anger.

"Well, Dr. Patou, unless you are suggesting that sloppy technique in the Willowbrook has created a bug which, in the past two weeks, has traveled all over the city—despite your actions here—and is now infecting other people, I can't see how your position is tenable."

Patou shot him a withering glance.

"Dr. Ford, I really don't think this is a time for cheap point-scoring. It really doesn't matter who is right or wrong. The important thing is to deal with the situation."

Ford stood up.

"Well, actually, Dr. Patou, it does matter. I have been *suspended* on the assumption that I am in some way guilty for what is happening here. So it matters a great deal."

Patou rose from her chair.

"Dr. Ford, you have been suspended pending an investigation into your supervision of Officer Denny's admission into the critical room of the Emergency Department."

This was too much.

"That's just *bullshit*, and you know it. I've been suspended as part of a PR exercise, because the health authorities don't want the public to know what's going on in this city."

He had raised his voice. The anger with which he had expressed himself seemed to hang in the air for a moment. Both Lee and Patou were staring at him as if they expected him to start breaking up the furniture. Patou moved to the door.

"Well, I suggest you take *that* up with the county health depart-ment," she said, and she walked out of the room.

6

Ford left the hospital in the late afternoon, having watched Sunny's transfer to an isolation room. She was now on vancomycin. It was a last-ditch attempt to clear her system of the botulinum. There was a considerable risk of increased toxin release due to cell destruction, but Lee was gambling on the CDC antitoxin countering the effect of any poison buildup. Because of the cardiac fibrillation episode, she was now under close surveillance at all times, and while this was reassuring as far as it went, Ford remained deeply apprehensive. Even if she did pull through, there was a chance that the drug itself would cause lasting damage.

Ford felt like an empty shell, a husk. Drifting forward with the freeway traffic, he stared blankly at a bank of dark thunderheads building up over the San Pedro Channel.

Out of nowhere a red Nissan pulled across in front of him. He had to brake hard and swerve.

"Jesus Christ!"

He shouted at the driver, an obese Hispanic woman, through his open window.

"Watch where you're driving, you maniac!"

She didn't even look at him. She was wearing earphones, her head bobbing to some gangsta rap junk or other. Defiantly Ford flipped on the radio and pumped up the volume on a Haydn string quartet. See how she liked *that*. Nobody around him seemed to mind. They were all roaring ahead, eyes front, all going to hell anyway.

Then Ford realized how hungry he was. He hadn't eaten all day, and it was now after five. He would have to stop somewhere on Pico to pick up groceries because there was absolutely nothing in the house apart from frozen pizza. The thought of having to shop and then wait another hour before he finally put something in his belly was intolerable. He started to drift over to the right-hand lane, looking out for restaurant signs.

He came off the 105 at the next exit, missed a turning, and found himself on Crenshaw going in the wrong direction. He pulled into a Sizzler and parked.

The Sizzler was almost empty. Just a few truck drivers being served by bored-looking waitresses. Ford installed himself in a booth, ordered a cheeseburger and fries and sat staring out at the deepening gloom. He wondered how soon it would be before the press got wind of the other outbreaks. It would probably be on the news that night. He smiled with grim satisfaction. They were going to find it harder to point the finger now. Like Patou, they were going to have to cast the net wider, find other reasons for what was going on.

And what was going on? He couldn't help feeling that the outbreaks were linked. It seemed impossible that a variety of very different pathogens were developing multiresistance spontaneously. There had to be something, some kind of transfer of a particular trick between the different species. It had already happened in Japan with *Shigella*. Then it came to him that he should call Novak immediately, tell him all about it, see what he had to say. He reached into his pocket for some nickels, but then the thought that he was going to be seeing him anyway made him change his mind. He was too tired. They could talk about it when they met at his condo. . . .

"Hey there!"

It was his waitress. She was smiling down at him, waiting to place his meal on the table. He had fallen asleep again.

"Oh!" This was becoming embarrassing. "Yeah. Thank you! Thank you."

"Looks like you could use a vacation," she said.

He ate hungrily, wondering, as he finished the fries and the bread *and* the coleslaw, what Novak was going to make of the news. Thinking about him, he recalled the first time they had spoken on the phone, recalled Novak saying that he needed to talk with some people before . . . how had he put it? Before he *got into it* any further. Got into what? And who were these *people*? Outside there was a flash of lightning in the dark, charged air. Ford finished his watery soda. Novak was probably just referring to some group of academics.

Then he remembered Wingate.

It had been such a traumatic day he had completely forgotten the scrap of paper Gloria had given him. He reached into his pocket now and looked at Gloria's girlish, round handwriting.

He called from his mobile phone in the Buick. Wingate picked up immediately.

"Dr. Wingate? This is Dr. Marcus Ford. I understand you've been trying to reach me."

"For three days, yes. Just one moment." There was a muffled crunch and the sound of Wingate closing a door. "Yes, I'm glad you decided to call me."

He sounded a little peeved.

"I'm sorry I took so long, I don't know if you've been following the news on the Willowbrook, but—"

"Yes. Yes, I have. I was very sorry to hear about your daughter. You've been having a rough time down there. When's the inquiry?"

"I still don't know. I'm hoping they'll drop the whole thing."

"Ungrateful bastards."

"Pardon me?"

"You spend your life stitching them up, making them well. Then you have an off day, and they want your house."

Ford was surprised by the man's tone. He had sounded more poised before, more in control. It occurred to Ford that maybe Wingate was facing litigation of his own, although it could hardly be serious. As he'd said in their last conversation, he had erred on the side of caution precisely in order to avoid liability.

"Do you have any news of . . . *um* . . ."

"The Turnbull boy? Yes, that's why I was calling you, in fact. I wanted to let you know about the results my laboratory people got. You remember they were looking at the clostridium?"

"Sure."

"Well, it turns out my worst fears were well founded. It's incredible. Nothing seems to affect it. Nothing antibiotic, I mean. We, I mean, they took it through the whole range of antibiotics from amino-glycosides to tetracyclines. I went to the trouble and expense of producing a full report of the tests."

He clearly had been threatened somehow. Otherwise why go to such lengths to validate his position?

"What did the Turnbulls say?" asked Ford, trying not to sound too disingenuous.

"I haven't heard from them lately," said Wingate. "There was a terse little letter after out last meeting. The mother realized she had nothing to threaten me with, of course, but that didn't stop her making trouble. We've lost a string of our regular patients already. That's how she gets her revenge."

"Revenge for what?"

"She said I took ten years off her life. Said I was irresponsible. Apparently she's been going around Beverly Hills saying that the only thing wrong with her son had been a sprained wrist and a throat infection. I actually produced the report in order to put the record straight. Even sent her a copy." He gave a tight, angry laugh. "So far she hasn't been in touch."

"But this isn't making sense," said Ford. "What happened to the boy?"

Wingate paused. It was as if he was only now considering the matter.

"I've no idea. Dr. Ford, the Turnbulls are rich and powerful people. When they shut their doors to you, you are left firmly *outside*."

Ford could imagine.

"But surely if he was infected with a multiresistant pathogen, he would have required further help, maybe even the amputation you recommended."

"Are you saying I was wrong?" snapped Wingate.

"No, no. I'm just saying it's intriguing."

"Yes, well. Anyway, whatever happened to him, I wanted it to be clear that my judgment is not in question. I wanted to know if you would be interested in seeing the report."

Ford realized now what his role was supposed to be in all this. He was on the point of referring Wingate to Patou, but then thought better of it. He would like to take a look at the report himself. Even if he could do little with it, Novak certainly could.

"Sure, I'd be very interested."

A disdainful snort exploded into the phone.

"A sore throat, indeed. Elizabeth Turnbull is going to have to do a little better than that!"

That was it.

Ford felt the hair prick up on the back of his neck. It was all he could do not to hang up on Wingate in mid-flow.

When the phone was back in its cradle, he sat for a moment staring out through the windshield at the lowering clouds. Behind him the lights of the Sizzler came on, throwing bars of pale yellow across the asphalt. He picked up the phone and called the critical room at the Willowbrook.

"Trauma. Six-three-one-four."

Ford frowned.

"Conrad, you still there?"

"Marcus! What are you . . . ? I heard about Sunny. I spoke to Lee, and he—"

"Conrad, I want you to do something for me."

"Sure . . . sure thing. Name it."

"I want you to get all the records of the resistance cases, especially the ones who have died. Can you do that?"

"Well . . . I'll have to go talk to Elaine Macaphery in records, but I can't imagine it'll be a problem. It's all supposed to be on the database now, but you know how slow they are entering that stuff."

"It doesn't matter if it's computer generated or handwritten sheets. Just get me as much as you can. I'll meet you in the staff parking lot in an hour."

"So are you going to tell me what it's all about?"

"I'll tell you when I see you."

"Okay. An hour might be a bit tight, though. Can you give me an hour and a half?"

"Just come as soon as you can."

"Don't come into the parking lot. There's still a lot of press hanging round. Meet me on the corner of One hundred twentieth Street, okay?"

* * *

Ford sat for twenty minutes at the intersection, nervously watching people as they walked or drove past. It was safe enough inside the hospital grounds, or when you were moving, but just sitting there behind the wheel of a stationary car, that wasn't recommended.

Finally Allen came strolling along the sidewalk. In his left hand he was carrying a battered briefcase and in his right a chunky-looking dossier. He climbed into the car, introducing a powerful smell of surgical soap. Ford felt safer having him next to him.

"So what's it all about?" Allen said, once he was installed in the passenger seat.

"I think I know why all this is happening."

"All what?"

"The outbreak, the superstaph, everything."

Allen gave a nod.

"Okay. So . . ."

Ford put a hand on his friend's arm. Using the Buick's map-reading light, he went through the files one by one, skimming, stopping here and there to be sure, getting a bad feeling when he came to Sunny's. It was as he had thought. He flipped off the light and leaned back in the seat.

Allen sat watching him. A car went past, lighting up his face.

"So are you going to tell me what this is—?"

Ford turned.

"Conrad. Remember the Shark? Do you remember his throat infection?"

Allen shrugged. Of course he remembered. He would never forget the sight of those wired teeth and the oozing pus.

"*Streptococcus,*" said Ford. "Remember Denny? I didn't even know he had an infection. That was because he was more or less over it when he was admitted. But that's what he had, strep throat. Do you remember Andre Nelson, the pneumonia case? Strep."

He riffled through the pile of dossiers.

"In almost every case strep is involved. I talked to Dr. Wingate this afternoon. Remember his patient with a multiresistant *Clostridium perfringens?* The guy also had a streptococcus infection. And Conrad, just before Sunny came down with the resistant botulinum—"

"She asked you to give her some medicine, some antibiotics, for her sore throat. I remember."

"*Streptococcus equisimilis.* It's the strep, Conrad. I'm sure of it. Somehow or other—maybe years of being bombarded with antibiotics— this little streptococcus has developed resistance to everything we have. Some harmless little throat bug that tends to stick around, people have hit it with every kind of thing. Wrong treatment, wrong doses, year in, year out. And it's learned to cope. We've *taught* it to cope. We've bred it to cope. And now it's sharing. It's sharing its know-how with every other microbe it meets."

Allen was shaking his head.

"But if you're right—"

"Of course it doesn't matter that the strep is resistant. It's just going to give you a sore throat. Your immune system can handle it. But conjugation, Conrad, that's the problem. This bug is too damned sociable. It's passing genetic material to other bacteria, to pathogens— *Staphylococcus aureus, Clostridium perfringens, Clostridium botulinum*— bugs that can kill if the body doesn't get help."

Allen was speechless.

"It's what happened with *Shigella* in Japan. It's happening here now, but with strep. Anybody with a strep infection who picks up a serious bug is at risk, because the bug will pick up the resistance. They're effectively out of the reach of modern medicine. If you even *try* and use antibiotics, you simply help the new resistant strains push out the old ones. You just speed up the process."

Ford fell silent. He was scared. Everything that was happening, the deaths, the confusion, his own growing sense of helplessness, it was just the beginning. They were being fast-forwarded into a future that none of them had prepared for, that none of them were *trained* for. He blinked. He didn't want to believe it. Maybe he was misinterpreting the data. Maybe Novak would set him straight. Maybe the correlation of strep and multiresistance was just a coincidence.

He prayed for Sunny's sake, for everybody's sake, that it was.

PART FOUR

ANTISENSE

1

CITY OF COMMERCE, EAST LOS ANGELES

"Look on the bright side, Duane. Prob'ly is a suicide, more 'n likely. You know how McNally is."

Sergeant Duane Ruddock gave his partner a stony look and yanked open the door of their '91 Chevy Caprice. It was all very well for Deputy Sam Dorsey to look on the bright side. He hadn't been on the job since Christmas without a single day's vacation. Dorsey hadn't even been at the Homicide Bureau that long. Six months ago he'd still have been at Vice, trawling for hookers and perverts, and probably getting off on it. It wouldn't worry him if some complicated case took them right through Thanksgiving and beyond. Working with the Bulldogs was still a novelty for him.

"Y'all got something planned for next week?" said Dorsey in a Texan drawl that seven years in LA had done nothing to weaken. "I mean, vacation-wise?"

Ruddock started the motor and cut a tight arc onto Rickenbacker Road, letting the tires squeak on the hot asphalt. The south end of Commerce was made up entirely of light industrial buildings surrounded by narrow grass shoulders and identical light industrial trees. The bureau had moved there in '93 after the earthquake wrecked the sheriff's department building downtown.

"I'd planned on the Rockies, as a matter of fact," said Ruddock. "Yellowstone Park or something. Anyplace, so long as there's no people."

"Hell, there's people in Yellowstone, all right. Trailers an' shit all over." A procession of heavy trucks went thundering by on Eastern Avenue, obliging Dorsey to shout. "Can't get out of your car half the time 'case a grizzly takes a bite out of you. I reckon you'd do a whole lot better—"

"Let me guess: I'd do a whole lot better in Texas. Is that what you were going to say?"

"Hell, yes. There's parts you can drive for a day and not see a living soul, if you've a mind to."

Dorsey reached into his top pocket and pulled out a pair of blue mirror sunglasses. Ruddock wished he wouldn't wear them on call-outs. With his neat blond hair, tight mouth, and arrowhead nose, he looked like a genuine surfer Nazi from hell. Just the sight of him could put some kinds of people on edge, and that could be very unhelpful in Homicide. Ruddock, forty-three, stocky, with a gray mustache and a perceptible spare tire round his middle, cut a more avuncular figure. It was easy to believe that all he wanted was to get the job done, that the last thing he was looking for was trouble. In his experience, people responded to that.

"Where exactly we headed, anyhow?" asked Dorsey.

"For the hills," said Ruddock. "Some place near Topanga. Green Leaf Canyon Drive."

"I thought Topanga was LAPD. Ain't it LAPD?"

"East of Topanga Canyon Boulevard is LAPD. West of Topanga Canyon Boulevard is county."

"And our man's west."

Dorsey took out a stick of gum and settled into his seat for the long drive to the Santa Monica Mountains.

They missed the junction the first time and had to turn around at a gas station three miles further on. Green Leaf Canyon Drive was little more than a dirt track that dipped and twisted through a wilderness of boulders and stunted, thirsty-looking trees. It was about as remote a part of LA County as you could find, an area favored by superannuated bikers and followers of holistic medicine. Ruddock had only been up there once before, about five years back. A young couple had stumbled on the body of a naked prostitute beside a track just like this one. She'd been strangled with her own stocking. At the time everyone thought the killer must have driven a four-by-four, a jeep, or a pickup, but when they finally caught the guy, it turned out he'd dumped the body from a regular sedan, rented at the airport. So Ruddock knew you didn't need a four-by-four, so long as you took it dead slow—despite the curses that came from Dorsey each time the chassis smacked the dirt.

The house lay at the very end of the track in a shady spot above a dried-up streambed. It was an old-style timbered house with a sloping roof made of red tiles and a wooden porch along one side. The wood had been painted pale yellow, but was badly in need of a fresh coat. Out front there was a patch of lawn that had turned to weeds and a dilapidated shed through whose open door several items of rusting machinery could be seen. The back of the house looked out over a shallow ravine, where the vegetation looked thicker and greener.

Ruddock parked the Chevy between a patrol car and a blue van that had GAUNTLET HOME SECURITY COMPANY written on the side. Further along stood a gray Lexus that Ruddock recognized as belonging to Dr. Juan Serratosa, the deputy medical examiner. That he had responded so quickly was a good start. On a busy day you could wait hours for the coroner's office to send somebody out.

Sergeant Pat McNally was giving instructions to one of the patrolmen when Ruddock and Dorsey walked in. McNally was six foot three inches, with neat brown hair, a smooth complexion, and a comic-book hero's jaw. He and his partner were on the desk that day, their job being to respond to calls from the patrol stations and make an initial assessment of the facts. They decided whether one of the nine other teams on the roster would be allocated to investigate. The discovery of a body was not enough in itself: suicide was not homicide, after all.

"Sorry to drag you out here, fellas," said McNally. "But this one needs a little digging."

Ruddock took a look around. They were standing in a dim hallway with a coatrack on one wall and an old, discolored mirror on the other. A musty smell of mothballs and sawdust hung in the air. There were doorways leading into a kitchen and a living room, and a polished wooden staircase going up to the next floor. The furniture and fittings all seemed to date from the I Love Lucy period: worn, utilitarian, a lot of beige and brown and eggshell blue. Apart from a pair of respectable-looking wooden cabinets, there wasn't a single item Mrs. Ruddock wouldn't have sent to the incinerator.

"Where's the body?" asked Dorsey, slipping his shades back into the top pocket of his jacket.

"Top of the house," said McNally. "There's a kind of study up there. Couple of PCs, books, and such. And an overhead beam. Dr. Serratosa's up there now with the crime lab people."

"You got a positive ID?"

"Got his wallet. Charles Novak, as reported. *Professor* Novak, as a matter of fact."

"Professor, huh?" said Dorsey. "Professor of what?"

"Not sure. Chemistry or some such, judging from the books."

"Who found him?" Ruddock asked.

"Couple of guys from this home security company. They were 'sposed to be fitting window locks today."

"They cut him down?"

"Yep. 'Fraid so. Loosened the knot too. Still, they say they didn't touch anything else."

"They say," added Dorsey with a shake of the head. "Dummies."

"It's natural enough," said Ruddock. "How do they know if the guy's dead or not? Anyhow, you got to talk to them, Sam. I'll do the scene."

"Sure thing."

"Through there," said McNally, pointing into the living room. "Their names are Arthurson and Roby."

Ruddock and McNally began climbing the stairs, which were covered by a worn gray carpet. On a small ledge halfway up stood a blue vase with a bunch of dried flowers inside. They looked as though they'd been picked around 1955.

"So this Novak guy was worried about security, huh?" said Ruddock, pulling on a pair of surgical rubber gloves so as not to disturb any prints. "Any sign of forced entry so far?"

"Not that I can see. And no sign of theft either. Front door wasn't locked, though. Anyone could have walked in. I've asked the deputies to check if he reported anything recently. Maybe something in particular made him want all these locks."

"He lived here alone?"

"Looks that way."

They were up on the landing now. Rays of sunlight from a window caught dust floating through the air. They passed a bathroom on one side, a bedroom on the other. Ruddock saw a dark red Chinese dressing gown slung over an unmade bed, a clutter of black-and-white photographs on a painted mantelpiece, a pair of brown slippers, one on its side.

"These security people, did they talk to Novak yesterday?"

"Not much. They said they knew what they had to do and just got on with it. Maybe Dorsey can get something out of them. It's one more flight, I'm afraid."

They went up another ten steps, steeper ones this time, uncarpeted and smelling faintly of wood preservative. McNally's heavy footsteps sent shock waves through the whole structure.

"Juan?"

The door swung open and Juan Serratosa appeared, dressed in disposable paper overalls that were too big for him. Serratosa was a small, lean man with a dark complexion and a brilliant smile, which he used a lot for a guy whose business was the aftermath of unlawful killing. The fact that he was wearing protective clothing confirmed what McNally had said: that the circumstances of this particular death were far from clear. It meant they were probably going to have to check the crime scene for everything from skin flakes to carpet fibers—the so-called trace evidence. In the room behind him the crime lab team was hard at work, photographing the scene and dusting for prints.

"Hi there," Serratosa said. "I thought you were on vacation any day now."

"Starting Monday, I hope," said Ruddock. "Provided I can get this one cleared up nice and quick."

Serratosa wrinkled his nose as if he didn't think that was going to happen but didn't want to say so.

"So let's take a look."

Serratosa led them into the middle of the room, a spacious attic that had clearly been converted during the last few years. Lit from a single skylight, it had a stripped pine floor and shelves along one wall, many of which were only half full. On three long tables office equipment was arranged, including two personal computers, a laser printer, and a small photocopier. On one of the screens computer-generated tropical fish swam back and forth above a computer-generated seabed. Leo Nash, the lab photographer, looked up from his camera and acknowledged Ruddock with a nod.

The body lay sprawled out on a patterned rug, the head twisted to one side, a length of nylon rope still loose around the neck. Male, about sixty, tall, about two hundred and twenty pounds, gray hair, balding. Ruddock stepped closer, taking in the dark purple marks below the ears, the gray-blue skin of the face, then the open mouth, the bulging, motionless eyes, the eyelashes. The eyelashes were brown, except above the roots where, he noticed, there was no color at all. The flashbulb went off again, the dead man's expression suddenly vivid. To Ruddock it seemed to register not horror or suffering but something more like disgust or self-reproach, as if Professor Novak's last realization was that he had missed some very important appointment.

"Best keep off the rug, guys," said Serratosa. "It should've trapped any stray fibers. The rest of the floor doesn't look so promising."

Ruddock looked up at the overhead beam: about two feet of rope hung down from a knot, the end of it frayed from the hasty cut the workmen had made. On the ground a couple of feet away a plain wooden kitchen chair lay on its side. He wondered why Serratosa and McNally were so reluctant to treat this as a likely suicide. Homicides by hanging were extremely rare. In fact, in all his years at the bureau he could not remember even one.

"Can you give us any help on time of death?" he asked.

"Well, we've got almost complete rigor mortis," said Serratosa, brushing his nose against his forearm. "Given the size of this guy that would suggest that he's been dead at least twelve hours. But it could be a lot longer than that."

"How much longer?" said Ruddock.

"Well, it's pretty hot up here, so I'd expect rigidity to start disappearing maybe twenty-four to thirty-six hours after death. But that's only a rough guess."

"So the likelihood is he died some time last night."

"And he's wearing a sweater," said McNally, "which tallies."

"And we don't have a note or anything, Pat?"

McNally shook his head.

"Nothing anywhere obvious. 'Course he may have mailed one to somebody. Has been known."

Ruddock pointed to the computer that was on.

"You checked that too?"

"What, the fish?"said McNally.

"That's a screen saver. Comes on automatically after a few minutes. Stops you wearing out the tube."

He walked over to the computer and gently pressed one of the keys with his gloved finger. The computerized fish instantly vanished to be replaced with a word-processor screen. In the top left-hand corner of a document were written the words: TIME TO END IT. CHARLES NOVAK.

Ruddock smiled. "There's your note."

McNally came over and looked into the screen.

"Well, what do you know," he muttered.

"Maybe his hand was shaking too much to write," Ruddock suggested. "I mean on paper. Or maybe he just didn't have anything handy to write with."

"Better get that keyboard checked out for prints," said McNally, "and the mouse too."

Ruddock frowned and put his hands on his hips. Maybe his partner was right about McNally. Maybe he was a little too suspicious.

"Sure, we'll check it," said Ruddock. "But, I think this puts a slightly different angle on this whole thing, don't you? I mean, Juan, when was the last time you had a case of homicide by hanging?"

"I haven't," said Serratosa. "Not in five years and two thousand autopsies."

"Right. So the odds must be—"

"But I'm not sure this *is* a homicide by hanging," Serratosa added. "The way I read it, what we have here is most likely ligature strangulation."

"Strangulation, as in homicide?"

"Only kind there is."

Ruddock looked at McNally. So that was it.

"Okay. Why?"

Serratosa squatted down beside the body and sighed. For him a

corpse was like an ancient artifact, something to be interpreted, understood. It was a messenger from the past; only it spoke in a language that
only the expert could understand. It didn't matter what state it was in
or whom it had once belonged to. All that was part of the game. Ruddock suddenly felt he understood how Serratosa was able to smile as
much as he did.

"There's no one thing," Serratosa said. "Just a lot of little things.
For one, the slip knot here. With all the suicidal hangings I've seen, the
knot's found at the side of the neck: left-hand side for right-handed
people and vice versa. If you're tying a knot yourself, it's a lot easier to
reach at the side." He demonstrated, grasping an imaginary rope over
his left shoulder. "But this knot's at the back of the neck, like a regular
judicial hanging. I've never seen that before."

"Maybe Novak just liked things neat," said Ruddock.

"Are you kidding?" said McNally. "Just wait till you see the
kitchen."

"And then there's the bruising pattern," Serratosa went on. "Here,
take a look. You got enough now, Leo?"

The photographer nodded and stepped back from the corpse,
making way for Ruddock.

"If everything's just the way it looks—if the guy got up on the
chair, tied the rope, and jumped off—you wouldn't expect to see such
extensive bruising. It would all be over too quickly." Serratosa reached
down with a gloved hand and gently loosened the nylon cord further.
"See here? Around the sternomastoids? And we've got more bruising
here, on the strap muscles around the larynx, and there's a kind of
rash—maybe a rope burn—on this side."

Ruddock knelt down for a closer look. There were deep horizontal
bruises following the line of the rope.

"But if he's dancing around, enough to kick the chair over,
wouldn't he get marks like this?"

"I can't say for sure. It's just not something I've seen before. And
just look at the whole area above where the ligature was: you've got
generalized anoxia, petechial hemorrhages. Just look at the conjunctivae. This is what happens when you get pressure on the veins and the
trachea before the carotid arteries. It all says he took a little while to

die. My bet is that when we do the autopsy, we'll find fractures in the thyroid cartilage. That's a classic sign of homicidal strangulation."

It could take two or three days, maybe more, for the results of an autopsy to come through. In the meantime, they would have to pull the place apart looking for a lead. So far, it didn't look promising.

"If this was a murder, Pat, then it looks awful clean. It would have to be at least two guys, possibly professionals. That means they ain't gonna have left any traces."

McNally shrugged. Vacations were never very high up on his list of priorities.

"Looks like you could be in for a long day," he said, checking his watch.

The body was removed half an hour later. Then the real work began: the measuring, the noting, the labeling, the cataloging, the plowing through papers and correspondence. Ruddock didn't know what he was looking for, so he had to cast the net wide. His best hope was to come across something that indicted illegal dealings of some kind, because if Serratosa was right, Novak's killers had to be professionals. And retired professors of biochemistry did not tend to get mixed up with such people in the normal run of things. But all the papers pointed to was a lonely old guy who liked to keep his biochemical hand in—read scientific journals, occasionally correspond with academics and PhD students on various campuses. He lived on a company pension, had been married and divorced twenty years back, had no kids. He didn't keep anything valuable at the house, yet he was apparently worried about break-ins—getting a little paranoid probably, the way old people often did. In short, he was the sort of guy who might just get depressed enough one night to put a rope around his neck and jump. He was the kind of guy who might type TIME TO END IT on his PC and end it.

The sun was well below the hilltops when Ruddock returned to the room at the top of the house. A white taped outline now marked the place and position in which Novak's body had been found. On the computer screen the tropical fish had returned. From the darkness they stared warily at the world beyond, as if they had witnessed a little of its suffering and violence and were afraid.

Ruddock went over to the table and tried to save Novak's message. The computer informed him that the document had no name and would have to be given one. He chose the word *Evidence*. When the file was closed, he began to search the word processor for other documents, hoping to find something more helpful than the old papers he had been sifting through all day. But there were few letters, and certainly nothing suspicious. He stood up straight and stretched. His back was beginning to act up again. It happened most evenings nowadays, especially when things weren't going the way he wanted them to: a tightness, like an iron fist closing around his spine. He needed a change, a rest. Above all, he needed a vacation.

"Duane? You up there?"

It was Dorsey. Ruddock could hear him coming up the stairs. He would want to know what their next move was, who they should talk to next. In the normal course of events, it would be the neighbors, to ask if they'd seen anything suspicious. But out here there were no neighbors. And whom did that leave? Ruddock didn't have a clue.

He was about to shut down the system when he saw a little folder icon he hadn't noticed before, tucked away in one corner of the screen. It called itself *Diary*. He opened it with a few clicks of the mouse and started scrolling through the pages.

The door swung open and Dorsey walked in.

"So what's the next move, Duane? We're all but finished here, I reckon."

Ruddock smiled.

"Well, it seems our professor had an appointment for tomorrow night at nine o'clock," he said, writing the name and details down in his notebook. "With one Dr. Marcus Ford."

"No kidding?" said Dorsey. "That son of a bitch? You know I read about him in the paper."

2

Ford came to with a bitter taste in his mouth, his back aching from where he had been slumped unconscious in the hard plastic chair. Helen Wray was there, leaning forward, holding Sunny's hand, saying something he couldn't make out.

For the past few days she had been coming in during visiting hours to keep him company. And it bothered him. He found he didn't want her to see his anguish. Sexual intimacy was one thing, but to share a family crisis with someone you hardly knew—it felt wrong. And there was a personal reckoning going on too. Something he would have preferred to go through alone.

Sitting by Sunny's side, hour after hour, watching her cling to life, he felt as if he were being forced to come to terms with years of error, years of living by the wrong principles. Memories of her early years brought feelings of painful tenderness. He saw her in the back garden playing on an old check blanket, saw her feeding at Carolyn's breast, her blue eyes pressed shut against the light, remembered chubby hands pushed against his mouth as he lifted her from the baby-fragrant bed. He thought of what Conrad Allen had said—about his responsibility to his family—and stroking Sunny's unwashed yellow hair, thought about what she deserved, thought about what he owed *her*.

In the midst of all this, it was difficult to have to deal with Helen, to look up out of the depths of his private world at someone who seemed to him barely more than a stranger. By now she had gotten to know Conrad Allen and several of the nursing staff, but that didn't help. He pulled himself up into a more comfortable position.

Helen turned. Smiled.

"You've got a real gift of sleeping upright. Did you know that?"

For a moment he took in her pale face. There were dabs of shadow under her dark eyes. She looked exhausted.

"How long have you been here?" he asked.

She shrugged.

"Thirty minutes, maybe." She let go of Sunny's hand. "How's she doing?"

There was no good answer to this. Ford looked down at the floor. He couldn't bring himself to say that his daughter was probably dying, was already dead but for the machines. Helen touched him on the shoulder. Waited for him to look up.

"I spoke to Gloria. She said you didn't go home last night."

Gloria had finally prevailed upon Patou to be allowed to care for Sunny—another indication of Loulou's changing attitude to the crisis. At four in the morning she had persuaded him to go lie down, but it had been no use. Being in the next room was just as bad as being on the other side of town. He had stared up at the ceiling for an hour or so and then gone back through to Sunny's bedside.

"I didn't want to leave her," he said.

Helen gave a little exasperated sigh.

"Marcus, they're doing all they can here. Exhausting yourself isn't going to help Sunny."

She took his hands in hers.

"Come on. Let's go get some coffee."

They walked out of the cafeteria into the harsh morning light. The media was now firmly established at the front of the building—they even had generators going out there—still covering the crisis, but they were denied access to the staff parking lot by the safety police. Ford and Helen leaned against Russell Haynes's Lexus and sipped their coffee unharassed.

"I appreciate your coming by," said Ford after a moment. Helen touched him lightly on the wrist.

"What are friends for?" she said.

"No, but it's a long way for you to come. I hope it's not screwing up your schedule."

"Oh, forget the schedule, Marcus. I kind of make it up as I go along anyway. I do have a lunch, though. I've got to be over in Santa Monica by around twelve-thirty."

She pushed at a piece of grit with her toe.

"In fact, I was hoping you'd drive me."

"You didn't bring your car?"

She shook her head.

"I don't like bringing it down here. I worry it'll end up dented like yours. I took a taxi."

Ford shaded his eyes against the sun and took a long look at her face.

"Helen, is this something you cooked up with Gloria?"

She looked hurt for a moment.

"What do you mean?"

"Well, she's been trying to get me to go home for the past two days. Now you turn up needing a ride."

"Marcus, you have a suspicious mind. Did you know that?"

Ford dropped his hand, let the sun heat his face for a moment. They were probably right anyway. He had to ease up. Just a little.

"Okay," he said. "Okay."

The sun was behind them as they took the freeway back to West LA, light flaring in rear windows, pushing hard blocks of shadow ahead of the speeding traffic. Helen told him what the LA media were saying about the situation in the other hospitals.

"It's like you said the other night. They're focusing on the human-tragedy side of things. But the county health department has made a couple of statements about working in close consultation with the CDC."

"They're probably hoping it's just going to blow over," said Ford.

Suddenly he had a terrible pain in his head, as if he were trapped in a diver's suit, sinking fast, the pressure building up behind his eyes. He moved his head around, flipped on KKGO, got the climax of something overblown and symphonic—flipped it off again.

"Are you okay?"

"I just need to get some sleep."

Helen rubbed gently at the nape of his neck.

"There's something else, isn't there? Something you're not telling me."

Once again she was inside his head.

"I think I know what's happening," said Ford.

Helen removed her hand.

"Pardon me?"

"I think I know how these bugs are developing resistance."

And he told her his idea about the streptococcus. Told her about Allen bringing him the records of the infected.

Helen said nothing for a moment. Then she reached forward and turned up the air-conditioning. "So these reports . . . they all showed—"

"From the data I was able to get hold of, you would have to say there's a correlation," said Ford. "It's hardly a statistical sample, but—"

"How long have you . . . ?"

"A couple of days."

"So . . . I don't understand. Why didn't you say something?"

Ford nodded. He had asked himself the same question.

"What difference would it make?"

"What do you mean?"

"Well, assuming I'm right. Assuming there is some kind of link. What difference will it make? I mean, one way or the other."

"I can't believe you're saying this."

He frowned.

"In a way, neither can I. A week ago and I would probably have gone straight to Patou or the county health department. But with all this . . . with Sunny . . . I realized that what I had to do was to stick close to my daughter for a change. To *be* there for her."

He looked at Helen's face. She was staring straight ahead.

"I mean what was I going to do? I wasn't going to go to Patou, anyway. Nobody in the Willowbrook is going to enter into a serious discussion with me about this idea. I'm suspended, for Christ's sake. Even Conrad had a hard time accepting what I had to say."

"He said that?"

"I could see he had his doubts. The only way this thing is going to be tested is in a laboratory. So who do I go to? I'm not going to run myself into the ground trying to get somebody at the health department or the CDC to listen. It could take weeks, and I . . . Sunny doesn't have weeks."

"But you have to tell somebody. I mean even if you're wrong. It might be important."

Ford sighed.

"Look, I told Conrad."

"No, I mean somebody who has the time and the knowledge to make something of it."

"Well, there is Professor Novak. He's the only person who seems to share my point of view on these things. But the way I see it, there's not much anybody can do even if I am right. We're just going to have to roll with it."

"But you are going to tell him? You are going to talk to him."

Ford nodded.

"Sure. We have an appointment. I'll tell him. He'll probably just give me some sound reason why this is all bullshit, anyway. And I . . . well, there are things he said to me."

"What things?"

"He said he had information for me, research. He said if I used it in the right way, it might be very helpful to me. He said it could be helpful for both of us, in fact."

"Helpful? What did he mean? Help you with the Willowbrook inquiry?"

Ford considered this for a moment.

"I don't know. Maybe that's all it was. But I suppose I was hoping he meant something . . . I don't know—*bigger*."

"Bigger?"

"I mean, maybe he knew something about what was happening in LA. Maybe the work he did at Helical, the research he's done since, could throw light on the resistance problem. Maybe he's found an answer. Maybe . . ."

Helen pushed back into her seat.

"Oh, Marcus," she said softly.

"What?"

He turned to look at her.

"*What?*"

"I can . . . look, I can see where you're going with this. And I under-stand . . . but—"

"Helen."

"You think somehow . . . You think *somehow* Novak will be able to help . . . with Sunny."

Ford looked back at the freeway. He had pushed the Buick danger-ously close to the back of a trailer. He eased off the gas. Breathed for a moment.

"Does that seem so crazy to you?"

Helen brushed the hair away from her forehead.

"I don't know," she said. "In your position maybe I'd feel the same."

Ford gave an emphatic nod.

"Damn right you would. I've got to hope for . . . I've got to feel I can *do* something. Otherwise . . ."

"I understand."

For a while they drove in silence. Ford got onto the 405, where the traffic slowed to a crawl. The air-conditioning was freezing his hands to the wheel. He switched it off.

"*Both* of you?" said Helen.

"Pardon me?"

"He said if you used this information, whatever it is, in the right way, it would be helpful to both of you?"

"That's right."

"And he didn't say how or why."

"No, but I'm hoping he will."

Helen's tired face was framed momentarily in the doorway. She reached across the passenger seat and stroked the thickly growing stubble on Ford's chin.

"Try to get some rest," she said simply.

"You too," said Ford, but she had already closed the door.

He watched her walk across the lawn and up to the building where Stern housed its sales and marketing operation, 11111 Santa Monica Boulevard. It was all steel and glass—more like an investment bank than a pharmaceutical company. He started the engine and then pulled round on Sepulveda to head back east.

It had been three days since he had slept for more than a couple of hours, and the thought of stretching out on his bed was, to say the least, appealing. He would sleep until six and then drive back to the Willowbrook.

Turning into Kirkside Road, he braced himself for the barrage of cameras. The media had eased off a little since the beginning of the staph outbreak. Now that there were cases all over town, they had other people to hound. But a few stragglers still remained, hopeful of hearing some bad news about the inquiry or the state of Sunny's health.

When he saw the black-and-white parked at the bottom of the drive, his first thought was that some neighbor must have called to complain about the reporters blocking the road. But, getting out of his car, he was confronted by two officers identifying themselves as Sergeant Duane Ruddock and Deputy Samuel Dorsey. They were from Homicide. And he was the one they wanted to talk to.

Rather than have their conversation broadcast on the Channel 4 News, Ford invited them into the house. They went into the kitchen, Dorsey, the younger of the two, appearing to check everything out from behind a pair of spooky reflector shades. Ford offered them iced tea, which they refused. It was Ruddock who spoke first.

"We're real sorry to bother you at this time, Dr. Ford, but we were hoping you might be able to help us with a case we're working."

"Surely," said Ford. "If I can. It's not a murder, I hope." He covered a nervous smile with his hand.

Dorsey took off his sunglasses and fixed Ford with a cool, speculative stare.

"Wouldn't be here if it wasn't," he said.

Ford had a momentary vision of Raymond Denny stretched out on the operating table minus his left leg. Could this be related to *that?*

"But who . . . ?"

Ruddock squeezed into the breakfast nook, and Ford found himself sitting down.

They were quiet for a moment, Ruddock giving him the same blank look of scrutiny. Ford felt as if he were some kind of specimen in a glass case. A fly had gotten in through a window screen and was buzzing back and forth in the heavy air. Eventually Ruddock spoke.

"Dr. Ford," he said, bringing his meaty hands together on top of a dog-eared notebook, "what is your relationship with Professor Charles Novak?"

Ford swallowed hard. The pain was back behind his eyes. It was new to him. Unfamiliar. Like a sudden increase in pressure. He was diving again. Going down.

"My . . ." he had to cough—clear his throat. "We only met . . . Is he *dead?*"

Again Ruddock stared. Ford looked across to Dorsey, who had remained standing. The shades were back on.

"I'm afraid so," said Ruddock. "We found him up at his house in Topanga Canyon yesterday evening, wearing a rope."

"Wearing a . . . ?"

"Hanged. He was hanging up at the top of the house. Dr. Ford?"

Ford was on his feet. He walked across to the sink and turned on the cold tap.

"We don't think he hanged himself," said Dorsey. "We think somebody strangled him, then put him up on the beam to make it look like he hanged himself. But in fact, he didn't."

"Hanged himself," said Ford. His head was pounding. He put a tumbler under the flow of cold water, watched it fill and overflow onto his hand. Dorsey and Ruddock exchanged a look.

"No," said Ruddock, "didn't hang himself. It wasn't suicide; it was murder. Ligature strangulation."

Ford looked at him.

"Professor Novak—"

"He was strangled with a rope, Dr. Ford. Then he was put up on the beam like a hanged man. There was even a note written on his computer. 'Time to end it.' You know the kind of thing."

"Jesus. Jesus Christ."

Ford drank thirstily, spilling water down his shirtfront.

"Dr. Ford, can you tell me how you knew Professor Novak?" Ruddock asked again.

"We met at a conference a few weeks ago. He was interested in a paper I wrote."

"Have you seen him since then? Been up at the house, maybe?"

"This is just . . ."

He couldn't take it in. What did it all mean? He tried to recall every scrap of conversation he'd ever had with Novak, everything Helen had ever told him. His mind was racing, but he couldn't make sense of what he was being told. It had to be random. Some nutcase breaking in and then . . . But why fake a suicide?

"Dr. Ford?"

"*Hey!*"

Ford turned to look at Dorsey. He had raised his voice. Shouted at him as if he were some kind of hoodlum. Ford splashed water onto his face and reached for a hand towel.

"I'm sorry," he said. "I'm sorry . . . I . . . I actually hardly know the guy, hardly knew the guy, but I was supposed to be meeting him tonight."

"Why?" It was Ruddock now. Still sitting at the table. "What were you meeting him for?"

Ford frowned. They were treating him like a suspect.

"It was something . . . a technical matter. It's difficult to . . . I don't think you'd be interested."

Ruddock's eyelids came down just a little, so that the light went out of his eyes.

"We're just looking for a little help here, Dr. Ford," he said, letting a little cold steel come into his voice in a scary, practiced way.

Ford looked down at the yellow hand towel.

"Well, it had to do with what is happening at the Willowbrook. I don't know if you've been following all—"

"The Denny thing?" It was Dorsey now. "The officer whose leg you cut off?"

Ford felt his face grow hot.

"No," he said, his voice barely audible. "No, it had nothing to do with that."

"So what did it have to do with, Dr. Ford?"

Ford stared at his reflection in Dorsey's shades. He'd had about enough now.

"Plasmid transference. Jumping genes."

Dorsey smiled, took the shades off. It didn't make him look any more friendly.

"That's interesting," he said. "What does it mean?"

"Microbiology," said Ford. "Medicine. I am a doctor, in case you hadn't heard."

Ruddock gave his partner a tight, irritable look and took over the questioning again.

"Just prior to his death Professor Novak had been making a lot of improvements to his home security," he said. "Have you any idea why that was?"

"Of course not," said Ford. "I hardly knew him. We talked biology. I never went near his home."

Ruddock wrote something down in his book.

"Just so that we're clear about this, Dr. Ford, can you tell us where you were yesterday evening?"

He *was* a suspect.

"I was at the Willowbrook hospital with my daughter. She's very sick. I've been there for the past three days."

Ruddock nodded, wrote a little more.

"Okay, at the hospital. Got it."

He put the notebook away and slowly pushed himself up from the table.

"We can check that out easily enough," said Dorsey. "In the meantime, we'll need your prints. Just so we can exclude any prints you might have left at the house."

"I already told you," said Ford, "I've never been there."

Dorsey's mouth pushed into a hook. It was his cynical cop's smile. His lightless eyes held Ford for a moment.

"Yeah, that's right," he said. "You did say that."

3

"I don't understand it, Marcus. They're certain it wasn't suicide? They actually said that?"

Ford pulled open the refrigerator door and stood staring into it, trying to remember what it was he was looking for, trying just to concentrate on the next thing he had to do. He'd called Helen again and again, but she had been tied up in meetings all afternoon. He couldn't rest. He had to try and make sense of what was happening, to understand why every time he thought things couldn't get worse, they *did* get worse. How every avenue of hope was blocked off before he could reach it. He felt suffocated, encircled. He needed to know he was not alone. The truth was, he needed her. At last she had arrived, looking almost as tired as he did, still in her work clothes. He felt bad about having resented her presence at the Willowbrook. She was only trying to help, to support him in his hour of need. And here she was again. The very least he could do was give her a drink.

"It was meant to look that way. That's what they said. But it was definitely murder. Ligature strangulation." Helen instinctively put her hand over her throat. "They wanted my fingerprints and everything. I really think the sons of bitches have me down for a suspect."

He reached into the fridge and took out two cans of Budweiser, then remembered that it wasn't beer Helen had asked for, but coffee. He was going to make fresh coffee for them both.

"They fingerprinted you right here?" she said. "Just like that?"

"No. They wanted me to go with them, all the way over to Commerce. I told them if they wanted my prints, they could send someone out here. They said they'd do just that. I don't think they liked me too much."

Helen sat down on the sofa. The news of Novak's death seemed to have shaken her, more than Ford had thought it would. After all, it wasn't as if she knew him. She had only met him once. But then again, Ford thought, as a trauma surgeon maybe it was different for him. In his line of work meeting people who were about to die was an everyday occurrence. And besides, he had Sunny to worry about.

"Did they . . . Did they say anything else?" she asked. "Was there a break-in? Was anything stolen?"

"I didn't ask. But I don't think so. I mean, who ever heard of a thief going to that kind of trouble? What would be the point?"

For a while neither of them spoke. He'd been hoping that she would say something, suggest something. She knew about Novak. Maybe his death *meant* something. But all she could do was sit there on his sofa, her hands pressed together between her knees, going over the same obvious questions. But then, what more could she do? What more could anyone do?

It was already nighttime outside. Over the yard the sky was a dark rectangle of streetlight on smog. Ford felt as if the darkness were gathering around him, congealing, pressing in on him until there was nothing left but to lie down and surrender. He was so tired. He wanted to sleep, to sleep the night through and wake up to find that nothing had changed after all, that the last two weeks had never happened. He wanted his old life back: his job, his team, his purpose, above all, his daughter. Yet it was his old life that seemed now like the dream, a structure built on sand. And he knew that if he did lie down to sleep, it would be a new, darker life that he would wake up to.

Helen reached over and turned on a light.

"Did you tell them about the apartment?" she said.

"The apartment?"

"At Haverford Avenue. Where you and Novak were supposed to meet."

"No, I . . ." Ford thought for a moment. "No. I guess I just assumed they knew about it. They knew about the meeting, so—"

"But they found Novak at his house, right? In the mountains."

"That's right. I'm sure they ... Yes, in Topanga Canyon. That's what they told me. Hey, we could go there," he said.

He stood up.

Helen frowned. "Novak's apartment? Why?"

"Because the police may not know it exists. And maybe someone there can tell us something. Maybe ... It's a long shot, but maybe Novak had a girlfriend there or something. She might know what he wanted to talk about."

Ford took the wallet from his discarded jacket and checked inside. The slip of paper was still there: *Novak 9pm 15500 Haverford Ave Apt 12 Code—XA 3747.* He held it up between two fingers.

Helen looked at him. There was an intensity in her gaze. In her dark, dilated pupils he saw both exhilaration and fear. Just as on their first date, at the seafood place on Ocean Boulevard, he sensed a complexity, an inner world of impulses and desires that her outward behavior rarely more than hinted at.

Lights went on in the house opposite. From the other side of the fence came the sound of a door opening, the friendly bark of a dog.

"Okay, let's go there tomorrow morning," Helen said. "Maybe Novak—"

"Let's go now. Why wait?"

Ford grabbed his jacket.

"Marcus, we can't ... You're in no state to—"

"Helen, maybe the police don't know about the apartment yet, but they're bound to find out. The morning could be too late. You coming?"

"Marcus, wait."

She came over and took hold of him by the arm.

"Marcus."

She reached up and touched his unshaven face. She felt for him, pitied him; he could sense it. But he didn't want to be pitied. He wanted to do something.

"Marcus, you go over there looking like ... like this, and you're gonna scare the hell out of people. At least get cleaned up, take a shower. We have to do this right, or else we could ..."

She put her arms around him and held him for a moment. *Or else we could end up like Novak,* was that what she was going to say? And it came to him, even through the exhaustion and fear, what a step this was for her, what she was prepared to risk for him.

"Okay," he said, letting her slip the jacket off his shoulders. "Okay. A shower. And coffee."

They took her car, a red BMW convertible. They went west on Santa Monica Boulevard, then followed the Coast Highway north. She drove, Ford sitting in silence beside her, sheltering his eyes from the glare of the oncoming traffic. He tried not to think about Sunny, about her lying there at the Willowbrook, fighting for her life. It made him want to turn the car around and go back right away, just to hold her hand, to let her know that he was there. The thought that she might wake up and find him gone was unbearable. But as Gloria had told him, he had to be stronger than that. He had to find a way to stop what was happening—just in case Dr. Lee and the Code Blue team couldn't. He rolled down the window and breathed deep the salt air. A stiff wind was driving line after line of breakers up the beach, throwing foam into the air.

"Helen, I know you think . . ."

Helen turned to look at him.

"What?"

Ford kept his eyes on the road.

"Suppose, just suppose, a pharmaceutical company came up with a new generation antibiotic. Like the synthetic DNA drug you told me about. Omega."

Helen pursed her lips. Ford could sense her stifling a sigh.

"Could there be any reason why they wouldn't come out with it? File patents, start production? Any reason at all?"

Helen didn't answer at once. She reached for the dash and hit a button on the air-conditioning, then another.

"In theory," she said when she was done. "Sure."

"In theory?"

"I mean there *could* be circumstances in which you might delay an announcement, but Marcus, at Helical—"

"What sort of circumstances?"

This time she did sigh.

"Well, first of all the company would have to be pretty confident that nobody else was going to beat them to it. Otherwise it would be suicide. But, assuming that was the case, then commercial considerations might come into play."

"Like what, Helen?"

Helen checked the mirror. A big truck was coming up behind them. She began to accelerate.

"It's like this. A drug takes between eight and ten years to develop, typically. Including trials and everything, that translates into an upfront cost of maybe three hundred to four hundred million dollars, sometimes more. When you're making that kind of investment, you want the maximum market impact for the longest possible time."

"But a patent gives you a fourteen-year monopoly, right?"

"Sure. But by the time you get through the Food and Drug Administration, do the marketing, fend off half a dozen bogus lawsuits for patent infringements, the most you're likely to end up with is eleven years. After that all your competitors can make the same product—they call them generics—except that they haven't got all your development costs to pay off. So they can undercut you, take away your whole market."

"Just what sort of market are we talking about here, Helen? I mean, what would it be worth? Roughly."

"Well, let's see. Among antibiotics, Ciproxin's the number one seller at the moment. That's one of Bayer's products. Generates about one and a half billion dollars in sales."

"You mean every year? One and a half *billion* dollars every year?"

"Roughly. Of course antibiotics is a very crowded part of the market, because the underlying biotechnology is mostly pretty old. I shouldn't think Cipro's total market share is much more than three and a half percent—four percent at the very most."

Ford tried to do the math in his head. It meant that the total size of the antibiotics market was nearly forty billion dollars per year. How much of that market could a new-generation drug expect to take? One percent? Ten percent? Twenty? Until now it had never occurred to Ford to think about the money. He'd always thought about medication in terms of problems and solutions—medical problems, scientific answers. He thought about Omega the same way, in terms of what it could do for a patient, what it could do to save a human life. Sure, he knew that drug companies liked to push their products, that doctors in general practice tended to rely on them too heavily, but that was different somehow. You could put it down to laziness or ignorance or even simple overenthusiasm. But the way Helen was talking, he began to sense something more threatening. Once again he felt himself passing through the shadow of a world of high stakes and hidden purposes, where he was a stranger.

"But I still don't see why you wouldn't want to file your patent as soon as possible. I mean, why wait?"

"Like I said, Marcus, you probably wouldn't."

"But there could be circumstances. You said—"

"Okay, yes. We're talking antibiotics. Okay. You could take the view . . . I mean, it's a fact that the market for new antibiotics is getting hungrier every day. This resistance problem has been on the increase for years, and . . . well, as we know, the old drugs are getting less and less effective. Remember, you've got your patent for a fixed period only. After that, everybody can make it."

"So . . . you're saying you might decide to stay out of the market until . . ."

"Until Cipro, Augmentin, Rocephin—as many of the market leaders as possible—become unreliable. It would be a very risky strategy. And I sure as hell wouldn't recommend it. But, in the end, it might pay off."

Ford turned to face her, bracing himself against the dash.

"So the rumors about Omega could have been true. Helical could have—"

"No, Marcus, not Helical. They were a young company. They needed a breakthrough. It was a matter of survival for them. There's no way—"

"But they could have sold their research to somebody else, a bigger company. Maybe they sold out, made a deal in secret or something. Maybe they didn't want to wait for a surge in the share price to get rich."

They were heading inland now, climbing through parkland towards the hilltops of Pacific Palisades.

"We're almost there," Helen said, checking her watch. It was coming up to ten o'clock.

They found 15500 on the northernmost section of Haverford Avenue, a secluded stretch of road that looped around a line of Scotch pines and cedars. The building was a condo development, four floors high with tall windows and a distinctive white-and-gray stone facade, suggesting a marriage between the classical and the modern. It looked classy, even by the standards of the area.

"Hey, wait a second," said Helen, squinting up through the windshield as she cut the engine. "I know this place. It's a Fred Johnson. Won a whole stack of awards."

"A Fred who?"

"Johnson. He's pretty big. I saw it in a magazine. Built to six times earthquake standards or something." The place looked at least half empty. Some of the windows had an X of duct tape over them. "Marcus, these apartments start at . . . must be three quarters of a million. Are you sure you got the number right?"

"He said it was a new building. This has to be it." Ford unbuckled his seat belt. "Listen, you wait here, okay?"

"Marcus, I didn't mean—"

"I know. But one trespass charge is enough. At least I've got an invitation."

Helen sighed.

"Okay," she said. "But . . . just watch yourself, will you?"

Ford got out. The street was empty, silent but for the stirring of the trees. A carpet of pine needles deadened his footsteps as he crossed over and headed for the entrance at the corner of the building.

The security cameras were already in place, one on the front of the building, another just inside the glass doorway, looking out. There was no way of knowing whether they were working or not. Ford cupped a hand against the glass and stared into the lobby. There were stacks of tiles leaning against one wall, a pile of heavy-duty paper bags, a spool of electrical cable. Opposite the elevator was another camera. A faint yellow light shone down from above the stairwell, illuminating the bottom steps.

The keypad was to the left of the door, next to a set of buzzers numbered one to twelve. It was just as Novak had said. Ford reached into his wallet for the entry code, holding the scrap of paper towards the streetlight behind him.

He was about to tap in the numbers when he heard a car approaching. Ford took a couple of steps back into the shadows. It was a Jaguar, black. It slowed down to a walking pace as it coasted past the building—a thump of loud music suddenly audible—then sped away towards Sunset. Ford stepped out again into the light, glancing back at Helen in the BMW. The polished glass of the windshield hid her face.

A faint click told him that the code had been recognized. Ford pushed open the door and stepped inside. Magically, a light went on over his head. The camera stared down at him expectantly, as if he were some exotic insect under a glass. He could see his tiny distorted reflection in the lens. He went quickly to the elevator and pressed the call button, aware now of the adrenaline pumping through his system. What was he going to say if he found the police waiting for him? Keeping an appointment with a dead man wasn't an easy thing to explain. They'd question him, maybe take him in if they didn't like the answers, take him away from Sunny. He stepped away from the elevator. The stairs would be better. He climbed slowly, treading softly, looking up above him for any sign of movement. As he reached each new floor invisible sensors picked up his presence, turning on banks of discreetly recessed lights.

The hallways were marble. Marble on the floors, marble on the walls, with some kind of pink stone inlaid in a Roman-style pattern. The grainy hardwood double doors were six feet wide, with heavy bronze fittings, promising something grander on the other side than regular two-bedroom apartments. Ford listened for voices, for music, the sound of a television, but there was nothing. Novak had planned on a very private meeting.

Apartment 12 was on the top floor, opposite a single window that looked out over the treetops towards the black ocean. On the horizon the lights of ships fluttered and winked like drowning stars. There came the muffled clunk of a car door, hurried footsteps on the road. From under the canopy of swaying branches the hood of the red BMW was visible, but no patrol cars, no people. The street was still deserted.

Suddenly the hall lights cut out again. Ford turned and edged his way back towards the apartment. From somewhere below him came a faint mechanical hum, a tiny vibration—another automated system, probably. The building bristled with technology, only most of it wasn't working yet, or wasn't working right. That was why Novak had given him the entry code. The only odd thing was why he should want to meet here at all.

Ford was sure the doors would be locked. The whole building seemed empty, barely ready for occupation. He took a firm hold of one of the handles and turned it.

The door wasn't locked.

Ford raised a hand to knock, but something made him hesitate. The was no light coming from inside, no sound except the wind whistling over the roof. Was the building so new they hadn't even fitted the locks? He ran a finger up the side of the door. Around the catch the wood was cracked and splintered. *Forced entry.* Maybe whoever killed Novak had come looking for him here first, found him gone, moved on. Ford pushed back the door and stepped inside.

It had to be the biggest apartment in the building. A split-level penthouse, the main room gave onto a broad balcony overlooking land-scaped gardens and was crowned with a domed skylight twenty-five feet overhead. It had to be worth millions, design awards or not. But Helen was right: it didn't square with the awkward, badly dressed man they had met at the NIH conference. It didn't square with anything they knew about Novak. But then, neither had his death.

There was no furniture except for a single office chair on casters. Next to it, on the ground, lay an answering machine, an empty bottle of scotch whisky and a couple of plastic cups. The red eye of the machine winked slowly on and off. Someone had left a message.

Ford crouched down, searching for the replay button. But it was too dark. He needed light. He stood up again, was about to head for the door. Froze.

There was someone else in the apartment.

He could hear movement, hear a metal drawer open, the rustle of papers. It came from a passageway leading off the main room. And now he could just make out a faint yellow light thrown across the polished wooden floor.

He edged back towards the phone. He had to call the police. But could he do it and not be overheard? Helen had a phone in her car. He could make a run for it. But then the police might be too late—too late for him, too late for Sunny. He picked up the whisky bottle and walked slowly towards the source of the light.

The door was ajar. Ford saw gloved hands, a glimpse of denim, the top of a jogging suit, the hood pulled up, saw papers and files being thrust into a black plastic sack.

He stepped back. It sounded as though there was only one of them. He would wait for the guy to leave, then hit him from behind at the base of the skull. He would wait at the end of the passage, around the corner, aim for the occipital bone. A bruise would be enough to render him unconscious, so long as he wasn't high on something. No need for a fracture. Ford turned, anxious to get back, to get in position before the guy was finished. He didn't see anyone behind him until it was too late.

The effect of the pepper spray was instant. It felt as if his eyes were on fire, melting in their sockets. The pain was unbelievable. He couldn't see, couldn't breathe. He tried to cry out, dropping to his knees, choking, gasping for breath.

The last thing he sensed before he blacked out was somebody barging past him, knocking him on his face.

4

―――――――――

"Breathe, breathe. Just try to . . ."

Ford pulled hard, air rasping in his seared throat.

"That's right. In and out. Try to fill your lungs."

It sounded like Helen's voice. He squinted up at the face looming over him but could see nothing through his streaming eyes.

"Hel . . . ?"

"Don't try to speak. Breathe."

"You're . . . You're telling . . ."

Ford coughed, retched. He blinked the tears from his eyes, but they filled again immediately,

It was ten minutes before he could get to his feet.

Helen took him through to the kitchen and pressed a tumbler of cold water into his hand, watching as he drank thirstily, tumbler after tumbler. Finally he could make out her worried face.

"I got nervous waiting in the car," she said. "So I decided to come up. What the hell happened?"

Ford refilled the tumbler under the faucet. His hand was shaking, and it was painful to swallow.

"Jesus. I thought . . . I thought I was going to die. I think it was pepper spray. LAPD uses it. Jesus." He took another gulp of water. "I came in . . . The door was open, so I just came in. Helen, there was somebody *in* here. I saw them stuffing papers, documents into a bag."

"And they zapped you with the spray?"

"No. I was waiting for them to come out of that"—he gestured towards the doorway—"that room down there. Then somebody else jumped me from behind."

"My God. Did you get a look at him?"

Ford shook his head.

"No . . . no, I . . . Like I said. I was looking at this guy and the next thing I know my eyes are on fire and I can't breathe."

"Poor baby." She pushed the hair from his forehead. "I think if you wash your eyes with water, it might help."

When Ford came out of the bathroom five minutes later, he found Helen standing by the window in the huge living room, looking out into the gardens. Tall firs dipped and swayed in the wind, throwing shadows across a landscape of winding paths, fountains, and flowering shrubs.

Ford walked over to the answering machine. The red light was no longer flashing.

"I already listened to it," Helen said. "There's nothing. Just the sound of someone hanging up."

"Pity," said Ford. He looked around the room. "Can you believe this place? Must be worth a couple of million, at least."

"Maybe he inherited some money."

"Right," said Ford, making a wry mouth. "He just inherited a couple of million and sank it in a superdeluxe condo he doesn't use. I mean, there's nothing here. No furniture, no pictures, nothing."

"It could have been an investment. Palisades came through the earthquake more or less untouched. Maybe he got burned on the stock market, decided to switch into real estate."

"I don't know." Ford looked away, shaking his head. "I don't think so somehow."

Helen walked through to the study. Ford could see that she was buzzing with suppressed excitement. He followed her, standing in the doorway, still rubbing at his throat.

There were filing cabinets, heaps of books, a desk, a lamp. Papers and floppy disk covers were strewn all over the floor, and something, a chart maybe, had been ripped from a bulletin board. Scraps of paper were still snagged on the pushpins.

"Well, even if he wasn't living here, he was using it for work," said Ford.

"Yeah, but why? Why not work at home?"

"Wait a second. Those Homicide cops told me Novak had been beefing up his home security. Maybe he was doing something . . . I don't know, something he wanted to keep secret. He'd stand a better chance in a modern building than in some rickety old house in Topanga."

"Well, if that was the reason, it didn't exactly work out. My guess is whoever broke in must have known what they were looking for. I don't think your typical thief is interested in this kind of material."

She took a book down from a stack on the shelves and gave a low whistle.

"Look at this stuff: *National Institutes of Health Study on Antibiotic Resistance Worldwide.* Sanders and Sanders—*Beta-Lactam Resistance in Gram-Negative Bacteria: Global Trends and Clinical Impact.*"

"How about this?" said Ford, flipping through another stack. "*Methicillin-Resistant Staphylococcus Aureus in U.S. Hospitals 1975–1991, Infection Control and Hospital Epidemiology.* Cohen—*Epidemiology of Drug Resistance: Implication for a Post Antimicrobial Era.* He was really on top of this."

"But why? What was he trying to do up here?" Helen put down the book she was holding.

"What's that?"

She was pointing to a map that had been taped to a bare wall. In fact, it was four large-scale maps stapled together showing Los Angeles and its neighboring areas, going up as far as Kern County and south to San Diego. They crossed the room to take a closer look. Cotton threads radiated from a galaxy of colored pins. All around the map were tiny cramped notes that gave dates and locations followed by three-digit numbers.

"An epidemiological study?" said Helen, touching a finger to her lips.

"One time when we spoke on the phone, he asked me about an etiologic agent—said he was looking at a descriptive epidemiology sheet. Maybe the staph cases at the Willowbrook . . ." Ford peered closely at the South Central area. There they were: not the staph, but the *pneumoniae* cases. The Willowbrook was marked with a red pin. Following a cotton thread out to a scrap of paper, Ford read "Lynwood, Vernon, and Huntingdon Park." Against each location, there was a date and then a number. "It's all here," he said. "What do you think the numbers refer to?"

"Files, maybe." Helen turned and looked at the room. "In those cabinets. Or maybe on the computer."

Ford continued to look at the map.

"There are cases going back nearly ten years here, if these numbers are dates, I mean. Look, 'Loma Alta Pasadena, 8/1987. r. 143. Coronado Street, Placentia, 5/1988. r. 481,' and then a question mark in brackets. Why . . . Why was he going to all this trouble?"

"We need to find out what the numbers refer to. There's going to be a lot more detail there."

They started with the filing cabinets. But whoever Ford had surprised had got there first. The cabinets had been all but stripped. Of the documents that remained, the latest cases dated from 1983. Either the intruder had taken everything after that date, or Novak had started to put his data onto computer at that time.

The computer was a chunky Compaq with floppy disk and CD-ROM ports. Helen flipped on the machine, but after several minutes of keying in instructions, pushed back from the desk in frustration.

"I think someone's tampered with it."

Ford took Helen's place in the cheap swivel chair. But it was no use. They could get the operating system up, but as soon as they tried to access any of the utilities, the whole system crashed.

"He must have fed in a virus or something. Damn it!" He slammed his fist against the table. Papers slid to the floor. "We're so close to . . ."

Helen was watching Ford from behind.

"To what?"

"I don't know. But this has to mean *something*—all this . . . all this stuff." Ford looked around at the office with all its teeming detail and information. "What the hell was he doing?"

He pushed a hand back through his hair.

"Okay, okay. Let's be . . . Let's try to be logical."

He got up from the desk. Helen watched him as he walked back and forth.

"Let's start with what we know about him," said Ford. "He came to me at the conference. He was interested in my paper. He was interested in the cases at the Willowbrook. Okay. He was putting the data into his . . . into his study. He was doing an epidemiological study of resistance cases in the area. He's been doing it for a while. Maybe as far back as . . . it doesn't have to go right back to the first cases, but my guess is he's been doing it for a long time. Maybe even since he left Helical."

He stopped pacing and looked back at Helen.

"You say he just dropped out of the picture after Stern bought Helical?"

"As far as I know. He didn't take any other position."

"And that was in . . . ?"

"Ninety-two."

"Okay. So let's say he's been doing this for a few years, at least. Following all the specialist press, getting as much detail on cases as he can without actually being inside the CDC. And he's worried about somebody else finding out what he's been doing, whatever it is he's trying to prove."

He stopped for a moment. Thinking about it didn't help. It was just giving him a headache.

"So what was he trying to prove? I just can't see . . . Wait."

He started pacing again. Helen stayed where she was, watching him go back and forth, a serious, almost hostile, look on her face. She wanted to get out of there.

"He's in touch with a group of people. The people he referred to as 'the others' when we spoke on the phone. No, that's not right. What did he say to me? 'I have to talk with . . . *some people.*' Yes, that's what he said. '*Some people.*' He said it was a matter of professional etiquette, of protocols. I remember thinking he was some kind of Freemason, you know? Some kind of lodge member."

"Right," said Helen with cynical emphasis. "Freemasons."

"Well, who—?"

"All I know is, we're sitting in the apartment of a man who has just been choked to death. We're sitting here, having broken in—I mean that's the way the police would read it—with the lights on. I feel kind of vulnerable."

Ford looked at Helen's tired face.

"Helen, I can't leave here until I find something. I don't know . . . some kind of . . . There has to be something."

He crossed the room and leaned against the map, staring at the scores of entries. There was no discernible pattern. No particular spread. He recognized the names of a number of retirement homes in the Beverly Hills area. Old people. People with depleted immune systems. There were drug rehab facilities too. And hospitals—public ones, private ones: Harbor USC, La Pacifica, Southwestern Healthcare Corp.

"Helen, take a look at this. There are nine, ten, at least a dozen sets of references here from this year, from this *summer*. If these are resistance cases, nearly half of them have cropped up during the past two or three months."

Helen came over and stared at the map, scrutinizing the notes down each side.

"But they've nearly all got question marks beside them. Looks to me like they're only *possible* resistance cases. It's just a hypothesis, Marcus."

"A hypothesis that says—Jesus, Helen—this thing's all over the place. It isn't just the Willowbrook. It was *never* just the Willowbrook. It's been spreading right through the city."

"Oh, come on, Marcus. It *can't* be that bad. I mean if a hospital had a rash of resistance cases, why wouldn't they tell everyone? Why would they just keep quiet about it?"

"It isn't always that simple, Helen. People come in sick from some other disease or with some terrible wound. It isn't always easy to tell what exactly kills them in the end. Besides, if you were running a private hospital, would you want the whole world knowing you'd had a staph outbreak among your patients? What good would it do you?"

"All right, all right. Suppose Novak was right. The problem's bigger than we realized. I still don't see how that helps us. I don't see how it explains anything." She sighed and sat down behind the desk.

Ford studied the map once more, running his fingers over the stiff paper. At Box Springs Mountain Park in East LA there was a fold in the map that caused the heavy paper to bulge, making it difficult to read the scribbled note there. Ford pressed it flat, hoping to see better.

"Wait a minute."

Helen turned in the chair.

"What?"

"There's something here. Underneath."

Helen stood up, but she didn't move from where she was.

Ford turned back to the map and, detaching one of the taped corners, pulled it away from the wall. Pins fell. Scribbled notes fluttered to the floor. He had the terrible feeling he was destroying any chance of reconstructing Novak's work.

Then he saw the photograph.

It was in a beechwood frame, the frame itself fixed to the wall with brass screws. A group of maybe ten men smiled out of the picture in oddly-saturated color. Most of them were in shirtsleeves. Written at the bottom of the picture were the words *Helical, January 1992*.

Helen had joined him at the wall. Ford could feel her warm breath on his neck.

"It's just a photograph," she said, sounding almost relieved.

Ford stared at the three rows of faces. There was Novak, sitting down in the front row, an empty wine glass in his hand. Next to him was a thin guy with a crew cut. They had been celebrating. But what?

"It's the Helical team," said Ford, blankly.

"Novak, Finegold." Helen pointed. "That's Walter Auerbach. There's Lewis Spierenberg just behind Novak. Scott Griffen. They're all there. Novak was part of the Helical team. We already knew that."

"It's the only picture," said Ford reflectively. "The only picture in the whole apartment. And he's gone to the trouble of fixing it to the wall with brass fittings."

He looked at Helen. Nervous exhaustion and extreme anxiety plucked at the corner of her right eye.

"They're all holding wine glasses. It's a celebration, Helen. What were they celebrating in January 1992?"

"I don't know. Maybe they had just finished some important project."

Ford smiled.

"Omega, maybe. Maybe they'd just . . ."

Helen was already turning away. Ford went after her, taking hold of her by the arm.

"Maybe they had just finished some preliminary trials."

She looked up into his eyes.

"Marcus, we've been through all this. Stern *bought* Helical, remember? Omega was just an idea, a good one maybe, but just an idea. It never really got off the drawing board."

"So how come Novak has just been killed? How come somebody broke into his apartment?"

"Look, Marcus, we're standing in a multi-million dollar condo that belongs to a dead man. We don't know what he was up to. Maybe he just got mixed up in some dodgey real estate deal, borrowed money from the wrong people and paid the price. Isn't that the simplest explanation?"

Ford was no longer listening. He stared at the photograph.

"Helen, what if the people he wanted to talk to were the other members of the old Helical team?"

"What?"

"When I spoke to him on the phone, he said he had to talk to some people. Maybe it was the guys from Helical." He turned to her.

"I don't see what difference it makes."

She put her hands flat on his chest.

"Marcus, we have to get out of here. The police could turn up here any—"

They both froze, staring at each other wide-eyed. The telephone was ringing.

Ford hurried back down the corridor towards the main room. The phone kept ringing.

"Don't answer it!" said Helen. But Ford was already there.

He picked up the phone on the ninth ring.

"Hello?"

Helen came after him. She was shaking her head, willing him to put the phone down. Ford pressed his ear against the handset. A man's voice. Out of breath. Annoyed. A man who called himself Scott, a man who thought *he* was Novak.

"Jesus Christ, Chuck, I've been trying to reach you all day. I'm fed up with hearing your voice on that damned answering machine." There was a long rasping sigh, and then the sound of a cigarette being lit. Ford was about to say something—he didn't know what—when the man went on. "Anyway, I've talked to the others. They've all been contacted, just like I thought. And the message is loud and clear: as things stand, the protocol will not be invoked. That's the decision. And we're all expected to abide by it. They're watching, Charles. So if you're still planning to short-circuit the system, you can count me out, okay? Charles? Charles, are you there?"

Ford gripped the phone, tried to think of something. He felt the blood pulsing in his temples. All he could blurt out was—"*Yes.*"

What else could he say?

There was an agonizing pause. Ford thought he heard the man draw on his cigarette. Then the line went dead.

Ford put the phone back down. Helen was on her knees beside him, a document trembling in her right hand, her left hand still pressed against her mouth.

"Who was it? What did they say?" she said, her voice shrunk to a whisper.

"He said his name was . . . Scott."

"Scott?"

"Yes. I'm sure I've . . . Wait a minute, Helen. The photo. It was Scott Griffen. Griffen, right?"

"Could be. What did he say?"

"He thought I was Novak. He said he'd talked to the others about this . . . this decision. About some protocol. '*We're all expected to abide by it,*' he said."

"Abide by it . . ." Helen repeated the words, trying to make them fit somehow.

"And, Helen, he said something about Novak wanting 'to short-circuit the system.' "

Helen stared at him in silence. They both stood up.

"I think we'd better leave," Ford said.

5

Ford was climbing out of the Buick when he saw Gloria Tyrell hurrying down the steps into the staff parking lot, carrying stacks of empty cardboard boxes. She was followed by Marlene Fuller and Norma Jackson, two of the junior Emergency Department nurses.

"Gloria?"

"Huh?"

She lost her footing for a moment and stumbled. The boxes went skidding across the asphalt.

"Oh, Lord!"

Ford knelt down to help her gather them up again. Gloria was panting. A bead of perspiration ran down her cheek.

"Gloria, what the hell is going on?"

"I don't know. I just don't know, Dr. Ford. It's crazy. It's all gone crazy in there."

He thought for a second she was going to burst into tears.

"Haynes fired the catering company," said Marlene Fuller matter-of-factly.

"What?"

"This morning. They're gone."

"They were gone anyhow," said Norma Jackson. She'd only been with the Willowbrook for about six weeks and was still very much under Gloria's wing. "That's why he fired them. They wouldn't come in. Said it was too dangerous."

"Said they had responsibility to their staff," said Marlene.

Ford looked at the three women.

"So—what?—You're going *shopping?*"

"Then we gotta make sandwiches. For three hundred people."

"Ain't no one else to do it," said Gloria, getting up again. "We're missing people from all over. Even some of my nurses. Everyone's taking off, Dr. Ford. Everyone's scared."

"Case they catch something," added Marlene. "Press too."

She nodded across the parking lot. It was true. Where the crush of TV crews and outside broadcast vehicles had been a couple of days earlier there was now just an empty space, littered with fast-food debris and old newspapers.

"There was a story in some magazine," said Norma.

"Called us a 'plague ship,'" said Marlene. "'Plague ship adrift in South Central,' that's what it said."

"On the cover," added Norma.

"Way everybody's been callin' in sick, you'd think it was true." And Ford saw that in spite of her dismissive tone Marlene Fuller was scared too.

"What about . . . ?" He gave Gloria's arm a squeeze. "What about Sunny?"

Gloria looked crestfallen. It was clear that in all the chaos she had momentarily forgotten about his daughter. She smiled, trying to be encouraging.

"Dr. Lee's been keeping a real close eye on her. She . . . She had a peaceful night. Don't worry about all this. You go on up now."

And she scurried off, leaving Ford standing there with an unsteady feeling in the pit of his stomach.

The lobby was in chaos. Most wards had been closed to visitors, but the visitors refused to go home. They crowded around the reception desk, demanding to know if their loved ones were all right, shouting at the two beleaguered women trapped behind their transparent Perspex screens. Two security officers looked on, powerless to intervene.

Most of the overnight cleaning staff hadn't come in. On the landings and corridors the waste bins were full to overflowing. Outside the elevator Ford almost stepped in a pool of coffee that was slowly spreading across the linoleum floor. On the other side of the fire doors he came across one of the pediatric nurses and a porter arguing at the top of their voices about whose job it was to do what. Outside ICU an Hispanic woman, a complete stranger, blundered into him and ran away before he could even ask what she thought she was doing there. Ford had never seen anything like it, not even during the '92 riots. Back then they had been short-staffed—the hospital had been in the middle of a war zone and many people just couldn't get there—but everyone had kept their heads. There had been a camaraderie in the face of adversity that had made him proud. But something about the present crisis seemed to have the opposite effect. Maybe it was just that this time the enemy was *inside* the hospital, instead of outside on the streets. The Willowbrook was tainted—as much a part of the problem as a part of the solution—*a plague ship*, as the magazine had said, adrift and rudderless. Yet no one knew how or why. It was no wonder morale was starting to crack.

He hurried on towards pediatric ICU, squeezing his way past a trolley piled high with laundry being wheeled down the corridor by one of the Code Blue team surgeons. Sunny's room was at the end of the corridor. A large red notice had appeared on the door, emblazoned with a black biohazard symbol and the words ISOLATION WARD—KEEP OUT. Ford peered through the glass window. Sunny's bed was screened off behind plastic sheeting. He could just make out the impression of her motionless body beneath the bedclothes.

The door opened. It was Simon Lee. He looked exhausted, his eyes bloodshot, his face shiny with sweat.

"Dr. Ford. Good morning, I was—"

"How is she?"

Ford went to the bed, pulling back one of the plastic sheets. Sunny lay there, her eyes tight shut, a vacant, death-mask stillness in her features. He stroked her hair, looking into her face.

"I'm here now, honey," he murmured.

The noise of the ventilator was loud beside him.

"She's not . . . I think she's asleep at the moment," said Lee. "She seems to drift in and out of consciousness. It isn't . . . It's getting difficult to tell."

Ford looked back at him.

"Difficult to tell?"

Lee looked down at his clipboard.

"The paralysis seems to be spreading. She's lost the use of her arms completely, and we haven't seen any movement in the lower body since last night. It may be that she is conscious, but just can't . . . very easily . . ."

The idea that Sunny was awake, conscious, but unable even to open her eyes, was trapped inside a body that would not respond, was almost beyond bearing. Ford let his fingers drift down across her skin, over her eyes, moving the lids, so that the pupils became visible for a moment. Could she see him, hear him? Could she feel his touch?

"What about the antitoxin? Isn't it working?"

"Yes, it is, up to a point. Only . . . Dr. Ford, do you mind . . . ? Do you mind if we step into my office?"

Ford sighed and kissed Sunny's forehead.

"I'll be back in a minute, honey, okay?"

He stayed there for a moment, hoping to see something, anything that could be interpreted as a response. But Sunny remained perfectly still.

In Lee's office Ford refused coffee and took a seat opposite the desk.

"Just as well," said Lee. "The machine's out of cups, and there's no milk left. I could wash one up if—"

"Please, just tell me about Sunny. What's happening?"

Lee ran his fingers around the inside of his collar. It was hot in his office. He glanced at the air-conditioning unit by his window, but seemed to think better of adjusting it.

"The truth is we're entering uncharted territory here. I have to be honest with you, with each day that passes the existing data on this type of problem becomes more and more . . . well, irrelevant. I mean, we caught this infection very early. Normally we'd have licked the problem by now. But we're six days in and, well, at best we're holding our own."

"But you said the antitoxin was working."

"I believe it is effective. We saw a big dip in her toxin level after the first dose was given to her. I should have another set of test results by now, but . . ."

"But what?"

"The lab . . . They've had problems. I don't know."

"Jesus Christ!"

"Supplies they were expecting didn't show up, they said. And some of their technicians, they—"

"Called in sick, I suppose."

"I've been on them all morning. The problem we have is that the *botulinum* itself is still there in her gut. It's still releasing toxin. And my hunch is the amount of toxin being produced is rising. That's why the paralysis is spreading. I think the bug may actually be replicating in Sunny's gut—maybe only slowly, but"—he sighed—"you must see the implications."

Ford locked his hands together and stared down at his feet. He didn't want to think it through, but he had to. He had to know how much time he had. The botulinal antitoxins were extracted from enzyme-treated equine serum—horse serum. A substance that was so entirely alien to the human body was always likely to produce an unwelcome reaction in humans treated with it over any length of time. For twenty years the medical profession had called for the development of a treatment based on human biochemistry, but the pharmaceutical industry had declined to oblige.

"How much more antitoxin can she take, Dr. Lee?"

"That's impossible to say. She's had two doses so far. That's forty mils in total. But I'm afraid we are beginning to see signs of hypersensitivity. In particular, there seems to be generalized abdominal swelling. I'm sure this is due to edema, and I'm prescribing a diuretic to deal with it, but . . ."

"Go on."

"But my main concern is that this edema, this buildup of fluid, suggests that Sunny had—or is developing—an allergic reaction to the antitoxin. Edema is a classic early warning of anaphylaxis. To be blunt, I'm afraid if we keep on pumping the patient—I mean Sunny—with this antitoxin, we could push her into anaphylactic shock."

Ford felt as if the breath had been sucked out of him, and he hadn't the strength to take another. Anaphylaxis was simply an abnormal reaction to a particular foreign substance, one in which histamine was indiscriminately pumped out into the system causing dilation of blood vessels and contraction of smooth muscle—the type found in the heart and lungs. Anaphylactic shock was an extreme version of the same thing. It could involve violent constriction of the bronchioles, heart failure, collapse of the circulatory system, death.

"Normally, there'd only be a very slim chance of such a reaction," Lee went on, "five or six percent at worst. But normally you'd never have to take the antitoxin treatment much beyond the forty-milliliter level. Normally the toxin you start with is the only toxin you have to deal with. But this damned bug . . . *It's still there.*"

Ford stared. The bug was slowly killing Sunny, and now Dr. Lee was telling him that the only treatment would also kill her before long. He took a breath, struggling to keep his voice steady.

"What do you recommend, Doctor?"

Lee leaned back in his chair, closed his eyes for a moment as if in pain, sighed.

"We can't let the toxin just build up. We can't simply surrender the entire nervous system. We have to . . . We have to . . ." For a moment it struck Ford that the man opposite him had nothing more to say, nothing more he could say. "We have to find a way to get this bug out of her system."

Ford stood up.

"How much time do we have? In your opinion?"

Lee shook his head.

"Marcus, I don't know. As things stand, days . . . a week perhaps. Then we may have to look at more drastic measures. Like I said, this is something new. There just aren't any case histories to draw on."

"Thank you, Dr. Lee."

Ford started to go.

"Dr. Ford?"

Lee was standing. He looked defeated, lost. What he was about to say was clearly difficult for him. In his own quiet way he was a very proud man, proud of his skills, his profession—just like Ford himself.

"I'd be the first to admit that I'm not . . . that this is not necessarily the best place for Sunny to be right now. There may be other hospitals, other teams, specialists, who've more experience with this kind of thing. Especially since we're . . . since we're having all these practical difficulties. What I'm saying is, I'd entirely understand—I'd give my backing—if you wanted her moved elsewhere."

* * *

Ford found his office locked up, and he didn't have a key. He had to use a pay phone outside the kitchens. He called Helen's direct line at Stern, but her secretary told him that she was not in, couldn't say when she would be back. He called home, hoping to find a message on his answering machine, but Helen hadn't called. She'd promised to let him know the moment she found out where Scott Griffen was. She was better placed to locate him, she'd said. He was supposed to have been a big fish, a leading light in the world of pharmaceuticals. Someone at Stern would know where to find him. Ford should leave that part to her. It was better that he went back to Sunny, while Helen located Griffen. *So how long could it take?* It was already midmorning and she hadn't called. What was she *doing?* Of course, it was possible that Griffen too had retired, just like Novak. That would make it harder. That would take a lot more asking around. And it was still only a quarter past ten.

"Marcus?"

It was Conrad Allen. He was wearing a smart black polo shirt under his lab coat, and it looked as if he'd had a haircut. He was the first person Ford had seen that morning who didn't looked stressed.

"Hey, how's it going?" His voice softened. "How's Sunny?"

Ford tried to smile.

"Not so good. She's . . . She . . ."

He couldn't form the words. Just hearing her name seemed to touch it off. It seemed to open up a chasm inside him, a glimpse into the void that life would be without her. An existence without hope. He covered his eyes with his hand. It was all he could do not to sob. Allen put a hand on his shoulder.

"I know, I know. I looked in this morning. Lee told me the story. If . . . If you need anything. If there's anything I can do, Marcus, just . . ."

"Thank you." Ford took a deep breath, then another. "I appreciate it."

"Why don't we get some coffee? They still have coffee back there— if you get it yourself, that is." He began leading Ford towards the cafeteria. "Maybe we can even find something to put in it. A little bourbon, maybe, or—"

"Conrad."

They stopped.

"Conrad, what you said, the other day—about moving Sunny to Cedars-Sinai." Allen nodded, then looked down at his feet. "I want you to arrange it. If you can."

"Marcus—"

"You were right. I was wrong. I shouldn't have . . . I want the best for her, Conrad. The best."

"Marcus—"

"I don't care what it costs. Can you do it?"

Allen sighed, ran his fingers across his forehead.

"Marcus, I already tried. I already talked to them. Yesterday. Just in case you changed your mind."

"And?"

"They won't do it." Ford stared, uncomprehending. "I'm sorry. They said they couldn't take the risk. It's the same everywhere. Nobody wants these resistance cases. They're afraid they'll end up with the same problem. We can't even organize transfers to other public hospitals. It's health department policy, apparently."

"What is?"

"No movement of infected patients. Marcus, they're trying to ring-fence the problem, stop it from spreading. Each hospital's gotta fight its own corner. I checked with Haynes this morning. There was supposed to be an announcement, but . . ." He shrugged, despairingly. "I don't know."

"But this problem is *not* nosocomial." Ford was almost shouting. "Haven't they grasped that yet? It's *out there,* coming *in here.* Staff, patients. They aren't going to escape it like this."

"I know, Marcus, I know."

"They want to keep this thing out, they'll have to close down completely. Either that or screen all incoming patients, turn away the infected ones. Leave them out on the street."

"Some of them already are. That's what I heard. Patients carrying that strep are on their own, as far as some places are concerned. Yes, that's right, Marcus, your strep checked out. I talked to the laboratory people. Had them take a look. It looks like your strep is the guilty party."

"So what are they going to do about it?"

"The health department is supposed to be talking to the CDC about some kind of game plan."

"Great. Meanwhile I can't even get into my fucking office."

"I'm sure that's only a matter of time, Marcus. They can't—"

"I don't have time. I don't have time." He turned and went back to the phone, lifted the receiver. "I have to find that drug. I have to find Griffen. How do you . . . ? How do you find somebody when you . . . ? How do you find somebody when you don't know where the fuck to begin?"

Allen rested a firm hand on Ford's forearm.

"What number . . . ? What's the fucking number for . . . ? How do you get—"

"Marcus. Calm down. Calm down." For a moment they stood in silence, Ford aware only of the pounding of his heart. "What exactly are you looking for?"

Ford replaced the receiver.

"I need to locate a man named Scott Griffen. Dr. Scott Griffen. He works in pharmaceuticals, or did until a few years ago. I think . . . I think there's a chance he could help Sunny."

Allen looked at him. Ford sensed the inevitable skepticism. How could Griffen help? Wasn't Ford just clutching at straws?

"All right," Allen said. "Then I suggest we start with the in-house pharmacy people. God knows, they're not too busy right now. Paloma Jimenez. She's been in the business for years. If she can't help you, nobody can."

6

Paloma Jimenez had been more than helpful. She'd given him a promotional document produced by a company called Apex Inc. The corporate headquarters, it turned out, lay just a few miles away in Century City. The brochure was entitled *Apex Horizons*, and it was supposed to get you excited about the company's research-and-development effort. There were lots of photographs of people in white coats looking through microscopes or working with brightly colored chemicals, interspersed with pictures of happy, healthy children, pregnant women, and squeaky-clean senior citizens. On the first double-page spread was a picture of three executive types in dark suits gathered around the end of a shiny boardroom table. The caption read *"Dr. Arthur T. Ross (Director, Healthcare Policy), William B. Donnelly (Chief Executive Officer, Apex Inc.), Dr. Scott R. Griffen (Director, Research & Development)."*

Ford raced back up the freeway, stopping by his house on the way to Century City. Somewhere in the garage was a gun. It had been Carolyn's. Their first summer in LA, a friend of hers had been mugged downtown, and Carolyn had gone right out and bought one without even consulting him. They'd had a fight about it. Ford had wanted her to take it back. He knew exactly what guns could do to flesh, to bone. And he knew that people who owned them were more likely to end up shot. *"I won't have that thing in the house,"* he remembered saying. And so, in the end, they'd compromised on the garage. Carolyn could keep her gun so long as it was well out of reach.

He found the box at the back of the metal cabinet, behind an old portable heater and a jumble of tire tools. Brown cardboard, it was covered in dirt with a big smear of grease across the top. The make and model was printed in plain black type along the side: SIG-SAUER 220 .38 CAL. He yanked off the lid. The Sig lay cushioned in foam. Despite seven years of neglect, it looked as pristine as the day Carolyn had bought it, the metal smooth and hard, like polished black glass. It felt heavy in his hand, powerful. Cheap at two hundred dollars. "*Your basic automatic,*" the guy in the shop had told Carolyn.

The clip lay beneath the trigger, already loaded with its nine rounds. Ford snapped it into place, yanked the slide, took aim at his shadow on the back of the garage door, and tried to imagine himself pulling the trigger.

He drove back up to Pico and then headed north on Avenue of the Stars, his heart thumping hard. He had already decided what had to happen next, but that didn't make his part in it any easier. What it came down to was talking to Griffen. If anybody knew what Novak had been up to, *he* knew, and if anything was going to help Sunny . . .

He flipped on the radio, tried to breathe deeply, tried to slow his heart. He didn't want to think of Sunny's chances, about his chances—about the odds stacked against them.

Griffen was the next step. Not a step forward necessarily, but a step, an alternative to standing still, to waiting for bad news. He was going to ask the man a couple of questions, questions which, he realized, Griffen might not want to answer. If the money was as big as Helen had said, if the stakes were high enough to warrant Novak's execution, if Griffen had *learned* by now of Novak's death, then he might not want to cooperate.

That was what the gun was for. If Griffen didn't want to help, Ford intended to put the gun between his eyes, *make* him talk. Or maybe in his mouth—let the guy taste the cold metal. Ford checked his own tired eyes in the rearview mirror. Two days without a shave, and a week without proper sleep had made him look like a person who could pull a trigger. He just had to hope that Griffen would believe in the possibility.

Fender to fender, the late afternoon traffic drifted forward through smoggy dusk. It seemed to take forever before Century City shimmered into view.

Ford pulled into the short-stay parking lot off Constellation Boulevard and sat looking at No. 1 Century Plaza, the forty-story tower in which Apex had its main offices. He had ten free minutes before the meter at the gate started to run. After that time he would be losing $2.50 every sixty seconds—expensive parking even for Century City. But despite the niggling time pressure, he found he was unable to move immediately.

He sat for a long time looking at the paper bag he had used to hide the .38. His heart was still pounding, and despite the air-conditioning, he felt hot and clammy. He put his hand inside the bag—carefully, as though expecting to be bitten—then slowly withdrew the gun, feeling again its coldness and weight. Looking at it, his heart seemed to grow heavy, to sink. He knew there was no way he was going to be able to put it against a man's head, let alone shove it in his mouth. Then, just as clearly, he realized there was absolutely no question of driving away, of going home. He pressed his eyes shut—wished he could talk to Helen, could let her know what he had in mind. There was always the possibility that she had already found something out. But why hadn't she called? Why hadn't she left a message on his answering machine? Surely she would have found out about Griffen by now. After all, all you had to do was look in the Apex brochure.

But there was no time to get into that now. He had to focus. He considered the gun in his hand as though it were part of a puzzle. He could always put the safety catch on. The problem with that was Griffen might know enough about guns to see it. He would call security. It would all be over. For him. For Sunny.

Then Ford had an idea. It was so simple, so stupid it made him smile.

He dropped the magazine out of the grip and removed the bullets one by one, letting them fall into the paper bag. Then he snapped the magazine back into place. The gun looked exactly the same, but it was different now, no longer an instrument of destruction. Now he could be as threatening as he wanted—nobody was going to get hurt. Leaning forward, he pushed the gun down the back of his pants.

* * *

Inside the elevator, Ford pressed the button for the twenty-seventh floor and then looked down at his feet as though they had just been pointed out to him. His shoes looked dusty, and he was ashamed to see that the left toe was spattered with something—coffee maybe. The other shoes he could see near to his own, but—was he imagining it?—turned away from him, at a slight distance to him, these shoes had a rich double-welted corporate luster. The building was full of attorneys, insurance brokers, accountants. He didn't know how many people were in the elevator, but he was sure they were all looking at him—the bum with the .38 down his pants.

They rode up to the twentieth floor. People got out. One guy, a technician of some sort in blue overalls that stank of perspiration, got in. Ford tried to stand so that the .38 didn't press against his spine.

But for a vase of lilies discreetly lit by a recessed spotlight, the Apex reception area was smugly unadorned. A woman behind a black melamine counter, her smile framed in the triangular logo of the corporation, stiffened as Ford made his way across the marble floor. Ford tried to smile himself. His clothes might be a little rumpled, but he was still head of trauma in a major city hospital. There was no reason to feel intimidated.

"Can I help you, sir?"

"Yes, hello. I'm Dr. Marcus Ford, trauma director at the Willowbrook Medical Center."

The woman continued to stare. She had pale unblinking blue eyes like a seagull's.

"I'm here to see Dr. Scott Griffen."

The corporate smile was replaced by a frown.

"Do you have an appointment, Doctor?"

Ford realized with a jolt that he was unprepared for this. He had been so focused on the moment in which he would point the gun at Griffen that he had completely forgotten about how he planned to get into Griffen's office in the first place. He looked beyond the woman—saw a series of closed doors.

"I . . ."

"Because Dr. Griffen just left."

"Left?"

Ford refocused on the face.

"Yes."

The woman pointed past him to the elevators.

"He just went down."

Rushing out of the elevator on the ground floor, Ford almost ran into Griffen's ostrich-hide attaché case. Griffen had placed it on the ground in order to chat with a colleague. Trying to look composed, Ford walked past the two men towards the Constellation Boulevard exit. He stopped at the door and made a show of checking something in his battered address book. Counted to five. Risked a glance at Griffen.

He looked leaner than in the brochure, and he had a regular golfer's rich tan. Obviously not spending too much time in labs these days. Looking at Griffen, Ford noticed the exit on the other side of the lobby. It led through to the plaza. That was where the underground parking would be. If Griffen went that way, Ford was going to have a hard time following him.

Then it occurred to him that he actually stood a better chance of getting close to Griffen in the parking lot. Nobody would see him pull the automatic with all the cars in the way. He could even abduct him, make him drive to some quiet place. Ford was trying to think how this might work out when Griffen reached down for his attaché case. The two men shook hands, and then Griffen turned. He started across the lobby to where Ford was standing.

As casually as possible Ford went out of the building and over to his car. He opened the door and got in. Taking his time. A valet wearing a red waistcoat had appeared from nowhere. He was holding open the door of a blue Mercedes.

"Dr. Griffen! How are you this evening?"

Griffen mumbled something in reply, keys jingled, and he climbed in. Ford watched from behind the wheel. Clearly Griffen wasn't the kind of man to go to the trouble of fetching his own car from the underground lot. His time was too precious. His time was *money*.

Ford followed the Mercedes out onto Constellation. They made a left on the Avenue of the Stars and another onto Santa Monica Boulevard, Ford staying a couple of cars behind, keeping his eyes on the back of Griffen's head. As they turned right into Beverly Glen, he noticed the Mercedes's license plate: 2 HELIX. It was the insignia of a man who had made it to the top of the biotech ladder, a man who probably knew all about playing hardball.

They were climbing now, crossing Wilshire, going up to Sunset. The properties on either side of the road were getting steadily smarter, the vegetation in the front yards becoming thicker until suddenly the house fronts were no longer visible, hidden behind lush cascades of bougainvillea and manicured spruce.

They entered Bel Air, Ford holding back now, giving Griffen plenty of room, going through big iron gates, past signs advertising the presence of Bel Air *Armed* Patrol. There were no police visible, but Ford became acutely conscious of his budget car with its smashed bodywork. He reached across and put the bag hiding the .38 into the glove compartment.

The road wound upwards, the taillights of the Mercedes disappearing from time to time. Then Ford was passing Griffen, Griffen sitting tight, his curly head tilted slightly, waiting for the electronic gates to his substantial-looking property to ride open.

Ford drove on a little way, hoping to God that Griffen hadn't recognized him from the Plaza parking lot. Then he pulled over. For five minutes he sat listening to the engine cool, his headlights extinguished. Nothing had gone according to plan, but here he was—so *close*. Entering Griffen's world, albeit marginally—seeing his car, his house, *sensing* his money—somehow it made Omega seem more real.

But now that he was here, he didn't know what to do. He couldn't go back and ring the guy's doorbell. That would be even more suspicious than turning up at his office unannounced. Then the thought that Griffen might have a study similar to Novak's, a study packed with information—about the resistance problem, about Helical, maybe Omega itself—the idea of this possibility started his heart thumping again.

He pulled the car round and went back up to where he had seen Griffen stop, slowing as he went past to read the house number stenciled on the curbstone. He drove another hundred yards and then came back, looking for a place to park now. There were a couple of large trash containers standing by the side of the road and next to them a shadowy space overhung by eucalyptus trees. He didn't want to find Bel Air Patrol waiting for him when he got back, and there was always the risk that they might come by while he was creeping around. So the shadows looked good. He cut his lights and put the Buick into reverse.

He had the wheel hard over, was trying to squeeze in behind the trash cans, when there was a jolt and the flat pop of busted plastic.

"Damn it!"

He tensed up, expecting the inevitable car alarm. But nothing came. Then he got out of the car and took a look. Somebody else had already parked there. It was a blue Pontiac by the looks of it—pushed into the shadows nose first. He had taken out the right rear taillight with his twisted fender. Leaning through the door, he took his car out of park and rolled it forward a foot. Fragments of plastic fell onto dry eucalyptus leaves. A bumper sticker on the Pontiac read IF YOU THINK EDUCATION IS EXPENSIVE, TRY IGNORANCE.

Ford stood absolutely still, listening to the chirping of crickets and the distant whoop of a police siren. There was no sign of anybody coming out of the houses to investigate the noise. He took the gun out of the glove compartment.

Fifty yards away, Earl Rothenburg, Scott Griffen's nearest neighbor, looked up from the bundle of old newspapers he was tying. It had sounded like an accident—someone parking sloppily and clipping someone else's bodywork. He had bought his two-story hacienda to get away from the LA traffic, but these days the cars were everywhere. And the drivers were getting worse all the time. He decided to go take a look.

The gates to Griffen's house were set in imposing granite posts. On either side there was a thickly growing spruce hedge, which hid a chain-link fence. Ford moved along the hedge, trying to find some sign of a gap, or a place where he could climb over, but it looked more or less impregnable. He was on the point of turning back when he saw dirt on the road.

He bent down to take a closer look. It was fresh, still slightly moist. Turning, he noticed that at the base of one of the spruces someone had dug at the earth until there was a gap under the fence. He looked up and down the road. Kids maybe? A dog? He thought of the Pontiac hidden in the shadows, but dismissed the idea of a connection.

It was a tight squeeze, but he got through, tearing his shirt and grazing his back quite badly. He touched at the spot and felt blood. Just as he started to get to his feet, he saw headlights approaching along Bel Air Road. *Police.* The car slowed to a halt outside the property. After a moment Ford heard the gates open with a low hum. The car rolled on up the driveway. At the same time the front door of the house opened. Ford thought he heard a man's voice, but it was impossible to see anything because of the shrubs and bushes. He pressed himself against the hard ground, waiting for whoever it was to go into the house.

Then he could smell chlorine. Faint but distinctive. That meant a pool somewhere, and patio windows maybe . . . possibly unlocked. He started to skirt the perimeter of the property, keeping his eyes on the house.

It was built in a money-is-no-object modern style somewhere between Frank Lloyd Wright and Mies van der Rohe. Through enormous windows, Ford could make out warm colors of old leather and terracotta punctuated by the occasional canvas. Griffen liked his art big and abstract. Towards the back of the property, Ford heard the sound of the pool filter pump. Being extra cautious now, he started up the slight incline towards the house.

He found cover behind a low box hedge. Slowly—his whole body shaken by his thumping heart—he rose until he was looking at the back of the house. He took in rough-hewn stone slabs, an unlit pool, scattered deck chairs. And windows. A sliding patio window had been pushed back to let in the cool evening air. He could see the corner of a richly colored Turkish rug, a coffee table, and then Griffen.

He was standing with his back to Ford, a drink in his left hand. He was talking to somebody—lifting his drink to his mouth, gesticulating in a jerky, agitated way. Beyond Griffen, Ford could make out a woman's bare, suntanned legs. He needed to move if he was going to see who it was, but feared exposing himself to view.

In the end, it was Griffen who moved. Taking a step to the right, he reached for a decanter. What Ford saw brought him upright, rigid, no longer thinking of concealment, unable to believe his eyes.

It was Helen.

She brought a glass to her lips, sipped, and then nodded, agreeing with what Griffen was telling her. Griffen moved back. And she was gone from sight.

Ford dropped to his knees, his mind racing, flashing through jumbled images of the past two weeks. There was a moment of terrible clarity in which he understood that he had been betrayed, *felt* it—felt constricted, unable to breathe. Then, as if a voice had spoken inside his head, he knew that he must be mistaken, that Helen had not betrayed him, that she was simply doing what she had said would be necessary— talking to Griffen. And, unlike him, she had obviously found some clever way of doing it, some way that did not involve blundering around in the dark with an empty gun. Because only a fool would do that. If she hadn't called him, it was because she had been too busy working her leads, following up, closing in. Despite these attempts to rationalize, Ford felt weak. For a long time he crouched by the hedge, rocking back and forth, looking at the gun in his hand. Finally, when he was ready to move, he made his way back down to the car.

And he drove. Drove without stopping, following the sweeping curves of Sunset down to the Pacific Coast Highway, where he turned north, drove as far as Ventura, made a U-turn, came back down the coast towards Santa Monica. Lights changed, traffic slowed, stopped, and he responded—mechanically, unable to think, feeling only the need to keep moving, to keep going forward, as if he were surfing a tow- ering black wave that would otherwise engulf and drown him.

He ate a greasy hamburger in a roadside diner, trying to fill the emptiness that was growing inside. Then he found himself on Lincoln Boulevard, and he *had* to stop, *had* to think. The car had brought him, as if of its own accord, to 940, Helen's apartment. There was no sign of her car and no light on in her front room. Sitting in the warm dark,

Ford forced himself to go back—think back to the moment he had first seen Helen Wray at the conference—so confident, so beautiful. He remembered how, later, she had turned up at the hospital, remembered his own confusion, his instinctive rejection of the idea that she could be attracted to him. And he had been *right*. He saw that now. Because she had never been interested in him. It was Novak she had wanted to get close to.

He recalled Novak's reticence: one minute open and communicative, the next—when Helen came back with the coffee—clamming up, anxious to be gone. And Novak had clammed up because he had known—had known that Helen was a Stern employee, had known that what she wanted was to get to the bottom of the Omega rumors, to find out if Stern really had been fucked over by Helical five years ago. She had probably already tried to get to Novak and had found him elusive. What was it she had said? *He's a difficult person to get to see.* She obviously hadn't been having much success with him at the conference. Then, once she had realized that Novak was opening his door to the zealous doctor from South Central, he, Marcus Ford, had become useful to her.

The rest was bullshit.

A wave of scalding humiliation swept through him as he remembered their moments of intimacy, the tenderness, his unquestioning belief in her sincerity. And even now, now that he understood, it was hard to believe the *depth* of her deceit, her ease and smoothness in manipulating him. *Sometimes bad means bad,* she had said, and she had meant it, had meant it as a warning—a warning that she knew he, with his lover's blinded eyes, would never see. *Sometimes bad means bad.* She had said it looking him in the eye, showing him her naked body, and thinking . . . Ford clutched the steering wheel, pressing his teeth together until his jaws hurt. He recalled the talk of his healing hands, of his reaching into the bodies of the sick—saw that she had just been having fun, being creative, being good at her job. She had reached into his mind in that way that came so naturally to her; she had reached in and come up with what she knew he would like to hear. *The wounded surgeon plies the steel* . . . It was unbearable, but Ford could not stop himself now, remembering everything, remembering the night they had slept in her bed, the intense pleasure of being there, the sleekness of her fragrant body . . .

Then there was something else. The beginning of something else—an idea that made him catch his breath.

He recalled the moment when he had left the bed, had crossed the room to make sure he still had Novak's entry code. He was making connections now, bringing everything together.

How had she been able to enter Novak's building? Without the code, it would have been impossible. He recalled the slamming of the car door, the footsteps on the road. If they were her footsteps, then she had followed almost as soon as he entered the building. She must have made a note of the code from his scrap of paper. And the person who had attacked him from behind . . . *Did you get a look at him?*

A cold feeling of animosity brought his head round so that he was looking up at her window, a taste in his mouth of cheap meat from the burger. Without thinking, he reached across and took out the .38. Then the bullets, feeding them into the clip. He was like someone falling from a building—unable to stop. If it was Helen who had jumped him, then she had been working in concert with the man who had been rifling Novak's apartment. *I think if you wash your eyes with water, it might help.*

Ford brought both hands to his face.

"Oh, Jesus, Helen."

It was unbelievable, unbearable.

But once you looked at it that way, everything fell into place. She had sought to delay him—*At least get cleaned up, take a shower*— she had asked him to get cleaned up *in order to give her colleague time.* Once she had assured herself that the apartment had been stripped of all useful information, all she had wanted to do was get out. All she had wanted to do was *get him out.*

"Oh, Jesus."

And now she had turned to Griffen, still using her dazzling smile, still in pursuit of her quarry. She had finished with Dr. Ford. She would never smile at him again. He would probably never even see her again, never hold her again, never breathe her rich, waxy perfume. She had used him. He had allowed himself to be used. He pressed back against the seat, drowning, his face distorted by the intensest self-pity.

He sat like that for a long time, the gun in his hand, unaware of cars going past. A young couple coming out of one of the houses dropped their car keys, went down on their hands and knees to search. There was some drunken laughter and then a cheer. A kid in a baseball cap went past, talking to himself in a low, angry voice. But Ford heard nothing. Saw nothing.

Just after midnight he checked his wristwatch. There was still no sign of Helen's car. He allowed himself to imagine her screwing Griffen for information—lying on her back, looking up at the ceiling, doing it for Stern, doing it for the money.

And then it came to him that if she was screwing Griffen, it was because there was something worth screwing for.

PART FIVE

THE CZAR

1

SANTA MONICA

He was woken just after dawn by the sound of breaking glass. A garbage truck was stopped alongside him, grinding down a block's worth of refuse in its big metal belly. The sun threw bands of yellow light across the empty street. Ford blinked, yawned, then noticed with a jolt that there was a gun pointed directly at his leg. He had fallen asleep with the Sig in his lap, his finger still wrapped around the trigger. He had been sitting outside Helen's apartment all night, with the barrel of a gun lodged against his femoral artery.

Stiff and disheveled, Ford climbed out of the car. There was no sign of Helen's BMW, but it was possible she'd come home in a cab. There was even a chance she'd seen him sitting there, had pretended *not* to see, and gone inside. He walked up the steps and rang the bell.

There was no answer. He leaned into the door, listening for the rustle of bedclothes or the slap of bare feet on the stripped pine floor. He could picture the spartan rooms on the other side of the door, the couch he'd sat upon, the herb-smelling kitchen, the bedroom, the bed. He imagined himself there again, imagined her, lying there in the bed where they'd made love. It seemed like a long time ago now, a last taste of something sweet and comforting. And yet it still seemed real. He had to remind himself that it had all been a pretense, just a step in the strategy, a part of the plan. There hadn't been a relationship; there hadn't even been an affair, just the empty shell of one, as bare and empty as the apartment itself.

From the next-door apartment came the yapping of a small dog. Ford punched the bell again, but there was still no answer. It occurred to him that maybe even the house was a front, a temporary address from which she could disappear once her mission was accomplished. Was Helen Wray even her real name?

"She's not in."

He turned. It was the woman with the dachshund. She was looking at him through her part-opened door, holding the dog under one arm. She was wearing jogging pants and a pastel pink sweatshirt. There was no rebuke in her voice, in spite of the hour.

"Did she say—?"

"Business trip, I expect. She travels a lot on business, Miss Wray. I'll tell her you dropped by, if you like."

The dog watched him intently, its ears pinned back in expectation.

"Yes, thank you," Ford said. "Tell her I was looking for her."

"Is it something important?"

Ford took a couple of steps towards the street, stopped.

"No, not really," he said.

He crossed Wilshire and headed for the freeway. The traffic was just starting to build, the early birds making a quick dash to work ahead of the crush. Standing at a red light, he picked up the phone and punched in Dr. Lee's number at the Willowbrook, hoping to catch him before he started on his morning rounds. Lee picked up the phone at once.

"There's been no improvement, I'm afraid," he said. "But we do have the tests from the lab."

"And?"

"It's pretty much as I thought. The antitoxin is effective, but only for as long as it remains in the system. Once it starts to break down, the toxin levels rise again."

Ford put the car in drive and accelerated across the junction. He wanted to get down there quickly, if only to hold Sunny's hand, to stroke her hair, her face. To let her know somehow that he was there.

"When does it break down? How soon?"

There was a loud rustling of papers.

"Er . . . the half-life is normally around six days, at least."

"Normally?"

"Well, the first treatment seems to have given us a respite, but not for as long as that. I think we got about four days. Then the toxin started to reappear. So it looks like we were right to administer a second dose."

"Which should have bought us another four days, right?"

"*Mmm*, not necessarily. I don't know, but there's a chance the rate of replacement is accelerating."

It was what Ford had feared. If the *botulinum* was able to replicate in the acid conditions of Sunny's gut, the volume of toxin that would be produced would grow. That, in turn, would make it necessary to administer more of the equine serum.

"Are you saying you want to increase the dosage of antitoxin, just in case?"

Lee took a deep breath. It didn't sound as steady as Ford would have liked.

"I . . . I'll need to make some consultations about that. Normally the answer would be no. Beyond twenty mils there isn't usually any point in injecting more. That should be more than enough to cover any level of toxin that isn't . . . that isn't fatal. On the other hand . . . It all depends on what the bacteria are doing. If they're breeding fast enough, we may have no option. At this stage I really can't . . . The fact is, we're feeling our way here. I don't feel comfortable making any assumptions without more information."

Ford felt a surge of anger. He felt an impulse to shout. *I don't feel comfortable.* Who gave a damn if Lee was comfortable or not?

He held the phone against his chest and took a couple of breaths. It wasn't Lee's fault. The truth was the staph cases had left him feeling just the same way: helpless, cut adrift from the bedrock of experience and knowledge. For the past fifty years medical training had been built on the assumption that microbes were dumb, passive even. In the face of human inventiveness they didn't stand a chance—because if there was one thing humanity was good at, it was finding ways to kill. But now the foundations were shifting. The concept of *routine infection*, an accepted accompaniment to a huge range of medical treatments, was beginning to seem dangerously complacent. Now it was the doctors' turn to adapt, and they were none of them proving very good at it.

"Listen, Dr. Lee. You said before it might be advisable to get Sunny moved, maybe to someplace where she could get specialist help. Have you—?"

"I know I did, but the health department says no. They won't allow these patients to be moved. They're afraid the problem will spread."

"So I heard. I was just thinking—"

"I'm sorry. I wasn't told about the policy until yesterday. But I'm keeping in daily contact with the CDC. They know as much about *botulinum* as anybody. All the same, I do think we should sit down sometime and discuss the . . . the options."

Ford closed his eyes. He didn't want to discuss the *options*, not yet, not now. He didn't even want to hear what the options were. He didn't want to hear what desperate measures Lee had dreamed up or that Sunny might soon slip into an irreversible coma. He still needed to believe—just for a little while longer—that she might be well and whole again.

"When you come in, I mean," Lee added. "Maybe later today."

"All right, then," said Ford reluctantly. "I should be there in half an hour."

He came to a halt at another red light, waiting to turn onto the Santa Monica Freeway. He couldn't help thinking about Griffen and Apex and Helen Wray, about how he could get to them. There had to be a way.

"Dr. Ford?" Lee was still on the line. "I hope I didn't give you the wrong impression yesterday, when I mentioned the idea of moving your daughter. It was just . . . an idea. I assure you Sunny's getting the best treatment available right here. No effort is being spared."

He was trying to put a brave face on things, trying to give Ford hope. It was a tone of voice Ford had heard a hundred times. Doctors used it when they knew the odds were against the patient surviving, but didn't think the relatives were ready yet to hear the truth. There had been times when Ford had used it himself.

"Of course," Lee went on, "if there is somewhere in particular you'd like to have Sunny moved to, I'll do my best. But I'm afraid the county's calling the shots on this thing."

"The county," Ford repeated.

"That's right. They might be a little heavy-handed, but at least they're taking the problem seriously." The car behind Ford honked its horn. The light was green. "Well, I'll see you shortly then, Dr. Ford."

"No," Ford said. "I have to go talk to someone first, downtown. Do you have the health department's number there, Dr. Lee?"

Marshall West stood with his back to the room, looking down on Figueroa Street as it dived beneath Temple and the Four Level Interchange. He hadn't said anything for several minutes, just stood there with his hands behind his back, taking in the ninth-floor view, his well-built frame masking the sun. Ford had a feeling the silence wasn't a good sign, but he kept on talking, explaining everything, grateful just to be heard. From the walls a gallery of one-time political celebrities smiled down at him in black and white: Mayor Ed Koch shaking West's hand, Hillary Clinton on the campaign trail, Senator Hal Burroughs, who'd given West his first job, California congressman Henry Waxman, and Jack Kennedy, adopting a relaxed pose for Irving Penn's celebrated camera. It was a relief when West himself finally turned to face him again.

"Marcus, I'm going to have some coffee sent in. How do you take it?"

Ford blinked. The sun was in his eyes now.

"*Um*, white. No sugar. Marshall—"

"How 'bout a Danish or something? They're not bad. We get them in from some Hungarian bakery hereabouts."

He reached down and pressed his intercom button.

"No," said Ford. "No thanks, I'm—"

"Sally, could you bring us two coffees and one Danish? Thank you."

West released the button and sat down again in his high-back swivel chair. Ford watched him intently, trying to read some reaction in his face. Did West believe any of what he'd just been told? Had he even been listening?

West sighed, as if trying to decide about something, then rapped the edge of the desk with his index fingers. He yanked open a drawer. It struck Ford how easily his old med-school classmate had slipped into the crisp mannerisms of the fast-track, time-is-money executive.

"Let you in on a secret," West said. "I take these sometimes."

He put a small bottle of pills down in front of him.

"What are they?"

"Tranquilizers. Pretty mild. But when things start getting especially hectic, I find they help. Now, you're the doctor, but from where I'm sitting you look like—"

"I know what I look like, Marshall. I look like I slept in a ditch, but—"

West held up a hand.

"You look like you haven't slept for a week. And I'm not surprised, with all you're going through. I just thought they might help you to . . . keep it together, that's all."

"I appreciate it, Marshall, but I didn't come here for a prescription. I need your help to—"

There was a knock at the door, and West's secretary appeared carrying the coffee things on a tray. For a few moments the discreet chink and clatter of cups, saucers, and teaspoons was all that broke the silence. Then the secretary left, giving Ford a cozy, hearth-and-home smile.

"Please, go ahead," said West, pushing the Danish towards him on its white china plate.

Ford ignored it.

"Marshall, I'm certain this drug exists. I'm certain Apex has developed it. I don't know when exactly—maybe years ago, maybe just recently—but it *exists*. That's why I'm here. I need that drug. Sunny needs it."

West dragged one of the cups of coffee towards himself. He looked troubled. Ford just hoped the guy didn't think he was crazy.

"I can see . . . I can see from your point of view"—West took a sip from his cup—"why you wouldn't want to leave any stone unturned. That's only natural."

"It isn't just my point of view. There are scores, probably hundreds of people at risk right now. And the way things are going, it won't be long before every major hospital in the county is affected. We could be talking about a lot of lives."

West nodded slowly, acknowledging, not agreeing.

"I know the situation is serious, Marcus. Tragic, in many ways. But

I don't think we should get *too* alarmist about it." He spoke softly, reasonably—calm-in-a-crisis, as his reputation said he was. "As I understand it, the situation is being brought under control. Of course, I'm not involved in the daily running of the department—you know that—but the director is confident that if precautions are taken, if incoming patients are screened—"

"Marshall, you can't screen trauma patients. Most of them would be dead before you ever got the results. And what about the women in labor, the stroke victims, the heart-attack victims? These aren't people you can just turn away on suspicion."

"Nevertheless—"

"It's bullshit, Marshall. You could close every hospital in the county, you could sterilize them all from top to bottom. A week after you reopened, you'd be back to square one; I guarantee it. This strep is all over town. And it's handing out multiple resistance like candy at Halloween. Until it burns out you're gonna have hospitals going down all over the state and probably beyond. Just like the Willowbrook."

Ford stopped himself there. West had agreed to see him virtually on the spot, even though, as far as the department was concerned, Ford was little better than a troublemaker. Under the circumstances, it was more than he had a right to expect, old classmate or not.

"What I'm trying to say is, we need a new drug. We need to stop this thing in its tracks. And there's a chance we can."

West was leaning back in his chair, one finger pushed into his cheek.

"I thought you didn't believe in magic bullets, Marcus. At the NIH conference, for example, I seem to remember you saying we spent too much time looking for magic bullets, and not enough—"

"That was different, a . . . a general point about not squandering vital resources, vital tools. It's all a question of appropriate use."

West smiled.

"Appropriate use? I'd a feeling you'd say something like that. In my line of work when you see the word *appropriate*, it just means somebody's passing the buck. Take the appropriate steps, frame the appropriate response, and, while you're about it, take the heat when it all goes wrong."

"It can't be appropriate to let people die, Marshall, not while there's a chance you can save them."

West's smile faded.

"I know what you must be going through," he said softly. "When I think about my two"—he nodded towards the family photograph propped up on the side of his desk—"it makes me . . . Well, if there's anything I can do, you know you can count on me."

Marcus leaned forward in his chair.

"We need to get into Apex. We need to find out if they've developed this drug. We need to get hold of it. For a lot of people it could be the last chance. For Sunny it could be the last chance."

West frowned.

"Marcus, we can ask them about it, but I doubt if—"

"Asking's no good. There isn't time to ask. We have to go in there and look at what they've got. We have to make them hand it over."

West shook his head in disbelief.

"Marcus, you don't know what you're saying. These people have rights. You can't march into a major company and take what you like just because you *want* it. This isn't North Korea. We need grounds, evidence of criminal activity. Otherwise, how is anyone supposed to get a warrant?"

"Marshall, they *stole* this technology. By rights it belongs to Stern Corporation. When Stern bought Helical Systems, they bought the rights to all its R and D work as well. But Novak and Griffen and their friends, they took the best of it away with them—Stern themselves reached that conclusion, even if they couldn't prove it. Then, sometime later—my guess is when things had died down a little—they made a deal with someone else, a big deal for a lot of money."

"And you think that someone was Apex?"

"Who else? I talked to our in-house pharmacy people yesterday. They told me Apex badly needs a breakthrough. They've spent a ton of money on research, and they've got nothing to show for it but a handful of specialist treatments. A genetically engineered product like Omega is just what they're looking for. And besides, Scott Griffen is in charge of research, for Christ's sake."

Ford saw the muscles flex on either side of West's jaw. He had the impression that he was talking to someone who wanted to give the impression of listening but who *did not want to hear*. It was West's job, his chosen role, to persuade people, not to be persuaded.

"If what you say is true, then maybe, just maybe, Stern could pursue some kind of claim against Apex. But we've no real evidence that Omega even exists, not really. All we can be confident of is that Stern's people *think* it exists, or maybe just suspect that it does. I hate to dent your hopes on this, Marcus, but we have to be realistic."

Ford looked down at the pale green carpet, at his dusty, spattered shoes. West wasn't going to help him, maybe just couldn't help him. The evidence *was* circumstantial. And if Stern hadn't been able to prove anything, what hope did he have? But then, why should it matter if things were proven or not? If there was a chance that lives could be saved, it was worth trying anything.

"Look, Marshall, Novak was killed because he wanted to make the drug available. I'm certain of that. He and Griffen were going to shortcut whatever deal they'd made because they saw the need for it. Sooner or later the police are going to find that out. I'll tell them myself if I have to."

"These theories aren't enough, Marcus, compelling as they are."

"The point is—"

He was interrupted by a sharp buzz on the intercom. West deliberately reached over his desk and pressed a button.

"Yes, Sally."

"Your car's downstairs, Mr. West."

"Thank you. Be right there. Marcus, I hate to rush you, but I've a meeting at City Hall in twenty minutes."

West began gathering papers and files together. Ford stood up, planting a hand on the desk.

"My point is, we don't have to worry about who has legal title to Omega. Once we establish it's there, at Apex, we're in a position to call the shots, don't you see? Provided there's no publicity. We can make a deal with the company."

"Marcus, I don't see—"

"We get to try out the drug under whatever name they like—call it a clinical trial—in return for keeping its history out of the papers. If Apex cooperates, they retain ownership. If not, we let the whole story out, how they've been keeping the drug back, even when people were dying on their doorstep. At best it'll be bad publicity, at worst they lose the drug to Stern and half the board goes to jail."

West put an attaché case down in front of him and released the catches. Then, avoiding Ford's gaze, saying nothing, he began placing his documents inside it. For a moment everything in the office was quiet. Then suddenly he stopped, closed his eyes as if in pain, sighed.

"What you're asking . . ." His voice was little more than a whisper. "These are powerful people. The kind of favors I'd have to . . ." He shook his head. "You have no idea, Marcus, no idea."

Ford slowly straightened up.

"It's my daughter's life," he said.

West nodded to himself, then got to his feet.

"I'll do everything I can. It isn't going to be easy, but I'll try. You have my word on that."

2

Scott Griffen came out onto the patio carrying a bowl of coconut chicken soup to find two men standing by the pool—looking into the pool as though they had lost something. The one with the gun was dressed in a lightweight gray suit and had short red hair. The other, similarly dressed, was lean, balding, with the wholesome look of an astronaut. For a moment Griffen was so shocked he couldn't speak.

"Smells good," said the man with the gun. "*Tom ka gai*, right?"

Griffen nodded.

"Thai food," said the man, nodding, "absolutely my favorite and I'm including French here. People say French. They say haute cuisine, but I think those Thais have it down to an art."

"Spicy though," said the astronaut. "A little on the hot side."

The gunman raised his eyebrows.

"Not from my point of view."

It was as if they had arrived at his poolside by accident. As if his being there was of no importance to them one way or the other. Griffen took a step backwards. Realized he was wrong.

"Where *you* going?"

The gunman was pointing his automatic, a small pistol with the teat from a baby's bottle on the business end.

"I said where the *fuck* are you going?"

Affable. Just wanting to be kept informed.

Griffen put his free hand up, spilling a little soup as he did so.

"I was just . . ."

"Don't go back into the house," said the astronaut. "Stay with us. Eat your soup. It must be getting cold."

Griffen looked down at the bowl.

"Seriously," said the astronaut. Meaning it. "Eat. I'd hate to see it go to waste."

Griffen, keeping his eyes on the teat, spooned some of the milky soup into his mouth. Ten minutes ago he had been starving. Now he could hardly swallow. All he could think about was what had happened to Novak—what the woman from Stern had told him.

"It's nice up here," said the astronaut. "I'm down in the Valley. The air's better up here."

"What do you want?" asked Griffen, finally able to speak.

The men approached the round patio table where Mrs. Menendez, the housekeeper, had set a place for supper. Griffen was mesmerized by the gun and its soft rubber nipple. Were they going to ask him to suck it?

"How come you do the cooking?" asked the gunman.

"I don't, not . . . not normally. When my wife's away, I like to cook. Thai food. My wife can't eat spicy food. It's not good for her."

"So what's wrong with the housekeeper?"

"I'm sorry?"

"The housekeeper," said the gunman. "How come she don't cook?"

"Mrs. Menendez doesn't especially like cooking Asian food. She doesn't like the smell."

The gunman was shaking his head in disbelief, looking at his partner.

"Can you believe that? Fucking greasers. All they know is garlic and onions."

"So you sent her home early?" asked the astronaut.

Griffen nodded, his eyes still on the gun. There was a moment's silence.

"What?" said the gunman. Following Griffen's gaze, he lifted the pistol and considered the teat. "This?"

Griffen nodded.

"Great, isn't it?"

The gunman was looking at the teat with an expression of amused wonderment.

"Fucking incredible, but it really cuts down on muzzle blast. Mind you, this is just a .22. Be no good on a bigger gun." He looked at Griffen now, and Griffen could see that the pupil of his left eye had a flaw of some kind and was pulled into a shape like a comma. "You walk around with a suppressor—a silencer?—get caught with one, say, by the cops, they want to know what line of work you're in. But nobody minds a little titty. Course you take it off when the gun's in your pocket or holster or whatever. Hell, you can even swallow the thing if you have to."

"You get close enough," said the astronaut, leaning forward, "you put the hole in the right place, you don't need a big gun. Pop the guy in the head with a .22? The bullet doesn't come straight out. Whirls around inside. Scrambled egg. You find a nice soft spot—love handles are good or a big stomach—the target soaks up the noise. On a night like this? Little breeze in the trees, nobody's going to hear much. You understand what I'm saying?"

Griffen put the soup down on the table.

"Is that . . . Is that what you're here to do? Shoot me?"

The astronaut smiled, shaking his head.

"Now, don't get all worked up. I'll tell you what, why don't we sit down."

Griffen sat. Waited for the men to take seats opposite.

"So what . . . what is it you want?"

Putting both his hands on the table, the astronaut looked at Griffen's face with a calm, almost friendly expression.

"Naturally, you're right," he said, affably. "We are, of course, here for a reason. In fact, I wanted to ask you a couple of questions about Apex. Hear your views on a matter which concerns me. It won't take more than a minute, and then we'll be out of your hair."

Griffen looked from one man to the other, wondering for the first time who they were with. Novak had always feared that word on Omega would get out, that other parties might come sniffing around. That was why he had moved his office to the Palisades address.

"Sure," he said. "What do you want to know?"

"Well, we were hoping you could tell us a little about your work. On antisense."

Griffen relaxed a little. At least now he knew what they wanted.

"You're going to have to be a little more—"

"Specifically what interests me . . . what interests my employer, is the work you're doing on synthetic DNA, particularly synthetic DNA drugs designed to deactivate or kill bacteria."

"Antibiotics?"

The astronaut nodded, giving Griffen time but no longer looking so friendly.

Griffen drew a breath. "I'm afraid—"

He stopped short, staring at the astronaut's raised index finger.

"Now, I should explain here," said the astronaut, "just to save everybody time, that there is a right answer and a wrong answer to this question."

He smiled and leaned back against his chair, giving Griffen a friendly go-ahead nod. Griffen swallowed hard.

"Well . . . I . . . I don't know what you would consider the right answer. I can only tell you the truth, the truth as far as I know it. Apex *is* interested in antisense and triplex agents, but we have always . . . we have tended to focus more on human cells with a view to dealing with . . ."

The astronaut had turned. He was looking at his partner. His head came back round, and Griffen could see that he was unhappy. Then the soup bowl slammed into his face, the astronaut reaching across the tilting table, pressing hard, twisting. Griffen made no attempt to move, just leaning backwards as the other man pushed.

Just as it had started, it stopped.

The bowl was back on the table, empty now, the astronaut brushing a spatter of soup from his sleeve. Griffen blinked through the warm broth of coconut and chicken. It ran down his neck and into his shirt. With trembling fingers, he detached a strand of lemongrass from his mouth. There was a taste of blood.

"Please don't hurt me," he said.

The gunman raised his pistol and sucked gently at the teat, watching Griffen's face.

"Scott," said the astronaut after a moment, sounding disappointed. "Scotty. Does the name Charles Novak mean anything to you?"

Griffen froze.

"Sure, he's . . . he was . . . I worked with him at Helical Systems back in the—"

"Helical," said the astronaut as though remembering the name. "Right . . . right. Well, it's a terrible thing, it's a terrible thing to have to say, but the slob croaked."

"Yes," said Griffen, trying to think whether or not the murder had been reported in the press, whether or not he should know what he knew. "Yes, I heard."

"Guy killed himself," said the gunman, taking the teat out of his mouth to speak.

"And Helen Wray?" asked the astronaut.

"She's dead?"

"Not as far as I know. Not yet."

The astronaut watched Griffen for a moment.

"You seem upset."

"I . . . No, I'm just trying to understand."

"No, but when I said Helen Wray. You thought she was dead. Why would she be dead?"

"She came here last night," said Griffen.

The astronaut raised his eyebrows.

"You're not making any sense, Doctor."

"I'm sorry. For a moment—when you said her name, I . . . She was here last night, and I thought you were telling me—"

"Did you fuck?"

"Pardon me?"

"I said did you fuck. You and Miss Wray. Did you have sexual intercourse?"

"I never met her before last night."

"That's not what I asked."

"No. No, we didn't."

"Must have been a nice surprise for you, though. Your wife being away and all. Good-looking woman like that just happens to stop by. What did she want exactly?"

Griffen looked away.

"Now, Scotty," said the astronaut, lowering his voice, "I know this is difficult for you to talk about, but that's why I didn't just pick up the phone. That's why I didn't fax you a list of questions. That's why I . . . why *we* went to the trouble of coming up here. Because I knew you would find it difficult."

He paused for a second, letting all this sink in.

"Now, I'll ask you again," he said, his voice a soft growl. "What—did—Helen—Wray—want?"

Still Griffen looked away, his whole body taut, trembling. He did not want to repeat what Helen Wray had said to him because that would mean getting into a discussion that was strictly taboo. His mind raced as he tried to come up with a plausible lie.

"Let's go inside," said the astronaut, mildly.

They walked him into the house, closing the outside door as they entered the kitchen. The gunman placed him next to the sink, propping him up as if he were a target. Griffen saw the big kitchen knife, the remains of chopped vegetables, strips of chicken skin, a piece of fresh galingale. He saw a note from his wife on the refrigerator door. *Don't forget the grapefruit!* Elements of his former life—receding from him at the speed of light.

"They did a beautiful job," said the gunman, looking around the kitchen.

The astronaut walked over to the microwave. He pressed a button and the door popped open. Then he pushed it shut again, tried to set it to defrost.

He looked over his shoulder at Griffen.

"How do you set this up? Say you want to cook some meat."

"From . . . from frozen?"

"No, not frozen. Fresh."

Griffen crossed the Mexican-tile floor, so scared he couldn't think straight, pressed a button. Then another.

"That's for the temperature; that's for the time."

"Okay," said the astronaut. "Okay."

Griffen was pulled back to the sink. He watched as the astronaut picked up the big kitchen knife. The gunman pushed air out through his nose. He put the gun against Griffen's head, touching his temple with the cool teat, and waited.

It was the astronaut who spoke.

"Okay, Scott. I'll tell you what I'm going to do."

He pointed with the knife.

"You're left-handed, am I right?"

Griffen nodded, showing his delicate left hand.

"I noticed when you were eating your . . ."

"*Tom ka gai*," said the gunman.

"Your *Tom ka gai*, right. Okay. Now, what I'm going to do is, I'm going to cut off your right hand." Again he pointed with the knife. "I'm going to cut it off with this knife, and I'm going to cook it in this neat little Japanese microwave."

He looked at the gunman. Then back. Smiled.

"How does that sound? Understand me, this is in case of any more wrong answers. I'm going to *microwave* your fucking hand, and then you are going to eat it. How's that?"

Griffen felt a sudden release of heat into his crotch. He looked down in disbelief, tears of fear and shame stinging his eyes. Then he was blubbering—out of control.

"Please, dear God oh God oh Jesus oh God . . ."

The astronaut crossed the brightly lit space and pressed the flat of the knife against his face, careful not to cut him. There were to be no marks.

"It may not be Thai, Scotty, but it'll be interesting. It'll be a first."

"Please please please please please . . ."

"Okay, Scott, here comes the question."

"He's peeing in his pants," shouted the gunman, looking down at the floor. "Don't step in it, man."

"Shut the fuck up!" snapped the astronaut.

"Now! For the right hand and a weekend for two in Acapulco. What did Wray want? And don't give me the wrong answer, Scott. Not this time."

"She works for Stern," blubbed Griffen. "They want Omega."

"There," said the astronaut, stepping back. He breathed quietly for a moment.

"I *knew* you could do it, Scotty. Now, that wasn't so bad."

Griffen shook his head.

"That wasn't so bad," echoed the gunman.

Then Griffen was shaking convulsively. A bitter taste of bile surged into his mouth, and it felt as if his legs were going to give way.

"Okay," said the astronaut. "Okay, nearly over now."

He came close again, holding Griffen's jaw with his left hand.

"Now, Scott. *Scott!*"

Griffen struggled to control his trembling body.

"I want you to tell me what she said. And I—"

"Stern Corporation . . ." blurted Griffen. "The Stern people feel Omega belongs to them. When they bought Helical . . . the drug was already a viable product at that time. There was testing to do, trials, but the groundwork . . . it was already done. It should have been part of the Helical purchase, but it was . . . it was hidden."

"But Ms. Wray wasn't appealing to your sense of justice, right? She was here to make you an offer."

Griffen shook his head.

"No, not an offer. It was a warning. She said if Apex made the drug, they would litigate, I mean against us personally."

"Us?"

"The Helical people. The team. She said she could prove we stole the technology. That we kept it from them."

"And are you?"

"Are we what?"

"Is Apex making the drug?"

Griffen was confused. It was as if the guy knew all about Omega already. All he seemed to be interested in was the players—Stern and Apex. Again he asked himself who they were with.

"No."

Then the astronaut was smiling.

"But you could, couldn't you?" he said quietly. "You've had the information all along. You and Novak."

There was a moment of complete silence. Griffen shook his head.

"Sure," said the astronaut. "Kept it for a rainy day, right? Thought maybe it would come in useful some time."

"Who are you?" asked Griffen. "Who are you working for?"

The astronaut took a step back so that the overhead light struck a bar of shadow down from his nose.

"So does Stern have the drug now?"

"No," said Griffen. "No, how could they?"

"You're sure about that? You're sure you're going to say the same thing when you're through eating?"

"Please, I swear."

The astronaut put the knife down and looked at the ground for a moment, thinking.

"Okay," he said. "Take off your clothes."

3

The meeting had been scheduled six weeks in advance, and CEO Bill Donnelly had made it clear that he expected everyone to be there. On her own initiative his personal assistant, Carla Samuels, had rung the offices of the various directors and department heads the day before, just to make sure that nobody was planning to be anywhere else. In an ordinary company it probably wouldn't have been necessary, but with some of these Apex people you could never be sure: most of them had come up through the technical side of the business, she reminded herself, and while they might know all there was to know about DNA and protein synthesis, they weren't above a little creative absent-mindedness when it suited them. Thankfully, this time everybody was planning to be there, or so they said.

The meeting was scheduled for nine o'clock, but at a quarter past there was still one chair empty. Donnelly and Arthur Ross talked sotto voce about yachting—they both kept boats down in San Diego—while Carla tried to locate the absentee. It was the R&D director, Scott Griffen. Apparently he hadn't shown up at the office that morning and his secretary hadn't been able to raise him on the phone. Secretly Carla wondered whether Griffen wasn't trying to make a point by staying away. After all, he was very much on the technical side of the company. Maybe he knew what was coming and wanted no part of it. Carla didn't know much about Griffen, but by all accounts he was pretty stubborn and didn't like anybody telling him what to do. There was also a rumor that he was thinking about retirement.

Reluctantly Donnelly got the meeting under way. Carla positioned herself on his right—not actually at the table—and got ready to write. Just as she had expected, Donnelly began by talking about how the company was perceived in the market. The idea was gaining ground, he said, that Apex was hostage to fortune, more than was appropriate or desirable for a venture of its size and maturity. It was essential to the continued independence of the company that this perception be reversed. And then he began to unveil the new resources allocation system he wanted to introduce, with its targets and regular performance assessments.

Donnelly was still talking when the phone rang. Carla hastily put down her pad and hurried to pick it up, annoyed that anyone should have the nerve to interrupt the meeting. It was Marcia Burridge, the new girl on reception.

"Pardon me, is Mr. Donnelly there, please?"

She didn't sound very sure of herself.

"Mr. Donnelly is in the middle of a meeting. He is *not* to be disturbed."

Donnelly turned back to his colleagues and went on talking.

"Oh," said Marcia, "but you see there's—"

"Marcia," Carla hissed. Some of these girls just had no idea. "This is a *board* meeting. You do not interrupt board meetings. You can get whoever it is to leave a message on my voice mail. Now good-bye."

"But, Miss Samuels, there are two gentlemen here"—her voice dropped to a whisper—"from the F-B-I. They're right here."

"The FBI? Are you . . . ? Just . . . just tell them to wait a moment."

Carla put down the receiver and stood there, trying to decide what to do. Donnelly was in full flow now, punctuating his speech with little karate chops against the polished walnut tabletop. Should she interrupt him? She decided not. It was probably just a routine inquiry, something that concerned an ex-employee more than likely. No need to get excited. Just deal with it.

"Excuse me," she murmured and slipped out of the room.

There were only two men in the reception area; so it had to be them. They were trying to look like everyday visitors, one of them standing, leafing through a company brochure, the other sprawled out on the black leather sofa, gazing down on Century Plaza two hundred feet below. They were dressed like businessmen—dark suits and white shirts—although there was something incongruous about the brass tie clasps they both wore. They were big men, and one of them had a sandy-colored mustache. As Carla approached, Marcia looked up from behind the desk and nodded in their direction, her eyes as big as saucers.

"Can I help you gentlemen?" Carla said in her best strictly-business voice. The man who had been sitting stood up. "My name is Carla Samuels. I'm Mr. Donnelly's personal assistant."

The two men looked at each other.

"Good morning, ma'am," said the mustache. There was a touch of the South in his accent. "I'm Agent Monroe. This is Agent Buford. We're from the Commercial Crimes Section, FBI."

Two of the junior managers from Marketing appeared, laughing as they headed for the elevators. Carla waited for the heavy glass doors to close behind them.

"Do you have some identification?" she said.

Monroe reached into his jacket and produced an ID card fixed inside a black leather wallet. Carla examined it closely, even though she had no idea what an FBI agent's ID was supposed to look like.

"Well, what exactly can we do for you?" she said, unable to keep the indignation from her voice.

Monroe tucked the wallet back inside his jacket. Carla glimpsed a fine leather strap running vertically from his shoulder and realized with a jolt that the man was armed.

"Ma'am, we have a federal warrant for the removal of any and all documents in this company's possession relating to research and development activity carried out at, or on behalf of, Apex Incorporated. I would like to present that warrant to Mr. Donnelly so that we can proceed."

Carla blinked, unable at first to take in what she had been told.

"You . . . You have a warrant? What's the charge?" she stuttered, realizing immediately how stupid the question was.

"There's no charge, ma'am," said Buford, one side of his mouth tightening to a smile. "We're not here to arrest anyone."

Carla straightened up. A bunch of people—she recognized Lisa Wallbach and Greg Tanner from Corporate Affairs—were rubbernecking from halfway down the adjoining corridor. A door slammed and rapid footsteps receded into the distance. Carla shot a hostile glance at Marcia Burridge, who immediately ducked down behind the reception desk.

"Anything relating to research and development would be *highly* confidential. You'd have to talk to the director concerned, and he's . . . he's not here at the moment." The thought flashed through her mind that maybe this had something to do with Griffen, with his absence. Was he some sort of fugitive? "In any event, I . . . I must ask that you talk first with our senior in-house legal counsel. "I'll . . . Just one second."

She hurried back to the reception desk. Marcia looked up at her guiltily, her hands pressed together between her knees.

"Get Frank Pellegrini on the line," Carla hissed, "*now*. And keep your mouth shut otherwise, missy."

Marcia got the senior counsel on the line, then handed over the receiver.

"Frank? It's Carla Samuels." She tried to sound calm, set an example. "I'm sorry to bother you, but I'm in reception with two gentlemen from the FBI. They say they have a warrant to take all our documentation relating to research and development."

From the receiver came a strangled shriek of disbelief. Then Pellegrini was shouting at his secretary—Carla had to hold the phone away from her ear—telling her to call "Phil at Kirkland" right away. Then the phone went dead.

Carla handed back the receiver. She felt a little steadier, knowing she'd done the right thing. When in doubt, leave it to the lawyers; that was the rule. But then she was struck by a new anxiety: what was it all about? "Commercial crime," they'd said. It sounded serious. Was it serious enough to damage the company? Serious enough maybe to cost jobs, *her* job? And who'd want an ex-employee of a bent company? No job, no insurance coverage, no pension plan, no *health-care* plan— elements of the impending catastrophe loomed up before her like warning signs on a road she wasn't meant to be on. It was a road that led to exclusion. She'd be out there—instinctively she cast a glance towards the low-rent sprawl of Central LA—on her own. She could end up like one of *those* people, people you knew about, knew were there, but never actually met, spoke to, touched, people you paid money to keep away from.

Frank Pellegrini came hurrying down the passage in his shirtsleeves, one cuff hanging loose at the elbow.

"Where are they?" he demanded, as if it were difficult to spot them.

Carla shook herself and escorted him to where Monroe and Buford were standing, their hands buried in their pockets. Pellegrini's head just about made it to the height of their shoulders.

"I understand you gentlemen have some kind of a warrant?" he said.

Monroe took an envelope from his side pocket and handed it to him. Pellegrini read the contents, making loud sniffing noises as he went. Carla got the feeling this wasn't the kind of situation he'd had much practice with.

" 'Technology acquired through illegal means'?" he said. "Is this some kind of a joke?"

Buford planted his hands on his hips and looked down at the floor, as if trying to restrain himself from saying what he wanted to say.

"No joke, Mr. . . . ?"

"Pellegrini, Frank Pellegrini."

"The warrant is effective immediately. We have six more men waiting downstairs. Now, we just need to know where the documents are located so that we can remove them as quickly and with as little disruption as possible. I'm sure that would be in everyone's best interests."

"Remove them? Those documents are . . . are of huge potential value to our competitors. There is *no way* we can let them off the premises. How do we know . . . ?"

There was a commotion behind them. Donnelly, Ross, and half the board were marching towards them.

"What the hell is this, Frank?" Donnelly demanded.

Monroe took his hands out of his pockets and put them behind his back. Buford didn't.

Pellegrini handed over the warrant. "They want to take away the research data. Some bullshit about stolen technology."

"*What?*"

Pellegrini turned back to the FBI men. "This is an outrage. We are going to seek an injunction preventing you from removing any confidential information from these offices. I have someone working on that right now. In the meantime, I would like to know who the hell—who the hell in *Washington* authorized—"

"I'd love to stand around here talking about it," said Monroe. "But I'm afraid I'm gonna have to make a start with the execution of that warrant. It's also my duty to warn you that any attempt to conceal or destroy documents of any kind likely to be of interest to this investigation may constitute a criminal offense punishable by fine or imprisonment."

For a moment there was silence, then a sudden loud buzz from the direction of the main doors. Everybody looked round: a messenger boy carrying a large brown envelope stared back through the glass.

"Now, it would be much appreciated," said Monroe, "if you could tell us where to begin."

4

Sergeant Ruddock was halfway through a king-sized pot of instant noodles when Pat McNally came over to his desk holding the latest batch of teletypes.

"Jesus, what is that, Duane?" he said. "You're stinkin' the whole place out."

"Spicy Chinese chicken," said Ruddock, defensively. "Just thought I'd give it a try."

"Smells like a dog's breath." He pointed at the splashy Chinese characters on the side of the pot. "Jesus, I'm right. Chinese dog's breath flavor."

Sam Dorsey looked up from his side of the desk and sniffed at the air.

"Hell, I thought that was you, Duane. California armpit flavor."

Someone on the other side of the room let out a single snort of amusement. Ruddock sighed wearily and put the noodles down.

"So what have you got for me, Pat?"

McNally tore off one of the teletype sheets and handed it to him. The report was about ten lines long and listed the preliminary details of a homicide investigation. Like all the reports the different police forces put out, it was designed to highlight peculiarities that might suggest a link with cases in other jurisdictions. With so many different police departments working in such a small area, the teletype system, while far from high-tech, was an indispensable tool for detectives of all kinds, but most especially those dealing with violent crime.

"This one just came in from LAPD. Possible one-eighty-seven in Bel Air, a drowning."

"Only possible? Does that mean they think it could've been suicide?"

"Doesn't say. This is what's interesting, see?" He pointed to the beginning of the second paragraph. "The victim, Dr. Scott Griffen, was a senior executive at a pharmaceutical company and had a *PhD in biochemistry*. They actually put that in there. Must have thought it meant something."

"Sounds like they're as desperate as we are," said Dorsey. "Have they checked his computer for messages?"

Ruddock ignored the joke.

"Pharmaceutical companies make drugs, right? All kinds of stuff."

"Sure," said McNally.

"And biochemists know how to make 'em, the refining and cutting and all that."

"I guess."

"Wait a second, Duane," said Dorsey. "You think this could be a narco thing, now? Thanks for sharing."

"It's just a thought. Maybe there's been some moonlighting going on. It would explain a lot of things."

"Better give 'em a call, first," said McNally. "It isn't much of a connection. Just thought you needed all the help you can get." He began to walk away. "Don't let it spoil your lunch, though."

The senior LAPD detective assigned to the case was Sergeant Jim Tolbert, a linebacker-sized black man with a brisk, confident manner and a habit of rapping his fingers on the tabletop when he talked. Ruddock had worked with him on a serial-killer case a few years back and, despite the minor intrusions of professional rivalry, couldn't help but be impressed by the way he operated. His lumbering, heavyweight appearance concealed a quick mind, and he was good at getting people to talk to him, even pimps and hookers, who were not always inclined to be helpful. It was something to do with his demeanor: being around him, you felt safe. As a team player, though, he left something to be desired, preferring to trust his own judgment rather than anybody else's. Ruddock left a message, and Tolbert called back a couple of hours later.

"How you doin', Duane? You take that vacation yet?"

"No," said Ruddock, reaching for his pen and notebook. "Sore point, actually. What about you?"

"Yeah, just got back. Went to visit my mama in Florida. It's nice down there, once you get away from the tourists. So what can I do for you?"

"That case you got in Bel Air. It's ringing a few bells. Can you talk me through it?"

"Sure, just a second." He cleared his throat. "Okay, let me see now. Scott Griffen, fifty-one years old, research director at Apex Inc. That's in Century City. Married, son in college, daughter married, living in San Francisco. The wife was visiting up there when it happened. Housekeeper found him at the bottom of his pool, nude. That was two days ago, about half past nine in the morning."

Ruddock listened carefully, making notes. The way Tolbert talked, his brisk, businesslike delivery, made the whole thing sound banal, no more compelling than a parking violation. But then, Ruddock reminded himself, that was the way Tolbert was. He liked to be in control, to stay cool whatever.

"The teletype said *possible* one-eighty-seven. You think he might just have drowned by accident?"

"Could be, but I doubt it. For one thing, there were bruises on his arms and around the shoulders and minor lesions on the fingers—all consistent with a struggle. 'Course, he could've got them someplace else. We're still waiting on the autopsy report. But we also got signs of forced entry on the perimeter fence and several sets of fresh footprints in the earth round about."

Ruddock finished writing and circled the word *several* with his blue ballpoint.

"Anything else?"

"Well, I'm still not sure what to make of this, but we couldn't find his pants."

"His pants?"

"Yeah. The guy strips off to go swimming, but all we find inside—I mean that wasn't clean and pressed and put away—was a shirt, a tie, and a pair of socks. They were in this laundry basket. But no pants and no underpants. It's like they walked off on their own."

Ruddock pushed himself back from the edge of the desk, trying to figure out if anything tied in with the crime scene in Topanga Canyon. There was nothing tangible, but the feeling he got, the feeling of things not quite stacking up, was the same.

"Anyway," Tolbert went on, "we've got the lab people crawling over the whole place looking for trace evidence. The pool itself looks promising. We got several different samples of human hair, including half a dozen strands of red hair, most with the roots attached. We already know it doesn't match Mrs. Griffen's. If we can eliminate any other recent visitors, we could have a very usable sample of the killer's DNA."

In spite of himself Ruddock was impressed. It was quick work, but a DNA sample was no good without a suspect to go with it. At least Tolbert didn't sound as though he'd got very far with that yet.

"Are you checking the scene, and maybe the used clothes you do have, for traces of narcotics?"

Tolbert laughed.

"Great minds," he said. "I thought the same thing when I found out what Griffen did for a living. That's why I put the biochemistry thing on the teletype."

"And?"

"Not a whiff so far. It'll take time to check everything, but it looks like if that was the deal, he didn't take his work home."

"Have you been down to his office?"

"Planning to. And guess what: the Feds have been down there this week already."

Ruddock sat up.

"The Feds?"

Dorsey looked up from his side of the desk. This was something even he couldn't ignore.

"I'm still trying to get the details, and the company itself isn't being exactly helpful. But from what I heard, the Commercial Crimes section's been digging around, removing documents and stuff. I'm not sure why, but I should have more on it later. So what's your angle?"

Ruddock outlined the facts of the Novak case, which didn't amount to a whole lot more than he'd learned on the very first day. The crime scene had yielded nothing new, certainly no unidentified hair samples or fingerprints. Checking the man's financial records revealed the only surprise: sometime shortly before his retirement he had made a number of sizable investments both onshore and offshore. The sums involved amounted to at least three and a half million dollars, yet the origin of the money was a mystery. The most likely explanation, that he had simply inherited it from some wealthy relative, was not supported by any documentation yet discovered.

"Griffen wasn't short of money, either," Tolbert said. "You should see that place they got: six or seven bedrooms, a bathroom you could get lost in, pool, views over Stone Canyon Reservoir. I don't even like to think what it cost."

"Might be worth checking what it *did* cost. See if everything adds up."

"I'm already on to it," said Tolbert. It sounded as if he was writing now too. "Any other suggestions?"

"Not yet, except we should try and find out if Griffen and Novak knew each other. I'll check again for that. We've got all Novak's personal papers."

"O-kay, sounds reasonable. I'll do the same. I haven't had much time with Mrs. Griffen yet. I'll start with her. Meanwhile, for reference, we're trying to trace two unidentified vehicles seen parked in the vicinity of the house a day or two prior to Griffen's death. Neighbor saw them while he was sorting out his trash for recycling. Said he heard what sounded like a collision and went out to take a look. *Didn't* take any license plates, of course."

"Uh-huh," said Ruddock. "Fire away."

"One blue Pontiac, *probably* blue."

"Probably?"

"It was dark. And a white Buick Century. He was pretty sure about that one. Guess an American car would kinda stand out up there, especially one all smashed up at the front."

Ruddock closed his eyes, trying to remember something. Then it came to him.

"Smashed up left front or right front?"

"Huh? Er . . . the right fender, he said."

"Jim, that car belongs to Dr. Marcus Ford. I've seen it myself."

There was a moment's silence on the line. Ruddock was pleased to be giving Tolbert something to be impressed about, for a change.

"Don't tell me, another microbiologist?"

"Nope. This one's a real doctor, or was. Let a cop die. Got himself suspended."

Dorsey was watching him as he spoke, a tight grin on his face. Hearing that Dr. Ford was back in the picture seemed to please him.

"You gonna go talk to him?" Tolbert asked.

"You bet," said Ruddock. "I'll keep you posted."

"All right," said Tolbert. "All right. When you find him, get him to give you a hair sample, okay?"

5

The investigation into Apex Inc. was covered by several of the Los Angeles dailies, though only the LA *Times* felt it rated the front page. Featured below an extensive update on the resistance problem facing the city, the *Times* article stated the facts as far as they were known and speculated about the investigation's purpose. It ended with a pithy comment on the precarious nature of the biotech industry and was topped by a grainy photograph of three men emerging from No. 1 Century Plaza carrying boxes.

Ford read the piece, sipping coffee in an Au Bon Pain on Pico Boulevard. He felt as if he was, at last, getting somewhere. West had been as good as his word, and Ford only wished that he had gone to him earlier. But the whole process was going to take time. Whatever the imperatives of his personal timetable, whatever the gravity of Sunny's predicament, the investigation would take as long as it took. All he could do was hope for some quick answers. In the meantime . . . He folded the paper and stood up. He couldn't postpone seeing Dr. Lee any longer.

Entering the Willowbrook, Ford was struck by the clear signs of further deterioration. Someone had kicked a hole in one of the doors of the staff entrance, and there were pieces of glass all over the floor. Buckets and mops stood in the corridors next to waste bins that looked as if they had not been emptied for a week. The elevator linking the abandoned Emergency Department to the first-floor ORs and ICU was out of order—pieces of machinery and what looked like gears were scattered across the dirty blue linoleum. Ford walked up to the first floor.

He found Lee on one of the wards set aside for resistance cases. All of the nurses and attending physicians were wearing lightweight plastic visors, plastic gowns, and rubber gloves. The plague ship and its crew.

Lee came down the central aisle, gesturing for Ford to go back. He waited until they were outside the ward to push up his visor.

"Didn't you read the sign?"

He pointed to a sheet of computer paper taped to the door on which someone had scrawled ISOLATION—OBSERVE STRICT BARRIER TECHNIQUE.

Ford apologized.

"Every time I come here, the place seems to have gotten worse."

"Tell me about it." Lee sighed.

He picked up a staff telephone and punched in a number.

"I just need to . . . Yes, yes, Dr. Allen? Dr. Ford is with me, so if you can . . . In the little cupboard near to radiology, right."

They set off along the corridor.

"We've had CDC people in with Patou trying to do something about cross infection. Naturally they do the easy things like make everybody put on masks and gowns. But our real problem, as I see it, is waste collection. I mean, did you see the state of the corridors?"

He pointed to a pile of what looked like dirty dressings outside the inoperative elevator. Ford shook his head.

"It's the subcontractors," said Lee. "The sanitation people are worried about lawsuits from their staff in case somebody comes down with something. Personally, I think they're just scared."

They entered a windowless room in which there were two plastic chairs and a small autoclave unit that looked as though it had been dropped from a great height.

"What happened to your office?" asked Ford.

Lee opened the autoclave and took out a sheaf of papers held together in a torn binder.

"It's currently housing around two thousand TV dinners."

"Wow."

"Absolutely. It feels like the whole place is about to collapse in on itself, you know? Like a neutron star? Haynes is calling us in every day. Pep talks. Warnings about the media. We've still got no caterers."

"I know."

"I've gained a pound in the last three days eating subs."

There was an embarrassed silence. Lee gave his tie a little tug. Then checked his watch. It was obvious he didn't want to get into a serious discussion any more than Ford did.

"Dr. Allen will be joining us any moment," he said, flipping open the dossier to reveal a page of cramped notes.

"In the meantime, why don't we . . . I've put this material together so that you can have a clear view of the situation."

He pulled the dossier round on the desk, and Ford sat forward, pretending to look at the page.

"How's she doing?" he said.

Lee glanced up from his notes.

"You haven't been in to see her?"

"I came straight in to you. I wanted to get this out of the way first thing. It's been hanging over my head ever since you mentioned that word *options* a few days ago. I mean with respect to Sunny's treatment. I can't believe any of them are very attractive."

Lee gave a little shrug.

"I understand," he said. "Well, in answer to your question, she's about the same this morning. Like I told you before, we're having limited success with the current treatment. We got a breathing space, but that was all. The toxin levels remain consistently high even after forty mils of the CDC antitoxin. And the bug, as you know, seems to be impervious to any of the antibiotics we have."

He looked down at his notes for a moment.

"What you have to understand is . . . I mean I dare say you worked this out already, but . . . well, this is uncharted territory. We are effectively . . ."

He turned over his empty hands in a gesture of helplessness.

"In the dark," said Ford.

"That's right. Feeling our way. My worry is that at some stage Sunny's body will react to the equine serum, and then I think we'll be facing the *um* . . . well, a *crisis*. Which is why I wanted to talk to you about alternatives."

There was a brief silence in which Ford stared at the broken autoclave.

"I'm talking, of course, about surgery," said Lee.

Ford sat back and brought his hands together on his lap. He had considered this possibility, had even decided it was the most likely next step, but so far had been unable to muster sufficient courage to contemplate exactly what might need to be done.

"I know it's not what you want to hear," said Lee, "but that's where we're at."

Ford nodded. It was not what he wanted to hear, but, after all, it was only what he had recommended for Denny—what he had recommended to Denny's wife. *Amputation is really the only alternative, Mrs. Denny. I urge you to consider it.*

"But it didn't work," he said under his breath.

"Pardon me?"

Ford took in Lee's frowning face.

"How do you know surgery will work?"

The other man shrugged.

"I don't. But we're fighting for Sunny's life here. My belief—and there is nothing in any of the tests I and the CDC have carried out to indicate the contrary—my belief is that this bug is reproducing in Sunny's gut, precisely speaking, in her large intestine. I fear that if we don't do *something* . . . something radical, we're going to lose . . ."

He stopped himself, but Ford knew exactly what he had been about to say. *We're going to lose this one.* He had heard it said a million times. It was part of the rough-and-ready vernacular that kept all the Willowbrook medical staff at one crucial remove from the suffering around them. For Lee, Ford realized, Sunny was one of many. His discomfort might be greater because Sunny was the daughter of a colleague, but she was still part of a larger picture—necessarily so. The Willowbrook was full of people facing similar choices every day. Thinking about it now, Ford wondered how he had ever been able to do this job. How he had ever been strong enough to use a scalpel. He was not strong enough to be the father of a patient—that was becoming increasingly clear. He framed the beginning of a question.

"So . . . ?"

Lee placed his hand flat on his loose bundle of notes, pressed down, as though swearing by *his* bible.

"So . . . So I've been considering this possibility. I have discussed it with Dr. Allen. He agrees that—"

"Conrad?"

"Yes. Conrad Allen. Obviously I wanted some expert input on this. As I say, he'll be joining us to give his—"

"Yes. Of course. What is it that you . . . What do you have in mind exactly?"

Lee pushed his hand back through his hair, and Ford could see that he was working himself up to saying what had to be said. "I think we have to consider a *colectomy*."

Ford blinked. They were going to cut open Sunny's belly, cut through her sleek child's body, reach into her, cut out her bowels.

"Colectomy," he said in a barely audible voice.

Lee averted his eyes for a moment.

"We've gone into this in great detail, Dr. Ford—considered it from every angle. Dr. Allen agrees with me that Sunny's best chance is, in fact, with a panproctocolectomy and ileostomy."

Ford gasped.

"What?"

"The simultaneous removal of all the colon and rectum and the construction of a spout ileostomy on the anterior abdominal wall."

"I know what it is, Dr. Lee. I'm just having a little trouble . . . I can't quite . . ."

"We're just talking now," said Lee putting up a hand. "You know we have to talk. We owe it to her."

"Yes," said Ford, trying to keep a grip, trying to be reasonable. He had seen ileostomies done, had even assisted in one or two. It was a long complicated process that came down to pulling the end of the small intestine out through the abdomen to allow the excretion of waste. If all went well, the patient survived on a special diet and regular care. Sunny would be left with a little spout—the stoma—protruding just below and to the right of her navel. Out of nowhere phrases from a manual pushed into his mind—*the edge of the everted bowel being sutured to the skin . . . when completed the stoma is inspected to ensure it is pink and healthy.* A stomach spout to shit through. They wanted to do that to his baby.

He was on his feet.

"Dr. Ford."

But he could no longer hear. There was too much pain, too much anguish to just sit there and take it. He felt as though he were being torn in two, ripped open. He tried to breathe, pressed both his hands against his face, pushing back against the chair.

"This . . . this is . . ."

He tried to say what it was, but the word, the *term* was buried too deep, hooked deep inside, already part of him like a rib. He would never be able to say what he felt about the cruelty, the arbitrariness, the ugliness of what was happening to his daughter—it was literally unspeakable.

Conrad Allen was in the room.

Then Ford was drinking Lee's bourbon again, taking a long drink and holding out the plastic cup for a refill. For a while nobody spoke. Ford drank thirstily, feeling the heat build inside, not even wiping the tears from his face. Allen had taken a seat on top of the autoclave.

It was Ford who eventually broke the silence.

"I won't do it," he said simply. Then, addressing Allen: "I won't allow it."

Allen sighed, kicked his worn crepe heels against the autoclave for a moment.

"Yeah, you will," he said gravely. "You'll do it."

Ford looked at his friend's face. He saw tiredness, compassion, but also determination.

"Why?"

"Because it's her only chance," said Allen.

"Dr. Lee is staking his reputation on this thing replicating in Sunny's colon. We can't hit it with a drug. We know that much. If we take out the colon, take out everything *below* the colon, with a little luck this . . . this *bug* goes too. Sunny lives."

Ford closed his eyes, thought of the life Sunny would have. The years of readjustment. Inch by inch. The *humiliation*, the suffering. The reconstruction of her whole personality around one terrible fact. A beautiful young girl on the brink of womanhood . . . with all her vitality, her drive, her ambition. *When completed the stoma is inspected . . .*

"Lives?" he said.

Allen nodded slowly. Then he reached over and took a drink of the bourbon himself. He sat staring down into the plastic cup.

"Yeah, lives. Not the way you'd planned, maybe. Not the way she'd planned, I realize that. But . . ."

He finished the sentence with a shrug.

"Bad things can happen," said Ford.

Allen held his gaze for a moment with an expression of deep sadness. Then he looked away.

"That's right," he said.

The three men sat quietly for a while longer. Then Ford stood up.

"Give me a little time," he said. "I need to think."

Lee was putting the bottle and his notes back into the autoclave.

"Don't leave it too long," he said.

He stood over Sunny for twenty minutes, willing her to open her eyes, but she slept on, her narrow chest rising and falling in time with the machines. It was just as well. If she'd been awake, she might have read the anguish in his face and realized how bad things must be. The idea of having to explain to her what Lee proposed to do was unbearable.

She was losing weight. There was a pinched look to the bridge of her nose that was familiar to him somehow, but not in Sunny. Then he knew whom it reminded him of—Carolyn. He had an abrupt sense of Carolyn's presence in the room. It was eerie enough to raise the hair on the back of his neck. So close to death, he thought, it wouldn't be surprising. The hiss and click of the respirator grew momentarily sinister. Then he shrugged his shoulders. In all his years working at the gates of death, working long nights when there was *only* death, when every admission to trauma had died, working with cases where patients had actually threatened to come back and haunt him—and *meant* it—he had never had the slightest inkling of a world beyond the stopped heart or the cold brain.

He bent forward and kissed Sunny's hair.

"It's just you and me, sweetheart," he said, tears starting to well again.

Then, like an apparition, but an apparition that favored pungent handcreams, Gloria was standing next to him. She said nothing for a moment, just stood there, looking down, breathing noisily.

"That doctor called again," she said.

She sounded tired, her voice coming out low and flat. Ford touched her shoulder in a silent greeting.

"Which doctor?" he said.

"Winget is it? Called twice this morning."

"Oh, Wingate—right. Did he say what he wanted?"

"Just said he wanted to talk to you. He wanted your home number, but I said it was against hospital policy to give out the personal numbers of staff."

Ford nodded. He tried to recall where he had left things with Wingate, but too much had happened in the last few days. He certainly couldn't face calling him now—couldn't face hearing him bitch about his Beverly Hills clients—not with so much on his mind. He looked at Gloria, then back at Sunny's blank face.

"If he calls again, you can give him my home number."

"Okay. If you say so. Oh . . . and that lady called, Miss Wray?"

Ford turned.

"When?"

"Lord," said Gloria. "You look awful tired. But I'm glad to see you're shaving again."

"Gloria, when did Miss Wray call?"

"This morning."

"What did she want?"

"She just wanted to know how Sunny was doing. I told her there was no change."

Ford looked back at Sunny. He couldn't understand it. Why would she call? She hadn't called him since their visit to Novak's condo. Then he realized that none of that mattered anymore. He had to focus on Sunny now. Forget Wray and her scheming. He had to make a decision on his daughter's behalf.

"She's doing real well," said Gloria. "She's a real fighter."

Ford nodded. If positive thinking ever cured anybody, Gloria was the person to have by your bedside. He had seen her struggle with some borderline cases for hours, some kid hit by a truck or a stabbing victim, struggle to help right up to the last breath, and then, when the life was gone, sigh and pick herself up and get on to the next case. It was something he had never quite gotten used to or been able to take for granted, this instinctive drive to care and cherish that he saw in the nursing staff.

Ford took Gloria's hand. They had never touched in this way before. She had given him her big momma-bear hug on different occasions, at end-of-year get togethers and so forth, but he had never touched her in this direct and simple manner. She returned the pressure of his grip, saying nothing. They stood looking down at Sunny like that as if in prayer. He had never noticed what powerful hands Gloria had. They were inspiring hands, the kind of hands that you could believe might pull you back from death itself . . . but, Ford realized, strong hands and a big heart could do nothing for Sunny now. She was way beyond that. She was going to have to face some of the sharper compassion that Helen Wray had once cited.

He let go, and, in answer to Gloria's inquisitive expression, said blankly, "They want to operate."

Gloria sighed and looked down at the bed.

"All the girl wants is a fighting chance," she said.

Fifteen minutes later he was on the 110 heading north. He would make a decision. He would get back to Lee before the day was out. But first he had to satisfy himself that he had exhausted every line of inquiry regarding a nonsurgical solution. He owed Sunny that much.

He got lost in downtown LA as usual, but finally got on to Figueroa going in the right direction. He stopped in a no-parking zone at the front steps of the county health services building. Climbing out of the car, he was startled to see West no more than twenty feet away. He was on the point of leaving, helping his attractive assistant get into a black limousine.

"Marshall!"

When West saw Ford making his way towards him, he frowned momentarily, as if he didn't recognize him, and then produced a warm smile. He said something to the assistant and then came to meet Ford on the sidewalk.

"You know, they're pretty strict around here about keeping that area clear," he said, pointing to Ford's car.

"I wanted to talk," said Ford. "It won't take more than a—"

"You're lucky you caught me," said West, tucking his tie inside his vest. "I was on my way. I've got a meeting with some Orange County people in Santa Monica."

As usual West was immaculately turned out, but Ford could see signs of strain. There were dabs of shadows under his eyes and a nick on his right cheek from a hasty shave.

"What's the news at the Willowbrook?" asked West, the smile replaced by a look of concern.

"I've just come from the hospital," said Ford.

"And?"

"They're want to operate."

"Jesus, you mean . . . ? Jesus Christ."

West looked away for a moment at the traffic. He drew his hand across his mouth.

"I'm real sorry to hear that, Marcus. Real sorry."

Then he looked back, and Ford could see that he was genuinely upset.

"I guess you find it hard to look on the bright side right now," said West, "but at least they're still in there—still pitching."

He put his hand on Ford's shoulder.

"And they're good people down there. Nobody knows that better than you."

For a moment Ford thought he was going to lose it. He pressed his jaws together, riding out the wave of emotion.

"Marshall, I came up here to ask if there was any news on the Apex investigation. I know it's kind of premature, but . . ."

West checked his wristwatch.

"Well, it is a little early, Marcus. Just getting qualified people to go through all that stuff has been a nightmare, and there are just so many strings I can pull—"

"So how long before—"

"And I have to say, I'm not very optimistic about getting a positive result."

Ford searched West's face for meaning. It was too early to be making statements, West had said so himself, but already he seemed ready to give up.

"What are you saying?" said Ford. "Apex wasn't looking at antisense?"

West picked at a loose thread on the sleeve of his pinstripe suit.

"That's right. I think . . . You know I hate to admit it, but I think we struck out on this one. Not that they weren't looking at antisense— they *were*, but not in connection with anti-infective agents."

He checked Ford's face for a reaction and then grimaced.

"This whole Omega thing is looking increasingly . . . what's the word?"

He clutched at the air as if miming the impossibility of holding smoke, bringing his theatrical skills to bear on the problem.

"But I *know* they have it," said Ford, taking a step back.

West looked over his shoulder at the limo. Blue exhaust curled from the tailpipe. The assistant was sticking her pretty head out and pointing to her watch.

"All I'm saying is, it doesn't look good." West gestured back to the assistant. *Won't be a minute*, the gesture said. "I'm sorry, Marcus, I really am."

"But I . . ."

He couldn't think of how to go on. Until that moment he hadn't realized how much he had staked on this chance, how much he had counted on it. He felt as though his last thread of hope was finally broken.

"Look, Marcus"—West looked down at his shoes—"you've . . . We've all been here before. There comes a time . . ." He looked up and down the street. "Jesus, I know this isn't the time or the place, but . . . there comes a time when you have to . . . when you have to accept, when you have to *let go*. There's a limit to what medicine can do. We all know that. We just kind of forgot for a while, didn't we?"

Ford looked down at the ground. West's voice seemed to come to him from a long way off.

"Don't think I haven't moved heaven and earth over this. Just read the press this morning. Front page of the LA *Times*. County health administration officials leaving Apex. Jesus, the company's spitting blood. We had a fax from their legal people more or less implying that Etienne Kempf or Stern had put us up to it. But, hey, it was worth a shot."

Ford looked up. He reached out and touched West's sleeve.

"Don't think I don't appreciate what you did. I know I owe you one."

West watched him for a moment and then took a couple of steps back.

"Forget it. Marcus, I wish I could give you more time right now, but—"

"Have you talked to Griffen?"

West looked confused for a moment.

"Who?"

"Scott Griffen, the director of research."

"Don't you listen to the radio? It's all over the news this morning."

"What is?"

"About Griffen. They found him in his pool. Drowned."

"What?"

Ford felt momentarily stunned.

"But, Marshall, don't you see? This is all part of the same thing. The same conspiracy."

West stroked his tie, drawing it between his fingers of his right hand.

"Marcus, look. I went down that road with you. And who knows, maybe with Apex we'll strike it lucky. Like I said, we're not very popular with them right now, but we got all their technical documentation, and that's what counts. If they're working on a new antibiotic, Marcus, we'll find out. That kind of technology isn't the sort of thing people carry about in their heads."

"But surely . . ." said Ford, coming forward, "surely Griffen's death . . . I mean, he was the director of research, for Christ's sake."

"Marcus, you're forgetting that—"

"He wanted to go ahead with . . . I believe he wanted to release the drug. He and Novak. Now they're dead."

A tight smile flickered on West's lips and then disappeared.

"Marcus, this is all getting a little wild. I understand you're upset because of Sunny, but what . . . I mean what are you saying? Are you saying we're not doing a proper job? Come on. Be reasonable. My people know everything there is to know about inspecting R and D facilities."

"But . . ."

He had taken hold of West's arm, his fingers pushing into the light-weight wool. West looked down and gave a short laugh—not of amusement. Then, seeing Ford's distress, his expression softened.

"Marcus, listen. You . . . You have to face up to reality. What is happening to Sunny . . . it happens to people *all* the time. *Every* day. People get sick and sometimes they get well again. But . . . *Christ*, it's so fundamental to medicine they should work it into the Hippocratic oath: *you can't cure all of the people all of the time.* It's that simple, Marcus. That brutal."

Ford let go of West's sleeve. He was right. *God grant me the serenity to accept the things I cannot change.* That was why Haynes had the plaque on his desk. It was something you had to keep at the front of your mind.

"And Sunny's getting the best care there is," said West. "You know that."

6

H e reached Kirkside Road just after two o'clock. The street was empty. The residents were at work, their kids in school. He had an overwhelming feeling of unreality. The harsh, flat light, the dusty-looking trees, the distant sound of a television game show, everything seemed utterly alien.

He went into the house and got himself a beer from the kitchen. Then he walked through to Sunny's bedroom. He stood for a while, looking at the pink floral wallpaper peeping through the patchwork of posters—Madonna and Whitney Houston holding their own against a variety of bands—heavy metal, acid house, gangsta rap. There was a scarf pinned over the bed on which the words DIRTY BLACK SUMMER had been stenciled in thick paint. Ford took the teddy bear from the top of the dresser and sat on the narrow bed.

There was a little bald patch between the bear's ears where Sunny had sucked and chewed through those formative years. Ford brought the toy to his mouth. It had a smell from . . . he couldn't make out what it was exactly. There was a dustiness, a faint fruitiness that seemed to recall the past—afternoon light through closed curtains, Sunny playing on the floor in the middle of her scattered toys. Ford wished he could go back to that innocent space.

He woke at four-thirty in the afternoon on Sunny's bed. Looking up at the ceiling, he realized he had made the decision.

When Lee finally came to the phone, he sounded agitated, out of breath.

"Is everything okay?" asked Ford.

"Yes, well, no. Not really. Mary Draper has come down with something."

"What?"

"Yes. I know she was one of your key people. Apparently she picked up some kind of bronchial condition. They've just isolated *Staphylococcus pneumoniae* in her sputum."

"Oh, my God."

"Of course everybody is praying it's not a resistant strain, but . . . Well, there you have it. Have you thought about what you want to do?"

Ford tightened his grip on the phone.

"I want to go through with the operation."

"Okay. Good. As per our discussion?"

"Yes."

"The panproctocolectomy and ileostomy?"

"If that's what you advise."

"Good. Yes, I do."

"And Conrad will . . . ?"

"He's already agreed to take that responsibility."

"How soon do you want to do it?"

"I think the sooner the better. I'll talk to Dr. Allen about the OR schedules, but I'd be aiming for tomorrow morning."

That soon.

"Oh . . . okay," said Ford. "Dr. Lee?"

"Yes."

"I appreciate all your efforts on Sunny's behalf."

There was a pause. Then, putting a little steel into his voice, Lee said, "We'll get her through this."

He hung up.

Eighteen hours, thought Ford. Then they would cut Sunny open. He sat immobile for a time, vaguely aware that he was hungry.

It was only then that he noticed the answering machine. It lay on a separate shelf under the telephone. The red light was winking on and off, indicating two messages. *Helen.* Her name lit up inside his head like a neon sign and was followed immediately by a rush of bitter feeling. But maybe she had found something out. Maybe she had only just gotten a chance to call him. Holding his breath, he pressed the messages button.

The first caller had left nothing on the tape. There was a rustling noise, what sounded like a sigh, and then whoever it was hung up. The second call was from Dr. Wingate.

"I'm sorry to bother you at home, Dr. Ford. It's just that . . . well, I heard something about Edward Turnbull. You remember? My patient? I thought it was something you might be interested to know."

He left two numbers.

Ford went through to the kitchen and got himself another beer. He couldn't believe the news about Mary Draper. This was how it was going to be from now on. They were all on the front line.

He went back into the living room and picked up the phone.

Wingate picked up almost immediately. He sounded more relaxed than the last time they had spoken. He asked about Sunny, and Ford, not wanting to get into the details, said there was no real change.

"Apparently you've been calling me at the hospital."

"Yes, a few times. I keep getting this lady . . ."

"Gloria, yes, that's right. I told her to give you my home number. She said you had something to tell me."

"Well . . . yes. Yes, I do. I don't know what to make of it, to tell you the truth."

"To do with Edward Turnbull?"

"Yes. As you know I'd been having a little trouble with his mother, Elizabeth Turnbull. I can't say things have improved in that department. But . . . well, to get to the point, I was contacted by a Dr. Lloyd a few days ago. He was after Edward's medical records."

"Did he say why?"

"Oh, yes. He's treating Edward now. It's a private hospital, the Aurora, up in Mandeville Canyon. Do you know it?"

"No, I don't."

"Well, neither do I, very well. It's small and, you know, *very* exclusive. Anyway the point is, after I sent the records, I followed up with a couple of calls. You know, I all but brought Edward into the world. I've known him since he was a baby. I wanted to know how the operation had gone."

"And?"

"And they told me the treatment had been successful and that he was *on the mend.*"

"The treatment? You mean the operation?"

"No. That's just it. I managed to ascertain that there had *been* no operation."

"He's getting better *without* the amputation?"

"Apparently, yes. Of course I asked for more information, but as I think I said before, the Turnbulls and the circles they move in put a premium on discretion. I was lucky to find out what I did."

"So . . ."

Ford didn't know what to say. He had no real sense of Wingate's character or the extent to which he could be relied on. It was an intriguing piece of news but perhaps no more than that.

"Dr. Ford?"

"Yes, I'm still here. I'm trying to get a sense of how important this—"

"Well, it may be nothing, of course. It may be that the boy's immune system came out on top. I mean, stranger things have happened. All I'm saying is, the last report I had of Edward Turnbull he was very sick with a multiresistant infection. You had to see his hand to appreciate what I'm saying."

"I see. But, as you say—"

"Well, I suppose what I'm really saying is, I would be intrigued to know what kind of treatment they were giving the boy, that's all. It's just a feeling I have. I mean, if anybody is going to have access to the latest medical treatment, it ought to be Edward Turnbull. Do you see what I mean?"

"I'm not sure I—"

"Well, quite apart from his family's financial . . . resources, his uncle more or less *runs* LA County."

"Pardon me?"

"I mean the health administration in LA County. His uncle runs it."

"And his uncle is . . . ?"

"Marshall West. You know, the czar. So, you can—"

"Yes. Yes, I can."

Wingate continued to talk, but Ford was no longer listening. All he

could think of was Marshall West's face as he'd stood there on the
street and told him it was time *to face up to reality.* What had he said?
Sunny's getting the best care there is. You know that.

Maybe that wasn't exactly true.

"Hello? Hello, are you still there?"

Ford gave himself a shake.

"Yes. Dr. Wingate, I have to go now. I really appreciate your
keeping me informed about this."

Wingate started to say something, but Ford just hung up. He sat
still for a moment, his mind racing. Then he got to his feet. *You can't
cure all of the people all of the time,* that was what West had told him.
All of the people some of the time, and *some of the people all of the
time.* Yes, thought Ford, keyed up now, looking through his desk for the
big LA County road map, *some* of the people—that was a different
matter.

PART SIX

OMEGA

1

Mirage Valley

Helen Wray looked at herself in the mirror and managed a nervous smile. She was about to meet the CEO of Stern Corporation, Randolph Whittaker, and wanted to look her best. Whittaker was a well-known ladies' man, and while he had several good reasons to be delighted with her efforts on Stern's behalf, that was no reason not to give him another. She turned her head slightly, tried a complicit smile bordering on the flirtatious. Even by her own exacting standards she looked terrific. The exertions of the past few weeks had taken her a couple of pounds under her ideal weight, bringing out a distinctly feline quality in her face. She gave her dove gray Gucci jacket a little tug downwards and smiled again, getting it right this time: a friendly smile, warm with just a hint of playfulness.

The Stern Corporation laboratories were located twelve miles east of the town of Lancaster in the extreme north of LA County, not far from Edwards Air Force Base. From a distance the building had the look of a high-tech grain silo, except that it was surrounded not by rolling wheatfields but by scrubby desert and a scattering of Joshua trees.

Stern Corporation undertook the business of anticipating the requirements of the twenty-first century protected by an air-conditioned steel-and-glass envelope. The labs themselves, while packed with state-of-the-art equipment, were no more than functional, providing a stark contrast with the executive suites, boardroom, and reception rooms on the fourth floor. The move to Lancaster had been voted during a stock-holders' meeting back in the mid-eighties, and a disgruntled board had insisted that if they were to be stuck out in the desert, then at least let it be in comfort. The designers and architects had taken them at their word.

Wray's meeting was scheduled for three o'clock in Whittaker's office, but before that she planned to call in on Murray Kernahan, Stern's R&D head. She had always cultivated Kernahan as a contact because it was useful to know what was coming down the pipeline. The imminent arrival of a new beta-blocker or analgesic might require some shift in her sales focus, even in the kinds of clients she was developing. For his part Kernahan had always been very receptive, claiming an interest in hearing what the clients were saying about Stern products, though Wray suspected that his openness was, at least in part, social.

Having notified Whittaker's personal assistant of her presence in the building, Wray took the elevator down to the first floor and, using her security pass, entered the first-floor laboratories through the double glass doors.

Kernahan was, as usual, up to his ears in work. He liked nothing better than to get into his lab coat, all the more since the nature of his work—interfacing between the upper tiers of management and the research teams—didn't allow it that often. Not surprisingly, he had insisted on being directly involved from the outset with the development of the antisense material recently "recovered" by Stern.

Like everybody else at Stern, or at least those people who knew anything about it, he took the view that the company should have had the material back in '92, at the time of the Helical takeover. The fact that Stern had decided to take an unorthodox route to reacquire Helical's work was seen as a reflection of market reality. Charles Novak's death was a clear indication of the harsh nature of that reality—proof that there were other interested parties ready to play even dirtier.

A ripple of discomfort had gone through senior management when news first reached them of how the Helical technology had been "reacquired." But that was soon forgotten in the ensuing excitement. For the R&D people lucky enough to be working with antisense technology, the material, the *ideas*, were like a sudden rush of pure oxygen.

For the first few days the team under Kernahan's supervision hardly ate or slept, running on pure adrenaline and instant coffee.

Kernahan was pouring himself his fifth cup of the morning, his eyes glancing to a computer printout, when Wray entered his office.

"Murray?"

Kernahan looked up and smiled.

"Helen, hi! I heard you were coming in."

Wray pointed to his cup.

"Stern should take a position in coffee futures."

"You want one? It's instant."

Wray accepted, though she had no intention of drinking. They ground their own beans on the fourth floor, and that was how she liked it.

"So," said Kernahan confidentially, "you're in to see the man."

"That's right. He tells me you are making great progress with Ribomax."

Stern had already decided on a brand name for the new drug.

Kernahan jabbed his thumb over his shoulder.

"These guys are having the time of their lives," he said, keeping his voice low, although there was nobody in earshot. "What a buzz, I'm telling you. 'Course it helps having worked in the same area for so long. We find that we were pretty much in the ballpark with a lot of the ideas, but I have to admit, Novak was one hell of a chemist. I mean, talk about lateral thinking." He stroked his beard for a moment, considering. "The way he could step back from a problem, from a discovery, and then come at it from a whole new angle. The way he used knowledge. It's been an education, I can tell you."

"How far away are you from producing the first . . . ?"

Kernahan opposed his fingertips and smiled.

"Everybody who comes down here asks the same question. Here we are riding the roller coaster, and all you guys want to know is when are we going to get off."

Wray shrugged.

"That's business, I guess. So are you anywhere near . . . ?"

"It's already done," said Kernahan.

"You're producing it?"

"Sure. Not industrially of course. That's going to take a lot longer.

We're talking to our plant-design people about that. And anyway, the board has to decide what they want to do with this thing first. How they want to play it. My guess is they'll want to keep the whole thing under wraps until the patent comes through. That could take a couple of years."

"But you've actually made some?"

Kernahan smiled and reached down beside his desk.

"Helen, let me put you out of your misery."

He brought up a small cardboard case of the sort used to store vials of serum. Wray could see the small bottles inside. Kernahan took one out.

"Voila," he said, presenting the bottle as though it were a fine claret. "Chateau Stern '97."

Wray reached across the desk and took the bottle. It was such a small thing. A slender bottle containing a clear, slightly viscous fluid. Omega. Ribomax. Billions of dollars in sales.

"Have you tested it?"

"We've shown it to a few cultures."

"A few?"

"Well, a few thousand, actually."

Kernahan shook his head in admiration.

"It's radical. You pick up the petri dish the next morning, and, well . . . the bacteria are dead in their tracks. They just stop dividing. A day later and they start to die. Like I say, *radical*. And the funny thing is . . . at the heart of it, it's so . . . intelligent, subtle. I'm not expecting many adverse side effects."

"So the rumors about Omega were true?"

Kernahan shrugged.

"Rumors schmoomers." He paused for a moment, considering Wray's delicate clavicles, then leaned forward a little. "And if you want a piece of free advice, don't bother mentioning the O word around here. People get a little antsy."

"I'll bet."

She considered the bottle again.

"Is that the form it's going to take?" she said.

"A serum, you mean? Yes. Synthetic RNA does best in that medium. It's fragile as hell, actually."

So fragile, thought Wray, but strong enough to burst the market wide open, to fly into the heart of the market and detonate like a nuclear warhead—billions of dollars of sales flying out like shock waves. It was going to change everything, including her life. In half an hour from now, Whittaker was going to give her the biggest bonus in her life, but more than that, he would hand her a block of options on Stern stock. He'd already hinted as much. When Wall Street got wind of Ribomax, the stock would go critical, making her a millionaire at least. Stern was going to go through the roof and she was going to be riding it. She could almost feel the pressure of money building up.

"I can't believe I'm holding it," she said in a quiet voice. "I've dreamed about it for so long."

"I know exactly what you mean," said Kernahan. "It's going to make a hell of a difference to a lot of sick people. I only wish we could get it out to the hospitals right away."

Wray looked up as Kernahan took the bottle from her hand.

"Yes," she said. "I . . . I guess that's right."

The phone rang. Kernahan picked up.

"Kernahan. Yes . . . Yes, she is."

He handed the phone across the desk.

It was Whittaker himself. He sounded as if he were high.

"Helen, I really appreciate your coming in. I wanted to express my gratitude personally for . . . for all your hard work."

"That's very kind of you," Helen said, the beginnings of a blush rising to her cheeks.

"Now, listen, Helen, the way things have turned out . . . I think it's time we sat down and . . ." He burst into a hard, euphoric laugh. "Look, this is ridiculous," he said. "Just come up to my office right away."

Wray handed the phone back to Kernahan. Her hand was shaking. Kernahan smiled.

"You look like you just won the lottery," he said.

Wray shrugged. "It kind of feels like that," she said. She stood up.

"Look, Murray, I've got to go up to see Randolph now. But . . . can I come back down afterwards? There's a few things I'd like to sort out."

Kernahan smiled.

"Just can't stay away, huh? I understand. The only problem is I've got a meeting this afternoon with some of the other directors. They want to be briefed on the technology."

He tapped the bottle.

"I'm taking it up for them to admire. Just the one, mind you. I can't afford to have them break the whole case. You know what they're like after a heavy lunch. They'll probably drop it."

Wray nodded.

"Oh, well, another time, then."

"Sure," said Kernahan, getting to his feet. "My blast-proof door is always open."

2

The late afternoon sun flared against the dirty windshield as Ford turned off San Vicente and headed across Sunset into the shady mansion-land of Brentwood Heights. The Buick took the speed bumps with its usual nonchalance, bucking and lurching like a bull at a rodeo, but Ford didn't slow down to the statutory crawl until a patrol car turned out into the road behind him. It stayed there for three blocks, watching him, keeping him in its sights, probably checking his plates. Then it cut a U-turn and headed back the other way. Ford watched it disappear in the mirror, then hit the accelerator again.

On the seat beside him lay a black doctor's bag. It was an item of medical paraphernalia he'd owned for years, although he'd never actually used it for work. His godparents had given it to him when he'd graduated from med school, presumably in the belief that he would soon be making housecalls. Since then it had served as a lunch box, a camera bag, and once, when he and Carolyn had first started dating, as a makeshift champagne cooler. Now it concealed a Sig-Sauer .38 and an assortment of family medicines hastily swept from the bathroom cabinet. He'd thought about putting on a white coat too, but had opted instead for a jacket and tie and a proper wet shave. The coat he left ostentatiously draped over the back of the seat.

Mandeville Canyon snaked its way north through the fringes of the Santa Monica mountains, which divided West Los Angeles from the sprawling suburbia of the San Fernando Valley. It was quiet: no traffic on the road because most people used the nearby freeway, no people on the sidewalks because this was still LA. The houses were comfortable here, not ostentatious, except that now and again, halfway up a hillside, or tucked away at the bottom of a private drive, Ford glimpsed more substantial properties, homes of movie stars, maybe, who were tired of the stalkers and paparazzi in town.

Sky Valley Road lay at the top of the canyon. On the road map it was a tiny black line, no more than a quarter inch long. The entrance to the Aurora Clinic lay at the end, behind a screen of tall cypress trees that formed a neat semicircle right around the property. The building itself was two stories high, red-brown brick, part-timbered with verandahs and ornaments that gave it an oriental resonance. As he drove up to the gates, Ford wondered how many patients it could accommodate. It was a quarter the size of the Willowbrook, but then the community it served—if *community* was the right word—was probably one percent the size of the Willowbrook's, if that.

The gates were not manned. Ford rolled down his window and found himself looking into the lens of a security camera. It was mounted on a concrete post, hidden away between the cypresses and the brick wall behind them. There was another one on the other side, and a third mounted directly above the gates. There didn't seem to be a bell or an intercom. Was he supposed to show the cameras some identification? He was reaching into his jacket for his wallet, when, without warning, the gates opened.

There was a visitors' parking lot at the side of the building, the bays shaded by flowering acacia and citrus trees. In one corner a man dressed in gray livery was polishing the side mirrors of a Rolls-Royce Silver Shadow. As the Buick went by he stared at the crumpled fender as if it were something catching. Ford parked in the opposite corner and climbed out onto the gravel. It was cooler up here than in the city, and the breeze wore a subtle perfume of lemons and something sweeter that he couldn't place. As he was walking towards the sign marked VISITORS, carrying his bag, he noticed a young woman standing in one of the windows on the second floor: a nurse in a pristine white uniform. She was folding something. She watched him for a second and then turned away.

The reception area was hexagonal, with passageways going off to left and right. The desk stood in the middle, with a glass atrium directly behind it, complete with an ornamental fountain and several species of dwarf trees, including one that looked like a miniature cedar of Lebanon.

"Welcome to the Aurora Clinic. How may I help you?" said the receptionist.

She wore the same uniform as the girl in the window, a tailored white coat, the collar finished off with a thin stripe of royal blue. She was maybe twenty-five, blonde hair, piercing blue eyes. Her name badge read Lauren Heller.

Ford forced a smile, tried to make it warm, relaxed.

"Yes, I'm Dr. Marcus Ford." He made the statement sound like a question, as if she was supposed to know who he was. "I'm here to give a second opinion. The patient's name is Turnbull. Edward Turnbull, I believe."

The receptionist showed him a white smile and an easy ten thousand dollars of orthodontistry.

"Thank you. I'll just check the schedule."

She swiveled around to a computer terminal and tapped in a few keys. Ford gazed around casually. A security man in a blue sports coat came out of a door by the main entrance, took a look at him, then wandered off down the corridor. Before the door swung shut, Ford glimpsed a row of television monitors and at least two more men dressed the same way.

"I'm sorry. We've nothing scheduled for Mr. Turnbull this afternoon."

Ford frowned.

"I understood from Dr. Lloyd that it was a matter of some urgency. Postinfective pharyngeal dysphagia, in fact. Perhaps he didn't have time to log it in."

A flicker of confusion registered on Miss Heller's wrinkle-free face.

"I suppose . . . I'm afraid Dr. Lloyd's not here right now."

Ford stared.

"Is there any reason why he should be?" he said.

"Well, I don't . . . Didn't you want to check with him?"

"No," said Ford. "A second opinion. I'm to give a second opinion, an *independent* opinion." The receptionist nodded blankly. "Independently, you see? So if you'd just direct me to Mr. Turnbull's ward—I mean, his room—I can get on with it."

Miss Heller tapped a few more keys. Three little parallel creases had appeared in the middle of her forehead.

"But we've nothing on the schedule," she said, looking at the screen. "We're not supposed to—"

"Listen, Lauren," said Ford. He leaned onto the counter, trying to keep smiling. "I've come all the way from Santa Monica to check on this patient. On rather short notice, as a matter of fact. Now, personally, I'd be quite happy to turn right around and go back, but I don't think the Turnbulls would be. You know, they're old Oscar Turnbull's family, and, well"—he lowered his voice to a whisper—"litigious as hell. So I think for Dr. Lloyd's sake . . ."

Miss Heller looked around, as if in need of help.

"Oh . . . well. I guess if it's urgent."

"It certainly could be."

She pointed down one of the corridors.

"I'll give you a visitor's pass." She handed him a green clip-on badge. "Take one of the elevators to the second floor. Turn left. He's in Suite C-three."

Ford attached the badge to his lapel and walked away. As soon as he was out of sight, the receptionist pulled out a list of phone numbers, found the one she was looking for, and dialed.

"Hello? I'm sorry to trouble you. This is Lauren Heller from the Aurora Clinic. I wonder, is Dr. Lloyd there by any chance?"

There was an upright chair outside the room, with a folded copy of *Newsweek* magazine and glass tumbler of mineral water resting on top of it. Ford checked up and down the corridor. Through a pair of open fire doors he glimpsed a nurse wheeling a trolley away. There were voices, laughter, then silence. He reached for the door handle and turned it.

The venetian blinds were half closed against the setting sun. It was a big room, furnished like a modern hotel. There were neatly arranged flowers in blue vases, an occasional table, upholstered chairs, a magazine rack, a big television in one corner. A small strip-light in a brass fitting illuminated a reproduction impressionist landscape. Another door led off into a private bathroom, from which a faint hiss of plumbing was audible. Instead of the pungent hospital smell of phenolic disinfectant, Ford thought he could smell lavender.

Turnbull lay asleep on his bed, his arms by his sides. Wingate was right: there had certainly been no amputation. In fact, a gauze bandage wrapped around the boy's right hand and a drip at the left wrist were the only obvious indications that he had ever been sick.

Ford moved closer. The fingers of the right hand were still swollen, he could see that now. The skin was stretched tight around the finger joints, and there was a general yellowish discoloration between the knuckles, although that could have been iodine. The skin around the wrist was also blue and puffy, and on the underside of the forearm there appeared to be the aftermath of a petechial rash: at some point the boy had begun to hemorrhage into his skin. The bacteria had eaten right through a blood vessel. That must have happened sometime after Wingate's final diagnosis, but given the absence of a fracture, it all squared with his account of a life-threatening infection—but an infection that had apparently been beaten.

"Who are you?"

The boy was sitting up. The pitch of his voice was scarcely deeper than an adolescent's. He sounded scared.

"Hi, there. I'm *um* . . . I'm Dr. Ford, Dr. Marcus Ford."

The boy lay back again, smiling.

"I'd shake your hand, Doc, but, as you can see . . ."

Ford smiled back, keeping up the bedside manner. He wasn't sure how best to go about this.

"That's all right, Edward." He put his bag down on a chair. "No need for formalities."

Turnbull yawned.

"Am I getting out of here soon? Dr. Lloyd said I'd be out by the end of the week, but my mom says she's not gonna take any chances. If she has her way, I'll be laid up here till Christmas."

Ford turned on a light above the bed. Letting patients' relatives decide when to vacate a hospital bed wasn't a concept he was used to.

"I'm sure tomorrow will be fine," he said. "How long have you actually been here now?"

"About ten days," said Turnbull. "Did Dr. Lloyd send you over?"

"Yes, that's right. He wants a second opinion."

"About what? I feel great. All I need is a drink."

He reached over for a torpedo switch that lay on top of his bedside cabinet. Ford guessed it summoned a nurse—or was it just room service?

"Wait a second," he said, pulling the switch out of Turnbull's reach. "No fluids for the moment. It could interfere with the tests."

The boy looked at him for a moment.

"What tests?" he said. He sounded wide awake now.

"Well, yours is a very unusual case; you probably know that. We can't be too careful, can we?"

"Dr. Lloyd did say I *was* very lucky," Turnbull said, looking down at his arm.

"Did he . . . Did he explain why? I mean, why you were lucky?"

The boy blinked and appeared to reflect for a moment.

"Well, the infection was real bad, I know that. Dr. Wingate—my regular doctor—I think he got quite worried about it. It did get pretty gross, actually. And it hurt like hell. Ached real bad. But you people up here, I guess you've got all the latest stuff, right?"

He yawned. Ford smiled reassuringly. It sounded as if the possibility of amputation had never actually been put to the boy. Probably Wingate hadn't had the guts to tell him or hadn't been given the chance. Officer Denny, on the other hand, had been spared nothing: the amputation had gone ahead and he had died anyway, died from an infection that nothing could stop—or so everybody thought. Ford felt a surge of anger. Denny had been a hardworking, decent guy, with friends and family. But they had let him die.

"Listen to me, Edward. Has Dr. Lloyd kept you fully informed about your treatment here? Has he explained to you what he's doing?"

"Kind of. I was given papers to sign. My mom too. Some kind of liability waiver. It explained things. To tell you the truth, I didn't read it all. I mean, I wasn't in great shape at the time."

"Do you remember anything about it?"

"It's some kind of experimental treatment, right? A drug."

Ford nodded. "That's right."

Turnbull smiled. He was a confident young man, strong, good-looking, his attention fixed on whatever bright future he had imagined for himself.

"I guess I was like a kind of guinea pig. As a matter of fact, I'm surprised Mom went along with it. Where her kids are concerned, she's what you might call risk averse."

"Edward, when was the last time you had to take these drugs?"

Turnbull coughed.

"I'm taking 'em all the time. Three times a day. They come and stand over me while I swallow." There was a flicker of alarm in his eyes. "Is everything okay? There's no problem, is there?"

"No, no problem. I'd say you're healing up very well here. Remarkably well."

"The swelling's gone right down. It still aches a little, and I get these bad twinges. But I feel much better generally."

"That's good. Now, tell me, who administers these drugs? Do you know where they're kept?"

"Well, the nurse comes around three times a day. She . . . Wait a minute." He stopped, slowly eased himself up again. "You want to know where they're kept? Why would you . . . ?"

Something about the situation got him worried.

"Who are you?"

He reached over for the torpedo switch, but Ford got there first, pushed it out of reach.

"Look, I don't have time to explain."

The boy was looking increasingly alarmed.

"Who the hell are you? What do you want?"

"Just listen to me. That drug you were given, I have to get hold of it. Right now. There are people dying *right now*, and that drug, the drug that saved your arm, can save their lives. It's their only chance."

"You don't even work here, do you?"

"What difference does it make? What I'm telling you is true. This drug is being withheld from people who are dying."

"Christ, I bet you're not even a doctor. What are you, some kind of—"

"Sure I'm a doctor." Ford opened his bag, reached inside for the Sig. "Here are my qualifications."

"Jesus Christ!"

There was a sharp knocking at the door. A muffled voice from the other side.

"Everything all right in there, Mr. Turnbull?"

Ford put the gun against the boy's temple.

"Everything's all right," Ford said through clenched teeth. "Say it!"

The boy looked at the gun. Ford's hand was shaking.

"I'm fine," he called out. "No problem."

Ford took the remote control from the bedside, turned on the television: cowboys in plaid shirts were shooting at each other from behind water troughs and wagon wheels. He turned the volume up high.

"I'm sorry it has to be this way," he said, taking a step back. "But there isn't much time."

"He told me you'd called him in specially, for a second opinion. Pharyngeal dysphagia, I think he said. Something serious, anyway."

The receptionist blushed as the voice at the other end of the line switched from a tone of disbelief to one of anger. Pharyngeal dysphagia was, apparently, a type of sore throat.

"Yes, of course, Dr. Lloyd. Yes, yes, right away. I am sorry. Yes, good—"

Dr. Lloyd had hung up. Immediately the receptionist punched in another number, this time just four digits.

"Hello, Security? This is Lauren Heller. I'm afraid we have a problem."

"Sure," said Turnbull, "sure. Whatever you say."

"Just tell me—"

"They're down there. In the cabinet. All my medication is right there."

The cupboard was part of the bedside unit. Ford rummaged through packets of sterile dressings and needles, cotton wool, gauze, a tube of centrimide disinfectant, and then at last he found it: a brown plastic bottle, with no label. He unscrewed the cap.

There were thirty or forty bicolored capsules, half pink and half yellow. Hastily Ford emptied a few of them into the palm of his hand. Then he was looking at it—Omega. Somehow he had expected something more, something clearly and demonstrably *unique*. Yet it looked just like any other oral antibiotic, just a handful of capsules. It struck him as ludicrously prosaic. Like penicillin, and its hundreds of successor drugs, it was a lifesaver, a miracle cure. Yet it looked no more miraculous than a handful of candy. Perhaps it was no wonder antibiotics had been so quickly and universally taken for granted, misused, squandered. They were just products, demanded by people, supplied by business. And that was the way they would stay until the supply finally dried up, for good.

Ford held up the bottle. "Are these the capsules you take?"

"Yes, yes," said the boy. "Three a day."

The boy had been in for ten days, had been all but cured in that time. There were enough capsules left to do the same for Sunny. And that was all that mattered now.

Ford put the bottle inside his black bag. All he had to do was get out and away. He took the torpedo switch and yanked it clear of the wall. But how could he hope to keep Turnbull quiet? There was no way he could bind him and gag him. There was nothing there to do it with.

"Look," he said. "I'm sorry about the gun. But it's my daughter. My daughter's life. I need to get to her before it's too late."

The boy stared, said nothing.

"If you call out right away, before I'm out of here, there's a chance I won't make it. And then my daughter may die." Ford hid the gun inside his jacket pocket. "She's thirteen years old, Edward. She deserves the same chance you had, don't you think? Even if she doesn't have quite the same . . . connections that your family has. Because that's what this is all about. Who gets healed and who doesn't. Who lives and who dies. Do you understand what I'm saying?"

Turnbull's lips parted as if he were about to say something, but nothing came.

"Well," said Ford, turning back towards the door. "I guess it's up to you."

The man outside was standing with his hands behind his back. Hearing the door, he turned. A tall man in a gray suit.

"An excellent recovery," Ford said, his grip tightening on the gun in his pocket. "Mr. Turnbull should be out of here in a couple of days."

"Glad to hear it," the man said, watching him coolly.

Ford smiled and turned towards the elevators, afraid that Turnbull would call out any moment. But there was no sound. *The boy was going to wait.* Ford was about to press the call button when the steel doors slid open. Two security men in the blue sports coats were waiting on the other side.

"That's him," said one. "Hey, you!"

Ford stepped back, pulled out the gun.

"Don't move or I'll—"

It felt as if he'd been hit by a truck. He pitched forward, a pair of muscular arms locked round him. It was the guy in the suit. The weight drove him over, down. He landed hard on the tiled floor, shoulder first. One of the blue coats stamped on his wrist, kicked away the gun.

"Call the police, Jack."

Ford tried to speak, but the fall had knocked the wind out of him. He thought for a moment he was going to vomit.

"Fucking psycho," someone said.

Jack got on his radio, started talking. The man in the suit pinned Ford's arms halfway up his back.

"Wait just a moment there, please, gentlemen."

A third man stepped out of the elevator. He was balding and built more lightly than the others. The way he carried himself, he looked as though he was in charge.

"I don't think we need the police just yet."

"But, Mr. Denman, the guy pulled a gun," said Jack.

Mr. Denman knelt down next to Ford. There was a smell of after-shave—Cool Water or something sporty.

"That's true," he said, turning his head so that it was in line with Ford's. "It is a serious matter. But I still think we can get it all cleared up without the need for charges. Don't you think so, Dr. Ford?"

3

Right out of the blue he had offered her Paris.

Driving towards the bloody sunset half an hour later, Helen Wray relived the moment once again. Whittaker had been standing when she entered the room, looking out across the desert towards the purple haze of the Shadow Mountains. He'd turned and looked at her. He was actually rocking up and down on the balls of his feet. She could sense his excitement. Then he'd smiled and said, "Helen, how do you feel about Paris?"

And she knew then that they weren't just going to reward her for what she'd done. They needed her, *valued* her. Because Paris could only mean one thing: head of sales and marketing, Europe. And that was a big job. In fact, it dawned on her now, she would be ten years younger than anybody else at Stern with that level of seniority. The *only* woman.

She had mumbled some incoherent answer, and then Whittaker had begun to outline "the package" he had in mind. Her salary would double, naturally, but that was just the beginning. She would be issued a block of stock options, options that would already be worth a good deal in the market, but which, he added with a complicit smile, would probably be a good idea to hang on to for a couple of years, *given what we now know* (she liked the way he said *we*). And when she did not respond immediately—it was all too much to take in—he'd added that the options were in no way conditional upon her accepting the post. Moving to Europe was a big step, and there were always personal considerations, he recognized that. And, of course, her bonus position would not be affected, the bonus in question being a reflection of past—and recent—achievements.

"Helen, we just feel you're the best person for the job," he'd ended by saying, almost defensively. "You've earned it."

She'd managed to get out of his office with a reasonable degree of composure. But no sooner had the door closed behind her than the elation took over. Hurrying past Whittaker's personal assistant, she dove into the nearest bathroom, just to steady herself, just to let the emotion out for a moment, unobserved. She'd felt light, giddy, and, at the same time, invincible. It was a feeling she'd worked and fought and struggled for, and now it was there, done, delivered. She'd splashed water on her face, drank from the palms of her hands. It had spoiled her makeup. Laughing, she'd taken the rest off with a paper towel, leaving her face looking flushed, her skin shiny.

She'd gone back out to the fourth floor, helped herself to a cup of coffee, sipped at it once, and then sat alone for a while in an empty meeting room staring at the aluminium grid on the ceiling. She remembered that she had to get back to Marvyn Lennox, the guy who had helped with Novak's apartment. If it hadn't been for his good work, she would never have gotten Novak's records. But it had been impossible to sit still for long. Almost right away she had gotten up again, and without saying anything to anyone, left the building.

Now, gripping the wheel of the BMW, she was struggling to keep her speed down. Every time she thought about what was happening to her, about all the infinite possibilities now opening up before her, she found herself leaning on the accelerator. It *was* the executive fast track. It *was* life in the fast lane. She felt as if she were being hurled into the future. And she realized that now she could do whatever she wanted. Her success was no longer conditional upon anything or anyone. *They* needed *her*. And it didn't matter if she never worked again. She was free.

But then the road was running out. The asphalt surface was split and buckled. Loose grit rapped the underside of the car. Then the impact with a pothole almost threw her against the roof. She put on the brakes and slewed to a halt just short of a junction. A small metal sign read 150th Street East, although there was nothing for miles around but Joshua trees and scrub. She was somewhere on the outskirts of Lancaster, a city of a thousand square miles—planned, but never built, except for a huddle of housing developments by the Sierra Highway. A distant cluster of sodium streetlights marked the spot.

She sat for a while, unable to understand what had happened. She knew this road so well, and for a moment she had the impression that the road itself had changed, had reverted to what it must have been twenty years ago. She checked her wristwatch. Then she turned and looked back at the ruler-straight track and her own drifting dust.

There was something she had been meaning to do. She remembered now. With all the excitement she'd put it out of her mind, hadn't wanted it to cloud things. But now . . .

Staring out at the desert, she picked up the car phone, and keyed in the number for the Willowbrook's pediatric ICU. It was Conrad Allen who answered. His voice sounded as though it were coming from a long way off.

"I thought you'd be gone by now, Conrad," she said. "Aren't you supposed to be starting at Cedars-Sinai?"

"Yeah, well . . . Helen, can you hang on just a . . ."

Helen listened to muffled voices. A woman's, urgent, distressed; then Allen's, explaining something with exaggerated calm.

"Sorry about that. The ICU's blood gas machine is on the fritz. So naturally everybody has to start screaming. What was it you were . . . ? Oh, yeah, the job. Well, you know. What with one thing and another, I . . . what's the expression? Well, *I changed my mind*. I don't know. I guess I didn't think it was the right move for me in the end."

Helen felt a vague wash of irritation—a confusing feeling that was almost like physical discomfort.

"But I thought this was what you had been waiting for," she said. "Marcus said you were all set."

Allen sighed into the phone. It had obviously been a long day.

"Yeah . . . Yeah, I was, but . . . I didn't want to leave just yet. Not with all this going on. I mean, the problems."

"You're staying *because* of the problems?"

"Well"—he laughed, seeing the funny side of it—"we're supposed to make things better, right? I mean, doctors. That's what we train for. Besides, their . . . the approach they have up there, in those kinds of places, I'm not altogether happy about it. I don't think it's for me."

Helen cut the engine.

"It sounds like you're staying for good."

"Well, nothing's forever. Anyway, we'll see." There was a pause, a crackle on the line. "So was there anything . . . ?"

There was one Joshua tree that was bigger than the rest. Its silhouette stood out stark and black against the sky. It looked dead, but it came to Helen that the species was, in truth, prolifically fertile. It had to be because of its environment, the white-hot days, the freezing nights. Kernahan had told her that.

"Helen?"

"Yes. Sorry, I was just . . . I'm fine, fine. I called . . . I wanted to know about Sunny Ford. Is she . . . Is there any change?"

There was a long pause. Helen could hear the noise of activity in the ICU.

"No," said Allen eventually. "I'm afraid not. In fact we're going to operate tomorrow morning."

"Operate? You mean, surgery?"

"Uh-huh. A colectomy."

"A colectomy? What does that involve?"

Allen hesitated.

"I'm sorry . . . Helen, but we're not supposed to give out those kinds of details. Only to immediate family."

Helen stared hard at the Joshua tree.

"Yes. Yes, of course," she said.

"It's just one of those rules."

"Sure, I understand. Will you be . . . ?"

"Operating? Yes."

"Is Dr. Lee there?"

"I don't . . . No, I don't think he is. But I'll tell him you called, if you like."

She wanted to say something, something more, but no words came.

"Yes, please. Well, then . . ."

She frowned, trying to find something appropriate to say, but what was there? What could you say in the face of such bleakness?

"Good luck, Conrad," was all she could manage.

She hung up and then sat for a moment listening to the silence. Outside, the sunset had deepened into scarlet and indigo. She climbed out of the car and was surprised by the coolness of the desert air. Overhead the stars were shimmering in a cobalt sky, but away to the south she could see big nimbus clouds building. She told herself that she had never seen anything so beautiful.

Then she suddenly wanted to walk, to walk out into the desert. She wanted to feel its emptiness, to feel the space. She took a couple of paces off the road—lost her footing, stumbled. She looked down at her Ferragamo shoes and was surprised to see that they were covered in dust. Tears pricked at her eyes. She was just overwrought, she told herself, dabbing at her lashes with the back of her hand.

4

They kept him in a bare, windowless room with two plastic chairs on either side of a Formica-covered table and a line of laundry bins next to a chute. High up on one wall a fan turned behind a steel grille, blowing a stream of warm, detergent-smelling air across his forehead. A poster of Yosemite National Park was pinned to the back of the door.

He had tried to argue with them. All he needed was half an hour. All he needed to do was get across town, get to the Willowbrook with the drug, and Sunny would be all right. He had been so close, had held Omega in the palm of his hand. He had pleaded with them, offered to go with them, to pay them, anything, but they hadn't listened. There had been a brief, unceremonious search in which they had taken his wallet, his car keys, his black bag, and then the bottle of capsules.

It was Denman who had stayed with him in the room, flicking through a copy of *Newsweek*, looking up at him occasionally and smiling.

At ten minutes before eight he heard footsteps outside in the hall. He thought at first it was the police. Then somebody was asking questions, getting answers from the big guy in the suit who'd been standing outside Edward Turnbull's room. Their voices were subdued, as if they didn't want to be overheard. Denman put down the magazine and got to his feet.

"Who's that?" Ford asked. "Your boss?"

Denman raised a warning finger, but said nothing, just stood there, watching the door until it opened and Marshall West stepped into the room.

Ford got to his feet. He'd expected somebody from the hospital, the medical director or the CEO. The flood of relief he felt at the sight of his friend immediately gave way to confusion. It didn't make any sense. West came into the room until he was standing directly opposite Ford on the other side of the table.

"Hello, Marcus," he said. There was weariness in his voice and disappointment. He gestured to the empty plastic chair.

"Mind if I sit down?"

He looked different from the way he had that morning. His skin was shiny and the shaving nick was red and angry as if he had been scratching at it. Ford watched him sit down and then lowered himself back into his chair.

"We found these on him," said Denman. He put the bottle of capsules on the table.

West eyed Ford for a moment, picked up the bottle, and unscrewed the cap. He emptied some of the pink-and-yellow capsules into the palm of his hand and closed his fist around them, as if weighing their worth.

"Where did you get these?" he asked.

And then Ford understood. Denman and the others were working for West. *He* was their boss. And they were here to guard the very thing Ford had come looking for.

"Where do you think?" he said.

West nodded slowly.

"Ah, yes, my nephew." He began putting the capsules back one by one into their bottle. His hands were shaking. "He's a good kid, you know. I think he'll go far."

"Further than he would have with one arm, that's for sure."

West smiled, let the last capsules drop into the bottle. Then he screwed the cap down and put the bottle back on the table.

"And how did you know . . . ? What made you *think* it was worth visiting him? I'm assuming this wasn't a purely social visit."

It was Ford's turn to smile.

"What difference does it make? Word's out, Marshall. Soon everybody will know about Omega. Soon everybody will know how you had the drug and how you let people die."

West fell silent, his mouth clamped shut as if there were things he wanted to say, but couldn't.

"As a matter of fact," he said at last, defiance creeping into his voice, "I don't share your pessimism on that count. I think we're still well within the"—he paused to savor the phrase—"parameters of plausible deniability. Provided everybody keeps their heads."

"Keeps their heads? I think you mean holds their tongues. What have you got going, Marshall? Some nice little deal with Apex? Or is this just another one of your fund-raising schemes for the county?"

West looked momentarily perplexed.

"Oh, I see." He nodded to himself. "You think this is about money."

"What else?" said Ford.

West considered him for a moment, slowly shaking his head.

"You of all people, Marcus. Surely you can see there's more to it than that. How long ago was that conference we went to? Three weeks, a month?"

Ford looked across at Denman and then back.

"A month ago," said West, "you were telling us how the drug industry was failing us because all it cared about was profits and market shares. How we needed to regulate before it was too late, how governments had to step in before we found ourselves defenseless against resistant microbes, before our hospitals became . . . became *plague ships*, if you'll forgive me using that phrase. Correct me if I'm wrong, but I think you were saying we had to find another way somehow. And, Marcus, I *agree* with you. A lot of people agree with you. More people than you know. Why do you think I got you invited to that conference in the first place?"

Ford looked up as West leaned forward in his chair.

"You and I . . ." he said, "we're on the same side."

For a moment it looked as if West was going to touch him, touch him on the arm, as if they were old buddies, old friends. Ford felt a shudder of revulsion. He pushed back from the table and stood up.

"On the same side? On the same side, you *sonofabitch!*" Denman stepped forward, but West gestured to him to stay back. "You *lied* to me. You told me to give up and go home. You told me to give up on my daughter because there was nothing that could be done. What was it you said? She was going to get the *best treatment*. You stood there, you sonofabitch, you looked me in the eye and said—"

West raised his hands.

"I know."

Ford was halted by the look of anguish in West's face. West drew a hand across his forehead.

"I know that's what I ... I didn't like doing that, Marcus, I didn't ..." He closed his eyes as if in pain. "I wanted to help you, believe me, but I'm not ... a free agent in this. There are *rules* I'm bound to observe ... protocols. The truth is, I couldn't take a chance on your keeping quiet. You weren't ... You weren't stable."

Ford searched the other man's face.

"Quiet about what? What are we ... What's this all about?"

West let out a short breath, almost smiled.

"Helical, Marcus. Omega. I'm surprised you haven't worked it out already. You seem to be so sure about everything."

Then he was suddenly comfortable. He stood up, took off his jacket.

"Christ, it's hot in here."

He slipped his jacket over the back of his chair and stood with his hands on his hips, considering Ford, who was still standing on the other side of the table.

"All right," he said. "I'm going to tell you everything. I'm going to tell you because I want you to understand. I want you to see we had no choice."

He gestured to Ford's empty chair.

"Please," he said.

He waited until Ford had sat down again before regaining his own seat.

"Nineteen ninety-two," he said. "April, I think. That's when Helical's research team made their big breakthrough. It came almost out of the blue, and much sooner than they'd expected." His eyes narrowed as he struggled to recall all the detail. "For years they'd been trying to find a way to kill bacteria by blocking the transmission of genetic information inside them. In effect, to stop them producing vital proteins."

"Antisense," said Ford, recalling what Helen Wray had told him.

"That's right." West looked up. "So you know about that?"

Ford shrugged.

"Well, then you'll know perhaps that Helical was trying to make an antibiotic based on oligonucleotides. You know what they are? Highly complex molecules made of DNA. They bind to specific sites on messenger RNA, effectively blocking their message. They're called oligomers for short."

Ford shifted in his chair.

"Yeah, I heard something about it."

"Well, Helical had a problem. These big molecules are delicate, they degrade quickly, and many bacteria's defenses can handle them. So the oligomers had to have extra chemical protection built into them, and progress on that was very slow."

"So Helical needed money. Let me guess: they approached Stern."

"They needed the support of a larger company. You see, everyone was beginning to run out of patience, the banks, the equity capital people, everyone. Then one day somebody—Charles Novak, actually—stumbled on a much simpler, tougher RNA molecule: a ribozyme. It's actually a naturally occurring genetic tool, but Novak saw that it could be biochemically engineered to recognize the same genetic sites as the oligomers. The key difference is, instead of binding with the RNA, blocking its message, the ribozymes simply cut the RNA in two, destroying the transcripts. And they're small, pass much more easily through the bacterial wall. And once they've done their job one time, they're free to pass on to the next messenger and the next. They won't rest until the bug is dead."

"A genuine magic bullet," said Ford under his breath.

"Tough, efficient, lethal. The ribozyme discovery knocked at least five years off Helical's research schedule, probably more."

"So? What happened to the drug?"

"What happened, Marcus, was that for the first time Novak and his team began to see what it might actually mean if their discovery were commercialized in the normal way, *made available* in the normal way. And they began to have second thoughts."

Ford tilted his head over to one side.

"A little late for that, wasn't it?"

"You'd think so. It was the big prize they'd been working towards for years. It was the reason they created Helical in the first place."

"So? I don't get it."

West smiled.

"Marcus, did you know that at the start of the Second World War most of the world's leading nuclear scientists were German?"

Again Ford looked at Denman, as if his reaction might help him understand what was actually being disclosed.

"Well, they all went to work for Hitler. Rolled up their sleeves and got busy trying to make an atomic bomb. And by rights, they should have got there first."

"I still don't—"

"Bear with me. When the Nazis surrendered, the British locked these guys away in an old country house. Let them read the news every day—including the news about Hiroshima and Nagasaki—and they bugged their conversations. The Brits couldn't figure out why the German team hadn't got further. They even suspected that some of the team—being decent, educated fellows—had been deliberately dragging their feet. But what they discovered was these men of science hadn't even *considered* the implications of giving Hitler the bomb. They'd never even discussed it. Why? Because they all assumed that the war would be over, one way or another, years before anybody could make such a weapon. It was only when they saw that somebody *had* that the arguments started between them."

"I don't see the connection."

West closed his hands on the table.

"What I'm saying is this. We're in a war, and we're losing. The bugs are way ahead of us. The old weapons get less effective every day. You've seen bacilli at the Willowbrook that can beat vancomycin. Believe me, you're not alone. I've seen reports—confidential reports— that would scare the shit out of you. Half the hospitals in Europe have suffered major outbreaks of multiple-resistant pathogens during the last eighteen months. The percentage in North America is probably higher, only no one wants to admit it because they're afraid of losing business. The situation—"

"I know what the situation is. I've seen it for myself."

West sat back, reining himself in. His voice returned to its normal calm, measured level.

"Well, Novak and his people saw it first. They saw it coming. They knew that what they'd come up with might be the last broad-spectrum antibiotic for a generation. That's why they started calling it Omega. The *last*, Marcus. And if it went the way of the others, if it was patented and sold, and exported and marketed and every goddam thing, then five years down the line it would be as useless as everything else. You'd think they might have considered the problem ahead of time, but they didn't, not until they were actually standing on the brink."

"So instead of going to the patent office, they went to you."

West nodded.

"They went to the government," he said. "I was at the Department of Health at the time. They presented us with the facts and asked us to intervene, to take control of Omega before the whole company changed hands. We accepted their analysis. In the public interest we had to act—to act fast, and in secret."

"But why? If you were acting in the public interest . . . ?"

"It had to be that way. It had to be secret because, for one, Helical's research people between them only owned about . . . fifteen percent of the company. The rest belonged to financial and industrial partners. We'd have had to buy the whole company, and with a product like Omega in the pipeline that would have cost billions. As it was we only had to compensate the research team. Christ, it cost less than a pair of F-sixteens."

Ford made a wry mouth.

"You just said this had nothing to do with money."

"Marcus, even the federal government can't spend a billion dollars without explaining itself. The existence of Omega would've had to be made public. How long do you think it would have been before we were forced to use it? Some little kid's going to lose a kidney or an eye or her front teeth or can't sleep at night because of earache. Can't you see it? We'd have newspaper campaigns, telephone polls, tearful parents on *Oprah Winfrey*. And how long do you think it would be before politicians started jumping on the bandwagon?"

"But if you regulate—"

"No!" West checked himself. "Once we lose control of this thing, it's *over*. There's too much money to be made, too much *demand*. We've never been able to control the narcotics trade. What makes you think we could control this? Start using Omega in every minor crisis, and two years down the line you'll be able to buy bootleg copies everywhere from Bangkok to Tijuana."

Ford fell silent. Everything West said made sense. It chimed with his own perceptions, his own instincts. Yet the secrecy, the deception, it *couldn't* be right. It still couldn't be right to let people die.

"Marcus, I'm not saying this technology must be locked away forever. Nobody's saying that. But we're entering a new age here, a new age for medicine. And we just don't know what to expect. Remember the flu pandemic of 1918? It swept around the planet in five months. That was *before* the age of air travel. Killed twenty million people, half a million right here in America. And what about tuberculosis? Scarlet fever? Measles, for God's sake? They all have the potential to become epidemics again. And if they do, we need something to hit back with, something that still works. Omega could be our last chance. And that means it has to be treated as a weapon of last resort. For genuine emergencies only."

Ford folded his arms. "Genuine emergencies like Edward Turnbull?"

West nodded silently, taking the hit as if he knew he had it coming.

"What do you expect?" He sighed. He ran his fingers slowly along the edge of the table. "I'm supposed to turn my back on my own nephew? My sister's only son? If I'd been in any doubt that I couldn't keep the matter confidential, it would have been a whole different story, but—"

"If your nephew is a genuine emergency, then so are my patients. What's the difference?"

"There *is* a difference. I—"

"Yeah, the difference between rich and poor, black and white. Is that what Omega's really for? A safety net for the good people of Beverly Hills?"

West planted his elbows on the table and pushed his hands into his hair.

"No, Marcus, it isn't. We established a clear set of guidelines governing the deployment of Omega. Everyone agreed to it. There was an understanding—a protocol. The drug would be deployed only in certain circumstances."

There was that word again. Every time he heard it, Ford couldn't help thinking of Novak. Like West, he'd claimed to be on Ford's side, yet he'd been silenced before he could share what he knew. Was that *why* he'd been killed? He'd always assumed that his death was all about money, but as West had admitted, there was more to Omega than that.

"So is that . . . is that why Novak was murdered?" he said. "He saw what was happening in South Central, downtown, all over LA County, in fact, and he wanted to invoke the protocol. That's what happened, isn't it? He felt the circumstances justified deployment. That was what Griffen said."

"Griffen?"

He could see it now, slowly opening up: a reason why Novak had to die, and Scott Griffen too. He felt giddy, sick.

"He wanted to invoke the protocol, but the problem was the victims didn't matter, not to you and your friends. They didn't count. Jesus, Jesus Christ. And you got scared he'd go public. After all, it'd been his discovery. His and Griffen's. With what they knew between them, they could get the drug made for themselves. Apex could make it, or Stern."

West was shaking his head.

"For God's sake, Marcus. This is all . . ." There were sweat patches under his arms. He looked very pale, his eyes bloodshot. "I don't know what games Novak was playing, and I don't care. If you ask me, he got a little loopy towards the end, and, yes, he might have been trying to make a deal with Griffen. It wouldn't surprise me. There are billions of dollars involved here, and plenty of people who'll kill to get their hands on it, not just Apex and Stern. Business is just the continuation of war by other means. Or hadn't you noticed?"

"So what are you saying, Marshall? My daughter has to die for the sake of your . . . of your fucking protocol?"

West picked up the bottle of capsules again, looked at it, put it down.

"No. No, that's not . . . We're not monsters here, Marcus. We've made one exception; we can make two." Almost for the first time, he looked Ford straight in the eye, hoping to see the impact of his words. "But I can't let you just walk out of here with Omega in your pocket, not on your own at least. For one thing, it could be dangerous. What happened to Novak could just as easily happen to you."

They were going to let him have the drug. Ford let it sink in for a moment. They were buying his silence with Sunny's life. But there was going to be a price, he knew that, and the price was betrayal.

"What's the matter? Don't you trust me, Marshall?"

"Sure," said West, standing up and reaching for his jacket, "like you trusted Helen Wray. Denman here will go with you to the hospital. Omega doesn't leave his sight. Once Sunny's treatment is complete, he takes what's left away with him and this whole thing never happened. You have to give me your word on that."

"What about the medical staff? Dr. Lee, the nurses? They'll be the ones who'll administer the drug."

"No, they won't, because you will. Your suspension will be terminated. I'll see to that."

"But there are others there, others who are dying. Some of them are my patients. Goddammit, Marshall, there are children. I can't just . . . I'm a doctor. I have a duty—"

"Sorry, Marcus, it's just too risky. I've explained the situation to you. I've explained everything, and you know now—you'll see when you stop and think about it—that what I've said adds up. There's just too much at stake to . . . to do everything we'd like to do."

Ford looked down at the ground. He didn't have the strength to argue. He was all used up.

"You can't save all of the people all of the time. Is that what you're trying to say, Marshall?"

West pulled his jacket from the back of the chair and slipped it on, anxious now to complete the transaction.

"We can save your daughter, though. We can save your daughter."

He rose and looked down at Ford.

"Do we have a deal?" he asked.

He was waiting for Ford's answer. Yet Ford could tell he already knew what that answer would be.

They went out a back way, past a line of private ambulances and a van unloading catering supplies. West's Mercedes was awkwardly parked in the corner of the yard, almost blocking in a blue Pontiac. It was after eight o'clock, dark.

"I want you to ride along with Mr. Denman," said West, gesturing to the other man, who was putting an attache casé in the trunk of the Pontiac. "I'll have somebody drive your car down later."

Ford paused for a moment.

"What's the matter?" said West.

"Why can't I . . . ?"

"You don't think I'm going to let you drive out of here on your own with this thing."

He approached Ford until he was standing so close, Ford could smell the faint sweetness of breath freshener.

"Marcus, don't be a fool. We're not Cosa Nostra, for Christ's sake."

Ford watched Denman get into the Pontiac. He turned on the lights and began slowly reversing out of his space.

"Remember, I'm going out on a limb here," West said. "Again, I hope you see that. Not everyone would handle things like this."

Ford kept his eyes on the Pontiac reversing slowly towards him, bathing them both in red light.

"I told you," he said. "We have a deal."

West looked Ford over one more time and walked back towards the clinic.

"I'll be in touch," he said as he went inside.

The Pontiac was just a few feet away now, slotting itself into the narrow space behind. Watching it come on, Ford read its bumper sticker: IF YOU THINK EDUCATION IS EXPENSIVE, TRY IGNORANCE. Denman stuck his head out of the window.

"Am I clear there?" he said.

Ford did not reply. He was trying to remember where he'd seen the sticker before, the broken taillight, the blue Pontiac itself. Something told him it mattered. Something told him to think.

"I said, am I clear?"

And then it came to him—Griffen's place. And what would muscle like Denman have been doing up there, unless . . . ?

"Say, wait a second," Ford shouted, raising a hand. His heart was suddenly pounding. He risked a look back at the building, but there was no sign of West.

Denman put on the brakes. "What's the problem?"

"You're . . . It looks like you're losing oil," said Ford, his mind racing. "It looks pretty bad."

"Oil? Back there?"

"Did someone run into you?" asked Ford, bending down close to the taillight.

With an impatient swipe Denman put the car into park.

"I can't believe this."

He was stepping out to take a look, one foot out on the gravel when Ford threw himself against the door.

"What the fu—!"

Denman screamed, leg and arm trapped, crushed against the frame. He strained back, pushed, face pressed hard against the glass, straining.

"Son of a bitch!"

With his free hand he was struggling to reach inside his jacket. Ford wrenched the door back, slammed it again. Denman bellowed with pain. With the trapped arm he tried to claw at Ford's face, his fingernails dug into his cheek, reaching up into his eyes.

Ford yanked open the door, grabbed Denman by the throat, dragged him clear with a strength he didn't know he had. Choking, Denman rolled out onto the ground.

And then there were footsteps, shouting. An alarm was sounding, high-pitched, oscillating. Lights went on up the side of the building. It was one of the catering people, a kid in white coveralls. He stopped dead, terrified of this crazy guy, this psychopath. And then there were others running towards him, blue jackets, the suit.

Ford jumped into the Pontiac and gunned the engine, showering the lines of luxury cars with gravel, narrowly avoiding another ambulance coming the other way. He could still hear them shouting as he raced through the narrowing gates and out onto the road.

5

"**D**amn!"

Gloria Tyrell looked down at her white sneakers—at the hot chocolate splashed *all over* her white sneakers—and then back up at the person who had come surging through the doors of pediatric ICU, almost knocking the drink out of her hand.

"What are charging around like that for, mister?"

"I'm sorry, ma'am, I hope you're . . . Can I . . . ?"

"I'll be"—Gloria pulled the plastic cup away from the reaching hand—"*fine*—thanks all the same. Just damn near ruined my work shoes is all. Now, are you going to tell me what you're doing in here? Or do I have to call Security?"

The man flashed a nasty smile and flipped open an ID card that showed a picture of him with a crew cut. Gloria checked out the tight mouth and sharp little nose. It was the same guy.

"Deputy Samuel Dorsey, Nurse . . ."

"Tyrell."

"I'm with the county sheriff's department. Homicide."

Gloria put her hands on her hips.

"Homicide. Well, our trauma unit's closed, if you're looking for hoodlums."

"Actually, I was hoping to have a word with Dr. Marcus Ford."

He looked behind him, pointing at an older man with a mustache who was coming along the corridor.

"Me and my partner, Sergeant Ruddock, want to ask him a few questions."

"So why've you come here?" asked Gloria.

Dorsey looked puzzled.

"Don't you know he's been suspended?" asked Gloria, raising an eyebrow.

Ruddock arrived, showing his ID.

"Dr. Ford isn't here?"

Gloria gave Ruddock a look.

"He isn't *working* here."

Ruddock could see that, once again, Dorsey had gotten on the wrong side of the civilian population. It was like a gift with him.

"We understand his daughter is here," he said, trying to look as avuncular as possible. "Little girl that's very ill?"

Gloria nodded.

"That's right. She's going into the OR tomorrow morning, first thing."

"We tried to reach Dr. Ford at his house," said Ruddock, "but he wasn't there. So we thought maybe he was down here visiting."

"I don't know whether he's visiting or not. I haven't seen him since this morning."

Gloria showed the policemen her plastic cup.

"I was just taking this to his daughter's room. She has a visitor, but it isn't Dr. Ford."

"Do you mind if we come with you, Nurse?" Ruddock asked.

Gloria nodded assent, turned, and with tremendous dignity set off down the ward towards the isolation rooms.

When she reached Sunny's room, she turned and faced the men.

"If you want to come in, you're going to have to put on masks. We're very strict about infection here."

She gave Dorsey a look that left him in no doubt about who she thought would be doing the infecting.

"Whatever you say," said Ruddock.

"In the meantime, I'm going to deliver what's left of this hot beverage."

She turned away from them and opened the door. Ruddock got a glimpse of a young woman sitting next to a respirator machine. She was wearing business clothes.

"How come she's drinking hot chocolate, but we have to wear masks?" hissed Dorsey.

Ruddock put a restraining hand on Dorsey's arm and watched as the young woman turned to accept the cup. She looked as though she had been crying.

6

The storm broke as Ford reached Sunset. Lightning flickered away to the east, and then the rain came down, a startling downpour that had him peering forward through the windshield trying to see the traffic ahead. Waiting at the intersection, he was suddenly aware of the pain in his right thumb. He held it up to the light and was surprised to see the nail rimmed with drying blood. He realized it must have happened in the struggle with Denman, but had no recollection of hurting himself. Staring at the damaged nail, he saw again Denman's face as he slammed the door into his body, saw Denman's eyes—so determined, so . . . *angry*. The presence of the Pontiac at Griffen's house, the disturbed earth under the fence, these things were suspicious in themselves, but it was the look in Denman's eyes that had convinced Ford, a look of resolute, focused, *professional* anger. It left him in no doubt. Denman was the killer. It was Denman who had killed Griffen. Novak too, more than likely. But why? And why did West need to employ such a man? The blast of a horn jolted him back to the present. He saw angry faces pressed against streaming glass. A raised fist. People were trying to get past him.

He rolled out onto Sunset and turned left, checking his mirror the whole time, expecting at any moment to see West or his people in pursuit. As he had so often in the past few weeks, he had the clearest sensation of being caught up in something so much bigger than himself, so much beyond his understanding. When he tried to focus on any part of what he was dealing with—Helen, Novak, Helical, West—all he got was a jumble of contradictory impressions. Yet what had to happen next, what he had to *make* happen, could not have been simpler. He needed to get to Sunny. He would explain to Allen and Lee what had happened. Explain everything he knew about the drug.

Omega. He looked down at the bottle of capsules in his lap. It struck him that he knew next to nothing about its effect on bacterial pathogens or its side effects on the human body. But then there was Edward Turnbull. The boy was living proof that the drug worked. *Clostridium botilinum* and *Clostridium perfringens* were not a million miles apart, and West had characterized Omega as an effective scatter-gun. Turnbull had said he was on three capsules a day. Ford would give Sunny the same and then monitor her progress.

Despite his predicament, despite his fear, the thought of Sunny's recovery lifted him with a sudden rush of elation. *She was going to be okay.* There would be no need to cut her open. She was going to come through this thing whole—unscathed.

He thumped up onto the access ramp of the San Diego Freeway and, despite the buffeting wind, immediately moved across to the fast lane.

Three cars behind him a dark blue Mercedes sedan effected the same maneuver.

"Maybe he saw us at the house," said Dorsey. "Saw the black-and-white parked in the street and just kept driving. Probably on his way to the airport right now."

"Just when his daughter's gonna have an operation?" said Ruddock. "I doubt it."

Dorsey looked out at rows of trash cans, illuminated by a single security light. Water sluiced down from a strip of broken gutter.

"Listen to that rain," he said. He turned to face Ruddock, his hands on his hips. "Yeah, well, maybe he's not such a great family man. If he's involved in some kind of racket . . ."

Ruddock considered the toes of his shoes and sipped at his coffee. Dorsey seemed pretty sure Ford was their man. However obliquely, he *was* linked to both crime scenes—so far the only person that was. Physical evidence may have been lacking at Novak's house, but forensics had lifted fingerprints and fiber from all over the Griffen property, footprints too. Dorsey was confident a piece of this evidence would eventually put Ford at the scene. When Ruddock had questioned Ford's ability to drown a grown man unaided—not without there being more signs of a violent struggle, anyway—Dorsey had developed the idea of a partner. Strands of red hair found in the pool were clearly not from Ford. So that meant he'd had help. Forensics had produced some good DNA shots from the roots of the hair. All they needed was for Ford to give up his partner and the case could be closed.

As to motive, Dorsey had gotten all steamed up speculating that Ford, as head of the Willowbrook Trauma Unit—being close to the street, close to the junkies, homeboys, and dealers of South Central— would be a perfect middleman for products coming down from Novak or Griffen. Once you accepted that, all you had to do was assume that something had gone wrong—as things always did in narco-land—and you gave Ford a motive for silencing the suppliers. Dorsey had put all these ideas to the gang and narcotics people, but so far there had been no response.

Ruddock levered a crust of mud off the toe of his right foot. It kind of made sense, but no more than kind of. Sure, he had doubts about Ford. For one thing it was weird that a white doctor with his qualifica- tions should bury himself in a public hospital in South Central LA— you *had* to wonder about his reasons for that. But Ruddock had trouble casting the man as the ruthless killer. Meanwhile, Dorsey kept cranking on about Raymond Denny's death, about how Ford had let him die because Ford was pro-black and, therefore, *necessarily* anti-police. It looked to Ruddock that his partner, as always, was taking things a little too personally.

Dorsey walked over to the door and looked out into the empty cor- ridor. The nurse had brought them down to the first floor, where the hospital was quiet, telling them to stay put until she called. As soon as Ford showed up, she was going to let them know.

"Where's she stuck us here?" said Dorsey to no one in particular.

Ruddock shrugged.

" 'Triage' is what she said. Somewhere near Triage—near the Emergency Department. It's better than being out in the waiting room with all the homeboys."

Dorsey started to hum as his hand went inside his jacket. Ruddock knew that he was touching his gun. He touched it all the time when they were out on the street, like it was a sore place he just couldn't leave alone.

"Ain't that the truth," he said.

Keeping his eyes on the broken taillight of the Pontiac up ahead, Denman drifted across to the middle lane and leaned on the gas.

"Don't get too close," said West. "If he sees us, he might panic. We'd be chasing him all over town."

Denman's eyes cut to the rearview mirror, where he could see West's pale face. He drew in a breath and winced with pain. The son-of-a-bitch doctor had broken one of his ribs; he was sure of it.

"We should have finished him off when we had him up at the clinic," he growled.

West let out an irritated sigh.

"Christ, is that all you people know? Killing?"

"I've got lime in the trunk. We could be driving him out to the Mojave instead of following him down to South Central."

"We wouldn't be following him now if you hadn't spooked him in the first place."

Denman gripped the wheel until his hands hurt. If there was one thing he could not abide, it was having his competence questioned. Especially by someone who knew nothing about operating in the field. He was good at what he did and only scared people when he *wanted* them scared—like threatening to cut off Griffen's hand, making the old fart piss his pants.

"I keep telling you it wasn't me that spooked him," he said. "He must have seen something."

"Yeah, right. Like that cannon you've got in your armpit."

Denman shook his head, his mouth pressed into a hard line. He didn't even pack a .45. It would be too bulky.

"There's no need for more violence," said West in a more concilia-tory tone. "Ford's no threat. He doesn't know enough to hurt us, not really. He knows nothing of the technology. That's what counts."

"How can you be so sure?"

"Look, all he wants is to save his daughter. He still needs us to do that."

Denman laughed a single harsh bark and then clutched at his injured side.

"I still can't believe he did that," he said. "He sure is a stupid son of a bitch."

"He's intelligent enough to cut a deal," said West. "That's all that matters."

"And if he isn't? If he doesn't want to?"

West said nothing for a moment. Denman checked the mirror again. He could see the pale face in profile. The great man was thinking, rummaging around in his soul for the right and wrong of it all. Sad son of a bitch. Then the face turned, meeting his eyes in the mirror.

"Well, in that case you get to use your lime," West said.

Dorsey looked at his watch.

"I don't know," he said. "Do you think we can trust her?"

Ruddock turned from the window, where he had been looking out at the storm. He checked his own watch. They had been waiting for forty minutes.

"I mean, she might be in on the whole thing. How do we know Ford hasn't come and gone?" Dorsey said.

Ruddock looked at his partner's flushed face, then checked his watch again, trying to make up his mind.

"We should have sat out front in the parking lot," said Dorsey. "We could have collared him as he entered the building."

"Oh, fuck it," said Ruddock. "I'm sick of watching you jump up and down, anyway. We may as well get up there."

They left the room and walked along the corridor to the elevators, one of which was out of order. Dorsey pressed the button and stood back. Ruddock watched his hand disappear under his lapel. He just hoped Dorsey had the safety on.

"You okay, Sam?" Dorsey gave an irritable shrug. "Because you look a little jumpy."

"I'm fine," said Dorsey. "Just don't like hospitals is all."

* * *

Ford entered the hospital through the main public entrance. The usual groups of anxious relatives and friends had been swollen by a cross section of South Central's street people—the disoriented lame, the addicted, the borderline psychotic—all sheltering from the storm, all clutching their broken umbrellas and bits of plastic, hoping to get some attention or hoping to go unnoticed—standing in pools of water, giving off rancid smells of poverty and neglect.

A few heads turned as Ford hurried past. But it was his appearance of purpose, of knowing where he was going, that singled him out, not his swollen lip and disheveled clothes. In the short run from the car, he had gotten soaked through.

Riding up to the second floor, he examined his damaged thumb. The nail was almost black now and it hurt like hell. He also noticed that the sleeve of his jacket was badly torn. He didn't like to think what his face looked like.

In pediatric ICU the first familiar face he saw was Gloria's. She was talking to another nurse who was clutching a bundle of soiled bedding. She didn't see him until he touched her arm.

"Holy God! What happened to you?"

"Where's Lee?"

For a moment Gloria was too stunned to speak. She shooed the other nurse away with her big hands.

"For Christ's sake, Gloria, where's Lee?"

She leaned forward, her expression suddenly furtive.

"A couple of homicide detectives came looking for you."

Ford brought the back of his hand up to his swollen lip. He couldn't help smiling at Gloria's face.

"It's all right, Gloria. I haven't killed anybody. Not yet."

"So what've you been—"

"Look."

He opened the bottle of capsules and held it out for her to see.

"Take a good look, Gloria."

"What?"

"I've got to get this to Sunny. This is the end of our problems."

Gloria's mouth dropped open. She took a half step back, looking at him as if he were a madman.

"Don't you understand?" said Ford. "She's going to be all right."

Warily, she took the bottle from his hand.

"This is Midrin," she said flatly.

Ford blinked. Grabbed the bottle. He shook out a couple of the capsules into his trembling hand. For a moment he stared at the distinctive pink-and-yellow painkiller in utter disbelief.

"I don't . . ."

Edward Turnbull flashed into his mind. He'd said this was what he was getting three times a day. Had it been a trick? Then Ford realized that Turnbull wouldn't know the difference between an analgesic and an antibiotic. *The boy wouldn't know any different.* Ford's hand closed in a fist. In his eagerness to get the drug, in the euphoria of believing that he was holding the drug that would save Sunny's life, he hadn't seen the capsules for what they were. He had poured them out into his hand, had *stared* at them, *but he had not seen.*

"Dr. Ford? Are you okay?"

"Oh, Jesus, Gloria."

Her beeper sounded. Keeping one eye on Ford, she picked up the nearest phone and punched in the number for the switchboard.

"Pediatrics, Tyrell."

Ford stared, blank, canceled, his hands relaxing, the useless medicine falling to the floor. It was a moment before he realized that Gloria was beckoning to him, holding out the phone.

He took it, hardly aware of what he was doing.

"Marcus? Marcus, are you there?"

It was West.

"Marcus, I thought we had a deal."

The anger seemed to bud in his throat. He couldn't speak. Suddenly all he wanted to do was get his hands on West. He would kill him with his bare hands. He would crush and squeeze his lying, cheating, murderous neck.

"Marcus? Hello?"

"Not for . . ." Ford tried to draw breath. His throat was so tight it hurt. "Not for *painkillers* we didn't."

West was silent for a moment.

"Marcus, *you* were the one who stole the bottle. I never said it contained the drug."

"You let me believe—"

"Yes, I did. I let you believe because it suited me. It gave me an edge. And now I'm going to give you the real thing. Not capsules, a serum. You, Marcus, administer it *intravenously*, or via injection. Whatever you need."

With a jolt of cognition, Ford remembered the drip in Turnbull's arm. He leaned forward against the wall, his injured hand pressed to his eyes. It hadn't been saline solution in that line . . . It had been *Omega*. He had been standing a couple of feet away from Sunny's salvation, clutching a handful of painkillers.

"I was *ready* to do a deal," said West. "Denman put the drug in the car. In the trunk. Remember Denman? The guy you assaulted?"

"What?"

"Marcus, it was in the trunk. Still is, no thanks to you. You should be more careful about locking up your car. Especially in neighborhoods like this."

He had left the key in the ignition.

"Denman's a killer," said Ford, but with no great conviction. He was confused, no longer clear about his position.

"Marcus, you have no idea. You have no conception of—"

"He's a killer. He killed Griffen."

"Look," said West leaning closer to the phone, his voice coming through in a conspiratorial whisper, "he's a lot of things, but he comes highly *recommended*. And I can't always . . . You can't always choose the people you work with. As I keep trying to impress upon you, I'm not a free agent in this. This thing is so . . . *important*—for the country, for the *world*. But you have to believe me, I never sanctioned any of the violence. It's just that this whole situation . . . it's become very complicated."

Ford closed his eyes against a sudden rush of nausea.

"I'm sorry to hear that, Marshall. I'm sorry to hear how *complicated* your life is. My life . . . *Sunny's* life is real simple. In fact she—"

"Marcus, you're not hearing me. I have the drug. Do you understand? I have the drug here with me. It's not too late for Sunny. I'm sitting out in the parking lot right now. We can still do the deal."

Ford looked up at Gloria. She hadn't moved an inch.

"Oh, really? You'd be going out on a limb there, wouldn't you, Marshall?"

"Like I said. Like I *said*, we're not monsters, Marcus. And giving Sunny the drug doesn't change the equation. Omega's efficacy is only compromised if it goes into mass production. Then you know what happens."

"So what's the—?"

"We'll give you the drug in exchange—"

"For my silence."

"If you agree to let us handle this whole thing in the proper manner."

Again Ford checked Gloria's face.

"And how do I know it's not just a trick? How do I know you won't kill me?"

Gloria brought her hand to her mouth.

"Why would I do that?"

"I don't know. It would be tidier that way. Easier. Less *complicated*."

"Marcus, it's a simple deal. I am buying your silence in exchange for the cure. I know you won't screw around with Sunny's life, not now . . . not later."

Ford felt the hair tingle on the back of his neck.

"What does that mean? Later? Are you threatening me, Marshall? Are you threatening my daughter?"

"All I'm . . . as a *friend*, Marcus, all I'm telling you is you should bear in mind the kind of people . . . the kind of *agencies* involved here."

"Agencies?"

"Do I have to spell it out? Wake up to the big picture, Marcus. Wake up to reality. Do you think Denman is on the payroll of the county health department?"

"I see," said Ford. "I think I see. So the Lord giveth, but he can also take away, is that it?"

"For Christ's sake, Marcus. We have an opportunity to do some good with this thing. Let's take it."

Ford pressed his eyes tight shut. He had no choice.

"Is the Pontiac where I left it?" he said.

He didn't even hang up the phone. Gloria watched him run down the ward, her hand clamped against her mouth. Then she picked up the swinging handset and punched in the number for Triage. She waited a moment, listening to the ring, her heart thumping hard. She had shown the older policeman the extension she'd be coming through on. They were supposed to be waiting in a room nearby. Now they were gone. She hung up the phone and started in the direction of the elevators.

Ford was surprised to see West standing out in the open, his only protection against the rain, a copy of the *Los Angeles Times* held over his head. He was standing under a broken streetlight, his face barely visible. When he saw Ford come to a halt twenty feet away, he lowered the paper.

"We chose a great place to meet," he shouted.

Ford paused, checking out the rows of empty cars. It was difficult to see with the rain drifting against his face.

"It's okay," said West. He tossed the paper away from him and showed his empty hands.

"So where is it?" said Ford.

"Well, do we have a deal, Marcus?"

Ford pushed the hair out of his eyes and came on another couple of steps. The wind was gusting and swirling over the asphalt, making it difficult to hear anyone that might try to sneak up on him. Instinctively he checked over his shoulder.

"You're holding all the cards here, Marshall," he said.

Still West didn't move from where he stood.

"It's right here," he said, pointing at the Pontiac. "Still in the trunk."

Ford looked hard at the car.

"Why don't you bring it out into the light," he said.

The smile went from West's face.

"Don't play games with me, Marcus. I'm risking enough just coming down here."

Ford advanced until he could see inside the car. It looked empty.

"So where's your muscle?" he said.

West took a step sideways, broken glass crunching underfoot.

"Where do you think? He's up at the clinic getting his ribs bandaged."

Ford looked up at the light. It wasn't just burned out. It had been shattered. West followed his gaze. Then he was shaking his head.

"These neighborhoods," he said. "Remember when we were kids? Remember how it was back then?"

"Sure," said Ford. "I remember. Manson. The Kennedy assassination. Napalm. They built this hospital after the Watts riots. Things weren't so much better."

West smiled.

"Yeah, but we still had Doris Day," he said.

Holding up his hands as if he were under arrest, he went over to the car and popped the trunk. Ford braced himself. If it was going to happen, it would be now. He watched, his heart thumping in his throat, as West reached into the trunk. He rummaged around for a moment and then came back upright, the rain dripping from his nose and chin, a pencil flashlight in his right hand.

"Come on," he said. "Come and take a look."

Ford walked towards the car. A gust of wind buffeted him from behind. There was broken glass everywhere. He couldn't remember it being there when he had parked, but he had been in such a hurry he might not have noticed.

Then he was looking at it.

Illuminated by West's pencil flashlight were three round glass bottles packed in black foam inside a bulky attaché case. The serum had a faint gold color.

"Just forty thousand IU per day," said West in a quiet voice. "That's all it takes. No venous irritation, no lasting side effects, and as far as we know one hundred percent effective. The pathogens we've tested it on—and we've tested it on some very clever organisms—show *zero* sensitivity. One minute they're . . . they're *seething*, the next minute—total stasis. It's like pulling a plug. Like . . ." He turned and looked at Ford for a moment. "It's like casting a spell. They just don't know what it is."

Ford looked down at the drug. He felt a strong urge to grab the case and make a run for it, get it into the hospital one way or another. Then he looked at West, saw a man who had struggled for years with the question of what to do. It was easy to forget West's medical background, to see only the politician, but there was something in his expression as he looked down at the bottles: it said the drug meant a lot to him too.

"I still don't understand," said Ford.

West frowned. Lit by the reflected flashlight, his face looked older. "Understand?"

"If this thing is as effective as you say . . . Well, then . . . Well, then all this is *wrong*. There are people in there . . ." He pointed away across the car lot to the hospital building. "There are people in there dying. In pain. They are dying, Marshall, and you're standing here with the cure."

West closed his eyes momentarily and then shut the case.

"Marcus, I don't think I can make it any clearer than I already have. I don't think—"

"I'm not talking about the technical issues. I'm not talking about the resistance question. I understand all that. I share your concern. But this is . . . this is about right and wrong. I'm talking about . . . I'm talking about your obligation, *our* obligation to help."

"You mean my sacred obligation not to harm my patients? Is that what you mean? The Hippocratic oath? Is that what we're talking about here?"

Ford looked down at the ground.

"Now you mention it . . . *yes*. Doesn't that mean anything to you anymore? Didn't it mean something to you when you went to med school? *I will prescribe regimen for the good of my patients according to my ability and my judgment and never do harm to anyone.*"

West shook his head.

"You always were a good student, Marcus. I'm surprised you still remember it. I seem to recall Hippocrates also said a lot about not screwing the patients, and the importance of keeping secrets that should . . . how does he put it?—*should not be spread abroad.*"

He lifted the case by the handle and stood it on its side.

"Unfortunately, Hippocrates knew nothing about antibiotic resistance. Nor did he understand the dynamics, the *imperatives* of the free market. If he had, he'd have taken the view I take."

He leaned forward a little, his dark eyes fixed on Ford's.

"What is my ultimate responsibility, Marcus? Is it to the people in

there, or to future humanity? Because we could be talking end games
here. Armageddon."

"Oh come on, Marshall."

"You think I'm kidding? Forget about the bugs for a minute. I'm
talking about the breakdown of the social order. Can you imagine the
effect a new plague would have on a city like Los Angeles? Given the
tensions, the anger, the volatility? This isn't fourteenth century Paris
we're living in—with a . . . with a docile underclass you can throw
scraps to. Our poor are armed. Can you imagine the riots, the chaos,
the burning?"

Ford took a step nearer.

"But Marshall, what . . . what happens tomorrow. . . . It's always
been that way. We've always relied on our ingenuity. When we run out
of ideas we'll become extinct, we'll be selected out. That's the world
we live in. But we can't second guess the future, we can't *sacrifice*
people for the sake of a future we can't even foresee."

West lifted the case out of the trunk.

"Well, listen." He squeezed the water out of his eyes. "Much as
I'd love to continue this edifying debate, the time"—

"*That's* your problem, Marshall. You, your people . . . you never
wanted this debate. This debate should have happened six years ago.
In Congress. People have a right to know what's going on. You could
have put the argument for restrictive distribution in Congress. *That*
was the forum for it. Not a parking lot, creeping around in the dark. But
you didn't. And do you know why?"

A band of muscle twitched in West's cheek. He was running out of
patience.

"Because you don't trust the people. You don't believe the people
can make the right choices."

West gave a dry, dismissive laugh.

"Yeah, and remember, *I'm a politician*. I see it from the *inside*. If
you think Congress is a democratic forum, you're more of a flake than I
thought. Marcus, Congress is where interest groups cut deals. Pressure
groups and lobbies—gun lobbies, farmers, distillers, ecologists. What
chance would we have had against the pharmaceuticals giants, against
Stern, Apex, Kempf? I'll tell you: no chance."

He held out the case, but Ford made no move to take it.

"So you conduct policy behind your mirrors," he said. "Like . . . like the politicians voting for war from the safety of their fallout shelters."

West let the case fall back against his leg, shaking his head, smiling. Then he was laughing, still shaking his head and looking at Ford as if he were the worst kind of fool. Ford felt his shoulders drop. For a moment he had thought he could carry West with him, could appeal to his decency. But it was hopeless.

"Marcus, I'm sorry, but . . ." West was still smiling, still amused. "Do you know what you've become? Do you know what working in this place has done to you? It has *radicalized* you. You're a fucking radical flake. You used to be a liberal flake, but now . . . And you think you're just the average Joe. The average decent guy. But you're right out there on the margin, Marcus, with the dingbats and the goofballs. Do you realize that?"

Ford stared at West's smiling face for a moment. Then something inside him snapped. He found himself grappling for the case, clutching at West's clenched hands, feeling knuckles under rain-slick flesh, the hardness of a wedding band, and then he was pulling back and away, the case magically his.

He took a step back . . . and froze. Denman was there, a .38 in his right fist. His rain-soaked clothes were covered in mud as if he'd actually come up out of the ground. He spoke through clenched teeth: "Put down the case, you dumb fuck."

West was massaging his hand, leaning back against the car.

"Fucking flake," he said with disgust. "You'd stand here arguing your bullshit morality and let your own kid die in that shit hole."

Ford started to back away, the case held across his chest.

"I'm not . . ." The words came to him as if somebody else were speaking them. "It doesn't belong to you."

Denman took aim.

"No further, Dr. Ford."

But Ford no longer had any choice. He kept walking, a step at a time, because he *had* to take the drug, he had to take it to Sunny.

Denman fired.

Ford was punched backwards, his chest split by intense pain. Red light squeezed his vision as he dropped to his knees, reaching up with the case as he went down, reaching up as if giving it to somebody above him. Denman fired again.

Deputy Samuel Dorsey turned at the sound of the first shot and, squinting through the downpour, saw the muzzle flash of the second. He raised his own weapon and began to run.

"Police! Put down your guns," he shouted.

From where he stood, Duane Ruddock watched in disbelief as his partner set off towards a line of cars barely visible in the gloom.

Denman picked out the advancing figure against the lights of the Willowbrook. He took aim. Fired.

Dorsey was hit twice. Once in the shoulder. Once in the groin. Between the first and second hits, he managed to squeeze off four rounds, one of which entered Denman's head through the left eye, tearing a dollar-sized hole in the back of his skull.

There was a car alarm. The sound of running feet.

Ford heard a man struggling to breathe—a harsh rasping he knew from the emergency room. And there was someone saying, *"Get it off me, get it off me"*—over and over. It felt as though a steel spike had been driven into his chest. He was drenched in blood. It flushed down into his groin as he sat clutching the case. It came to him that he was going to die now.

Then there were people, hands, voices,—*"Lie back."* . . . *"Are you okay?"* . . . *"Let go of the . . ."* *"He won't let go."* . . . *"We have to see where you're . . ."* *"Let go of the CASE!"*

It was wrenched from his grasp.

"No! It's . . . You have to . . ."

He reached after it, but the pain in his chest was unbelievable. He allowed himself to be pushed back. A mask was held against his mouth. He tasted oxygen.

"No . . ." he whispered. "The case. I . . ."

A mouth was close to his ear. Ford could hear urgent breathing. Fingers probed and palped. First his torso. Then his scalp.

"Not hit," said the mouth. "He's . . . I can't find any. There's no penetration. We'll have to check stool and urine for signs of internal bleeding."

Then Gloria was there.

"You're going to be okay," she said. She was struggling for breath. She must have run all the way. "The bullet went into the case you were holding. Broke a . . . broke a rib maybe, but you aren't losing any blood."

But he could *feel* the blood. He was *drenched* in blood. It wasn't rain. He could feel it on his hands, viscous, sticky. He could feel it in his clothes.

Then he realized what had happened.

"Oh, Jesus, no! Please, Gloria. I have to . . ."

He tried to pull himself up, but the hands restrained him.

"Gloria! For Christ's sake."

"You have to stay *still*, Doctor. You could have problems inside. You're just going to tear yourself up."

Ford blinked up at the falling rain. He could see the broad moon of Gloria's face. He breathed for a moment, trying to gather his strength, trying to focus through the pain.

"Help me up, Gloria. I'm okay. I have to check the case."

Gloria gave a snort of impatience and then turned away.

"Can we have that damned case? What's in that thing, anyway?"

"He was holding it when we got here," someone said. "Didn't want to let go."

"It's the drug," said Ford, tugging at Gloria's sleeve. "When I came into the hospital I thought I had it, but I was wrong. Gloria, you have to listen to me. It's an antibiotic. You have to give it to Sunny. Forty thousand IU daily. She'll—"

Gloria was easing him up into a sitting position.

"Take it easy," she said. "Let's just have a look at this thing."

In jerky flashlight Ford saw West leaning against the Pontiac, drinking water, his face spattered with blood. There were paramedics and doctors standing over two fallen men. Ford recognized Ruddock too, looking down at one of the bodies, his gun in his left hand. Somebody switched off the car alarm.

Then Ford had the case. He struggled with the locks for a moment. They popped open.

There was a faint woody smell. Of the three bottles, only the one on the left seemed to have survived. The others were just broken glass.

Ford pulled the third bottle out of the foam case and stared in disbelief as the last of the serum dribbled through a fine crack in the base.

He examined his trembling fingers. They had a faint oily sheen.

Omega, it was all gone. He looked across to West, and West saw what had happened. He smiled.

Ford brought his hands to his face and felt Gloria pull him roughly against her.

"It's all right, honey. Don't go upsetting yourself."

"West," he said. He started to struggle again. "I have to—"

Then there was another voice.

"Marcus?"

For a moment he thought he must be hallucinating, but then she reached down and touched him. She pushed the hair back from his forehead and tried to smile. Ford frowned. It was his head. It was playing tricks. It had to be.

"Helen, what . . . what are you . . . ?"

She leaned forward and put her mouth to his ear.

"Marcus," she whispered. "Say nothing. *Say nothing.*"

Duane Ruddock left the Willowbrook just after midnight, having taped Ford's statement concerning the shooting incident. He had also gone through the events of the past weeks, focusing particularly on Ford's whereabouts around the time of the Novak and Griffen killings.

Ford, despite being in considerable pain—he was X-rayed and then treated for damage to costal cartilage on his left side—had been more than willing to cooperate. He had solid alibis: he had been at the hospital watching over his daughter on the dates and times in question, a fact confirmed by several of the medical staff.

Regarding his presence in Bel Air just prior to Griffen's death, he explained that he had been following Helen Wray. To Ruddock this seemed promising: it at least indicated Ford's involvement in unorthodox goings-on, but further questioning created more problems than it solved. Two hours into the interview Ruddock realized he was up to his neck in the biggest can of worms of his long career.

West stated his belief that his bodyguard, Craig Denman, had clearly mistaken Ford for a mugger and that the whole thing had been a tragic accident. As to his presence in the parking lot, he said that he had simply come to discuss the outcome of the Apex investigation with Dr. Ford, who had a personal interest in its outcome. Asked to verify Ford's assertion that he had come to bargain over a lifesaving drug, he said that the intense stress of the previous weeks—first his suspension and then his daughter's illness—had left Ford a little unbalanced. At Ford's suggestion, the case and the shattered remains of its contents were taken away for laboratory examination.

Ruddock decided to call it a day. It was written in his personal rule book that when you find yourself in a hole, you stop digging. The only way the truth about that night's shootings was going to come out, if it ever did, was if a proper investigation was mounted. And that was going to take time. Ruddock cautioned all the parties involved that he would be seeking their assistance in the coming days and weeks.

He went from the Willowbrook directly to LA County USC Medical Center, where Samuel Dorsey had been admitted to the trauma unit.

For Ford, the time spent answering Ruddock's questions was the longest two hours of his life. He struggled to concentrate on what was being asked, but all he could think about was Helen, all he could see was her tearstained face as she told him that it was okay. "Say nothing," she had said, and there was nothing he could say, except, as the interview came to a close, that he needed to be with his daughter, a fact that Ruddock seemed to understand.

As soon as Ruddock was finished with him, he made his way to the second-floor isolation room where Sunny was being kept.

He found Helen sitting alone by the bed, drinking a glass of water. Sunny slept on in her deep sleep of sickness. He paused in the doorway, confused, unable to speak or move.

Getting to her feet, Helen handed him a small nylon traveling case.

"She'll need the next injection in six hours," she said, trying to avoid his gaze. Then she was pushing past him, trying to get out of the room without another word.

"Helen."

She stopped in the doorway and risked looking into his eyes.

"Marcus, I know you . . ." She looked down for a moment, at a loss for words. "I know it must be difficult for you to understand what happened. But I . . ."

Then she was pulling her hair back from her face, pulling hard, her fist clenched in the dark curls, her eyes glittering with unshed tears. He made a move towards her, but she stepped back, pushing out her left hand as though trying to placate him, trying to appease his anger. But Ford found that there was no anger, that he didn't know, in fact, *what* to feel.

"I'm leaving," said Helen. "I'm leaving . . . I just wanted to tell you . . . I wanted you to know that Sunny's going to be okay."

She turned and looked back at the bed.

"I explained everything to Gloria. She injected the drug directly into Sunny's lower intestine. It'll be working already."

Ford frowned.

"The drug?"

He was having trouble taking things in.

"Omega? Is that what you mean?"

Helen looked back at him.

"Ribomax."

"Ribo . . ."

"A rose by any other name," she said, trying to smile, but suddenly the tears came, and she was covering her face with her hands.

Ford watched her, understanding now that it was all exactly as he had feared. Helen had used him to steal Novak's work for Stern. Now they had gone ahead and produced the molecule. It would be packaged and sold, and in time, just as West had predicted, it would be copied.

But beyond that he remained confused. Here she was, after all. And with the drug. Suddenly he had to know everything.

"Helen . . . ?"

She lowered her hands.

"I don't . . ." Ford clutched at the air. "You'll have to . . . What did you *do*, for God's sake?"

She looked at him for a moment, before speaking.

"I went out to the Stern laboratories today. I went to see the director of research, Kernahan. He showed me the drug. They're not ready to mass produce yet. But they'd made some up on the bench. He had it in his office. In a carton, for God's sake. He showed it to me like a bottle of fancy wine. I knew he was going to be occupied elsewhere. So I went into his office, and I took a bottle."

She shrugged, still dabbing at her eyes.

"That's all there is to it. I stole the drug."

"But . . ." Ford pushed his hand into his hair. "I'm trying to understand why. After the past few days, I . . ."

Helen looked at him. He could see that she was as confused about this as he was.

"You know," she said, "that's harder than you'd think. To answer I mean. I . . ." She gave herself a shake. "Look, suddenly it was clear to me. I was driving along and suddenly it was clear. I couldn't stand by and let . . . let Sunny's life be ruined."

Ford took another step towards her.

"And . . . You're sure . . . I mean, there's no danger, right?"

She looked down at Sunny.

"It'll work. I wouldn't have used it otherwise. They've done tests at Stern. Marcus, this stuff, it's . . ."

Ford remembered West's words: *it's like casting a spell.*

"And I've been calling in a lot, talking to Lee. He's not that discreet, in fact. I know what he's been trying, and I'm certain there's no chance of interference with the other drugs."

She touched Sunny's hair.

"It's been inside her for about four hours."

"Four hours?"

"I came here directly from the laboratories. Came in here and told Gloria the whole story. She knew what to do. I know it's kind of a bizarre way of doing things, but I knew about Sunny's deadline, and I didn't . . ."

She paused. But Ford knew what she was going to say. She hadn't wanted to talk to him. She would have been too ashamed. A ripple of anger went through him as he remembered how she had treated him.

There was an embarrassed silence. Then he said, "And . . . what's going to happen? At Stern. They're going to know, aren't they?"

Helen gave a shrug.

"Kernahan will know a bottle's missing. He'll recall our talk. They'll check the digital inputs from the security-pass log. I'll be in there at six-fifteen, stamped and dated. I'll tell them I came back to get my scarf."

She looked at him.

"And they won't believe me."

"So . . . ?"

"Look, what are they going to do? They still come out winners. I know too much about this whole thing. There's no way they're going to litigate. For one thing, they'd have a little trouble proving this was all their own work. Their research notes'll only show they were barking up the wrong tree. It's going to be tough enough convincing the patent office. If anyone contests their application, they could have a real problem."

"So they'll just leave it at that?"

Helen sighed.

"They'll fire me probably. Or ask me to leave. But . . . I guess I was finished with them anyway. Don't worry, I don't come away empty-handed. Anything but. I'll still get the stock options they've promised me."

Ford gripped the rail at the end of Sunny's bed and looked at the bump made by her feet under the blanket.

"But what about the police? They'll find traces of the drug in that case, all over the parking lot."

"No, they won't," Helen said. "The active component of Ribomax is genetically engineered RNA. It's delicate. Fling it around a wet parking lot, freeze it in a forensics lab, and all you'll end up with is a soup of amino acids. Even if the Homicide Bureau's smart enough to have it treated like a regular DNA sample, they'll never work out what they're actually looking at."

Ford slowly shook his head. She was always ahead of him, anticipating, adapting. Again he had a sense of something almost predatory about her.

"So you get stock options, and Stern gets the drug."

"Yes."

"But it doesn't belong to Stern, Helen. They . . . You stole it from Novak."

He saw something contract in her, saw the hardness he had always found so attractive.

"Well, that's not exactly true, is it? They bought Helical when the drug was already a viable product. Novak effectively stole it from them."

She looked at him for a moment, and he could tell she was debating whether to say something more.

"Look, Marcus. I did this. I did this for Sunny, and I did this for you. I'm not expecting a medal or anything, but I . . . I *did* it."

"I understand. But . . ."

"What I'm trying to say is, I'm not such a great person. I know that. But I . . . I don't want you to think badly of me. That's very important."

"You walk away from the company, but you keep the money. Just as simple as that."

"That's about the size of it."

"And what about . . . ?" He opened his arms, indicating the hospital and everybody in it. "What about all the sick people here?"

"Stern will bring this to market as soon as they can," Helen said. "Especially if there are rumors about an antisense drug already being used. Here at the Willowbrook, for example. They'll have no way of knowing that Sunny was treated with the drug I stole. They know nothing of our . . . connection. For all they know, it might be the work of the competition. They'll be in such a hurry to stake their claim . . . I give it a month, at most."

She let this sink in for a moment.

"Now, if you walk out of here with Ribomax, tell everybody what you know, the whole thing could get tied up in red tape. There'd be litigation. Think of all those investors in Helical who never got their due. Stern wasn't alone in being cheated. It could be years before the drug got into the market."

Ford shook his head in disbelief.

"So even Sunny's recovery works in your favor."

He felt a moment of complete rejection, and total acceptance—the two feelings quite distinct, with no confusion between them. She had always been able to surprise him in this way, and in these moments he always felt the same loss of control, the same sense of her power.

"You think of everything, don't you?" he said.

And with her uncanny sense of what he wanted, Helen crossed the room and took his hands. But he couldn't move. The memory of all the badness seemed to freeze his joints.

"I know," she said. "I wouldn't blame you if you never wanted to see me again."

Ford looked away, swallowing the hot feeling of self-pity that rose in his throat.

"You played me for a fool," he said, "and I let you."

She leaned back a little at this.

"No, Marcus. That's not true. I mean, not really. I used you. I'm not denying that. At least that's how I started out. But the things I said . . . I meant every one of them."

She looked down at their linked fingers.

"What I said about your hands, that was true. What I said about you being a good man, that was true."

"What you said about yourself, that was true too," he said.

She looked up at him.

"What was that?"

" 'Sometimes bad means bad,' " he said. "Wasn't that it?"

The sun was coming up when they walked out into the parking lot. Helen turned to face him.

"You're sure you don't need a lift?" she said, unlocking the door.

Ford shivered in the chill dawn air.

"I'm going to stick around for a while. Make sure everything's going okay."

Helen tried to smile.

"You look as though you could sleep for a week," she said.

"When this is all over, that's probably what I'll do."

She got into the car and was about to close the door, when he spoke.

"Helen."

She looked up at him, and he could see her vulnerability.

"I'll call you," he said.

He watched her drive out towards Wilmington Avenue. The light traffic of LA's early risers kept her pinned in the entrance for a moment, and then she was gone, carried away like a piece of debris on a stream. He stood for a while watching the cold yellow light beyond the freeway. The storm had cleared the air, but there were banks of clouds away to the east. A battered compact pulled into the entrance and Ford remembered that his own car was still up at the Aurora Clinic. It could stay there, for all he cared. He checked his watch. It was just after six and the Willowbrook was beginning its new day.

He was turning back towards the entrance when he saw Conrad Allen's gray Sunbird. It drew up fifty yards from where Ford was standing.

Ford could see by the set of his shoulders as he came across the asphalt that Allen was not looking forward to his day. When he saw Ford, an expression that was close to actual pain passed over his face. Ford realized that his friend would rather be anywhere in the world than where he was right then. He took a step towards him.

"Conrad, are you okay?"

Allen shrugged.

"Didn't sleep much, that's all." He looked down at his shoes for a moment. "How about you?"

Ford smiled.

"What?" said Allen, putting his head on one side. "What is it?"

Ford touched him on the shoulder.

"Let me buy you a cup of coffee," he said.

EPILOGUE

Three weeks later, on November 3, Stern Corporation held a press conference at their offices on Santa Monica Boulevard. The conference was well attended, in spite of the fact that the press releases had been sent out only two days earlier. Many of the reporters and camera crews were forced to jostle for places at the back of the room or squat at the foot of the makeshift dais erected especially for the occasion.

The purpose of the conference was to announce the successful development of a "new generation" antibiotic, to be called Ribomax—this in spite of the fact that a patent had only that very morning been filed and was still many months away from being conferred. In his statement, CEO Randolph Whittaker explained that this highly unusual step was being taken in response to the "medical emergency" afflicting health-care facilities in southern California. Although clinical trials had not yet even begun, preliminary tests had indicated that Ribomax, a genetically engineered RNA molecule, was effective against a wide range of aerobic and anaerobic bacteria, including pathogens of the genera *Clostridium*, *Staphylococcus*, and *Streptococcus*. Provided patients and their families were prepared to sign liability waivers, Whittaker said, Stern would make Ribomax available to the affected hospitals upon request. Asked how long the company had been in a position to deploy the drug, prior to that day's announcement, Whittaker replied that the first laboratory tests had been completed just a matter of weeks earlier. The fact that Ribomax had come along at a time when such a drug was so urgently needed, he put down to "happy coincidence, or just possibly the hand of God."

For many of the journalists present, this explanation was less than convincing. During the preceding weeks there had been intense speculation that Stern was in possession of a lifesaving new antibiotic, speculation that the company itself seemed unwilling either to confirm or deny. According to rumor, a number of critical cases had been successfully treated with the drug at the Willowbrook Medical Center in South Central Los Angeles (although how medical staff had obtained it was not clear). The rumors were enough to send Stern's stock price up nearly thirty percent over the period. Commentators suggested that Stern had been forced into a premature announcement by the pressure of public interest.

Whatever the truth, the deployment of Ribomax during the following months probably saved the lives of hundreds of people. Many more who had been facing the prospect of dangerous or crippling surgery were spared the ordeal, although in some cases the progress of their infections had advanced so far as to leave them permanently disabled. By the end of February the following year, the county health department felt in a position to announce that the resistance emergency was, for the time being at least, over.

The questions surrounding Ribomax, however, were slower to die down. In January, following allegations of corruption and conspiracy involving public employees, the governor of California established a special commission to investigate official dealings in antisense research and development.

Among those who testified was Marshall West, whose involvement in a fatal shooting outside the Willowbrook Medical Center the previous October had given rise to much colorful speculation. West had described the death of Craig Denman, his driver and bodyguard, as a tragic misunderstanding, brought about by Denman's "overzealous" reaction to what he believed to be a threatening situation. West rejected out of hand suggestions that he himself had succeeded in gaining access to Ribomax or that his nephew had been treated with the drug. His version of events seemed to be confirmed when the

Aurora Clinic's records were produced. No mention of Ribomax, or anything like it, was found there. West admitted being aware of the rumors surrounding antisense research and being "passionately interested" in learning the truth, but he denied being in receipt of any privileged information, let alone the drug itself. If the drug had been in his possession, he asked, why would he have initiated the investigation of Apex Inc.? Executives at Stern Corporation, also interviewed, professed ignorance of any illegal or improper dealings and maintained that antisense research had been a field of particular interest at the company for a number of years.

The commission concluded that there had been no conspiracy either to illegally procure the drug or to conceal its existence. West nevertheless resigned his post at the county health department "for personal reasons." According to some newspapers, his unilateral initiation of the Apex investigation and persistent questions about his activities had combined to make his position untenable. West returned to the East Coast with his family and joined a public-relations consultancy specializing in political lobbying. Contrary to long-standing expectations, he never offered himself as a candidate for elected office.

The county sheriff's department and the LAPD continued to search for the killers of Charles Novak and Scott Griffen, but neither succeeded in making an arrest. Carpet fibers from Craig Denman's car matched those found at Professor Novak's house, and the LAPD were able to confirm that Denman had entered Scott Griffen's premises no more than forty-eight hours before his murder. However, the identity of any accomplice was never established. Nor did it prove possible to establish the source of the money Novak had obtained upon his departure from Helical Systems in 1992. After a decent lapse of time, both cases were transferred to the *Unsolved* files.

The county health department investigation into the death of police officer Raymond Denny at the Willowbrook Medical Center was terminated after just one day of testimony. Dr. Marcus Ford was immediately reinstated as director of the Trauma Unit, but resigned six weeks later in favor of a teaching position at LA County USC Medical Center. He was succeeded at the Willowbrook by his colleague, Dr. Conrad Allen. Ford's daughter Sonia made a full recovery, although it was not until after Thanksgiving that she was strong enough to return to school. She continued to suffer from weakness and lethargy for several months afterwards.

Ribomax finally received its patent in early March. Within weeks it was being marketed by Stern representatives in more than sixty countries. The continued impact upon Stern's stock price, and the cash flow generated, made it possible for the company to launch a successful takeover of Apex Inc. the following summer. This was followed by smaller acquisitions in Europe and Asia. The deals turned Stern into the third largest pharmaceutical company in the world.

By this time press interest in Ribomax had shifted from its immediate past to its long-term future. Journalists from the scientific press began to ask how Stern proposed to minimize the possibility of bacteria developing resistance to the new drug, as they had to the drugs that had gone before. In a magazine interview Randolph Whittaker declared that the company would take "every practicable step" to ensure that Ribomax was administered only "in appropriate circumstances and in appropriate ways." However, he refused to be drawn out on whether the company would insist upon the kind of directly observed therapy being recommended by the World Health Organization and others. He said that the company would continue to work closely with the medical profession, but was "not in a position to give orders." Regulation, he concluded, was a matter for governments.

One year after the interview was published, the first Ribomax clones became available over-the-counter from unlicensed traders in Shanghai and Hangzhou. . . .

• A NOTE ON THE TYPE •

The typeface used in this book, Transitional, is a digitized version of Fairfield, which was designed in 1937–40 by artist Rudolph Ruzicka (1883–1978), on a commission from Linotype. The assignment was the occasion for a well-known essay in the form of a letter from W. A. Dwiggins to Ruzicka, in response to the latter's request for advice. Dwiggins, who had recently designed Electra and Caledonia, relates that he would start by making very large scale drawings (10 and 64 times the size you are reading) and having test cuttings made, which were used to print on a variety of papers. "By looking at all these for two or three days I get an idea of how to go forward—or, if the result is a dud, how to start over again." At this stage he took *parts* of letters that satisfied him and made cardboard cutouts, which he then used to assemble other letters. This "template" method anticipated one that many contemporary computer type designers use.